P9-EES-707

Warriors of Wing and Flame

BOOKS BY SARA B. LARSON

Defy

Ignite

Endure

Dark Breaks the Dawn

Bright Burns the Night

Sisters of Shadow and Light

Warriors of Wing and Flame

WARRIORS OF WING AND FLAME

SARA B. LARSON

A Tom Doherty Associates Book
NEW YORK

This is a work of fiction. All of the characters, organizations, and events portrayed in this novel are either products of the author's imagination or are used fictitiously.

WARRIORS OF WING AND FLAME

A Tor Teen Book
Published by Tom Doherty Associates
120 Broadway
New York, NY 10271

www.tor-forge.com

Tor® is a registered trademark of Macmillan Publishing Group, LLC.

The Library of Congress Cataloging-in-Publication Data is available upon request.

ISBN 978-1-250-20843-9 (hardcover)
ISBN 978-1-250-20842-2 (ebook)

Our books may be purchased in bulk for promotional, educational, or business use. Please contact your local bookseller or the Macmillan Corporate and Premium Sales Department at 1-800-221-7945, extension 5442, or by email at MacmillanSpecialMarkets@macmillan.com.

First Edition: October 2020

Printed in the United States of America

0 9 8 7 6 5 4 3 2 1

For my sisters.
The greatest gift our parents
ever gave us was each other.

The great art of life is sensation,
to feel that we exist, even in pain.

—LORD BYRON

PART 1

WARRIORS OF WING

Before the beginning . . .

Memories were a tricky thing. They could elude you—or refuse to leave you alone. For so long, I only had the memory of Inara's birth to cling to from *before*. But as suddenly as my father came back into my life, so, too, did another memory return to me, a gift from before that fateful night.

The sun was warm on my back; I recalled the feel of it, and the way my dress swirled around my legs when I spun. The moment was only a glimpse, a hazy, sunshine-washed dream more than anything. It was my mother, fingers intertwined, turning with me. It was putting my palm on her swollen belly and feeling the baby within squirm, a foot or a hand pressing through her skin to meet my hesitant, wondering touch.

It was brilliant green blades of grass beneath my toes, and the brush of a gentle breeze on my sweaty cheek. It was blue skies overhead and birdsong nearby, a high harmony to the rush of the waterfall that I'd heard but never seen. Mere flashes of color and movement, wrapped up in feeling—in security and love and happiness that was warmer than any sunshine. But I didn't know to recognize and cherish the warmth until it was taken away—until *he* was taken away, leaving our world dark and cold, the sun banished to dreams.

During all the years of his absence, the memory grew fuzzier and harder to summon, until it was little more than a deep-rooted yearning that would surface when I stood beside Inara in her gardens, when her eyes flashed a particular shade of blue-fire that somehow reminded me of a different day standing on those grounds, a different *life* . . . when we'd been a family. When I'd only known the sun.

He was there that day, but his face had been taken from my mind as surely as he'd been taken from my life, so I only recalled the sensation of his presence, but not *him,* actually standing beside us as we spun and spun and spun, Mother's skirt billowing out like a flower blooming around us.

Until now.

He'd come back, and with his return, my father's face had also reentered my memories. So that a flicker surfaced, and I finally remembered him, too. How he'd watched us, his eyes flashing that same blue in the sunlight as Inara's; how he'd laughed, how he'd pulled us both into his arms and held us close.

A circle of sunshine, of love, of family.

But everyone knew that with any sunrise, there was also a sunset. Day must give way to night. We'd lived in the shadow of night for most of my life, and now, even though a glimmer of sunlight had been returned to us, I was still afraid.

Darkness still dominated, and with it, a fear that this time, the sun might never rise again.

ONE

Zuhra

Shadows crept across the floor, crawling up my walls and slinking across my bed. Silent, stealthy harbingers of the rapidly falling night. I sat halfway between the door and the window, on the same dingy sheets on the same sagging mattress where I'd sat countless times before, staring at the sun-faded walls and the worn dresser—all as familiar as my own reflection. This was the space where I had lived for eighteen years. I'd come there seeking solace, hoping the familiarity would help me shut out the horrific reality of the past few hours. And yet my room had never felt so foreign. Nothing had changed within the four walls . . . except for me.

But outside my door, *nothing* was the same.

Paladin once again walked the halls of the citadel that had been empty for so long. The magical beings who'd abandoned their home had returned, breathing life back into the stifling emptiness that had suffocated me. The citadel had come alive with their presence. Sounds of voices replaced the eerie groans and creaks that had always sent chills of foreboding over my skin. Hallways that once pulsed with menace, now vibrated with expectancy.

I'd dreamt of this moment; I'd *yearned* for it.

But not like this. Not with blood and terror and death in their wake. Yes, Paladin walked the halls again—and against all odds, my family was reunited—but at what cost?

So much of the death and destruction was my fault. My stomach churned with the guilt of it, compounded by the fact that despite it all, I couldn't deny being *glad* the Paladin had come. Or, rather, that *one* Paladin in particular had come.

Raidyn was somewhere within the walls that had been my prison for the vast majority of my life. I could open my door and possibly see him striding toward me, his long legs carrying him across the worn rugs I'd tread countless times, his blue-fire eyes glowing in the dark of nightfall.

But if I did open my door and saw him, would he be alone—or would Sharmaine be at his side?

The image of Raidyn rushing out to embrace her in the courtyard earlier that afternoon flared in my mind, the way he'd gathered her into his arms, how her fingers had tightened around his shirt, holding him so very close. But she and Sachiel, another Paladin general like my father, *had* just returned from trying to track down Barloc.

I still couldn't believe Halvor's uncle, the man we'd all believed to be a harmless scholar, had become a *jakla*—a Paladin word that meant "cursed"—after ripping my sister's power from her body, leaving her to die. I, too, was grateful Sachiel and Sharmaine were both alive and unharmed . . . especially after what Barloc had done to my grandfather.

His body had been taken to a room and covered with a sheet, prepared for burial tomorrow at dusk. I'd barely had a chance to get to know him before Barloc had taken him from me, using his unnatural power to kill my grandfather and then blasting his way through the hedge that had been impenetrable up until then.

I lurched to my feet, a fist pressed to my stomach, trying to keep the bile from rising at the memory of the hole in my grandfather's chest . . . of the blood . . . his glassy eyes staring up at a sky he would never again see, the fire gone out of them, along with his spirit.

I was afraid to open my door, to face what lay ahead, but I could no longer hide in my room—not without more memories assailing me, and the accompanying panic boiling hot in my veins, spewing acid to burn my stomach.

Inara. I should go check on Inara. She'd said she was fine when

I tried to speak with her after leaving Loukas's room, claiming to be so grateful she was alive, she wasn't upset her power was gone. But the *sanaulus* from healing her—the bond created between the healer and the one healed—gave me a direct connection to her emotions. Even without the extra insight into her tumultuous feelings, I knew my sister.

She was lying.

I hurried across my room, but just as I stretched out to grab the handle, a loud knock at the door made me jump back, gulping down a yelp. A tiny bud of hope bloomed—then withered when I pulled the door open.

Shadows swelled behind Halvor, standing a few feet away, his hands shoved into his pockets, narrow shoulders sloped. "Your father has called a meeting," he said without looking up. He'd been taller in my memory, but now, after my time in Visimperum with Raidyn and Loukas, he didn't seem as big as he once had. "He wanted me to come get you. They need everyone there." His eyes flickered up to mine, then away again, a flush touching his jaw.

Was he remembering the last time we'd been alone together—when I'd made it painfully clear I'd hoped he wanted me? I grimaced at the memory, at how wrong I'd been.

"Where?" I asked, hoping my blush wasn't as visible as his.

"The dining hall."

"All right. I'll come in a minute."

But he didn't move. "I was told to accompany you. They don't want anyone alone in the citadel."

My eyebrows lifted.

"I know I'm not much protection against my . . . against *him*." He stumbled over his words, a muscle in the corner of his eye twitching. "That blond Paladin wanted to come get you, but the redheaded girl pointed out he'd probably get lost. So your father sent me."

"Oh." I didn't know how else to respond to his admission. Raidyn had wanted to come get me—but *Sharmaine* had stopped him? I flushed even hotter, my neck probably turning as red as Sharmaine's hair. The Paladin girl who had grown up with Raidyn and Loukas, who had both of their love, who had always been kind to me. Then why had she refused to let him come get me? It wasn't *that* hard to find my room.

Shutting the door behind me, I stepped out into the hallway and followed Halvor back the way he'd come.

Awkward silence swelled thicker than the shadows that had always felt alive somehow, as we slowly walked side by side toward the dining hall. I couldn't help but remember the last time we'd walked through the citadel together alone—in the middle of the night, hoping to get into the Hall of Miracles. If only we'd known what havoc our actions were about to wreak upon both worlds.

And of course, that was also the night I'd basically told Halvor I had feelings for him—only to have him reject me. It was hard to believe that something that hurt so badly then only held the sting of humiliation now. I'd seen him with Inara; I knew something had happened between them. No matter how embarrassing it might be, nothing could be worse than allowing him to continue to feel that I still cared for him like *that*. My cheeks flushed hot. Unlike the heat Raidyn engendered—all melted and sinuous and delicious—this was itchy, uncomfortable, and unwanted.

"Halvor, I, uh . . . I just wanted to say that . . . er . . . that night before all of . . . when I thought that I . . . when I said that I . . . um . . ." Mortification chewed at my gut as I blundered through an attempt to explain myself.

"You don't have to—"

I tried to continue over his protest. "I'd never met a boy before and my mother made me think that I *had* to—"

"*Really,* Zuhra, you don't need—"

"I didn't know what I was talking about. I thought what I felt for you was . . . well, you *know*. But *now* I know—

"Please, *please* stop." Halvor reached out and grabbed my arm. I snapped my mouth shut, my face flaming so hot, I could only hope the deep tan I'd obtained from my time outside in Visimperum hid my blush. "You don't need to do this. We're friends, right?"

"Yes. Friends," I repeated, grateful and only a little bit miserable, as we continued toward the dining hall.

My gaze landed on a large bloodstain ahead, a crimson blotch on an otherwise gray rug, and had to suppress a shiver. I slid a glance toward Halvor to see if he reacted at all to the evidence of the destruction his uncle had caused. The death and suffering Barloc had brought upon us all.

Something in Halvor's expression tightened. Upon closer examination, I noticed the weariness in his eyes, the bruises beneath them, the exhaustion that bowed his shoulders forward. I'd never seen him so defeated. We'd all been so wrapped up in our own struggles—healing Inara, finding Grandfather's body, Loukas collapsing from a wound he'd concealed from everyone—had any of us stopped to think of what Halvor was going through? Barloc was his *uncle,* the man who had raised him after his parents' deaths. What was a shocking betrayal for us had to be a devastating one for him.

"I'm sorry, Halvor," I said as we neared the dining hall. The low murmur of voices, even though they were barely audible, was still a shock.

"You *really* don't need to apologize; I understand what you're trying to—"

"Not for that. I meant . . . for your uncle. I know you were close." I glanced sideways at him again. "I'm really sorry."

He shrugged, but I didn't miss the way his jaw clenched.

"Me too," he finally responded, low and gruff.

After several seconds of weighted silence, I couldn't help but ask, "Did you have any idea he knew how to do this? Was it in the books you studied?"

"Do you think *I* had something to do with it?" He stopped so abruptly, his hands clenching into fists, I had to skid to a halt to avoid walking right on past him. "That I helped him attack the girl that I—attack your sister?"

"*No*—of course not." We stared at each other, Halvor's eyes flashing in the dim late-afternoon light, his chest rising and falling as though prepared to fight—or flee. "I only meant . . . I wondered if you had any idea where he learned to do this. If you had studied it and knew of a way to stop him."

There was a tense pause before I saw my words sink in, the anger draining out of him, leaving him deflated once more.

"I didn't know a thing. I don't know how to stop him." He shuddered, and I wondered if he was picturing Inara as we'd found her—lying on her back, her throat ripped out, and his uncle's mouth stained crimson with her blood. "I'm sorry."

We walked the rest of the way to the dining hall in silence heavy with hopelessness.

TWO

Zuhra

Giant flames licked greedily at the pile of dry wood in the once-dank hearth, at the far end of the dining hall. The hiss and crackle of the fire devouring its fuel was a comfort, filling the cavernous room with warmth. Sami bustled around those at the table, setting platters of food in front of them. Her presence was familiar, soothing. As long as Sami was there, bringing us the meals she worked so painstakingly to make, things couldn't be *that* bad. Something in our world was still good, still *normal.*

Inara sat next to me, hands clutched together in her lap. After all these years, she was truly lucid—*permanently.* I longed to take her somewhere else, to talk to her alone, but it would have to wait until after the meeting that still hadn't begun.

Our parents sat on my other side, Mother next to me, her hands fluttering restlessly—from twisting her skirt in her fingers, to adjusting the silverware on the table, to pushing stray hairs behind her ear. Every time I glanced at her, she was looking at my father. I wondered if she longed to reach out and touch him, to assure herself he was real and solid and actually *there* at her side. I was still reeling at seeing them together—the sudden reality that our family was reunited after nearly sixteen years of separation. But what should have been a moment made radiant from dazzling joy was overshadowed by the carnage and suffering that had accompanied his return.

It wasn't just the four of us at the massive table I'd only ever eaten at once before, that first night Halvor had shown up at the citadel. Raidyn, Sharmaine, Sachiel, Loukas, Halvor, and two other Paladin were also there. A tense silence hovered over the room, a sort of foggy disbelief that made the gathering seem hazy and unreal. This couldn't possibly be happening; surely I was dreaming that *actual* breathing Paladin sat across the table from us. But every glance up confirmed the reality that this was no dream.

Finally, Sami placed the last dish—a tureen of soup—down on the table in front of my mother.

"Sami," Mother's voice broke through the quiet, and I flinched, expecting her to give her an order of some sort. Instead, she said, "Please, sit and join us."

"Oh, madam, I couldn't—"

"Sami, I insist. You're part of this family, and you deserve to be part of this discussion."

My eyes widened. The Paladin who had never known the mother I'd been raised by didn't show any sign of surprise at her invitation; my father nodded encouragingly. But Inara was astonished enough to glance at me, eyebrows lifted.

With a flush and a little nod of her head, Sami hurried down to the empty chair beside Sachiel and sat, her gaze lowered.

"Thank you for taking the time to prepare all this food," my father said as he reached out and spooned some roasted potatoes onto his plate. Everyone followed his cue, the next few moments filled with the sounds of cutlery and dishes clinking as everyone served themselves, though I wondered if they, like me, only did so not to offend Sami. The last thing I wanted to do was eat. Not when my grandfather still awaited burial tomorrow at sunset; not with the hole in the hedge still gaping wide, a wound the previously impenetrable plant seemed unable to heal; and Barloc still out there somewhere—powerful and dangerous, somehow managing to disappear into thin air, according to the Paladin who had gone after him and returned without news.

I glanced over at Inara and noticed her hand trembling as she spooned one tiny portion of steamed green beans onto her plate. The *sanaulus* from healing her enabled me to sense the tumult within her—a volatile mixture of hopelessness, pain, and fear. But she sat tall, her spine straight, expression benign, hiding her suffering as best as she could. Only that tremble in her hand, which she quickly folded back into her lap without taking a bite of the beans, gave her away.

A separate tug of awareness pulled my focus. I glanced up to see Raidyn watching from across the table, eyebrows pulled down over his brilliant blue-fire eyes. His concern was palpable even with the space between us. The *sanaulus* from when he'd healed me had grown even stronger after we saved Inara together, nearly draining us both. No one had ever been healed after having their power ripped from them before; she was the first known Paladin to have survived it—because of us.

After living my entire life believing Inara was the only one who had inherited our father's power, it turned out we'd been wrong.

In the hours that had passed since that death-defying act, Raidyn's eyes had grown brighter and brighter as his power rebuilt within him. There hadn't been time to ask why my eyes didn't glow, when it turned out I did have power after all. Though I really wanted to know, glowing eyes—or the lack thereof—was low on the list of questions that needed answering at that moment.

"So, what do we do now?" Loukas finally broke the silence. He sat stiffly, skin pallid and his temples damp. Raidyn had only partially healed his wound—sustained while fighting Barloc beside my grandfather—just enough to keep him alive. Raidyn and my father were hesitant to use any more power than absolutely necessary, needing to reserve as much as possible in case Barloc did make another appearance. But though Loukas was still in pain—at least until Raidyn finished healing him later tonight—he'd insisted on coming to dinner.

"How long will the *jakla*'s ability to absorb our power last? At what point can we *fight back*?" one of the two Paladin I didn't know asked. He was young, maybe only a couple years older than me. We weren't sure how many more had come from Visimperum; it had all been so chaotic. I had been so intent on my sister,

I only had vague recollections of Paladin and gryphons coming through the gateway before it had shut again, trapping us all here. Not all of them had returned yet; we knew that much.

"There's no way to be certain, Ivan," Sachiel responded. She'd cleaned the blood off the side of her shaved head, but she still looked more worn than I'd ever seen her; there was a tightness around her eyes and mouth that hadn't been there before the events of this day. "His ability to continue to absorb our power could last through the night . . . or even for a few days. It depends entirely upon how much power he already stole and how his body responds to the change." Her glance slid to Inara, then back to her plate.

My sister stiffened beside me; I sensed her misery intensify at the reminder of what had been done to her—what had been ripped *from* her. Raidyn and I had barely managed to save her life. The memory of that gaping hole within her, roughly patched together by our joint power, sat heavily in my belly, leaving no room for any of the food I'd put on my plate.

"Is there a chance he won't survive it?" The young Paladin—Ivan—sounded so hopeful.

"If he were fully human, there would be a possibility of his body being unable to handle it," my father answered this time. "But if, as he claims, he had a Paladin grandparent, the chances of him surviving the change are much higher."

"He claims to have had a Paladin grandparent?" Sachiel's eyebrows rose.

My father sighed, using his fork to push his half-eaten potato around his plate. "Yes. He said there have been other Paladin who have opened the gateway and traveled to Vamala at different times, and his grandfather was one who came with a small group about a hundred years ago. He didn't tell us why they came—but based on what he wants to do with the Paladin power he's claimed, I don't think it was anything good."

"What does he intend to do?" Sharmaine, who had remained silent the entire time, finally spoke. I tried not to think of Raidyn running out to her when she and Sachiel had returned, how he'd enveloped her in his arms.

"He said he was going to find other Paladin who feel the way he does. He believes we deserve to rule over the humans because of our power and strength. He intends to bring an army back here and show Vamala what the true might of the Paladin is, and he will be the one to unleash it on them."

Sachiel and Father shared a grim look. "You don't think he's part of the *Infinitium* sect . . . do you?" she asked.

The unfamiliar phrase sent a shiver over my skin, raising bumps on my arms, as though some deep, visceral part of me understood the direness of his speculation, even if my mind didn't.

"I don't understand how he could be . . . having lived here his whole life. But the fact that he knew how to steal Inara's power and the things he was saying—wanting to gather an army to rule over the humans—it's deeply concerning."

"That's an understatement," Loukas muttered.

Everyone fell silent. Who knew where he'd go or what he'd do now that so much of his plan had failed. But my guess was that he wouldn't stay away from the gateway for long. Not if an army was what he was after. I didn't know what the *Infinitium* sect was, but it didn't sound good.

"Halvor, he is your uncle. You knew him best." My father turned to Halvor, sitting beside Inara. He flinched at the reminder, his plate as untouched as the rest of ours. I wondered if his stomach was cramping, sick, like mine. "What can you tell us about him?"

"Nothing," he answered quickly, *too* quickly, his neck flushing. Some of the Paladin exchanged glances with eyebrows lifted. "I didn't know about any of this, I promise. He kept some of his books hidden from me—locked in his office. He said he would let me read them when I had proven myself a better scholar of their ways. But now . . . after . . ." His eye flickered to Inara, then away again, the flush spreading to his cheeks. "I wonder if he didn't want me to know what he was *really* researching."

"But he couldn't have known there was a Paladin at the citadel . . . could he? How could he have created a plan to come here and steal Inara's power if all of Vamala believed the Paladin to be gone?" Sachiel pointed out.

Inara's fingers were entangled in her dress, so tight I feared it might rip. I hesitantly reached over and put my hand on top of hers. She flinched at the unexpected contact, but quickly turned her hand over to thread her fingers through mine, clutching me as tightly as she had the fabric. And with that grip, her shoulders sagged infinitesimally, as though my touch were enough of a balm for her to release her guard, ever so slightly, the concealed truth of her suffering pressing down on her.

"My uncle—Barloc—the *jakla*—" Halvor stumbled over the words, his uncertainty and confusion evident in his every tone, the way his gaze moved from person to Paladin to person in the room, fear coating his skin like sweat. "He was connected to anyone in Vamala who had ever expressed an interest in the Paladin. Those who venerated them and wished they hadn't gone, and those who feared and hated them. Both groups had theories of their continued existence, hiding in the shadows. He spoke to me of rumors . . . stories whispered about a town at the base of the supposedly abandoned citadel, how the villagers spoke of Paladin living there, *hiding* there behind the hedge. That was part of why he'd wanted to come, why he asked me to fund our expedition. I thought it was to learn more about them, to possibly meet and *help* them, if they truly did live here. I never thought . . . I never would have . . ." He swallowed hard and broke off, his eyes dropping to where I clutched Inara's hand, our fingers interlaced, knuckles white. "I'm so sorry."

There was a long pause, before my father said, "We know you had nothing to do with his actions. You need not fear us."

Halvor looked up at him, a sheen on his hazel eyes—a reflection of firelight or tears, I couldn't say.

"Which brings us back to the question of what do we do now?" Loukas asked.

Halvor sagged back into his chair at the turn in conversation, the focus drawing away from him.

"I think we stay close to the citadel, run patrols, take watches, and wait and see. He'll show his hand before too long." My father looked to Sachiel, the other Paladin general in the room, and she nodded in agreement.

"We'll be safer in numbers, so I think staying close

together—and to the gateway—is for the best. At least for now. Though he won't be an expert at utilizing his newly gained power, he will have sheer will and strength on his side until the power settles."

"We'll divide into pairs, then, and take shifts. The rest of you try to get some rest." My father's pronouncement signaled an end to the meal—for the few who had managed to eat anything—and within moments, they were all pushing their chairs back and standing. I avoided looking at Sami, afraid she'd be upset by how little of the food she'd painstakingly prepared had been consumed.

"I'll take the first shift," Sachiel volunteered.

"I'll go with her," the other unknown Paladin, a female who looked Mother's age, added.

"Thank you, Lorina." My father nodded toward her and she inclined her head. "I'll take the next shift, then, in a few hours."

"I'll do it with you," Raidyn immediately spoke up and my father nodded.

My throat tightened at the thought of both of them out there, during the night, waiting and watching . . . not knowing if or when an attack might come. Barloc's eyes and veins pulsing blue—my sister's blood on his mouth and chin—flashed, a lightning strike of memory. A sudden pressure in my chest stole my ability to breathe.

"Inara . . . may I walk you to your room?" Halvor's hesitant question startled my sister, her fingers flexing against mine. But then she released my hand and stood with an attempt at a smile.

"Thank you," she murmured, but paused to glance back at me. I nodded for her to go. If she wished to be with him—if it would bring her any joy or comfort—she should go.

My father walked out the door behind Inara and Halvor, deep in conversation with Sachiel. My mother shadowed his every step as though afraid he might disappear into the darkness once more, his return nothing more than a phantom of her imagination.

It was impossible to believe this had all happened today. That this morning I'd been in Visimperum, standing by the *luxem magnam* with my grandfather, saying goodbye to the breathtaking room full of light that was the birthplace of the Paladin and their power. And tonight, his lifeless body lay in the citadel where I'd been born and raised in seclusion. A cold wave crashed over me, despite the waves of heat from the fire engulfing the stack of wood nearby. I shivered as Sami finished gathering the leftover food onto her tray, and the other Paladin divided up the night and next day into shifts. It was a burble of sound and activity that washed over me without piercing the pounding of blood in my ears. My body flashed cold then hot, my breath came faster and faster—

Someone touched my arm, and I jerked with a half-swallowed gasp.

"Zuhra, are you all right?" Raidyn's voice was a low murmur.

I blinked, shocked to realize everyone had gone, save for Loukas hovering by the door with Sharmaine at his side—both of them watching me.

And Raidyn. He'd stayed. His fingers still lingered on my skin; only the slightest pressure, but it was enough to bring me back to my senses, to interrupt the unaccountable panic that had seized me.

"I . . . I'm sorry," I finally responded.

"For what?"

I looked up into his glowing, blue-fire eyes, and lifted my shoulders slightly. I wasn't even sure; I didn't know what else to say after all that had occurred—knowing they were now trapped here with us.

After a beat, he said, "It's been a very long day. I think it might be best if you lie down, try to get some rest." His fingers curled around my arm, and he tugged, gently pulling me into motion, to my feet first, and then toward the door.

"I can't lie down. Not yet." A knot lodged in my lungs, trapping my breath at the mere thought of facing my empty room alone with the panic still simmering within me.

"I was going to check on the gryphons in the stables. Could you show me the way?" Sharmaine asked. "Then *you* can go finish healing this lout before he undoes everything you already did," she added, jerking a thumb toward Loukas.

"Did you just call me a *lout*?" Loukas's eyebrows lifted.

"Yes, I'll go with you," I immediately agreed. Anything to avoid my room—and the solitude that awaited me there.

"Great, it's settled." Sharmaine smiled at me, that same genuine smile I'd come to know in Visimperum.

Whatever was going on between her and Raidyn—or me and Raidyn—she continued to treat me like a friend. It made the jealousy I struggled to subdue all the hotter in my chest. It would have been so much easier if she were rude or unkind. I could have hated her and felt justified in hoping to win Raidyn's affections—taking them from her.

I averted my eyes from his searching gaze as I followed her out of the room, my cheeks and neck hot. My arm still tingled where he'd touched me as we left the boys behind us and silently began to walk through the shadowed hallway. Sharmaine paused after a moment and turned to me. "This place is . . . something else."

"That's one way of putting it." The wide, dark hallway gaped open before us, pulsing with oppressive menace. Nothing like the castle in Visimperum that was all light and bright white marble and shimmering diamonds. "Follow me." I took the lead, and we lapsed back into silence, passing the old, familiar statues, tapestries, and doorways I'd spent my entire lifetime with, but now experienced anew, as I tried to imagine what Sharmaine thought, how she saw the only home I'd ever known.

I took her to the back staircase, not wanting to pass the destroyed doors of the main entrance to the citadel—or the hole in the hedge looming beyond it. When we passed through the exit nearest the dilapidated but still usable stables where the Paladin had put their gryphons, I finally ventured the question that had been hounding me ever since I'd seen Sharmaine and her gryphon burst through the glowing doorway in the Hall of Miracles with the others who had come to Vamala.

"Why did you do it?" My voice was barely above a whisper, but I knew she heard me by the way she stiffened beside me. "What made you come here?"

She had to have known what a risk it was to come to Vamala—where, as she knew, Paladin were feared, hunted, and murdered for what they were. Why, then, had she steered her gryphon toward the gateway and come?

There was a heavy pause, as though she were weighing her words, or perhaps considering *me*—trying to decide what to confide and what to keep to herself. Though she had always treated me kindly and helped with my training, we'd never really spoken about anything of *importance*. It had been rash of me to ask such a personal question. Especially when I feared the answer had the power to shatter my heart: Raidyn.

"I came because I had to," she began slowly. "People I loved were in danger, and I am trained to protect those I love—or any innocent lives, for that matter."

People. Raidyn, yes, but not *just* him. I nodded like I understood her bravery, like I could possibly comprehend what must have gone through her mind in the moments it took between seeing Barloc burst through the gateway, attack them—including my grandmother—then leap back through it into Vamala, and her decision to follow after him. And not *only* her, so many others. At least seven or eight Paladin had come through, and possibly more that hadn't come back yet, knowing they were likely risking their lives. Not only from Barloc's stolen power, but because of the death trap they knew Vamala to be for their kind.

We reached the door to the stables and Sharmaine pushed it open. It was shadowed inside, almost too dark to see.

"We should have grabbed a lantern," I commented.

Instead of responding, Sharmaine lifted her hand. A split second later, her veins lit up with her power, until a small ball of light hovered above her fingers, illuminating the space around us. She glanced at me and smiled. "I think you know I can create a protective dome with my power," she said before I could ask, and I nodded. "That's what this is, only much smaller."

"That's . . . remarkable."

She shrugged. "It's a parlor trick. But it is useful sometimes."

A parlor trick. Even though I knew I had power now, her casual disregard for something so wondrous to me stung. My father and Raidyn had *seemed* awed by the fact that I was an enhancer. But

I'd never even be able to do a "parlor trick" with my power—I could only make someone *else's* abilities stronger. It had saved my sister, and I knew I should be grateful for that . . . So why did I look at the light Sharmaine lifted as she walked toward the stalls where the Paladin had put the gryphons for the night and feel a pang deep inside?

A soft hooting sound came from nearby, followed by other noises of gryphons moving and acknowledging our presence.

"It's all right, Keko girl, I'm here," Sharmaine murmured as she stepped closer to the nearest stall.

A gryphon with golden feathers lifted her head over the tall door and made another soft noise deep in her throat.

"Is she yours?"

Sharmaine nodded as she lowered the hand with the ball of light and lifted up on her tiptoes to press her forehead against Keko's.

I watched rider and gryphon silently. Keko closed her eyes and made a low noise deep in her throat. Sharmaine rubbed her hand down the gryphon's neck a couple of times, then pulled back.

"Sleep well," she said with one last brush of her fingers over the gryphon's beak.

"What are we going to feed them?" I asked as we moved down the row, Sharmaine peeking in on each stall. I wondered which one Raidyn's gryphon, Naiki, was in, or Taavi, my father's. But none of the other gryphons pushed their heads out to greet her, as if they knew it wasn't their Rider in the stable.

"I doubt you have anything for them here . . . so we'll have to take them out hunting. At least you live near these mountains. They should be able to find enough to eat without causing too much of a problem with the people of Vamala."

It was true, the mountains were uninhabited—with their sharp, unforgiving peaks, tangles of wild bushes, and trees clogging any possible path through them. I'd spent countless hours staring at them from my window. Trying to picture a flock of massive gryphons flying through them, hunting for dinner, was *almost* beyond the scope of my considerable imagination. If anyone in Gateskeep *did* notice them, who knew what they would think—or do. But that was a problem for tomorrow. We still had plenty to focus on for tonight.

"They all seem fine," she finally commented, after peeking into the last stall. "This place needs some work, but . . . it's better than being outside in the elements."

I glanced up at the cobweb-filled rafters, barely illuminated by the glowing blue light hovering over her hand. A gust of wind rattled the walls, but though it sounded questionable, the structure held firm against the onslaught.

"It's survived some terrible storms," I felt compelled to assure Sharmaine when her eyes widened, a flash of worry crossing her face. "It should be fine."

"I'm sure you're right." But she didn't look sure when another bout of wind sent the stables trembling beneath its might.

"Really, there have been a few times when it seemed like the *citadel* wouldn't make it, so I thought for sure we'd wake up to find the stables destroyed, but it hasn't collapsed yet."

She glanced back at me. "I really do believe you. If there were any danger of it collapsing, the gryphons would sense it and be agitated. But they're all calm. Well, as calm as can be expected after what they've been through."

"Right."

"We'd best head back in." She strode through the stable to the door we'd originally come through. In the brief time we'd spent inside it, night had settled more firmly over Vamala, shrouding the citadel and the grounds in darkness. I struggled to subdue a shiver as we hurried back the way we'd come. Sharmaine kept the light hovering above her hand and even brightened it a bit—as if she, too, felt the foreboding weight of nightfall pressing in on her.

Once we reached the security of the citadel, the door shut firmly against the oncoming storm, I sighed. If Barloc returned there was seemingly nothing and no one that could stop him, but being back in the citadel with all of the Paladin now residing within its walls felt like the safest place I could hope to be until they somehow came up with a plan to stop him.

Because that's what they *would* do—what they *had* to do. The alternative was unthinkable.

Sharmaine looked around and then with a little shrug admitted, "I don't know how to get back to our rooms."

"I can show you."

There was certainly no shortage of rooms in the citadel, but only some were in good condition. There had been no reason for Sami or Mother to maintain the others, with only the four of us trapped there. Mother had stayed in the room where she'd lived with Adelric before he'd been taken from us, even though it was in the wing on the other side of the kitchen, far away from where Inara, Sami, and I all lived—which only now struck me, how she'd secretly clung to the memory of him, even while professing to abhor him. Though the other rooms in the wing where the rest of us dwelt hadn't been lived in, they were still more habitable than the one poor Halvor had been forced to sleep in. The Paladin and Halvor were all staying in the same wing as us now, just down from my room, past Inara's.

Sharmaine followed behind me as we climbed the stairs and walked down the hallway, past my room, past Inara's, and the next and the next, until we reached the one where I knew Sami had aired out a bed for Sharmaine—next to the room Loukas was in. Raidyn was on the other side, one closer to mine.

"I think this one is yours." I gestured and she finally let the light above her hand die as she turned the knob and glanced in to find a fire burning in the hearth, her bed turned down, ready for her. The sheets were shabby and worn, but clean. I didn't hear any telltale scurrying of rodents, so I could only hope the room was free of unwelcome inhabitants. "It's the best we could do . . ."

"It looks warm and cozy," she assured me, "and I'm so tired, it could be a bed of stones for all I'd care and I'd still sleep for two days if I were able to."

I couldn't help smiling, even though the panic that had been somewhat subdued by the distraction of going to the stables with her was already rising, knowing she was about to close her door, to go to sleep, seemingly untroubled by the events of the day, leaving me to retreat to my room—alone with my memories and trembling hands. "Sleep well, then," I managed.

"You too, Zuhra." A flash of something—concern or sympathy—crossed her face, but I turned away before she could say anything further, not wanting to keep her from much-needed rest. I felt the shutting of the door behind me like an echo through my bones.

I paused in between the rooms where Loukas and Raidyn were staying, straining for any hint of sound—wondering if Raidyn had finished healing him and gone to bed, or if they were still together, perhaps talking of the day's events. But there were no discernible noises.

A throaty growl of thunder shuddered through the citadel. With a shiver, I forced myself forward. But rather than going to my room, I decided to go to Inara's. We'd barely had a moment alone together yet, and she was *alive* and completely lucid, and there was no way I was going to be able to sleep anyway.

I hurried to her door—but paused before reaching for the handle.

What if *she* were asleep already?

She desperately needed rest, to let her body heal. As much as I wanted to speak to my sister, I refused to be selfish enough to wake her. I was leaning forward to press my ear to her door when a click down the hall startled me. Straightening as if caught doing something wrong—though I didn't even know why—I spun, expecting to see Sharmaine coming after me. My heart skipped up to my throat when, instead of her red hair and smile, I found myself facing blue-fire eyes that glowed in the darkness and thick blond hair that looked as though a hand had been running through it continually as Raidyn stalked toward me.

I stood still, unable to move even if I'd wanted to.

"Zuhra." Raidyn uttered my name in a low whisper, as he halted close enough that I had to tilt my head slightly to meet his gaze. "I hoped to have a word with you before you retired for the night."

"Why?" I whispered back, the darkness swelling to envelope us like a cloak. Another angry clap of thunder crashed through the hallway, startling me. Raidyn lifted his hands—to steady me, perhaps—then paused, mere inches between his fingers and my arms. Likely it had only been instinct and he'd caught himself at the very last second. I wrapped my arms around my waist as he slowly lowered his hands once more.

"Why?" I asked again, a little louder this time.

He flinched. "I don't want to overstep my place, but I . . ." He paused briefly. When I didn't speak, he barreled on, "I'm worried about you. What you've been through—what you've *seen*—"

"I'm fine," I cut in, though I wasn't fine and he obviously knew all too well just how *not* fine I was, thanks to the *sanaulus*.

"Zuhra, the hardest part of any battle—of any loss, especially someone close to you—is not the heat of the moment. It's the quiet minutes afterward, when you're alone with your thoughts and the images that have been seared into your mind, when—"

"Stop," I cried out, heedless of who I might wake. "Please, just—*stop*." The vise of panic constricted, tightening around my heart, so I couldn't speak another word, my breathing shallow.

"I know what it's like. I know how hard it is." Raidyn was still quiet, and this time when he lifted his hand, he didn't stop, brushing the back of his fingers against my cold cheek. He took a step closer, swiping my hair behind my ear, and cupped my jaw, staring into my eyes, the warmth of his touch chasing away the chill.

"Can you make it go away?" My voice quavered. "Can you heal me?"

Raidyn shook his head silently, his gaze mournful. "This is not something I can heal."

The images began to cycle through my mind again, unbidden but unable to be suppressed. I trembled under the onslaught of death and carnage and pain. Inara lying on the ground with her neck ripped open, Barloc crouched over her . . . Grandfather staring sightlessly into the unfeeling sky, a hole torn through his body that no amount of Paladin magic could repair . . . that endless, terrifying blackness inside of Inara that Raidyn and I had barely managed to pull my sister out of . . .

"Look at me, Zuhra." Raidyn's voice sounded too far away, too quiet, over the roaring of my blood and the flood of terror that turned my legs weak and my arms inexplicably numb. My eyes burned and I gasped for air. "*Look at me.* Into my eyes." The hand that cupped my face tilted my chin up, his fingers firm against my skull and jaw. He laced his other hand with mine, lifting it up to press against his chest. "Feel *this.* Feel my heartbeat—and my hand on yours. Breathe with me. In and out . . . yes, there you go, just a little slower . . . in . . . and out . . . Look at me, Zuhra. Look right here and just breathe. You're all right. I promise, you are safe."

I succumbed to his gentle commands, staring up into his eyes, forcing myself to focus on the feel of his hand over mine, of the steady rise and fall of his chest beneath my fingers. I matched my breathing to his and slowly, slowly, the rush of blood in my veins calmed and my breathing slowed and my trembling stopped. I hadn't even realized I'd been crying until he brushed his thumb beneath my eye, to wipe away the tears that were still wet on my skin.

"Thank you," I whispered at last.

Raidyn's hand tightened over mine. "It won't always be like this," he said softly. "Even though it feels like it right now."

"I'm scared," I choked out, admitting the truth at last. "I'm scared to go to bed."

Normally, such an admission would have made my cheeks flame with embarrassment, nervous he would take my meaning wrong. But somehow, I knew he would understand.

"Would it help if I sat with you? Only until you are asleep," he quickly added. "Then I'll go back to my room."

His offer took the warmth from his touch and sent it straight into the depths of my heart. Oh, how I longed to say yes, except . . . "But you have to be up in a few hours anyway with my father. You need to be resting, not sitting with me because I'm such a mess."

"There is nowhere else I would rather be."

I didn't have the willpower to refuse him again—not when the fear and panic hovered, waiting to swoop in. My eyes dropped to where his hand clasped mine against his chest and I whispered "thank you" a second time.

Keeping our fingers laced, he rubbed his thumb across my jaw once more, leaving a trail of heat on my skin. Then he turned and guided me toward my door, opening it for me and keeping our hands intertwined as I followed him across the threshold and into my room.

"Do you wish to change? I can leave if you do, and then you can open the door when you are ready or call out for me."

"No," I quickly responded. "I'll go to bed like this tonight." I'd changed out of the bloodstained dress for dinner; the one I was wearing was clean and I didn't dare let him leave, afraid of how quickly the images might resurface if he did.

He nodded. "Would you like me to start a fire? It's chilly in here. That won't help."

"If you think so."

He had to drop my hand to place a few logs in the hearth. I stood a few feet back, my arms wrapped around my waist once more as he stretched his hand out. His veins lit with power, and then he sent a small blast of Paladin fire at the wood. The blue flames slowly morphed into normal orange and yellow as the logs caught and billowed warmth out into my room.

Raidyn turned to me. We stood there for a moment that drew out long enough to be both awkward and enticingly forbidden. We were alone, in my *bedroom*.

He cleared his throat and glanced toward the bed. "Why don't you get comfortable and then I'll tell you a story." Without looking at me again, he strode over to the lone chair by my desk and carried it over to the side of the bed.

"A *story*?" I repeated, though I did as he bid and pulled my covers down, climbing into my cold bed with a shiver, despite the spreading warmth from the fire.

"Yes, a story," he replied with a small smile—a true smile that lit his striking eyes with something even more powerful and beautiful than the Paladin fire in his irises. Something I'd so rarely seen that I couldn't help but smile back, even though I was trembling again. "Lie back, and give me your hand."

“I . . . I . . . can’t . . .”

“Trust me, Zuhra,” Raidyn murmured, sitting in the chair and resting his hand on the side of my mattress, palm up. “I promise to stay with you—to keep you safe. Give me your hand. Focus on the pressure of my grip and the sound of my voice. Wall yourself into this moment, with me, here, in this room. For right now, there is nothing else but you and me, and our hands, and this story.”

I inhaled deeply and then hesitantly lay down, my pillow compressing beneath the weight of my head. He nodded encouragingly, and I placed my hand in his. He squeezed it, firm but gentle.

“I can’t close my eyes. I don’t dare.”

“Then look at me. Look at my eyes. Listen to my voice. And just breathe. Slowly . . . in and out.”

“And if I don’t fall asleep?”

“Then I will keep telling you stories until the sun rises.”

I gripped his hand tightly, my throat thick with unspoken gratitude and so much more. I didn’t know why he was willing to do this for me—why he’d known to come, to be there for me tonight. Was it merely a sense of responsibility because of what he could sense through the *sanaulus* . . . or was it something more?

“Once, not so very long ago, there was a young girl who dreamed of flying,” he began, his voice low and smooth, the familiar melody of it washing over me as he spoke, my hand in his hand, his eyes on my eyes. I listened and felt and breathed and, miraculously, there was only Raidyn and me and his story and the warmth of the fire washing over us both as he wove a spell of comfort and calm.

And somehow, slowly, my eyes grew heavy, and my breathing steady, as he told me story after story, until eventually, I succumbed to exhaustion and was able to drift off to sleep, the memory of his blue-fire eyes on mine following me into my dreams, where I prayed they would keep the nightmares at bay.

THREE

Inara

Darkness crept across my room, stealing the final hint of daylight partially visible through my window next to where I lay, covers pulled up to my chin. Small noises came from the hallway, and I wondered if it was Zuhra. Part of me wished to go to her . . . but the other part of me, the part deep inside that was darker than the inky blackness spilling across the night sky, froze me in place.

Though I willed it not to, my heart began to thump hard, harder, *harder.* My face flushed hot; my arms went numb.

Terror.

Rising like a tsunami—something Zuhra and I had read about in a book years ago—a deceptively deadly wave that just kept coming, and coming, and coming, rising with unimaginable force, destroying everything in its path.

My breath burst out in short gasps, faster and faster, until the room spun along with my stomach.

You're safe. He's gone. You're safe . . .

I repeated the phrases to myself again and again, but they were feeble blockades against the relentless wave of panic, crumbling with barely a hint of resistance.

"Zuhra," I called out weakly, between pants. *Zuhra . . . come to me. Help me.*

It felt like I was dying again, not from a wound inflicted by a monster in the form of a man, from the monster *inside* of me.

The massive, prowling beast that stalked through the emptiness where my magic had once resided. The physical wounds were gone, healed by Raidyn and Zuhra's combined efforts. But not even their immense combined power could fix what his attack had done to me.

What it was *continuing* to do to me.

I threw off my covers, grabbed a dressing gown from my wardrobe, and began to pace my room. Sleep was not going to come, no matter how exhausted I was, no matter how drained my body might have been after the trauma I'd endured. I wanted my power back—*needed* it back. I would even have willingly accepted the roar again to have it returned to me.

I paused by my window, glancing out at the darkened grounds. The hole in the hedge was still there, a visible wound torn through our lives. The matching hole inside me throbbed, painful and raw, until everything blurred and I had to wipe at my eyes to clear my vision from the tears that kept gathering. Dizziness from breathing so hard and fast forced me to grip the window seal to keep myself upright.

I didn't know how long I'd been standing there when I noticed two tall, shadowed figures walking across the grounds toward the hedge. A rush of dread flashed through me; my nails gouged the window seal. Before the scream building in my throat could release, the clouds parted, and the silver light revealed my father and the Paladin who I was almost certain had feelings for my sister—Raidyn.

I watched them for only a moment before turning and rushing to my wardrobe. Sleep wasn't coming, that much was certain. And I couldn't bear the thought of standing in my room for who knew how many more hours by myself, lightheaded with panic. Instead, I hastily yanked off my dressing gown and nightclothes and pulled on whatever dress was closest. Without bothering to waste time putting on shoes, I left my room, my feet silent on the worn carpets and cold stones of the citadel's hallways. I hesitated by the door to Zuhra's room, but then hurried past it, hoping my sister was getting the sleep that eluded me.

The closer I got to the front entrance of the citadel, the colder it got; it wasn't until I stood at the threshold of the massive staircase and stared down at the darkness swirling where the heavy doors had once resided that I remembered Barloc had destroyed them as well as the hedge. A night-chilled wind lifted the hair from my neck, sending a shiver skipping over my skin as I hurried down the stairs and past the charred remains of the doors.

Even though the clouds had erased the moon once more, turning the night as dark as the soil beneath my toes, a strange sense of peace enfolded me once I was free of the citadel. I was exposed, and cold, and powerless . . . but I was outside, near the gardens and orchards I'd spent most of my life tending. My true home, more so than anywhere inside the massive structure behind me.

Finally, with a deep breath, I turned away from the gardens to face the ruined hedge, where Adelric—*my father*—and Raidyn still stood by the hole, their backs to me. Their voices were a low murmur as I drew closer. Before I could make out what they were saying, my father stiffened and spun, lifting a hand, his veins instantly lighting up with his power.

"Inara?" He quickly lowered his hand when he realized it was me, his shoulders relaxing slightly. "What are you doing up—and out here?"

"I couldn't sleep," was all I offered, and thankfully Adelric didn't push me. A muscle in Raidyn's jaw tightened, his gaze strayed to the citadel behind us then back to me, but he remained silent.

"You're barefoot—aren't you cold?"

Ignoring Adelric's question, I moved past them toward the charred wound in the hedge. When I lifted my hands up to one burnt leaf, the hedge fluttered half-heartedly, as though the inability to repair itself had removed its desire to even *try* to protect us any longer. The blackened edges crumbled beneath even the gentlest of touches, turning to dust in my palm.

"Why can't it heal? Nothing has ever been able to hurt it before—*nothing.* I don't understand how he did this . . . how he . . . he . . . *I don't understand.*" And suddenly, I was crying, the words choked to a halt by the echo of pain, of emptiness, of holes where there was once so much more.

My father stepped up beside me and gently put an arm around

me. I stood stiffly at first. Though he was my father, he was also little more than a stranger. But when he didn't let go, I slowly allowed myself to lean into him—a bit. "The *custovitan* hedge is nearly impenetrable, but nothing is invincible. Not even this hedge could withstand a blast of such massive, concentrated power, like the type a *jakla* possesses so soon after the change."

I shuddered beneath his arm.

"But it doesn't have to stay this way," he quickly added. "It merely needs a little help." When he lifted his other hand toward the hedge, his veins were already glowing with power. I turned my head away, squeezing my eyes shut.

"Sir, I'm not sure that's a wise use of—"

Raidyn's hesitant protest cut off. I refused to look, refused to watch my father use the power he'd gifted me—that I would never again feel burning within me.

The previously fresh night air took on an acrid bite. Awareness of power flowing from my father into the hedge raised the hair on my arms. Was he truly doing what I thought he was?

The arm around me tightened; I felt the strain within him. How much would it take to heal the hedge? Was it even possible?

A rustle of leaves. A flutter of movement that sent a cool waft of air over my cheeks. Unable to resist any longer, I finally opened my eyes to find an unbroken sea of green. The hole was gone. The hedge moved before me, well and whole once more, vines gliding over one another in celebration—in relief.

My eyes burned unexpectedly. I blinked a few times to clear them as my father let his hand drop back to his side, the glowing power in his veins dimming rapidly before disappearing completely.

"You see? He's not all powerful. Soon he will be just like any other Paladin. Then we can stop him and fix the damage he's done."

"Can we get my power back?"

There was a long, heavy pause. "No," he finally admitted. "It is truly a miracle you are even alive."

This time I clamped my teeth, keeping the words rising up, barreling toward my mouth, from escaping. I didn't want him and Raidyn—or anyone else—to know that a part of me almost wished Zuhra and Raidyn *hadn't* succeeded in saving me. Because without my power, I felt like a husk of my former self. Carved out, left empty and useless.

Instead, I stared at the hedge that had finally settled into stillness once more, and said, "Thank you for healing it."

He hugged me tighter, and we stood there together, little more than two strangers, no matter what blood bound us, staring at the hedge silently.

FOUR

ZUHRA

I swam through dark dreams shot through with glimpses of light, where the rich, melodic tones of Raidyn's voice transformed into a golden chord that I clung to as bloody teeth and torn flesh flashed past me, as shadowed beasts and beastly men stalked through my mind, hunting down any lingering peace I may have been able to clutch to my heart.

Being woken by the rising sun was actually a relief—to escape the horror of my nightmares by opening my eyes to the soft glow of a new day and my old, familiar bedroom. I lay in a ball on my side, knees pulled into my belly, my hands clasped against my chest. The chair where Raidyn had sat beside me last night was gone, moved back to the table where it usually sat. I was tempted to wonder if I'd dreamt his hand on my face, his fingers laced between mine . . . his compassion, his understanding, and his stories that had kept me from drowning in my panic—except I knew my dreams were not that kind.

Which meant he truly *had* stayed with me, alone in my room, possibly for hours, telling me story after story, until I drifted to sleep, his blue eyes a beacon in the firelight.

An unfamiliar warmth filled my body as I threw off my covers, despite the chill of the early morning air. I'd been too lost in the panic to question why Raidyn had known to come—why he'd stayed. But now, I couldn't help but wonder.

I rushed to change into a clean dress and drag a comb through my hair, quickly braiding it back, out of my face. The citadel was quiet, which meant Barloc must not have returned—thankfully. I left my room, not even sure what I intended to do or where I was going to go, but then I paused, glancing at Inara's room.

I hadn't heard any movement yet, but just in case, I moved to press my ear to her door. Silence. I wanted to see Inara—*needed* to talk to her—but it was a relief that she was getting the rest she desperately needed after all she'd been through.

Raidyn had always been up before me in Soluselis, but he'd been awake half the night by my side—and then had taken a watch with my father as well after that. Surely he was asleep in his room. Which meant I had no one to seek out.

Mother was like a different person now that Adelric was back in our lives . . . but I wasn't quite ready to face her alone. Nothing had been said yet about what I'd shouted at her, or opening the door in the Hall of Miracles that night that seemed like a lifetime ago, but in reality was less than two weeks ago—the night when so many of us had almost died, when our tiny little world in the citadel had been shattered as completely as the window of Paladin glass that Halvor had claimed was virtually indestructible.

If only there were a training ring here. It was amazing how quickly I'd grown accustomed to working off my emotions, how much I'd come to crave the accomplishment of pushing my body in ways I hadn't known it was capable of until I'd gone through that gateway into Visimperum.

Instead, I wandered aimlessly through the empty hallways. Out of habit more than anything, I eventually found myself slipping into the drawing room, where I'd spent most of my life.

"Zuhra! What are you doing up?"

Inara pulled her hand free from Halvor's and jumped to her feet from the couch.

I startled to a halt. "I thought *you* were asleep," I said, realizing it didn't answer her question but too surprised to find her there with him.

Inara shrugged. Even from across the room the dark bruises beneath her eyes were visible; her normally summer-bronzed skin had a wan undertone. A surge of anxious fear rose up my throat, so sudden and unexpected, I knew immediately it wasn't my own panic this time.

Without a word, I hurried across the worn rug to pull my sister into a hug. She stood stiffly, but I stubbornly held on. Finally, after several long moments, she crumpled into me, her body trembling. If *I* was dealing with debilitating panic, hers had to be worse—since *she* was the one who was attacked, *her* power ripped from her body. Had she been in her room, sleeplessly suffering the entire time Raidyn had been comforting me? Guilt-serrated teeth gnawed into my gut.

"Is everything all right?"

At the sound of our father's voice, Inara pulled away. We both turned to see him walking into the room, Mother right behind, clasping his hand in hers. She was rarely more than a few feet away from him whenever possible. I couldn't blame her, but I still couldn't get used to seeing them together.

Something crossed Inara's face, but she merely nodded and went to sit back by Halvor, who had watched our interaction silently.

"Were you able to get any sleep?" Mother asked.

"Some," I responded, when Inara remained silent.

"I'm glad to hear it." She and my father sat beside each other, across from Inara and Halvor, leaving me the only one standing—and companionless. "Inara? Did you sleep?"

My sister shrugged; my guess was she hadn't slept at all. Halvor reached for her hand and she let him take it, holding it tightly. My father watched, his expression inscrutable. When he finally looked to me, his normally brilliant blue-fire eyes were somewhat dulled, as if he had recently used a large amount of power.

I swallowed in the strained silence, wondering if I should sit on one of the empty chairs, or escape the tense room and continue my aimless walk through the citadel. Maybe I could go find Sharmaine and ask if she would be willing to spar with me—despite not having any protective leathers or padding. I couldn't remember which watch she'd volunteered for, but hoped she was done and awake and ready to work off some steam, like me.

Before I could decide, the door opened and Sharmaine herself walked in, followed closely by Sachiel and Loukas.

My father moved to stand, but Sachiel gestured for him to stop. "Nothing's wrong," she hurried to assure him. "We just switched watches. No sign of the *jakla* yet."

"Who healed the hedge?" Sharmaine asked as my father resettled on the couch beside my mother.

"What are you talking about?" I glanced at Inara, expecting her to share my shock—but her expression remained stoic, her eyebrows didn't even lift. In fact, it seemed I was the only one in the room who was taken aback by Sharmaine's question.

"The hole in the hedge is gone." Sharmaine speared my father with a pointed glare. "It couldn't have healed on its own," she continued as I rushed over to the window. "So someone must have done it last night."

The sun had barely crested the stark peaks to the east; jeweled rays of garnet and persimmon shot through the remaining clouds from the previous night's storm. And there, in the steadily increasing sunlight, was the unbroken expanse of greenery I'd known all of my life. Just as Sharmaine had said—the hole was gone.

"Raidyn didn't—"

"It was me," my father cut in before Sachiel could finish her thought—or accusation.

"Adelric, why would you *do* such a thing?"

At the surprisingly frosty tone to her voice, I glanced over my shoulder. Sachiel stood a few feet from my parents, her eyes narrowed.

"Didn't you think of the risk to use your power like that when we don't know when or how the *jakla* will attack again?"

"It needed to be done." My father's voice was even, but I noticed his hand tighten around my mother's.

"There is no possible justification for draining your power when that *jakla* could have shown up and attacked—leaving Raidyn to deal with him alone."

"Perhaps *you* don't think so, but I trust you will remember that I am perfectly capable of deciding that for myself."

"*Are* you? Because as I see it, you put all of us in danger for—"

"It was me!" Inara suddenly jumped to her feet, her neck

splotched red and her cheeks flushed. "It's my fault. He did it for me."

"Inara, stop, it's not—"

"No." She cut Adelric off and then turned to face Sachiel. "If you want to get mad, get mad at me. He did it because he was trying to prove a point."

"He did it to *prove a point*?" Sachiel's biting response was so sharp, even Sharmaine flinched. "Adelric, I understand you are upset that you've been separated from your daughters for so long, but you can't let that start clouding your judgment like this!"

"That's *enough*." I'd never heard my father's voice so cold. "I will not make excuses to you—and it is not your place to question me. We may not be in Visimperum anymore, but I am still your superior."

"You're right, we're not in Visimperum—and we may never be again." Her eyes flashed as her gaze roamed over the room; the well-worn, shabby furniture, the singed curtains, the threadbare carpet—all the items we'd tried to carefully tend, but were unable to do more than polish and press years of use into. I shifted my weight, the prickling heat rising up my neck spreading to my face at the disdain that curled her lip. "So, no, you are not anyone's superior," she continued at last. "Not anymore."

"Sachiel." Sharmaine reached out and placed a hand on Sachiel's crossed arms before my father could respond. "It's been a long night. Maybe we should go find something to eat and rest for a bit."

Sachiel shook her hand off, but turned on her heel and stormed from the room without another word.

"Sir, I'm sorry . . . I think she's upset about being trapped here and . . ."

"It's all right, Shar." He rubbed at his temple with his free hand. "Go ahead and go after her. Maybe you can help calm her down. I don't think she wants to talk to me right now."

Sharmaine nodded and hurried after the other general. Once they'd both gone, Inara's shoulders slumped forward and she dropped heavily back down to a seat on the couch. I remained frozen by the window, but even from where I stood, the trembling in her hands was visible when she clasped them together in her lap.

"I'm sorry." Her words were little more than a shaky whisper.

"Don't apologize," Mother finally spoke. "Don't let her upset you."

"But I put everyone in danger."

"No, *you* did nothing." My father shifted as though he would stand, but Inara stiffened and he froze. "I *chose* to heal the hedge—you didn't *ask* me to."

"And your father would never have done anything to put us in danger. Right, Adelric?" Mother turned to him, her hazel eyes lit up in a way I'd never seen except in glimpses of memory from before Inara's birth.

His gaze was trained so intently on Inara, I wasn't sure if he didn't respond because he was so focused on her obvious suffering, or if he didn't want to admit that he actually *had* risked putting us in danger for her.

"I'm sorry," Inara said again, but this time she jumped to her feet and rushed from the room.

"I'll go after her," Halvor offered, standing as well, but I stepped forward.

"No. *I* will." I summoned the commanding strength of my father's voice into my own. Halvor paused and I took his hesitation to my advantage, leaving him in the drawing room with my parents.

The door shutting behind me echoed through the empty hallway. How had she disappeared so quickly? I glanced left and right, trying to quickly guess where my sister had gone. I didn't know. The realization twisted through my gut. For fifteen years, I'd always known where she was, I could always guess where she'd go . . . We'd only been apart for a short time, but somehow those weeks of separation had changed us both in ways I still didn't fully understand.

Hoping she hadn't changed *that* much, I finally decided to head to her gardens. The sky I'd seen through the window was washed the crisp blue only visible the first sunny day after a long series of storms. Surely she would still wish to be outside, with her plants, if she was seeking solace or an escape. Wouldn't she?

I ran, praying I'd chosen the correct direction—because right before Inara had left the room, I'd felt a surge of black despair that had frightened me to my core.

Something was very, very wrong with my sister.

FIVE

Inara

The sunshine was warm on the top of my head and the back of my neck as I ran my hands over the leaves of my plants—and felt nothing except the slight stickiness of drying dew on my fingertips. Tiny plops of moisture dotted the soil, but it leaked from my eyes, not the cloudless sky.

I sensed my sister coming toward me. As she drew closer, I could hear her hesitant steps on the earth, but I didn't look up. Perhaps she wouldn't notice my wet cheeks if I continued to let my hair fall forward to curtain my face.

"Inara?" Her voice was soft, tremulous.

I stared at my plants that were still thriving without me—for now. But once the weather turned for the worse . . . then what? Would the other healers still be here? Would they make our food grow instead? Hopelessness tore the wound inside me even wider. A gaping maw that swirled with a darkness so deep, I was afraid to look into it, fearing I would sink and never emerge.

"I'm worried about you," she continued when I didn't respond.

"I'm fine," I lied.

"Inara . . . when I helped Raidyn heal you, something . . . happened." Zuhra spoke haltingly, her words coming out stiff and strange. She was never awkward with me, unlike everyone else. But everything else had changed; I guess I shouldn't have been surprised that even *our* relationship—something I'd thought indestructible—would too. "You healed Halvor, right?"

Her sudden change of subject, painful as it was, took me by such surprise. I nodded before I could think better of admitting it.

"Afterward, could you . . . feel things? Especially when you were close by him? Like . . . his emotions, maybe?"

I finally looked up. "Yes."

She smiled at me, a soft, gentle smile of understanding—and concern. "That's called *sanaulus.* It's what happens after an intense healing. That's why you could feel his emotions. Sometimes, even the one who was healed will be able to sense some of *your* emotions as well—though not as strongly as for the Paladin who did the healing."

"I didn't know that," I admitted, though it suddenly shed a new light on so many things. But I wondered if that, too, was gone now that my power was. I hadn't been near him most of last night, and this morning I'd been too absorbed in my own desolation to take note of whether I could still sense Halvor's feelings.

"That's why I know how . . . unhappy . . . you are right now," Zuhra continued carefully. "Why I'm so worried about you."

Oh.

Oh, *no.*

She could *feel* the darkness in me? The grasping, sucking despair that continued to grow stronger and stronger?

"I only wish I knew how to help." Zuhra stood close enough to reach out to me, but though her hand twitched at her side as if she *wanted* to, it remained by her side.

Can you get my power back?

There's nothing you can do.

Please go away.

Don't leave me alone.

I shrugged. "I probably just need time . . . to get used to it."

Zuhra's eyebrows knit together, and I realized even if I were the best liar in the world—which I most certainly was *not*—she would know I was lying because she knew what I was feeling. She knew just how deep the "unhappiness," as she'd kindly called it, burrowed into my heart, even my soul.

In an effort to deflect her focus, I blurted the first question that came to mind. "So, you're an enhancer?"

She blinked. "Yes, that's what Adel—er, Father—said."

For some reason, it was a little bit comforting that she stumbled over the word "father" even though she'd been with him the whole time we'd been apart, getting to know him.

"Then why aren't your eyes like mi—theirs?" Mine no longer glowed. They never would again.

"I . . . I actually don't know. There hasn't really been a good time to ask yet." Zuhra finally reached out, but to my plants, instead of me. She picked a ripe green bean from one stalk and rolled it between her fingers. "There's so much I still don't understand."

"What was it like there?" Even though it smarted to ask, I had to know. "How did you survive after . . ."

She stared down at the bean, a peculiarly sad, almost wistful look on her face. For Visimperum? Or something else? "The rakasa was trying to drag me away—to finish what it started. But the flare of power at the gateway drew the garrison on patrol to it, and thankfully they got to me in time." She finally looked up at me. "It was Adelric's garrison. I still can't believe it, but the first person I saw in Visimperum was our father."

While the rakasa in the citadel had nearly killed me and Halvor, while I was healing myself and then him, she was being rescued by our father. "So, *he* healed you?"

"No, actually. He killed the rakasa that attacked me—so he didn't have enough power left to heal wounds of my magnitude. He asked Raidyn to do it."

"Oh." I glanced past her to the citadel that was now inhabited by so many strangers, including Raidyn—the one who looked at her with eyes that burned with far more than just Paladin fire. The one who healed me—with her help. "Wait—the san . . . sana . . ."

"*Sanaulus,*" she repeated.

"Does *he* have that with me too?"

She paused just long enough for me to know the answer even before she nodded. "But don't worry—he's been trained not to use it to invade your privacy or anything like that. And he says he knows how to keep from getting confused about his emotions for anyone he has healed."

I could only stare at her, hot embarrassment rising up my neck. So not only could my sister feel everything I felt—which I wasn't thrilled about, but at least it was my *sister*—now her . . . whatever he was to Zuhra . . . could too? And then the second part of what she'd said sank in.

"Wait . . . *sanaulus* can make you confused about how you feel about someone?"

"That's what I've been told. It creates such a strong emotional bond between the person who was healed and the healer, that without proper training, it can be mistaken for a, ah, *different* kind of bond."

A fist of doubt pushed past my lungs to clutch my heart, compressing it to the point of pain. A sudden dizziness made my head swim. "How can you tell the difference? How do I know if what I think I feel for Halvor is . . . if it's real?"

Zuhra frowned. "I'm not sure. I . . . I think when it's real, it's more than just that connection. All I know is the difference between what I thought I felt for—a, um—different person, and Raidyn." She stumbled over her words, uncharacteristically hesitant. Who else had she believed herself to have feelings for? "With the, uh, first one, I was fascinated by him. Meeting him, *talking* to him, was exciting and different and I thought that meant . . . We'd read all those stories as girls but had never *met* any boys before, until—" She broke off, eyes lowering, and realization dawned on me with awful, sinking clarity.

Halvor.

She had believed herself to care for Halvor?

"But with Raidyn," she barreled on, while I tried to assimilate my shock, "it's so much *more.* I'm not just fascinated by the fact that he's a *boy,* I'm fascinated by *him.* Everything about him. I want to know him the way I know *you*—the way I can tell if you're upset or calm from a mere expression you make or the way you move your hands. I want to feel completely comfortable with him, the way I can share anything with you. With the other boy, I was . . . curious. But when I'm with Raidyn, my heart . . . it . . . it just *races*—like the feeling the moment right after a gryphon takes off and I'm terrified and exhilarated all at once. I want to be with him, all the time. And when he's gone, I wonder when and how I'll see him again. I want to have him hold me, to *want* me, the way I want him. I dream of him k—"

Zuhra stopped abruptly, eyes bright, the skin just below her ear flushed red—one of the only spots where I could see her blush because of her tanned, olive skin.

I stared at my sister. "Oh," was all I said.

Had she kissed Raidyn? Was that how she knew this? I enjoyed being with Halvor, I'd even kissed him, but it hadn't felt like *that*. Well, except for the whole blasting him to the ground with my power, which I supposed I no longer needed to worry about. But as for heart racing and wanting to be with him as much as possible . . . I couldn't understand *that*. Halvor comforted and calmed me. I was curious to kiss him again, to see what it felt like, especially with the threat of my power gone. But a part of my heart sank at the difference between what she'd described and what I felt. Was it just different for me and Halvor? Or was I confusing the effects of *sanaulus* with how I felt for him?

"Nara, I can't pretend to understand what you're going through." Zuhra finally put the tortured bean down and reached for me, thankfully changing the subject. Her fingers wove between mine and I found myself clutching her hand. She'd always been my lifeline, my anchor. No matter how much my world had changed, she was still the one steady thing to cling to, to stay afloat. "I want you to know you're not alone. I will always be here for you—no matter what. And at least we will always be able to talk to each other now."

"That's true." I looked down at my plants. The roar was never coming back—I would never be lost in it again. I should have been glad. Instead, new dots of moisture began to speckle the dry soil.

Zuhra stepped closer to me, so that we stood shoulder to shoulder, our clasped hands pressed between us. "I'm sorry, Nara. I'm so sorry."

We stood side by side, the sun bathing us in light and warmth, while I cried. A torrent of grief and fear released at last, with my sister as the only witness.

But then, right in the middle of the onslaught of tears, darkness crashed into me—so hard and fast, it felt like an actual, *physical* thing—as though Zuhra had shoved me in the chest, knocking me back. I stumbled away from her, my vision tunneling into black before a barrage of images flashed through my mind.

A boy staring up into the glowing blue eyes of an old man ensconced in a large armchair, his jowls heavy with a graying beard. "Our worlds were never meant to be separated like this. We were born to rule. Those who chose to create the divide were weak—and wrong."

A young man, consumed with grief, alone and supremely unhappy, stumbling into a large library to escape a deluge common for the area.

"You're late, Barloc," a stern voice came from the desk directly ahead; a tall, austere man stared down his long, beaked nose at him. The sorrow that consumed his every waking moment was pushed behind the crushing hatred that surged, as it did every time he had to make himself subservient to the cruel old man.

"I apologize, sir. My grandfather died and—"

"That was last week. You may no longer use that excuse. You will be on time, or you will be dismissed from the library."

"Yes, sir. Of course, sir. It won't happen again." And someday, I will never have to demean myself to worthless people like you again, *he added silently as he tromped toward his much smaller desk and the stack of books that needed sorting.*

A forest, bathed in shadow, only flickers of dappled sunlight glimmering between the leaves and branches above him. He stretched out his hand and loosed a blast of blue flame, consuming a huge bush entirely in moments, just because he could. *Burning, heady, intoxicating power searing through his veins—at long, long last.*

"Inara!"

I slammed back into myself with a jerk of Zuhra's hands on my shoulders, her voice nearly a shout. I was gasping for air, the emptiness inside me pulsing hot and painful.

"Inara—what happened? Are you all right?"

I blinked and looked at my sister, disoriented and terrified. "I'm . . . I'm fine," I finally managed. "I'm sorry . . . I just . . . I'm so tired," I added, aware of how absurd it sounded to claim it was only exhaustion.

"Are you sure?" Zuhra clearly didn't believe me, but she didn't press when I shook my head. "Perhaps we should go back inside. Lie down for a bit. Or go see what the others are doing."

"All right," I agreed, allowing her to thread our fingers together and walk hand in hand back toward the citadel. The sun was warm on our backs, but nothing could dispel the bone-deep cold from what I'd seen—and what it meant.

SIX

Zuhra

"Am I to understand there is an entire *collection* of Paladin books at this library you speak of?"

Sachiel's sharp question made Halvor flinch. "Yes. My uncle was studying them. At least, that's what he always claimed. He was a scholar. But, obviously, now I realize it was more than that." He sat perched on the edge of the chair as if preparing to jump to his feet and flee at any moment, his spine so straight, my mother would have cried tears of joy to see such proper posture—had she not been sitting beside Inara, her arm around her daughter's shoulders, glaring at him, as if she held him responsible for not knowing what Barloc had been planning to do.

The fact that *Mother* was the one comforting Inara during the meeting my father had called was unbelievable enough, but even more incredible was that Inara was *letting* her. Something between them must have drastically changed while I was in Visimperum. Either that, or whatever had happened to her out in the gardens, the frightening episode when her face had gone blank and she'd stopped responding—which she'd obviously lied about—had affected her so deeply, she hardly even noticed who was doing the comforting. I was still reeling from the fact that she had lied to me. I hadn't even dared question her because I'd been so stunned—and hurt.

"Why would a library in *your* world have *Paladin* books?"

"I'm not sure. My uncle didn't like lots of questions. He expected quiet obedience, and eventually rewarded hard work and study with answers. He'd promised me many answers after this expedition."

Sachiel's eyes narrowed, considering.

I'd hoped after the fiasco at dinner the night before, they would leave him alone. But when Inara and I had come back into the citadel, we'd seen him walking morosely toward the morning room, and she'd gone to him, all too eager to leave my side. He'd said he'd been summoned for more questioning, and she'd offered to go with him, leaving me no choice but to follow or return to my room alone.

"What name did you say he took here?" Sachiel continued her questioning.

"Barloc?"

"No, his family name—his surname. You name yourselves differently. What were his other names?"

"Ignulac. His full name is Barloc Ignulac." Halvor shrank back in his seat when Sachiel actually snarled in response to this revelation. Even Raidyn, who stood beside my father, winced.

"Ignulac?" my father repeated. "Are you sure?"

"He's my uncle—my mother's brother." Halvor's knuckles were white where he gripped his legs. "Yes, I'm sure."

My father spat a word in Paladin that I suspected wasn't one for polite society based on Sharmaine's flinch. "Sachiel, what can you tell us about any suspicious families near Fire Lake?" My father watched the other general closely.

"There is one family I remember," Sachiel said through clenched teeth. "A family strongly gifted with rare abilities—that were part of the *Infinitium* sect."

This time, Loukas cursed underneath his breath. A palpable chill descended over the room, like the visceral reaction I had when the name was brought up the night before . . . though I still didn't understand what it meant.

"They lived on a secluded farmstead on the edge of the forest, and groups of them would often go off into the woods for extended periods of time—you can imagine what they were searching for. They always returned, unsuccessful. But there was a rumor I heard when I was growing up—about one of the patriarchs of the family taking two of his sons and a handful of other family members decades before I was born; they left and never returned."

My father's hands clenched into fists. "That could be Barloc's connection." It wasn't a question, but Sachiel still nodded.

"Everyone in Ignulac believed they all died in the wilderness—killed by rakasa. At least that's what my grandmother told us. But what if they didn't? What if some of them actually *succeeded*?"

"Adelric," my mother finally spoke up, "can you explain what you're all talking about? Is Ignulac a place or a name?"

Sachiel's eyes narrowed as she pointedly said, "It's a place. It means 'fire lake'—and it's where I grew up."

"I see." Mother returned her glare for glare, some of her old fire returning at last—and for once, I was actually glad of her ability to make nearly anyone cower. "And what is the *Infinitium* sect?"

"The *Infinitium* sect is a fringe group of Paladin who believe our worlds never should have been separated—that the Paladin had the right to rule over the humans because of their superior power and abilities," Raidyn answered quietly, as if he bore the shame of *their* beliefs on his shoulders. "They often send groups of believers out to try to reach the gateway without being discovered by patrols and attempt to reopen it so they can come to Vamala and use their power to rule over your people."

When the meeting had begun, my stomach ached from hunger, but at Raidyn's words, that emptiness transmuted into acidic dismay. My mother drew back, stricken, and then turned her glare on Father. "Why did you never tell me about this?"

Before he could answer, I burst out, "Were the Five who succeeded—the ones who started the war—part of that sect?"

Everyone turned to me and I flushed.

"Yes, actually," my father responded, skipping my mother's question. But the look she gave him clearly meant *that* discussion wasn't finished. "They were caught attempting to get to the gateway by a patrolling garrison. The Five were all *jaklas* who had murdered other Paladin to strengthen themselves. They killed eight more Paladin in the patrol that caught them before they were subdued, imprisoned, and taken in to be tried and judged. But they were inordinately powerful, with rare gifts that enabled them to escape. The second time, they made it to the gateway and opened it—as you know."

We were all quiet for several seconds, absorbing what he'd said.

"So . . . Barloc's grandfather must have been part of the *Infinitium* sect, from Ignulac. And that's why he knew how to rip the power from—" Sharmaine cut herself off, flushing red, her eyes dropping to the ground when Inara stiffened.

"There's no way to know for certain," Sachiel said.

"What does that other word mean—the name of the sect?" Mother asked.

There was a pause, and then Father said, "It means unlimited power."

I shuddered. Raidyn's gaze lifted to me, no doubt sensing the emotion rising in my gut, boiling its way up, scalding my heart, my throat, my mouth.

"These secret books your uncle had." Sachiel shook off the reverie that had taken hold of her momentarily, her expression hardening once more as she turned back to Halvor. "We must assume they were brought by members of this sect from our world to yours. What's in them?"

"I don't know." Halvor stared down at his hands.

"How can you *not* know? Didn't you just tell us that you studied the Paladin with him—that you learned our language from him and his books?" Sachiel's voice rose again until Halvor cowered on the couch. I'd never seen him so diminished, so submissive. Not even by my mother at her worst. What his uncle had done to Inara had wounded him deeply, if not broken him entirely.

"Sachiel, that's enough," my father interceded. "Can't you see how upset the boy is?"

"We don't have time to be delicate about this," Sachiel argued.

"He knew a Paladin," Inara suddenly cut in.

"Excuse me?" Sachiel's eyebrows lifted.

Inara swallowed and looked up, her jaw set. "Barloc. He knew a Paladin. I don't know if it was his grandfather, but it was an old man."

I stared at my sister. "How could you possibly—"

"I saw him." Though Inara no longer had Paladin fire in her eyes, they still flashed when she lifted her chin and continued. "I saw him as a young boy, talking to an old man with glowing eyes. Telling him that our worlds were never meant to be split apart. That those with power should rule over those without."

"You *saw* him?" Halvor's voice was almost as quiet as hers.

Father and Sachiel shared a glance heavy with concern before Sachiel turned back to Inara. "Was it when he took your power? Did you see anything else?"

"I . . . ah . . . I'm not sure. I only remember seeing him with the old Paladin."

She was lying *again*. What was my sister hiding?

"If this is true, and the *jakla* did know a Paladin, who we must assume was part of the *Infinitium* sect, this is cause for even greater concern." Sachiel's mouth turned down at the corners.

"Why?" Mother asked, her arm still firmly wrapped around Inara, who had gone back to staring at the ground.

"As Adelric said, *Infinitium* means 'unlimited power'—which is partially because they believe Paladin should rule over those with less or no power. But also because they are willing to do *whatever* it takes to gain as much power as possible. Including performing the type of horrible rituals your uncle did to this poor girl." Sachiel paused and then barreled on. "There are rumors of other things they believe themselves capable of doing if they amass enough power—things even more terrible than what he's already done."

I shuddered at the thought of Barloc somehow doing things that were *worse* than ripping someone's power out.

"Do you think he might go back to the library?" Raidyn asked Halvor, though his concerned gaze was on me. "Now that his plan to get into Visimperum failed?"

"Maybe? I don't know where else he *would* go. I don't think he's ever traveled . . . before coming here."

"Then we must try to beat him there," Raidyn declared.

Loukas, sitting on a chair closer to the fire, turned to Raidyn, dismay on his handsome face. "You want us to go *farther* into Vamala? When you know what they did to your pa—the last time Paladin were here?"

Raidyn winced at Loukas's reminder about what had happened to his parents—two other Paladin who had never returned home before my grandmother shut the gateway at the end of the war, leaving many Paladin trapped in Vamala, including my father. But he didn't back down. Loukas's warning about Raidyn's intentions from that day by the *luxem magnam* rose once more—when he claimed to be worried that Raidyn was using me as a way to get to Vamala to see if his parents were still alive—writhing like a snake in my belly.

"I think Raidyn is right," Sachiel agreed.

"To what end?" Loukas shot back.

"To stop the *jakla*!" the female general cried out. "So we can go *home*!"

Silence followed Sachiel's pronouncement. My parents shared a glance. I forced myself to look at them, not Raidyn. Why had he suggested such a thing? If it had been anyone else . . . then the hard knot of distrust that had finally loosened last night wouldn't have resurfaced.

But it *was* back, and bigger than ever, crushing my hope that perhaps he truly did care for me as more than a means to an end. Loukas's theory that Raidyn hoped his parents had somehow survived and lived on, hidden in Vamala all these years, twisted my stomach as I listened to them argue.

"If he has books that taught him to perform the ritual—perhaps we can find a way to *undo* it?" Inara spoke again, her voice barely above a whisper.

There was an achingly long pause before Sharmaine gently said, "I wish that were possible. I truly do." Her eyes were full of regret but Inara didn't look up to see it, crumpling deeper into my mother's embrace instead. "But there is no way to undo what he's done. Plus, we still don't know for sure that is where he'll go. He may return here and attempt to get through the gateway again. He still thinks Inara opened it on her own, using only her power—which he now possesses. He never learned that Zuhra is an enhancer and that it was only their *combined* power that opened it, did he?"

"No, he doesn't know." Halvor also watched Inara, but she'd squeezed her eyes shut, so she didn't see. Her hands were clutched together in her lap, but they still shook.

"So, he thinks himself capable of opening the gateway with the power he stole. He claimed to be going to Visimperum to find others who felt the same way he did—he must have been referring to other members of the *Infinitium* sect. Perhaps even family, if the Paladin he knew was his grandfather as he claimed. We have to assume there's a high likelihood that he will return here."

I expected Sachiel to argue with Sharmaine, but instead, she nodded.

"You make a valid point. So perhaps it would be best if we split up—half staying here to defend the citadel and half traveling to this library in case he does return there."

"Splitting up is a risky move," my father said.

"So is leaving the gateway unmonitored," she countered.

My father finally stood, crossing to the couch where Mother and Inara sat, and placed a hand on his wife's shoulder. "Let's take the afternoon to think about it, and we can decide later before we start night watches again. After the burial."

Sachiel looked as though she were about to say more, but at the reminder that Adelric still had to bury his father, though her lips pursed, she remained mercifully silent.

"I believe Sami was preparing food for you all—it should be ready by now," my mother said. "I'm sure you're all famished after such a long night." She pulled Inara to her feet and guided her toward the door, Father right behind them.

The rest of the room cleared out, except for Loukas and Raidyn. I still stood by the window, the sunshine streaming through the clear glass pane warm on my back.

"Aren't you hungry?" Raidyn looked over at his friend.

"You know as well as I do that it would be better if I go find food for myself later. Last night was bad enough."

"That's not true, Louk. If anyone seemed tense, it was because of what happened yesterday."

He glanced to me, his unique green-fire eyes burning. I was suddenly acutely uncomfortable, as if I were eavesdropping on a conversation I wasn't meant to hear. A part of me had hoped to have a minute alone with Raidyn, but instead, I glanced away from both of them, then followed the rest of the group to the dining hall that finally had a use with all of the extra bodies staying in the citadel that needed food—something I could still barely wrap my mind around.

"Zuhra, wait," Raidyn spoke up, but I only paused for a moment before forcing my feet to continue to carry me toward the door.

"I'll talk to you later," I called over my shoulder. "I think you two need a minute by yourselves."

I didn't look back as I hurried out into the hallway, but I heard Raidyn say, "Did you do something to her?" and Loukas respond, "Of course not."

Last night, I'd been convinced Loukas had been wrong about Raidyn—his accusation that Raidyn was only interested in using me to get to Vamala in hopes that his parents survived and that he could find them. I didn't know much about friendship and knew even less about the relationships between a man and a woman . . . but I'd thought surely no one would spend hours comforting and soothing a person, at the loss of their own chance for sleep, if they were merely *using* that person. Would they?

After he suggested we travel to the library in Mercarum to try to find Barloc, my doubts had returned, however.

I was no longer hungry, and I didn't want to go sit beside Inara with her lie still between us, so I headed back outside, rather than going to the dining hall. I didn't really have a destination in mind, but found myself wandering toward the stables, where the gryphons were still in their stalls. The building sagged against the earth, squatting like an aged crone, stronger than it looked, having weathered many storms, just as I'd assured Sharmaine.

The door groaned, shuddering open beneath my hand when I yanked on it.

Inside, the stables were a mix of heavy, menacing shadows skulking between dazzling puddles of sunlight from the skylights. The door shut behind me with a resounding *thud,* encasing me in darkness. I stepped forward into the nearest square of sunshine and glanced around.

Silence.

No rustling, no huffing or clicking, or any noise to indicate the gryphons were awake—or even alive.

It hadn't occurred to me until that moment that it might have been dangerous to come out here alone. Barloc couldn't have snuck back in somehow and killed all of them during the night—could he? What if he'd hidden himself there—waiting to attack the next unsuspecting person who walked in?

"Good morning!" I called out brightly, forcing myself to act like nothing was wrong. Surely, if the gryphons still lived, they would react to me.

But there was no response.

Nothing but oppressive, chilling quiet.

My heart clawed up into my throat, gagging me with terror. Did I try to sneak back out, now that I'd just announced my presence? Or did I turn and run?

I was too frightened to do more than slowly slink backward, praying I made it to the door and escaped in time. To at least scream and alert the Paladin on patrol that something was wrong. I thought of Naiki, Raidyn's beautiful gryphon, and Taavi, my father's—their bright, intelligent eyes, snuffed out forever—and had to blink back futile tears.

Before I could stretch out for the handle, the door groaned once more, and daylight flooded around me, illuminating me like a target.

I spun to face the dark silhouette of a man, his face hidden by shadow, blinding sunlight haloing his head and body.

"No!" I cried, stumbling back to escape—but I was too late. He sprang forward and grabbed my arm.

SEVEN

Zuhra

"Zuhra? What's wrong?"

I fought to break free, until the sound of his voice penetrated the clamor of fear in my head—and realized it was Raidyn. I sagged with relief before catapulting forward into his arms; but rather than letting myself sink into his embrace, I grabbed his shoulders and pushed him backward, a sob breaking free as I shouted, "We have to go—*now*! He's here! They're gone—I'm so sorry, they're *all* gone."

"What?" Raidyn shoved me behind him, spinning to face the stables, his veins flaring with fire. A small orb of it almost immediately hovered above his hand as he stalked forward.

"No! Barloc is here somewhere." I grabbed his arm and yanked Raidyn back. "He killed them! He killed all of them!"

He glanced past my shoulder, realization dawning on his face. His eyes flared, a blaze of even brighter light pulsing through his veins. "*Naiki*," he uttered. And then he pulled free of my grip and charged into the depths of the stable.

"No, *Raidyn*!"

He let out a long, low whistle, a sound that mimicked a gryphon's, but that was so full of mourning it made my eyes fill with tears again.

Until there was a responding sound from within the stable, echoed all down the row of stalls.

Raidyn froze, then let his hand lower, the orb of flame winking out. The light in his veins dimmed. I stared in shock as first Naiki, then the other gryphons, all pushed their heads over the stalls, a cacophony of whistles and low hoots filling the previously silent stable.

"But . . . I don't . . ."

"Zuhra"—Raidyn slowly turned to me—"why did you think they were all dead?"

He should have been angry. He should have been yelling at me for scaring him like that. I could *feel* the anger simmering beneath the surface of the cool, collected tone of his voice. But he strangled it into submission and simply waited, while I gaped in disbelief.

"I . . . I went in to check on them and I didn't hear anything. I got scared and called out, but there was still nothing. They didn't even move. I—I guess I assumed . . ." It sounded so stupid now, but had felt so real, so certain before.

"They're trained to be completely silent when they're in unfamiliar places and it's not their Rider's voice or scent they recognize coming in," Raidyn explained, rubbing a still-shaky hand over his face and then pushing his hair back off his forehead, leaving it in disarray.

A flush crept up my neck and my stomach cramped. "I'm so, *so* sorry."

"You didn't know." Though his words were forgiving, he turned and walked away, toward Naiki's stall, away from me.

I stood in the doorway, watching as he reached up to his gryphon and stroked her feathered face, then leaned forward to rest his forehead against hers, his eyes squeezing shut. Scalding shame pulsed through my body. She was the only family he had left, and for a terrible moment, I'd made him believe she, too, was gone.

Mortified, I turned on my heel to rush to my room.

"Zuhra, don't go."

Despite myself, I paused.

"I came to talk to you."

"You did?" I slowly turned back to find him striding toward me.

He nodded, his eyes roaming over my face. "When I left last night, you were asleep. Were you able to *stay* asleep?"

My face grew hot again, but for a different reason this time.

"Yes. Until the sunrise, at least." I shifted on my feet, looking away from his blue-fire gaze, staring instead at his chest, to the muscles that shifted beneath the light material of his shirt. "I don't know how you knew . . . or why you were *willing* to . . . but I really can't thank you enough for doing that for me." It was such a meager excuse for the gratitude I owed him after what he'd done for me, but I had nothing else to offer except the paltry words.

When his fingers grazed my jaw, I jumped then went completely still. He gently pressed, lifting my face up until our gazes met again.

"You *truly* don't know?" His eyes seared into mine. "You can't *feel* why?"

I swallowed. He wanted to know why I couldn't *feel* why? Oh, how I *felt*. Quite a lot of things, actually. The tingle of his fingertips still lingering on my face, the heat in my limbs, liquid and languorous, tempting me to step closer to him and lift my face toward his. The heady rush of having his burning gaze focused solely on me. But beneath all that, there was something more, something deeper. A safety, a *security*, I'd never known before. A feeling that even though I'd believed this citadel to be home for all of my eighteen years, in reality, it had merely been a stopping place for me to grow and learn and bide my time until I found my *true* home—in him. Because if I were honest with myself, I couldn't picture a life that didn't have Raidyn in it.

But that was everything *I* felt. What could he—

And then it hit me, with such force I stumbled back a step, my eyes widening.

He watched me closely, an expression of such vulnerability on his face, it struck me like an arrow piercing me between the ribs, the target deep in my chest, making me ache. That, and the sudden swell of hopeful fear—emotions I recognized but couldn't claim.

His emotions.

"I can't hide anything from you, Zuhra. Not anymore."

The *sanaulus*. All those things I'd *thought* were my feelings and mine alone—the ones I was too afraid to name, even to myself . . . did that mean he felt the same things as me . . . was that even *possible*?

Could I truly trust myself to separate what was me from him? What if I had somehow twisted his true emotions into what I only *wished* to be true?

Every beat of my heart was laced with a painful, sharp hope; my head hurt from the confusion and longing that seized me.

"Can I ask you a question?" Raidyn's voice was soft, his fear rising over the tumult of emotions. At least, I was fairly certain it was his fear, not mine.

But it was so hard to tell, and I was so very, very afraid to let myself hope.

I nodded.

"Why don't you trust me?"

My mouth fell open, leaving me gaping at him wordlessly.

He looked to the ground as he quickly explained, "I apologize for being so blunt, but I don't know what I've done to make you think you can't trust me. I only know that you don't. And . . . now that you are aware of my feelings for you, I hope you will at least do me the honor of explaining what I did to deserve your mistrust."

My mortification grew even more acute, but though I opened and closed my mouth once, nothing came out.

When I didn't respond, he let his hand drop. My skin was oddly bereft without his touch, chilled and stretched too tight over my body.

"Do you know why Adelric has all three of us in his battalion—me, Sharmaine, and Loukas?"

"No," I finally managed, baffled by the question.

"We were all Riders, we all had gryphons choose us. But no battalion leader would take on me or Loukas. Sharmaine refused to abandon us, even though she had the opposite problem—nearly every single battalion *wanted* her to join them."

"But . . . why?" I had no idea why he'd changed the subject, but if his goal was to get me talking again, he'd succeeded. I was ashamed that I hadn't been brave enough to answer his question—especially after I'd made him think Naiki had died. I owed him an explanation, it was true, and doubly so after that. But the way he'd worded it made me realize just how unfair I'd been to him.

Because the truth was *he'd* never done anything to make me think he wasn't trustworthy. Only Loukas's accusations had planted those doubts, and circumstantial evidence had continued to make me wonder if it were true.

"Shar is smart, dedicated, and good at pretty much everything. Plus, her power to create a shield is highly coveted," Raidyn continued to explain. My stomach plummeted as he described the beautiful Paladin who had been in love with him for most of her life. "But she is also loyal to a fault, so she decided she'd rather not follow her dream to be a Rider with a battalion than leave me and Loukas behind."

Despite the jealousy I struggled to strangle into submission, I made myself say, "But . . . you're all those things too." I flushed when his brows lifted. "Why wouldn't every battalion leader have wanted you too?"

Raidyn grimaced. "Because after I lost my parents, I was hurt and angry, and I didn't know how to handle it."

I watched him closely, but there was no indication that he believed anything different—when he said he'd lost his parents, I sensed only sorrow and grief and even a little anger. But nothing else. No lingering hope.

I should have believed my heart, not Loukas.

"My grandmother did her best with me, but she, too, was heartbroken and she only lived a few more years after the gateway was shut. After that, I was old enough that I refused to move in with whatever distant relative the council deemed should raise me. Instead, I bounced between Loukas's and Sharmaine's homes and trained with Naiki, and eventually passed all my tests to become a full Rider. And then got rejected by every leader—except one."

My father.

"He took all three of us into his battalion, difficult as it was, because he, too, had suffered terrible loss. He knew how to reach a boy who had hardened his heart against everyone, afraid of being hurt again. He knew how to help me become . . . someone better than I was."

I remembered the pang of envy I'd felt when Loukas first told me that Adelric was like a father to Raidyn, after losing his own parents. But as I listened to Raidyn tell me what my father had done for him, when I sensed his gratitude for Adelric's influence, I couldn't help but feel thankful that not having my father in my life had meant Raidyn gained him in his.

"He saw past all my defenses and treated me like a person worthy of respect and kindness, which I wasn't at that time. He saw potential in me that I'd given up believing in long before that." He hesitated and finally looked back into my eyes. "I guess I hoped that perhaps his daughter would be able to see me that way too."

My knees trembled. "Raidyn, I—"

"And I know I'm not supposed to use the *sanaulus,*" he barreled on, "but when it comes to you, I must admit that I am not strong enough to resist trying to figure out what you're feeling—at least a few times. Which, I guess actually *does* make me untrustworthy, after all. But I've never felt like this before, let alone with someone I *healed,* and—"

"Raidyn." I stepped closer to him and reached for his hand, though it took every ounce of courage I possessed to do so. The deluge of words cut off with a snap of his mouth closing. His hand flexed around mine, his eyes widening as if just barely realizing how much he'd admitted. Embarrassment burned hot in my gut, but I recognized it as his this time, not mine. "You haven't done anything to make me not trust you. I'm sorry that I ever listened to Loukas; I should have known better."

His fingers tightened. "*Loukas?*" he ground out. His teeth clenched so hard, a muscle snapped in his jaw. It wasn't exactly the reaction I'd expected. Was he *angry*? "What did he say to you?"

"He, er, he said something about thinking you were using me to get to the gateway so you could come here and search for your parents."

"My *dead* parents? And you *believed* him?"

He was *definitely* angry.

"Well . . . my father was proof that it was possible to survive. And he thought maybe you still hoped your parents had too. And that you saw me as a way to get here and search for them." When his eyes narrowed, I rushed to add, "It made more sense to me than believing you could truly care for me. I know I don't have any experience with . . . with . . ." I faltered, gesturing between our bodies. "*Things* between men and women. But even *I* knew that it was extremely unlikely that someone like you could have wanted someone like me."

Raidyn stared at me for a moment before pulling his hand free of mine. My fingers closed over my palm, and I quickly yanked it back to my side. The sun overheard was unbearably strong. A dry breeze rustled through the courtyard, grazing my already-too-hot cheeks.

"And Loukas is the one who put these thoughts in your head?"

"Yes, but I—"

Raidyn turned on his heel and stalked toward the citadel.

"Raidyn, wait! I don't want to cause you to fight with your friend—"

He paused long enough to glance over one powerful shoulder. "Oh, *you* aren't causing anything. He brought this on himself."

I dashed after him, barely catching up before he made it to the door that was still slightly ajar from when he'd come out, apparently to find me. I grabbed his sleeve and tugged. "Please, Raidyn. It's my fault for listening to him. I should have asked you—I should have trusted you, like you said."

He looked down at my hand on his arm then up into my face. He lifted one hand to gently brush his fingers against my cheek. But instead of turning back to me—to finish whatever conversation he'd intended to have before I ruined it by admitting what Loukas had told me—he let it drop to his side again and asked, "Zuhra, do you know why Loukas has green eyes instead of blue?"

The unexpected question threw me off balance. I shook my head mutely.

"Ask him. It might explain a few things."

He moved toward the door again, but I grabbed his sleeve once more. "Tell me. Help me understand why you're so mad right now."

"It's not my place to say. Though the Light knows I don't owe him anything at this point." Raidyn's eyes glittered dangerously in the sunlight. "Now, if you'll excuse me, my *friend* and I are about to have a long-overdue talk."

This time I let him go, his lingering rage beating in time with my dread.

EIGHT

INARA

Mother hovered over me for most of the afternoon, but I didn't complain. She'd spent more time with me in the last twenty-four hours than my entire life. Plus, her constant chatter and fussing helped distract me—without all the questions Zuhra would have surely asked. I was terrified that whatever had happened in the garden might occur again—and the last thing I wanted was another glimpse into Barloc's life.

Thankfully, after the awful meeting with all the Paladin, Mother seemed afraid to leave my side, and for once in my life, I didn't want her to.

Adelric—*Father*—had stayed for a bit, but after a few minutes, he'd apologized that he was needed elsewhere and hesitantly came over to give me a hug. I had, even more hesitantly, hugged him back—briefly. Then he'd gone to Mother to *kiss* her (something that had taken me by complete surprise, though I supposed it shouldn't have) and left.

He hadn't returned yet.

Sami had outdone herself with breakfast, but I'd barely been able to eat a thing, so Mother kept going to get me plates of food every hour or so. I couldn't bring myself to do much more than pick at them.

All the while Sharmaine's words echoed over and over: *There's no way to undo what he's done.*

Not because of what she'd said—but because of the look on the other general's face when she'd said it. The dark-haired, dark-skinned woman named Sachiel. I needed to speak to her—alone. I didn't know how to make it happen . . . yet. But I had to figure it out. And soon, if they really did decide to split up or all leave in search of Barloc's library.

"Are you sure you don't want me to go check and see if there's any soup left?" Mother fussed with the blanket she'd tucked around my legs where I sat on the couch, trying to avoid looking out the window at the hedge Father had healed last night. I knew he'd been trying to show me that I, too, could heal. All it had done was prove how helpless I was—how *useless.*

But the only way to talk to Sachiel was to force myself to stop hiding in here with Mother.

"Actually, some soup would be nice," I said. "And maybe a bath? If it's not too much trouble."

"Of course! I should have thought of that. A nice, hot bath always helps me feel bet—relaxed," she corrected herself. Though she was obviously staying by my side because she was concerned, Mother seemed terrified to admit something was wrong with me out loud. She skirted the subject, refusing to talk about what had happened with Barloc, or the loss of my power, or the fact that I hadn't slept last night—something I was certain she and Father had discussed.

"I'll meet you in my room, then?"

"Yes," she agreed, jumping to her feet. "I'll be there as quickly as possible."

This new version of my mother was so strange, so foreign—but very welcome. My memories of her during all the years when the roar consumed me were of asking Zuhra where Mother was—why she wasn't with us, why she didn't want to be with me.

Why she avoided me.

Part of me wondered if she was only comfortable with me now because my power was gone, but I tried to silence that voice in my head, reminding myself that Mother had opened up to me even before Barloc ripped the Paladin half of me away.

Once Mother was gone, I made myself stand, even though I

was so exhausted, I wondered if perhaps I *could* nap. The panic from last night had subsided, and I longed for the release of sleep.

But I needed answers more.

Knowing my time was short, I hurried out the door. Rather than going to my room, I forced my feet to carry me toward the courtyard, where I knew Sachiel would be. I'd caught a glimpse of her on the back of her gryphon, flying over the hedge to the citadel, a moment before I'd asked Mother to draw me a bath.

I caught up to her as she was leading her gryphon to the stables. The massive beast still made me nervous, with its piercing hawk eyes, lion's hindquarters and tail, and razor-sharp talons. But I swallowed my fear and called out, "Sachiel!"

The older woman startled and turned. When she saw me, her eyebrows lifted. All the Paladin's glowing blue eyes were stunning, but hers were even more brilliant than the others, such a stark contrast to her dark skin and hair. "Did you need something?"

I forced myself to ignore the impatience in her voice and moved a little closer to her, though I made sure to still give the gryphon a wide berth. "Yes, actually. I need you to tell me how I can get my power back."

Sachiel's face was like a mask, except for a slight narrowing of her eyes. She reached up with one arm to wipe a drip of sweat off the bald side of her scalp, where she'd shaved her hair. The long braid down the center of her head swung with the movement. "I don't know what you're talking about," she said at last, turning away and continuing toward the stables.

"I saw you in the room earlier—when Sharmaine said there's nothing I can do. You didn't agree with her. I could tell." I followed, though my heart beat faster and my stomach had twisted itself up into a tangled morass of fading hope. I couldn't have been wrong—she *had* to know something. It was my only chance.

"Listen." Sachiel stopped once more and faced me. "I am so sorry for what happened to you. Truly, I am. I can't even imagine how terrible it would be." She paused but then with a slight shake of her head, continued, "But there is nothing you can do without the *jakla,* and he's missing. It's a miracle you're still alive. Try to focus on that. Though I know it is probably very difficult to believe that living without your power is a blessing, it's better than the alternative."

A dry breeze swept across the courtyard, ruffling the gryphon's feathers and blowing dust into my face. I blinked a few times to clear my vision. "Wait—what do you mean without the *jakla*? Does that mean if we had Barloc, there *is* something I could do?"

Sachiel crossed her arms, a tendon flexing in her biceps, visible beneath the material of her tight blouse. She wore a fitted leather vest and pants, with boots to her knees. She was formidable and strong and nothing like any other woman I'd ever known or read about. And though that wasn't saying much, with the secluded life I'd had in the citadel, somehow I knew that even if I had met *hundreds* of women in my life, she still would have been completely unique. As far as I knew, she didn't have a husband, no children, no reason to have any compassion for me. She was a general in the Paladin world, and I was just one pathetic girl, keeping her from her duties, or perhaps some well-deserved rest.

But she had an answer for me, I knew it. I *had* to convince her to share it with me.

"Please," I said. "You might think you know what it would be like to have your power ripped from you, but unless you've experienced it, there's no way you could." My hands began to shake at the audacity of questioning her and I clasped them together in front of me to hide it. "You say it's a miracle I'm alive . . . and you're right. It *is* a miracle. But . . . if I can't get my power back, I'm . . . I'm not sure I *want* to be alive." The trembling in my hands spread to my whole body as I spoke words I hadn't dared tell a living soul, not even Zuhra. The tightness in my chest returned, the gaping hole in me seemed to widen, as if it *enjoyed* hearing me admit the truth. "I might be alive, but there's this . . . this *emptiness* in me where the power used to be. And it's *awful.* A dark hole, so deep, so—" I choked on a rising sob and broke off. I tried to hold the tears back, but they were relentless, a tidal wave of anguish, and all I could do was repeat one word: "Please."

The skin of Sachiel's knuckles stretched tight; her fingers dug into her arms. She wavered—I felt her uncertainty. But then she shook her head. "I'm so sorry, Inara. Truly, I am. But Sharmaine was right. There's nothing you can do."

She spun on her heel, clucked at her gryphon, and disappeared with it into the stables, leaving me standing in the courtyard, dust from the summer wind sticking to the wetness on my cheeks.

Rather than go to my room and face my mother, I slowly walked through the orchard toward my gardens. I didn't know why I thought admitting the truth to Sachiel—a veritable stranger—would have swayed her into telling me how to get my power back. It had been a mistake. She would surely tell the others, and who knew how they'd react when they found out.

The only clue she'd given me was that getting my power back had something to do with needing Barloc. And he'd disappeared.

I ignored the frightening glimmer of memory of him in a forest, blasting a tree with his new power—*my* power. The forest was massive, spreading across most of Vamala. It was impossible to know where he was from that one, tiny glimpse.

"Inara?"

The hesitant question startled me and I spun to see Halvor standing across the courtyard, his hands shoved into his pockets.

"Are you all right?"

I thought about lying to him, trying to summon a smile and pretending. But I was exhausted and the wound inside me felt larger than ever, a pulsing darkness within that was growing stronger. I shook my head, my vision blurring yet again.

He crossed to where I stood, his long legs eating up the distance between us quickly. "I'm so sorry," he said and wrapped his arms around me. I sank into his embrace, pressing my face against his chest. I thought of what Zuhra had told me, of her racing heart and burning skin. The only reason *my* heart beat faster was my fear of Barloc—and Halvor's touch actually made it slow once more. He held me silently, calming me with every stroke of my hair as I sobbed, all the horror and pain and sorrow crashing through me, rending loose in a torrent of tears that left me weak and trembling.

Could love be made of comfort and calming, rather than need and heat?

When the storm finally passed, Halvor eased back, enough to look down at my face, keeping his arms around me. "I wish there was something I could do," he said quietly. I knew he held himself responsible for what had happened—he'd funded his uncle's expedition here, he had brought him into the citadel. But he hadn't known.

I stared up at him, into his warm, honey-brown eyes. He lifted a hand and gently wiped my cheeks, first one side, then the other. He couldn't take away my pain; he couldn't give me back what his uncle had stolen. But he could hold me. He could help push back the darkness with his touch, with the light in his eyes. Different from the glowing blue-fire of the Paladin, but no less remarkable. When he looked at me the way he was right then, it didn't make my heart race, but it made the widening maw of the hole inside me shrink a little bit, which was its own kind of power.

"Inara," he murmured, his voice low, his eyes searching mine. "I don't want to take advantage of you when you're exhausted and suffering so deeply."

Somehow, little experience as I had with people in general, and boys in particular, I knew he wanted to kiss me. That was what he meant. And . . . I *wanted* him to. I wanted to know what it felt like, I wanted to see just how much power he had to drive away the hopelessness within me. I wanted to feel fire in my veins again—even if it was from him, not my power.

"At least we know you won't get hurt this time." I tried to cover my nervousness, though the words caused a pang in my chest.

Halvor didn't laugh. Instead, he cupped my head with the hand that still lingered on my cheek. He swallowed, his gaze dropping to my mouth. But still, he waited.

"I want you to," I whispered, summoning any lingering courage I still possessed after my disastrous attempt to convince Sachiel to help me. "Please."

Halvor's arm tightened around me, and then he was leaning

forward. The distance between us closed, until I was pressed against him, watching as his head dipped toward mine. And then, finally, his lips touched mine. Soft, hesitant, and oh so sweet. Warmth unfurled in my chest, chasing away a little bit of the empty darkness inside. It wasn't what Zuhra felt for Raidyn, but I wasn't Zuhra.

I wrapped my arms around him, curving my body into his. His lips moved on mine, a slow give and take that I imitated. Halvor's kiss was made of its own kind of light; it was warmth, and it was powerful enough to drive the darkness away. It was the first time I realized, perhaps, even if I never got my Paladin power back, there was a reason to want to be here after all.

"Inara!"

The sound of my mother's voice jarred me back to reality, and we sprang apart. Halvor's shoulders curved downward, like a dog expecting to be scolded. I'd seen a picture of one once, tail tucked between its legs and ears drooping, in a book Zuhra used to read to me when I was younger and the roar receded long enough, usually in the winter. I reached out and took his hand in mine, holding it tightly.

"Thank you," I said.

"For what?"

"You said you wished you could help me—well, you did. So, thank you."

A small, hesitant smile curved his lips. "That helped?"

"More than you know," I assured him.

His smile grew wider. "Me too," he said softly. "More than you know."

I smiled back.

"Inara!" Mother's voice was closer now.

"I better go."

He nodded, but squeezed my hand before releasing it.

As I hurried back the way I'd come, the memory of Halvor's kiss burned brightly in my chest, holding the darkness at bay—at least for now.

NINE

Zuhra

Eventually I found myself in the kitchen with Sami, craving calm—*familiarity*. We cleaned and cooked, side by side, not speaking, but the silence was uncomplicated. Just being there, the aroma of spices and smoke from the fire wafting around us, melding together with the clink of dishes and Sami's comforting presence, brought much-needed peace.

As I was chopping some vegetables to put in the stew for supper, Sami finally spoke up.

"Was it very frightening? In Visimperum?"

My knife stilled over the carrot in front of me. "Only at the very beginning, when the rakasa had me. But my father's battalion was patrolling nearby and they saved me. I wasn't frightened after that . . . except that I'd never make it back home—that Inara and the rest of you might have all been killed by the rakasa that got into the citadel."

Sami nodded. "She *should* have died. And poor Halvor too. Her gift saved them both." There was a wistfulness in her voice that made the ache inside of me break open again.

"I wish I'd listened to my grandmother and left the gateway shut. I should have stayed in Visimperum." The carrot blurred on the cutting board. "I never would have seen my sister again—or any of you. But then none of this would have ever happened."

Sami paused from washing a pot in the large sink. "Zuhra, what's happened is done, and wishing for it to be different will only keep you trapped in the past. And who's to say what would have happened if you *hadn't* come back? Barloc was convinced Inara had enough power to open the gateway on her own. He would have attacked her eventually, I'm sure of it. And if you and that young man hadn't been there, she would have died."

I made myself resume cutting, even though the vegetables wavered in front of me.

When I didn't respond, Sami continued washing the pot. I thought perhaps she would remain silent, but after a few moments, she asked, "What was she like? Your grandmother?"

I must have grimaced, because Sami said, "That bad?"

After a pause to gather my thoughts, I said, "She was . . . hurt. And angry. And she didn't want anything to do with me."

"Oh, Zuhra," Sami murmured.

"I think she changed her mind in the end, but it was too late." I wondered if she had survived whatever Barloc had done to her. Loukas had said she was injured, that she took the brunt of a blast of Barloc's power when he'd found himself surrounded by hundreds of Paladin. But there had been many healers there—surely they had saved her. Though my feelings toward her were complicated at best, she was still my father's mother, and he'd already lost his father. He hadn't said a word about Grandmother, but I knew he was worried. I truly hoped she lived.

And that we would somehow see her again.

"I think that should be plenty." Sami eyed the pile of vegetables I'd amassed on the cutting board. "Why don't you go see if your mother needs any help with the preparations for your grandfather's burial."

I nodded, though I would have rather stayed with Sami. Did Mother even remember we were burying him tonight? It was hard to know; she'd been so focused on Inara. I wiped my hands off and handed Sami the knife to wash.

"Thank you for your help," she said.

"Thank you for always being there for me."

"I always will be." Sami reached for me with her free arm, pulling me into a brief hug. Before I could react, she'd released me and turned back to the sink.

* * *

Grandfather's body had been laid in an empty room, wrapped in sheets yellowed with age. It was all we had to offer, meager as it was. The plan was to bury him at sunset, after supper, as was the Paladin tradition. They believed the soul of the deceased would be caught up in the rays of the setting sun and carried with them to the Light in the afterlife.

I couldn't find my mother, so I slowly made my way to the room where he lay, not sure where else to look. Part of me hoped to run into Raidyn, to ask him what had happened with Loukas. But as I was walking through the hallways, I caught a glimpse of two gryphons taking off from the courtyard out the window next to me. I immediately recognized one of them as Naiki, with Raidyn on her back—and the other was Keko.

Sharmaine's gryphon.

A cold wave of dismay washed away the warmth from our earlier conversation. He wanted me to trust him, he wanted me to believe he cared for me—and I *thought* I'd felt his emotions. I thought, perhaps, there was a chance he felt the same way I did.

Then why had he gone to Sharmaine after talking to Loukas instead of me?

I closed my eyes and took a deep breath, willing myself to stay calm. *Maybe* she *asked* him *to go for a ride with her and he didn't want to be rude.*

I forced myself to turn away from the window and the view of the gryphons shrinking into the distance. The air was somehow heavier, pressing in on me as I walked on leaden feet to the room where my grandfather lay. Humidity had slowly built all day, until the citadel seemed less of a home and more of an oven, baking discontent and fear instead of food.

The door was slightly ajar. I pushed it open to find someone else sitting beside the bed, his head in his hands, shoulders shaking.

"Loukas?" I was so startled to find him there, his name came out before I had a chance to think through whether I wished to speak with him or not.

He immediately straightened, rubbing one arm over his face

before twisting in his chair to face me. The curtains were drawn, leaving only the impression of sunlight in the room; it was too dim for me to be able to tell if he'd truly been crying or not. His eyes flared bright green in the shadows, his jaw lined with stubble and his thick, dark hair in disarray, as if he'd been pulling it by the roots.

"So, apparently you told Raidyn about our conversation." His voice was as cold as the blood in my veins.

I flinched back from the icy rage billowing off of him. "He asked me why I didn't trust him. I wasn't going to lie. He would have known if I had."

"Ah, yes, because of the *sanaulus.* How convenient."

"Can we not do this here?" I glanced to the shrouded form of my grandfather's body and swallowed hard, once.

Loukas had the decency to look ashamed. He, too, glanced at the bed and his shoulders caved forward. "You're right. I'm sorry."

He sounded sincere, but I didn't have the luxury—or burden—of *sanaulus* with him to know for certain. If trying to decipher someone else's feelings could ever *be* certain, which I wasn't positive it could.

"You'll be happy to know he's furious with me now."

I cringed. "Why would that make me happy?"

His green-fire gaze burned into mine, making me unaccountably nervous. "He seems to think you don't know why my eyes are different."

"I don't."

"I find that hard to believe," he scoffed. "No one told you to stay away from me? Not one person you met warned you of what I could do?"

"No." The sudden realization that we were completely alone in a room far from anyone else in the citadel, with only my deceased grandfather as a witness, struck me silent. I'd never been nervous around Loukas—until now.

"You're afraid," he commented as if he were remarking on the weather. "That's good. You should be."

I crossed my arms, shoving my hands underneath them to hide their trembling from him. "Stop it, Loukas. You don't scare me."

He lifted one brow. "As an enhancer, you have a very rare gift. Your eyes don't glow because your power only works when you use it in conjunction with another Paladin's. If you'd been born in my world—with two Paladin parents, instead of a human mother to confuse things—everyone would have immediately known what you were. Just as everyone immediately knew what I was because of my green eyes. My gift is even rarer than yours—and far more feared. I'm a *mentirum.* I can control minds."

My mouth formed an *O* of shock. I hadn't even known such a thing was possible.

"So you see the problem. Raidyn, one of the only friends I've ever had, now believes I used my gift to control *your* mind—to force you not to trust him."

"Did you?" I managed to ask, though my throat was so tight, the words escaped as little more than a raspy whisper.

"Of course not, Zuhra! Don't you think you would know if I had forced you to believe something?"

I shook my head, my heart throbbing a terrified cadence beneath the cage of my ribs. "I—I don't know."

"I swear on my life, I didn't. I learned to control it a long time ago, and I almost never use it—not even on patrol. But most Paladin still avoid me, for fear of what I *could* do. All except for your father, Raidyn, and Sharmaine." His gaze dropped to the ground. "Until now."

Part of me ached for him, for the hurt he obviously held so close; but his revelation also terrified me. What exactly did it mean—that he could control minds? Could he only manipulate feelings? Or could he force anyone to do anything he wanted? No wonder Raidyn had been so upset by what I'd told him.

But when I thought back on that final day in Visimperum when he'd found me by the *luxem magnam* and warned me about his suspicions, I hadn't felt anything other than uncertainty that eventually evolved into suspicion. Surely, if he'd used his power, I would have felt an immediate, strong aversion to Raidyn—a *certainty* that Loukas was right.

A certainty that I still didn't have. About anything.

"I believe you."

He looked up, eyebrows lifted. "You do?"

I nodded. "You didn't force me to feel anything. I'll talk to Raidyn."

His jaw clenched, a muscle ticking in his cheek. After a long moment, he said, "Thank you," the words soft and low. The realization that he was trying to hold back his emotions—that *Loukas,* who seemed as indifferent as a person could be, was near tears simply because I *believed* him—hit me like a punch to the gut.

I finally walked into the room and took a seat across from him, in the empty chair.

I'd never really thought about it before, but what he said about the other Paladin avoiding him *did* seem to be true, when I searched through my memories with him in Visimperum. He was almost always alone, or with Raidyn and Sharmaine. I'd rarely ever seen him speaking with any other Paladin.

"Raidyn is even luckier than I thought," Loukas finally said, after several long minutes of weighted silence.

I glanced up.

"I've known you were something special since I first met you, that day in the stables, when you were determined to find a way back to your sister." He stared at his hands. "But no one has ever believed me so easily before—or been willing to stay near me—once they learned the truth."

Compassion, sharp and unexpected, twisted in my chest. "I'm sorry, Louk."

He shrugged and visibly summoned his normal apathetic guise, which I realized was just that—a front, hiding his true self, and his very real pain. "It's probably because they can't handle this level of handsome."

"Or that level of conceit," I teased, understanding his need for me to pretend with him, letting the heavier truths drop for now.

"Can you blame me?" He flashed me his most endearing grin and I shook my head.

After a pause, he stood. "I should probably let you have some time alone." He made it to the door, then stopped once more. "And I'm sorry for . . . before."

I nodded and he left.

Once I was alone, the reality that my grandfather was lying on the bed hit me—that he was truly gone, *forever.*

My fault.

Because I'd forced the council to open the gateway.

Even though the curtains blocked most of the sunlight, the room was still too warm. The shadows pulsed with dank summer heat that made my tongue thick and heavy in my mouth. I reached one trembling hand out to place it on my grandfather's shoulder, covered by the sheets. His body was strange, stiff and heavy and wrong.

Empty.

"I'm so sorry," I whispered, letting my head drop forward onto the bed next to him.

TEN

Inara

I stood at my window, a film of terror cold on my skin, chilled as the windowpane I pressed my fingertips to as I looked to the cliffs where a storm had begun to build. Mother had succeeded in forcing me to bathe, and even got me to drink some tea and lie down. Despite everything churning in my mind, I'd somehow fallen asleep much quicker than I'd believed possible. Until I'd finally woken, my tongue thick in my mouth and my head groggy.

She'd drugged me.

But not even that had been strong enough to fight off the demons in my mind for long. Once I'd woken, I'd gone to the window, hoping the cold would help shake the fuzziness from my mind. Outside, I saw the men digging the hole where my grandfather would be buried.

In a mere day and a half, I'd gone from thinking I'd been abandoned by my father and that my sister was lost to me forever, to having my sister and father returned to me, gaining a grandfather and then losing him, and nearly losing my own life. I wanted to grieve him, but didn't know how. How did one mourn a person they had never known—had never even thought to wonder about—but who was family by blood if not knowledge?

Killed by Halvor's uncle.

Killed by *my* power. Stolen by the *jakla*.

As I watched, lightning tore across the distant sky, raking across the dark cliffs on the horizon. I wanted to rip myself apart and force the lightning inside me, putting myself back together somehow, someway.

A miracle, Sachiel had said, and she was right. But I didn't want to be a miracle. I wanted to be *me.* The me I'd always been before the last day and a half.

My cheeks were wet when the darkness slammed into me again, with no warning other than a flash of ice across my already-cold skin. I vaguely heard the *skritch* of my nails dragging down the windowpane as I tried to grasp something, *anything,* to keep myself present, but there was no stopping the onslaught.

A boy lugging a huge book over to the man with the heavy, bearded jowls and glowing eyes. "This is from our true *home, Barloc. There are those who believe books have no value, but they don't realize how many secrets one can hide in plain sight in a book."*

A young man walked into his office in the library while he was poring over his latest find, a very rare Paladin book that a fellow enthusiast *had procured for him. The young man, his nephew, who was as lost and broken as he once had been, came over to him, his hazel eyes dull with grief, his brown hair too long, too unkempt.*

"It's time I taught you something," he said to the boy. "Something that was a secret just between your grandfather and me."

"A secret?" he asked, looking up, the first inkling of light entering his eyes since his mother had passed on to meet her husband in the Light.

"You like learning about other places, don't you, Halvor? You enjoyed sailing with your parents." Halvor nodded, cautiously interested. "I may not be able to take you sailing, but I can teach you about a whole other world—an entirely different people with power in their very veins. Power like you can't imagine."

"Really?" Halvor's eyes lit with excitement, and for the first time since being saddled with the unwanted ward, Barloc realized perhaps it had been a blessing in disguise. The boy did have an inheritance coming in a handful of years, after all. The means to finally make his dream a reality.

Wind whipped through the trees, on either side of the river he walked in, chasing him forward, the power in his veins sparking and burning, eager and willing to be summoned—to be used. *Not wasted like that girl, making plants grow. And then he felt it. The sensation of being watched—being followed. He should have been afraid; once he would have been. Terrified even. But no longer. Now his lips curled into a smile, his power surging up at his call as he rushed to face whoever had been foolish enough to find him. The two gryphons' eyes widened a split-second before the glorious fire erupted out of his hands and obliterated the screeches from their beaks before they could escape—*

I crashed back into my own body, my own mind, as though I had been ripped out of myself and then thrust back in again. Dizziness assailed me, dizziness and a violent wave of nausea. I clutched the windowsill so hard, splinters dug into my skin beneath my nailbeds. Painful, but not as painful as the horror of a knowledge I could no longer deny.

Whatever Barloc had done to me—which I'd miraculously survived—had created a connection between us, just as my power once had with those I healed. But this connection was all wrong. It crawled beneath my skin, like a disease burrowing into me, deeper with every strike. Instead of only seeing snippets of his life one time during the use of my power, it seemed I was struck with his memories *every* time he used it.

And a glimpse into wherever he was using his power at that moment.

Shoving one fist against my riotous stomach and the other against my mouth, I backed away from the window. I had to block him out. I *had* to.

It was yet another reason I *needed* to get my power back.

There had to be a way.

A knock at my door startled a scream out of me that I barely managed to muffle behind the knuckles still pressed against my lips and teeth.

"Dinner, Inara." Father's voice came through the door. "Are you up?"

"I'll be right there," I barely managed to force out past the wild thumping of my heart.

Sachiel knew something—she knew a way, but it had to do with having access to the *jakla* for some reason. Well, apparently, now I did. I needed to tell someone about what was happening to me. A little voice urged me to go to Zuhra—but though she would no doubt be gentle and concerned, she would also try to protect me somehow, like she always had. There was no way for her to stop this, though. And it was time I started protecting myself.

By convincing Sachiel to help me get my power back.

ELEVEN

Zuhra

Most storms blew in slowly, visible in the distance, taking hours to reach us. But occasionally, one would whip over the mountains, racing across the sky as though demons lashed it from behind, driving it toward the citadel with a speed that took my breath away.

I knew this was going to be one of those storms as soon as I heard the wind rattling the windowpane and glanced out the window of the dining hall to see eddies of dirt and leaves swirling through the courtyard. Menacing clouds clawed their way over the peaks on the horizon, monstrous and dark, low-hanging bellies swollen with rain.

We were supposed to have supper in a few minutes and then go outside for the burial. But if that storm hit as soon as I was afraid it might . . .

I kept looking out the window, marking the progress of the clouds, anxiously waiting for everyone else to show up.

I still hadn't seen Raidyn since that morning when he'd stormed away from me to get mad at Loukas. After his ride with Sharmaine, he'd stayed outside helping my father dig the hole to bury Grandfather for most of the afternoon. After I finished saying my goodbyes, I'd left the room where he was lying and found my mother. Sami had been right—she did need my help preparing the body. As we'd worked, she'd reported that Inara had finally fallen asleep after Sami added some sleeping herbs to her tea. I'd felt bad and relieved all at once to know that she was finally getting some rest.

The door creaked behind me, and I spun, breath held. It escaped in a *whoosh* when my parents entered the room.

My father walked over to me and gave me a tight hug—something he'd started doing every time he saw me or Inara, as if he were trying to squeeze a lifetime of hugs that he'd missed into as few days as possible. "Thank you for helping your mother this afternoon. I know that must have been difficult."

I embraced him back tightly, but didn't respond. It *had* been hard to help her wash and prepare Grandfather's body while Inara slept. He hadn't begun to smell yet, but I knew if we didn't bury him soon, he would. The water we'd used to clean any remaining blood and dirt from his face, arms, and torso had been scented with lemons from Inara's orchards. I wondered if I would always think of this day whenever I smelled lemons.

"It's really windy," my father commented as the citadel shuddered under another assault.

"A storm is blowing in." I glanced over at Mother. "I think it might be a bad one."

Concern flickered over her face. "We may need to do the burial before we eat, Adelric," she said hesitantly, coming over to his side.

He looked out the window. "It won't be sunset yet."

"By the time the sun is setting, that storm will be here, and if Zuhra is right and it's a bad one, you are not going to be able to be outside." Mother took his hand in hers. "I'm sure the Great God will hold his soul until the sun sets, and then make sure he is ushered into the Light."

My father stared out the window, his jaw set. The bump in his throat rose and fell when he swallowed hard, the tendons in his neck tightening. Even as we watched, lightning flashed in the distance, a jagged flare of warning.

"Sir, was that thunder?"

All three of us flinched at Sharmaine's voice behind us. My father took a deep breath and turned. "Yes. A storm is coming. We have to do the burial now, before it hits."

"But it won't be sunset," Sharmaine protested.

"We don't have a choice." He strode away from the window that rattled from another gust of wind. "Tell the others."

Mother hurried after him, but stopped short of the door.

"Inara?" she said, disbelieving. "What are you doing up already?"

My sister stood in the doorway, as pale as the alabaster wall, her hair hanging limply down her back. It looked like she'd dressed hastily. "I came for dinner . . . Aren't we eating?" Her gaze traveled quickly over those of us in the room; I wasn't certain but I thought I sensed a pang of disappointment go through her.

"There's a storm coming, we have to do the burial first," Mother explained. "You'd better come quickly, girls." She took Inara's hand and tugged her out the door, not seeming to notice the weak resistance Inara put up before her shoulders slumped and she allowed herself to be pulled from the room, leaving me and Sharmaine standing there looking at each other, her dismay obvious.

"Zuhra, now that we're alone, I—"

"We better go," I said and hurried out the door before she could say anything that would make this day any worse, the memory of her flying off alone with Raidyn still fresh in my mind.

Wind whipped through the courtyard, angrily pushing the charcoal clouds toward us, where we huddled around the hole in the ground. The scent of impending rain carried on the wind, mingling with the dust that blew up from the ground and stung my eyes.

Raidyn, Loukas, Ivan, and my father carefully carried Grandfather's body to where the rest of us stood. I wondered how they would lower him into the deep hole, until Sharmaine stepped forward and lifted her hands. Her veins lit up, and as the men drew closer and then held him above the hole, she created what looked like a blanket of glowing power that hovered just beneath Grandfather's body.

My father whispered something in Paladin, his voice choked.

Then the four men released him and stepped back. Instead of falling, Sharmaine's power caught him. As she lowered her hands, the glowing blanket beneath Grandfather's body dropped slowly down to the earth below, until he came to a gentle rest on the freshly dug soil.

My father nodded at Raidyn, who bowed his head and said something in Paladin, and then, after a pause, began to sing.

I'd always loved the sound of Raidyn's voice, but I'd never heard *anything* like his singing. Even in a different language, he somehow took the sorrow, the guilt, the pang of permanent loss, and transformed it into song that rose and fell into pure emotion. His smoky, musical voice shaped each note into something at once beautiful and heartbreaking. I didn't understand the words, but the haunting melody and the pure, mournful tone washed over me, summoning a fresh wave of grief that brought tears to my eyes again.

When Loukas, my father, Sachiel, Sharmaine, and even Ivan joined in, adding their voices to Raidyn's, my tears turned to sobs. I'd never heard so many voices joined together in music. In fact, I couldn't remember ever hearing a song with words before. Sami hummed sometimes when she cooked, so I knew music *existed.* But I'd never truly experienced it before—not like this. Even though I didn't understand the Paladin words, the beauty of their combined voices, and the tears flowing down their cheeks, felt more powerful than prayer.

I didn't want it to end, but all too soon, the last note faded away on the ever-increasing wind that whipped the wetness from my face, stinging my eyes with dust. Sami, who stood beside me, cried openly, even though she'd never known my grandfather. I wondered if it was from the music, or if she was thinking of her own losses—of her sister, whose death she blamed herself for causing. Even Halvor, who had also lost both of his parents, reached up to brush at his cheeks a few times.

Inara was the only one who remained dry-eyed, but there was a morass of darkness enshrouding her that sent a shiver of worry raking down my spine, as if the gathering storm above us were an echo of the despair swelling inside my sister. I reached for her hand and clutched her chilled fingers; she was as brittle as ice, on the verge of shattering.

"I know you didn't know him," I leaned over and whispered to her, "but he was very kind. He really wanted to meet you."

She didn't say anything, but her grip tightened on mine slightly.

As we watched, Father, Raidyn, and Loukas stepped forward to pick up shovels—there were only three that we could find in the stables—and moved to the large pile of dirt next to the burial site.

My father scooped up the first shovelful and held it out over the hole, his hands shaking so hard, little bits of dirt tumbled off of it. "Goodbye, Father," he said in Paladin, and then he closed his eyes and turned the shovel over.

I wasn't sure I'd ever forget the sound of that dirt hitting my grandfather's body with a low *plop.* It was so awful, so *final.* I shuddered as Loukas's shovelful and then Raidyn's joined the first. *Plop, plop.*

I tilted my face up to the clouds racing overhead, to the punishing wind, letting it slash the tears from my face. *Goodbye, Grandfather. I'm so sorry.*

Another gust tore through the courtyard, but this time, it was followed by the first few drops of rain. As I'd feared, the storm had reached us in the short time it had taken to gather everyone and bring Grandfather's body out for the burial. The thick, sable clouds surged through the ever-darkening sky, roiling into a teeming mass of destruction that would break loose at any moment.

As if recognizing the urgency, Raidyn and Loukas both turned to the pile of dirt and quickly began moving it. Each shovelful landed with that same terrible finality—the dull thud of soil on empty flesh made me flinch each time. After his first and only shovelful, Father merely stood there and stared as all that remained of Grandfather slowly disappeared.

Lightning, brighter even than Paladin fire, ripped through the clouds just beyond the hedge, close enough that a deafening crack of thunder exploded overhead within seconds. I barely swallowed my cry of fear, but Inara jerked beside me, her hand clenching mine.

The raindrops fell faster and faster, quickly moving through a drizzle into a downpour. The dry dirt the wind had flung into our faces all afternoon went from speckled to soaked in a matter of minutes. Raidyn and Loukas worked as quickly as possible, but there was no chance they could finish before the brunt of the storm hit.

Halvor stepped up to my father and gently reached for the empty shovel. "Let me, sir," he offered.

Father gripped the handle for a moment longer, then relinquished it to Halvor. Mother took Father's now-empty hand in hers. He turned away from the gravesite and wrapped his free arm around her, his shoulders and head curving down toward her, as Halvor hurried over to help Raidyn and Loukas.

The grave was almost three-quarters of the way full when the downpour turned into an all-out cloudburst, torrents of rain dumping from the sky.

"We need to go in!" Sami called out, over the howling wind. "Lightning could strike at any time!"

Before anyone could respond, the hedge suddenly moved, like hundreds of emerald snakes slithering apart, revealing the iron gate hidden beneath the thick greenery.

And standing behind it were two Paladin I'd never seen before.

TWELVE

Inara

The sky wept above us, rain slipping down my cheeks instead of tears. Alkimos's death was a sharp pain in my belly—the realization that I'd *had* a grandfather, and now I'd never get to know him—but for some reason, I was hollowed out by it, unable to cry. I stared at the grave, as the dirt slowly filled it, clutching Zuhra's hand, as I had so many times, but now there were secrets and lies between us, when there never had been before.

When the rain intensified, Sami said something, but her voice glanced over me without the words penetrating. Zuhra suddenly stiffened beside me, her hand tightening on mine. I felt a surge of shock go through her. I glanced up and sucked in a sharp breath. The hedge was open, the gate exposed, two Paladin—a male and a female—standing there.

"Cyrus? Melia?" Sachiel shouted to be heard over the increasing fury of the storm. "Where are your gryphons?"

The pair shared a look, their unfamiliar faces etched with grief.

"Gone," the male—Cyrus—said as he opened the gate and ushered the woman to precede him into the courtyard.

That one word made me go cold, the memory of Paladin fire blasting toward two gryphons seared in my mind.

"What do you mean 'gone'? What happened? Where have you been?"

"We need to get out of the storm!" my mother yelled over another deafening clap of thunder.

"She's right—it's only going to get worse!" Sami shouted.

As if to prove her right, lightning struck close enough that for half a second everything was lit bright white and then in the instant that darkness enveloped the grounds once more, thunder exploded around us, so loud I ducked, clapping my hands over my ears.

Adelric, who hadn't wanted to give up on finishing the burial, finally relented. "Everyone back to the citadel!" He waved his hands at the group, his words barely audible over the rage of the storm. "Tell us what happened inside!"

We all gathered in the dining room, where Sami had built a fire before the burial, and the food she'd prepared was waiting for us. It was vegetable stew tonight, simple but flavorful.

I put a few spoonfuls in my bowl to appease my mother's hawk-like gaze, but couldn't bring myself to eat, my stomach clenched too tight from what I'd seen in my room—that I hadn't dared tell anyone about yet—and my head fuzzy from the sleeping herbs Sami had snuck into the tea Mother forced me to drink.

The new pair huddled close together across from my parents, both of their eyes red-rimmed and bloodshot. They were covered in mud and what appeared to be partially dried blood splatters. Sachiel, at the head of the table, kept looking at them while everyone else quickly served themselves. Lorina, Ivan, Loukas, and Raidyn all sat on the same side of the table. Zuhra sat on my left and Halvor on my right, with Sami next to him. Whether consciously or not, somehow all the Paladin except for my father had sat together, facing the rest of us.

Once everyone served themselves, Sachiel looked to Cyrus and Melia. "What happened? Did you find the *jakla*?"

Cyrus was medium height and build, with brown hair and a sprinkling of freckles. Melia was shorter but stocky, with dusty blond hair and a sunburn on her nose. They held hands on the table, both of them trembling. At Sachiel's question, Cyrus's knuckles whitened.

"Yes. We found him."

Melia shuddered.

I wanted to leave. I wanted to hide. I could do nothing but sit there, frozen to my seat with guilt, bearing the weight of his atrocities, though I had no ability to stop Barloc.

"He . . . he was trying to hide his tracks by walking in the river."

No. No, no, *no no no no . . .*

"We set up a trap for him, thinking he'd completed the change and we could attack him." Cyrus paused and swallowed, his gaze on their clasped hands. "We were wrong."

Everyone stared in silence, the vegetable stew forgotten in front of them. Everyone except me—who had *seen* him in that river, had *felt* the moment when he'd known the Paladin had found him, had watched him attack two gryphons—

"I'm sorry to make you share something that is obviously . . . difficult." Sachiel's voice was as gentle as I'd ever heard it; I hadn't realized her capable of such compassion. "But we must know what happened."

I clutched my hands in my lap, willing myself to stay calm somehow as she spoke to the survivors.

A muscle in the corner of Cyrus's eye ticked. "There were four of us. Nicabar and Gen were the lure, and we were the closers."

Melia's shoulders began to shake; Cyrus wrapped his arm around her, pulling her in close.

"He found them before we got there and attacked. We got there as quickly as possible, but he slaughtered all of our gryphons and had Nicabar and Gen cornered. They tried to defend themselves, but he absorbed every bit of power they blasted at him. There was nothing we could do. We only escaped because . . . because Nicabar . . . he . . ." Cyrus's voice broke. He shook his head, unable to continue.

Sachiel tensed. "Are they . . . ?"

Cyrus stared down at the table, quaking almost as badly as the woman beside him. It took several moments before he responded. "They weren't dead when we fled, but . . . I don't know how they would have survived."

The plates and bowls on the table rattled when Sachiel slammed her fist down on the thick wooden plank with a guttural curse. I was hardly aware of anyone else's reactions to the ghastly news; the painful abyss inside me gaped open even wider from Cyrus's story, constricting my lungs, making it hard to breathe.

"I hate to be the one to point this out," Loukas said, low and apologetic, "but I can only think of one reason why he would have kept them alive."

Melia startled at the sound of his voice. When she glanced up and saw Loukas, she shrank back farther into Cyrus's embrace. Even Cyrus scowled at him, his arm tightening around Melia.

Loukas flushed and looked down.

It took a second for his meaning to hit me. I turned to my father, horror blooming in my chest, like a fresh wound. He would have waited to kill them to *use* them first. To drain them as he had me. If Barloc had ripped the power from both of them too . . .

Father swore, his face blanching. "Sachiel, what were their strengths? What powers could he now possess?"

The other general's teeth were clenched, her eyes flashing even brighter than normal. It wasn't until she blinked a few times that I realized she was holding back tears.

"They were both fire-wielders, nothing more. But they were both strong and good and—" She broke off with a harsh shake of her head.

Father moved as though he would reach out to her, but she jerked away. "I'm so sorry. I know how painful it is to lose members of your battalion."

Sachiel didn't respond.

"I've never heard of a *jakla* that ripped power from *three different* Paladin." Sharmaine almost seemed to be talking to herself, her face as white as the blouse she wore.

Raidyn put his hand over hers; she turned to look up at him, stricken. Zuhra stiffened beside me but remained silent.

"This is all my fault," Halvor whispered. "If only I'd refused to bring him here."

Even though I was struggling myself—the black hole within pulsing, painful, and bottomless—his acute guilt and misery skimmed the edges of my own suffering. Imitating Raidyn, I reached out to squeeze Halvor's closest hand, resting on his leg. He immediately grasped my fingers, clutching them tightly.

"What's done is done, and there's no use trying to assign blame." Father was the only one who responded, though his attempt at reassurance felt hollow. "You didn't know what he was planning."

I didn't even know what to say to Halvor. If they'd never come, no one would have died. Barloc would never have been given the chance to rip the power from me, leaving me empty and broken.

But . . . if they'd never come, I would have still been lost in the roar, the four of us still trapped behind the hedge we'd believed to be immovable. I wouldn't have met Halvor, wouldn't have known what it was to care about a boy the way I did for him, wouldn't have known how powerful a kiss could be. My father wouldn't have returned to us, Zuhra wouldn't have met our grandparents and Raidyn and all the other Paladin, and discovered that she, too, had Paladin power. Was all the suffering worth the good that had also come?

"If he somehow *has* absorbed the power from *three* Paladin . . . how will we ever stop him now?" Lorina asked.

The room fell completely silent, except for the *ping ping ping* of the rain lashing the windows.

Sachiel pushed away her untouched bowl. "I hate to agree with Adelric, but if we do this, then we need to split up like I suggested earlier. Half of us need to go after him, and the other half stay here in case he somehow makes it back before the other group catches him."

"What possible chance would only *half* of us have against a *jakla* wielding the power of *three* Paladin?" Sharmaine choked out.

"And how would they find him?" Ivan added.

There was a heavy pause before Sachiel announced, "We set a trap."

"A *trap*?" My father's eyebrows lifted, but the corners of his lips turned down.

Panic, part ice, part acidic fire, flashed through my body. I hadn't told her yet—how did she know? I didn't even know if I *could* find Barloc through the connection we had.

"Yes. A trap. We bait him with something he would be unable

to resist. And when he shows up, we kill him the old-fashioned way—with cold, hard steel."

"Bait," Father repeated slowly, his eyes narrowing. "What kind of bait?"

Sachiel's gaze moved past him to where Zuhra and I sat. "Your other daughter's power."

"No!" Mother gasped.

Zuhra sucked in a breath beside me. Raidyn's gaze snapped to her, the whites of his eyes visible all around his blue-flame irises.

No. Not Zuhra. I stared at Sachiel in horror. She didn't know then—she hadn't figured it out.

"If he learns she's an enhancer, he won't be able to resist trying to steal her power, as well. If we use Loukas to—"

Before she could finish, my father roared, "Absolutely *not*! How dare you even *suggest* such a thing!"

"Do you have a better suggestion? He *must* be stopped, Adelric!"

"You think I don't know that?" He shoved back his seat, jumping to his feet. "He killed my father and very nearly Inara. How *dare* you—"

"It would work!" she cut him off, just as furious. "And we can only pray to the Great God that he doesn't start attacking humans before we get to him!"

"Why would he attack *humans*?" Melia finally looked up.

Suddenly everyone was talking, yelling, gesturing, a cacophony of angry chaos that drowned out even the storm raging outside. As the voices rose louder and louder, I lost track of what anyone was saying. A strange buzzing started to accompany the painful beat of my heart and the tightness in my lungs that was making me completely breathless.

Before I could think better of it, I shoved my chair back and stood. Without a word of explanation, I rushed from the room. The empty hallway pulsed with shadows that undulated in the heavy humidity from the storm, as though the citadel were so nervous about the fury of the wind and rain lashing at its windows and walls that it was sweating.

I leaned against the wall, clutching at my blouse, struggling to breathe. I vaguely heard the door open and shut nearby, but I didn't even turn toward whoever it was. It took every ounce of my concentration just to stay on my feet.

"Nara." Zuhra's familiar voice was a soothing respite from the buzzing in my head. It was nothing like the roar; *this* noise was made of dizziness and not enough air, and blood pounding too hard, and emptiness where there should have been power. "Do you want to go lie down? I can ask Sami to make you some more tea, if you think that will help."

Her life had just been offered up on an altar by Sachiel, and yet here she was, coming after me, trying to comfort *me*. Though I should have found the strength to ask if *she* was all right, or what had been decided, or tell her what was happening to me, I couldn't resist her offer. I nodded. Zuhra gently took my arm and guided me through the dark hallways that felt as if they were closing in on us. Occasional bursts of lightning momentarily blinded me, making me stumble, but Zuhra was always there, holding me up, guiding me forward.

Until, after far longer than it normally took, we reached my room. Zuhra opened the door and ushered me in.

"Do you want help changing? Or do you want to lie down now?"

I stood in the middle of my room, trembling and still struggling to breathe. "I—I don't know," I barely managed to force out through my strangled throat.

"I think you should lie down," Zuhra decided. "Here, climb in, and then I'll hurry and go get you some more tea to help you rest."

She helped me crawl into bed and, just like when I was little—on rare nights when I was lucid and could remember her doing it—she tucked my sheets around me, cocooning me tightly in the safety of my bed.

"I'll be right back," she promised, softly sweeping a few stray hairs off my forehead. Her hand was warm and soft, and I didn't want her to go, but I couldn't speak, and with one last long look at me, her eyebrows knitted together, she hurried out the door.

I stared up at the ceiling, at the skeletal shadows of the trees outside when lightning sent their corpses skulking across my room, and the swelling darkness when the flashes of light receded. Thunder roared through the stone walls, and rain lashed at the windows; the storm seemed determined to tear the citadel apart, but though it shuddered beneath the onslaught, it held tight.

I'd always been afraid of the dark, but now it terrified me. Darkness brought *him*—it gave me glimpses into the mind of my would-be murderer.

I'd seen the moment before he'd slaughtered four gryphons and two more Paladin. I'd seen him in the river where they'd tracked him, moments before they died. And no one else knew that I had.

Just breathe, I told myself, with as much force as I could muster. But it wasn't long before I started to gasp again. Control was nearly impossible—especially because the pain in my chest kept creeping further and further out into my body, making it harder than ever to get enough air. Though Zuhra had promised to hurry, it still felt like an eternity before she finally came back, a teacup clinking against the plate she balanced.

"Oh, Nara!" She rushed to sit beside my bed when she came in and saw me struggling. "Here you go," she said, helping me lean up enough to be able to drink the slightly bitter concoction. Now that I knew it had sleeping herbs in it, they were all I could taste. "I'm sorry it took a little bit—I had to go get Sami from the dining hall."

I took another big sip, praying it would work again. "What did they decide?" I managed to ask.

Zuhra shrugged. "Don't worry about that right now." I could sense her fear, but my own was so much stronger, I could barely focus on her answer, let alone press her for more.

You have to tell her.

You can't ever tell anyone.

"Zuhra . . . I . . . I need . . ." I tried to force the words out, but my entire body began to shake, my stomach cramped so hard, I could barely keep down the little tea I'd swallowed.

Zuhra stroked a hair back from my clammy cheek. "Shhh," she whispered. "You don't need to talk right now. Just breathe. Do you want me to stay with you for a little bit? Until the tea takes effect? I can read you a story, just like I used to. It might help you calm down." She tucked the sheets in tighter around my torso, her hands firm, and warm, and sure, her presence a balm.

Despite myself, despite knowing I couldn't keep this to myself any longer, I nodded. First thing in the morning, when the sun was up, when the light of day chased back the shadows of the night, when I could breathe again . . . I would tell her. Nothing would happen tonight—not even Barloc could do anything in this storm. She was safe until then.

The same few books we'd read over and over as children were stacked on a shelf of my dresser from years gone by. Zuhra took one out and settled back into the chair beside my bed.

"There was once a young girl who dreamed such beautiful dreams they seemed real to her," she began, the words comforting in their familiarity, her voice soft, as the rain continued to pound against my window.

I closed my eyes and let the words flow over and through me, carrying me away from the storm, the pain inside, the tightness in my lungs, and the horror of the memories that still assailed me.

THIRTEEN

Zuhra

Only once I was certain Inara was completely out did I shut the book and gently set it down on the nightstand beside her. With her face relaxed in the release of sleep, she looked so much younger than when she was awake. She had an old soul; her eyes filled with far too much pain and suffering, aging her beyond her years.

I bent over and kissed her brow softly. Her eyelids fluttered, but she stayed asleep. I tiptoed from the room, shutting the door carefully. When I turned, someone was sitting in the shadows, leaning against the wall across from her room, his blue-fire eyes glittering in the darkness. I swallowed a gasp as Raidyn quickly scrambled to his feet.

"I'm sorry if I scared you," he said. "But I wanted to make sure I got to talk to you before we go."

My already-racing heart stumbled in my chest, sputtering at those two words: *we go.*

"Did they decide to do it, then?" Though my parents were both furious, I'd tried to force them to accept Sachiel's plan—telling them I would leave with *Sachiel* if they refused—when Inara ran out of the room. I hadn't heard their final decision because I'd gone after my sister. I knew it could quite possibly end with my death. But it was the only hope we had of trapping Barloc and stopping him. No one had any idea what he was capable of with the power of *three* Paladin. And I couldn't bear the thought of him hurting anyone else because my parents were too afraid of losing me.

I couldn't read Raidyn's expression in the darkness, but it looked like he grimaced. "Yes, they finally agreed."

I exhaled, long and low, equal parts resignation, relief, and terror.

"Loukas offered to use his power as the bait instead of yours, but Sachiel's plan hinges on his power being a surprise. If Barloc doesn't know he's a *mentirum*, Loukas can use it to force him to freeze, unable to draw on his power—even for just a few seconds—which will hopefully be enough time to cut his head from his body."

My lip curled at the gruesome image. "So, who is going? How will we make sure he finds out what I am? And when do we leave?" I asked faintly.

"Adelric refuses to let Sachiel be the one to lead the trap, not with your life on the line." The words seemed to strangle him. "She's staying here with her battalion members. It'll be both of your parents—because your mother refuses to stay behind, me, Shar, Louk, and you."

I nodded, hoping I looked braver than I felt. A flash of heat raced over my arms, immediately followed by a frigid shudder scuttling down my spine, my body rebelling against what my mind knew needed to be done. I'd just helped my sister through a panic attack, but now I was the one who needed help. My throat tightened.

"You don't have to do this, Zuhra. We can figure out another way to stop him."

Even though his words echoed my deepest wish, I knew it was a false hope. "There is no other way. Not one fast enough to keep him from killing others."

Raidyn winced. "We could try to lure him back here—then no one has to split up."

"And bring him back to the gateway? He might have enough power to open it on his own now." Caustic desperation burned in my belly. "Sachiel was right; we have to try to trap him *before* he comes back here." I shivered, a cold sweat breaking out on the nape of my neck.

Raidyn reached for me, taking my hand in both of his. "You're *freezing*," he said, rubbing it gently.

"When do we go?" I repeated, the words shaking with the rest of my body.

He didn't look up. "Tomorrow."

I stared at him. "So *soon*."

"I don't want to, but Sachiel made the same point you just did—he can't be allowed to come back here and open the gateway. If he does . . ." He continued to rub my skin, but even the heat of his touch couldn't chase away the chill of his words.

We were silent for several moments, except for the sounds of the storm still lashing the citadel, unrelenting and ferocious.

"When we go . . . I can ride with you, can't I?"

Raidyn stared down at me, my hand clasped between his. We stood close enough that when he breathed, his chest brushed my fingertips. "If that's what you want," he said, his voice low.

Lightning flared in the skylight overhead, instantly followed by a blast of thunder that reverberated through the stones beneath my feet, making me jump. Even Raidyn flinched.

"That's what I want," I said. "Please."

His thumb moved in slow circles on the pad of my hand, sending a small wave of warmth up my arm, nudging back the chill that still gripped my body. "What about Inara? Are you sure you can leave her?"

It was difficult to think clearly standing so close to him in the sweltering darkness. "She should come too. She can ride with Sharmaine or Loukas."

"I don't know if they'd be willing to do that. If we *do* find Barloc, they both have jobs to do to keep you safe. Shar is going to try to shield you, while Loukas takes control of Barloc's mind. It would complicate things quite a bit for them to have another person riding on their gryphon to worry about."

"Oh." I didn't want to put them in danger. But I couldn't stand the thought of Inara being left at the citadel, trapped once again.

"Maybe Loukas could stay farther back? So they won't be in danger?"

A dark shadow that had nothing to do with the storm flashed across Raidyn's face. "Possibly. But he has to be fairly close to the person to be able to fully control their mind. As you know."

"He didn't use his power on me. He never has."

"There's no way for you to know that."

"If he had, I would have been completely convinced you were using me to get here to search for your parents. But his words only put *doubts* in my mind. He didn't convince me of anything."

Raidyn exhaled. "It's not always that simple. He's very gifted . . . he can use his power more subtly than you may realize."

"Don't you think I would know if he had forced me to think or feel a certain way? Would I have decided I trusted you after all if he had?" I pulled my hands free of his and stepped back. "He's not the one making me doubt you—*you* are."

Raidyn gaped at me. "I don't understand."

"Why did you go to Sharmaine after you talked to him? I saw you two flying together. Instead of coming to find me, you went to *her.*" I hated how I sounded—but couldn't keep the question from leaving my mouth.

"Sharmaine is my friend—and she's known Loukas as long as I have." He shoved one hand through his already-disheveled blond hair. "I needed to talk to someone who really knows him, who could help me figure out if I should believe him or not."

"He told me about the three of you," I said. "How you both . . . you both love her." The words burned their way up my throat and out, too late to be smothered.

Raidyn reeled back as if I'd slapped him. "He told you *what*?"

I couldn't look at him anymore. The cold panic was replaced entirely by misery that was both hot and nauseating. "That . . . that you both love her. But that she loves *you.*"

"Zuhra." My name came out a strangled plea. "You have to believe me when I tell you that he's wrong. He's using his power to confuse you. I just don't know why."

"He didn't use his power on me!" I insisted angrily. "I've seen you with her—I've seen *her* with you. It's obvious you do care for each other. And . . . when we were healing Inara . . . I saw you . . . I saw the day when you found them kissing. I felt your anger, your hurt."

Raidyn flinched. "That was *years* ago, Zuhra. That was—"

Another clap of thunder growled around us, drowning out his words so he had to repeat himself.

"Yes, there was a time when I *thought* I cared for her that way. But Loukas is the one who is in love with her, not me. I love Sharmaine, it's true. But"—he rushed on, grabbing my arm to stop me when I tried to spin away—"as a *sister*. As the only family I have left."

I kept my head turned, even though his words chipped away at the confusion in my heart. "I've never had friends before," I admitted quietly. "I've never been around boys. I don't . . . I don't know what to believe. And it's not because of Loukas."

"Zuhra . . . please. I'm sorry I went to her first. Search my feelings. You can believe me." He touched my chin and gently tilted my face back toward him. "You want the *truth*? Yes, I talked to her about Loukas. But I was really asking her for advice. About *you*."

I swallowed. "About *me*?" I squeaked. Doing as he bid, I tried to search out his feelings—tried to separate them from my own. There was confusion, hope, an aching need that echoed the heat in my veins . . . and something deeper, something even more powerful than all the rest. It was similar to what I felt for Inara, a love so intense, it took my breath away, but different too . . . it did things to my heart and body that I'd never felt before.

His feelings or mine?

He cupped my face with one hand and took my other and pressed it to his chest. I could feel the thundering of his heart beneath my fingers. "Did you see anything else when we were healing Inara? Anything that had happened between *us*?"

The intensity of his gaze made my breath catch in my throat. The blue-fire in his eyes seemed to travel down his arm, through his fingertips on my face, and out into my body. My stomach tightened and my heart throbbed in the suddenly too small space beneath my lungs.

"Yes," I admitted, my voice trembling. "I saw our flight together . . ." I couldn't bring myself to say the rest. That I'd felt how much he'd wanted to kiss me. But he must have known, because his gaze dropped to my mouth. I could barely draw breath as he ran his thumb over my bottom lip.

"*This* is real, Zuhra," he said, the words low and raspy. "What you and I are feeling right now." Raidyn left my hand on his chest and wrapped his arm around me, pulling me into his body. I tilted my chin to look up into his face. "This is real," he repeated, so quiet, I wondered if it was more to himself than me.

Then, slowly, he bent his head toward me—*achingly* slow. Giving me the chance to stop him. When I didn't move or speak, his arm tightened around me and then finally . . . *finally* his lips touched mine, as soft as a butterfly's wings brushing my mouth.

As common as storms were, lightning had only struck the citadel once. I still remembered the charge in the air, how the hair on my arms stood on end in the instant before the room exploded with light and thunder and *heat*. Raidyn's kiss was like that bolt of lightning, cleaving the darkness in me. That brief, life-altering touch burned through my body, making my muscles tremble, so that I had to clutch his shirt to stay standing. He made a noise deep in his throat, and then he kissed me again, harder this time. The heat from his lips erupted into a blaze that scorched through me. I pressed into him as his mouth moved on mine. His hand slid down my spine, his fingers plying my lower back, sending a rush of sensation around my hips, straight into the depths of my belly. I wished I'd worn pants and a top like I had in Visimperum, instead of a dress, so he could have pulled my top up, allowing me to feel his fingers on my skin, as he had when we'd ridden on Naiki together.

Everything I felt was enhanced by Raidyn's emotions that flowed into me more fully than I'd ever experienced before. I wanted him closer, I wanted him to keep kissing me forever, and it was all compounded by the heat of his matching need, until we were consumed by it.

He suddenly started walking me backward, his mouth never leaving mine, until I bumped into the wall. Then he spun me around, our legs tangling together, so he leaned against the wall, and his hands could roam freely over my back. His mouth opened over mine. I moaned, feeling somehow completely weak and strong all at once. Growing braver by the minute, I slid my own hands off his shoulders and over the strong planes of his chest, down to his abdomen, feeling the ridges of his muscles beneath my fingers. He groaned and kissed me even harder, pulling me against him, trapping my hands on his stomach. His mouth left mine, but only to leave a scorching trail of fiery kisses across my jaw, to the groove below my ear, on my neck.

I gasped, lost in a mesmerizing sea of fire, and then a sudden scream split the night air.

We both froze and then sprang apart.

"Was that—"

"*Inara,*" I breathed and dashed for her door.

FOURTEEN

ZUHRA

I was still light-headed, my lips burning, when I shoved her door open and found Inara gasping for air, her eyes wide with terror, clutching her chest. Her lips were a terrifying lavender.

"Inara!" I cried, rushing to her side, all heat from kissing Raidyn draining away in an instant. I grabbed her shoulders. "What's wrong with her?"

She looked at me, the whites visible all the way around her pale blue eyes, making awful sucking noises with each labored wheeze, as though her lungs were full of fluid.

Raidyn came up beside me, his veins already lit with his power. "I don't know. But I'll try to fix it."

I moved out of his way. He put one hand on her shoulder and the other over hers where they still clutched at her chest. I stared at him, too frightened to look at my sister, to see if he was able to stop whatever was happening to her.

Raidyn's eyes shut, and within seconds of touching her, his jaw tightened, his teeth clenched together. The tendons in his neck strained while his power coursed through his veins, glowing nearly as bright as the lightning that still split the sky outside Inara's window.

Long minutes passed, while sweat gathered on his forehead, coating his hairline. I didn't know if I should reach for him and add my power to his or not. I didn't understand what was happening. We'd already healed her. She'd gone to sleep just fine, and we'd been outside her room the whole time—no one could have come in and attacked her again. *So why did it seem like she was slipping away?*

When his shoulders began to shake from the strain, I finally reached out and grabbed onto his hand.

His power exploded through me, lighting my own veins on fire. My fingers clamped over his. Awareness of Inara's room faded away, until it was just me and Raidyn, our souls intertwining yet again. Like the first time, I felt him recognize my presence. The relief that went through him was so deep and profound, I experienced it on more than one level: through our connected power and the *sanaulus* we already shared.

As before, in the space of a heartbeat, a series of memories flashed through my mind: Raidyn walking beside the Paladin I recognized as his mother from the first time I'd seen moments in his life, his small hand clutched in hers; sitting in a row of young Paladin all looking at a baby gryphon, and the baby turning to him and biting his hand with its tiny beak, drawing blood and filling him with joy where before there had only been dark grief; standing in a field with my father, practicing shooting at targets together with their power; and sitting beside me as I slept, his hand on mine, his heart so full, it hurt.

Then, with a gentle yet insistent tug, he pulled me forward into Inara. The same thing happened again, in the space of just one more heartbeat, a handful of her memories flashed through my mind. Curled up next to me in bed, reading a story one winter night when she was lucid long enough for books; running her hands over the hedge and feeling it respond to her, opening to let them out to warn the town below—the town that hated and feared her; Barloc leaning over her, his teeth covered in the gore of ripping through her flesh like an animal, his eyes flashing bright blue with her power; a kiss with Halvor, and the respite his touch gave her from the constant fear and panic inside, the darkness that spread inside of her like a poison—

Then we were pressing on, into that darkness. The "stitches" we'd made last time to fill the void her power had left were coming unraveled, the emptiness trying to steal her from us again.

Somehow I could tell Raidyn had been trying to fill that emptiness with his healing power, but it wasn't enough—he couldn't reach her. We had to do it together.

Just as we had the first time, Raidyn used my power to stretch his far enough forward to hold that darkness back, bridging the gap and reeling her soul back into her body, much like sewing a garment that had been torn apart, trying to pull the edges together—except with each of *these* "stitches," a stabbing pain went through *me.* It was the cost of using my power to enhance Raidyn's, and if it saved my sister, I would endure it over and over and over.

It seemed to take longer this time—either that, or knowing what was happening this time only made it seem longer. As the time passed, a growing weakness began to spread through me; it was all I could do to keep my hold on Raidyn. But I refused to let go, to fail. Inara's soul, the bright shining light that kept her alive, was dimmer than before, as though the ongoing battle inside her was taking a toll.

Together, stitch by agonizing stitch of our combined power, we managed to seal off that emptiness one more time, pulling Inara back with us. Right when I thought I could bear no more, when I didn't think I could hold on any longer, Raidyn reeled us both out.

There was a brief moment of just him and me together, a final tender stroke of his soul to mine that sent a shiver through me. It lasted less than a second, but I'd never felt anything more clearly than I did in that touch of our souls—of need, of peace, of power, of *home* . . . But then, before I could react, he unspooled his power from mine and suddenly I was back in my body.

I was vaguely aware of my hand on his, of Inara stirring beside us, of pain so intense, it shot down from my skull out into my spine.

Then there was only darkness.

FIFTEEN

INARA

I tumbled back into awareness like rain being spit from the clouds to slam against my window. Taking that first gasp of air and opening my eyes to my room was *painful.*

Both Raidyn and Zuhra sat beside me, her hand on top of his. She looked at me for less than the space of a breath and then her eyes rolled back in her head and she crumpled. Raidyn barely caught her before she fell to the floor, cradling her tenderly against his body as he carefully lowered himself to the ground.

"W-what's wrong?" My voice trembled and even though the terrifying darkness that had nearly taken me away again was gone, I was still too weak to do much more than just push myself up to my elbows.

"As the enhancer, it drains her more than me to do a healing that intense together. She'll recover, but it might take some time." Raidyn didn't look up when he spoke, his whole focus bent on Zuhra. He kept one arm around her, holding her against him, and using his other hand to softly brush her sweaty hair back from her face. The connection between us was even stronger than before. After healing me a second time, I could feel his emotions so strongly, they nearly overwhelmed me.

He *loved* my sister.

So completely, it actually *hurt.*

I knew it as clearly and undeniably as I knew that *I* loved Zuhra.

"She'll be fine," he repeated, barely more than a whisper, perhaps more to himself than me.

I had to blink back unexpected tears. "Is there anything I can do?"

"No," he murmured. "We just have to wait."

After a long pause, I asked, "Why did you have to heal me again?"

Raidyn exhaled. "What we did the first time wasn't enough. I was panicked. I'd never encountered something like that before, so I did the best I could—or so I thought. This time, I did quite a bit more. It should last longer."

"*Longer?* What do you mean 'longer'? This is going to happen again?"

He glanced up at me, his eyes dulled from the expenditure on his power. "I don't know. But I'm afraid it might."

"But . . . you *healed* me. Didn't you?"

Raidyn looked back down at Zuhra. Her hair fanned out over his arm, a thick, dark waterfall that gathered on the floor beside him. "No one has ever survived what happened to you before. What we did—it's unprecedented. I've never seen someone's healing fail, but then again, I've never seen anyone whose power was taken from them survive at all. This is new territory—for everyone."

I wanted to keep asking him questions, but Zuhra stirred then fell limp again, and we both went silent, his words ringing in my mind. I'd heard them say no one had ever survived what Barloc had done to me before . . . but I'd never realized how truly unique my situation was until that moment, as I stared at my unconscious sister and wondered how many more times she and Raidyn would have to do this for me.

If it would even continue to work.

Perhaps they'd only bought me time, delaying the inevitable.

Perhaps I really was going to die after all.

SIXTEEN

Zuhra

I woke up slowly, clawing my way out of the sucking exhaustion that filled my mind and body. Part of me wished to stay under longer, but the murmur of concerned voices began to pierce the muffled silence of oblivion, dragging me toward them.

I was lying down, my body cushioned by something soft . . . Was I on a bed? It took a massive effort to peel my eyes open; when I finally succeeded, it was to a room full of worried faces. Mother and Father, Sami in the corner, and Raidyn beside me, holding my hand.

"Zuhra," he breathed when he saw my eyes open, "you're awake."

"Praise the Great God," Sami murmured.

My tongue was strangely thick and heavy against my teeth. When I tried to speak, it was like talking through a mouthful of sand. "Is Inara . . ."

"She's fine. She's sleeping," Mother assured me.

"You gave us quite the scare, however." Father stepped forward to take my other hand in his.

"Why?"

Raidyn answered this time, his hand tightening on mine. "You've been unconscious for hours."

"*Hours?*" I repeated weakly. "What happened?"

My father and Raidyn exchanged a weighted glance, then Father turned to me. "I think it would be better to talk about it in the morning, when you've had more time to recover."

"I'm fine." I struggled to push myself to a sitting position to prove my point. "Tell me what's going on," I insisted, even though my arms shook and both Raidyn and my father had to pull the hands they held to help me.

Still, no one responded.

"If she wishes for answers, she deserves to know," Sami spoke up from the corner where she stood, arms crossed over her belly. "She certainly earned the right."

"It's not about earning it or not." Father couldn't quite keep the tightness from his voice. "She's barely woken up—and I've never seen a Paladin stay under for so long after a healing before."

Before anyone else could say something, I squeezed both of their hands. "Please," I whispered. "I need to know what's happening."

After a deep sigh, Father relented with a nod.

Raidyn exhaled slowly. "You know that no one has ever survived what Barloc did to your sister before, right?"

"Yes."

"When you and I healed her, nothing like that had ever been done before, either. It took the combined power of an enhancer *and* my healing to do it."

"I know that."

Raidyn's eyes were still dull from the expenditure on his power. "It didn't last. For some reason, the healing . . . it reversed. If we hadn't heard her cry out . . ."

I swallowed thickly, my mouth drier than ever. "She would have died?"

He nodded grimly.

If he hadn't been waiting for me outside her room, if we hadn't been kissing . . . I would have lost my sister. As if he'd read my thoughts, his gaze dropped to my lips briefly, but instead of any heat, my body went cold, my stomach clenched as if I'd been punched. "But she's fine—right? You said she's sleeping!"

"Yes—she's fine . . . for now. We healed her again," Raidyn assured me. "But . . . I don't know how long it will last."

His dismay and fear amplified my own. "Why won't it last? Why didn't it last the first time?"

"When we healed her, we were patching together a hole where her power used to be. And for some reason, that hole broke open again—negating our healing." He flushed, a stab of guilt darkening his emotions. Why would he feel guilty? "I did more this time, hoping it would last longer, but while it depleted me, it was almost too much for you. I had no idea . . . or I never . . ." He trailed off, his voice strained. His fingers tightened over mine. I remembered feeling like the "stitches" we'd created were coming undone, and that this healing took longer than the last time—that I'd barely been able to hold on to finish the job. I'd been right after all. "Because we did so much more, it should hold longer. But . . . I'm afraid we're going to have to keep doing this, over and over."

The reality of his words took a moment to sink in. "For the rest of her life?" I glanced at my father, who still clung to my other hand. He grimaced in confirmation. "You mean . . . if the healing reverses when we're not there, she'll . . . she'll . . ."

"I'm so sorry." Raidyn looked at our clasped hands, his powerful shoulders caving forward.

"What are we going to do?"

"I don't know, Zuhra. I really don't know."

It was a testament to how truly exhausted the healing had left me that I managed to sleep for a couple more hours, despite the awful truth that Raidyn had admitted to me before everyone left to try to get some more rest before morning came. Mercifully, my dreams were made of heat and lips touching and hands clutching—wonderful dreams, not the nightmares I was accustomed to.

But the moment the sun crested the eastern horizon, I snapped awake. As much as I wanted to continue to relive the heart-stopping kiss with Raidyn, my mind instantly whirred into action, running through what he'd said and what had happened with Inara, over and over. My stomach twisted, a den of writhing snakes. I had to go see her—to make certain for myself she was healed. They wouldn't lie to me, would they? To convince me to rest?

I pushed off my sheets and stood. The stones were cold beneath my bare feet, chilled by the damp night and the lingering humidity from the storm that had blown over sometime while I slept. After quickly switching into clean clothes—a tunic, leggings, and the boots Sharmaine had given me in Soluselis—and braiding my hair back, I hurried to Inara's room next to mine. I didn't knock, not wanting to wake her if she was sleeping; instead, I slowly slipped the door open, praying for it to remain quiet. In a stroke of sheer luck, the citadel complied for once; the door swung open silently.

When I saw Inara lying in her bed, dusky eyelashes resting on her cheeks, one hand on the pillow beside her, partially open, I exhaled in relief. Her chest rose and fell, gently moving the age-yellowed sheet pulled up to her shoulders. She looked so peaceful . . . and so young. Too young to have been forced to endure all that she had—and that she would continue to suffer if Raidyn and I couldn't figure out how to heal her permanently.

Something he didn't seem to think was possible.

My heart thumped painfully in my chest, heavy with the weight of her uncertain future. After thinking I'd lost her so many times already, I couldn't bear the thought that what we'd done—what we could continue to try to do—might eventually not be enough.

The supple leather of my boots made no sound as I moved to the chair still next to her bed and sat. *Please let her live. Please . . . help us find a way to keep her alive.*

Breakfast was a solemn gathering with everyone at the citadel, except for Ivan and Lorina, who had taken their gryphons out for exercise and to watch for any signs of Barloc.

I sat beside Inara, holding her hand in mine. Our twin fears and worries flowed between us, the *sanaulus* even stronger after the second, more intense, healing.

"We can't take Raidyn and Zuhra away from Inara—if this happens again, they *both* have to be near her to save her life," my father said, running a weary hand over his face. Between the loss of his father, the attack on Inara, his worry for his mother, the shifts during the night, and everything else that had happened, he'd seemed to age right before my eyes.

"There is no other gift here that he would want more—besides Loukas's," Sachiel responded. "And we've already agreed that his must be a surprise. We *have* to use her to set the trap or there's no guarantee it'll work."

Mother turned cold eyes on the other woman. "And how are they even going to make sure he hears about her ability and knows to come try to find us?"

"He has the power of three Paladin inside him now. Your husband should be able to sense him from miles away." Sachiel lifted her eyebrows at my father, as if daring him to contradict her. "Track him down, make sure he overhears you talking about Zuhra, and then wait for him to come. He will. I guarantee he won't be able to resist the chance to steal the power to enhance the abilities he already has."

"I can't take them away from Inara—not if there's a chance she'll die while we're gone." Father pushed the sliced strawberries on his plate around with his fork, not taking a bite of anything.

"Then take her with you!" Sachiel cried out. "But if we don't do something—and soon—he is going to either come back here and who knows how many of us will die . . . or he'll start attacking the humans!"

Inara stiffened, her fingers tightening on mine.

"Would one of you be willing to carry my daughter with you? I know that is asking a lot, but I can't . . . I can't bear to lose another member of my family." Father's voice broke, but he managed to wrestle his emotions into check and looked to Raidyn, Loukas, and Sharmaine—standing together near the windows.

Loukas and Sharmaine exchanged a glance that was difficult to read, but I felt Raidyn's dismay even from where I sat across the massive table from them.

It took me off guard when Loukas nodded. "I will, sir. I will take your daughter, if that is your wish."

For the first time since I'd woken that morning, the heaviness in my chest lifted slightly.

Sachiel shook her head, dark braid swinging, her lip curled with what looked like disgust, but she remained silent.

"What about me? It's my uncle that did all of this," Halvor spoke up, staring at Inara as he did. He sat on the other side of her, holding her other hand. When he'd found out what happened during the night while he'd been sleeping, he had gone pale and hadn't recovered his normal color yet—nor had he left her side. "I should be there when you . . . when he . . . when it ends."

"Absolutely *not,*" Sachiel bit out, before anyone else could respond. "Do you not realize what it will do to the gryphons to have all these extra bodies on them? It's ridiculous to bring Cinnia and Inara. Anyone not integral to the plan should stay here. Raidyn said the healing should last longer—trust that he's right. Go out there, finish this, and then come back as fast as you can."

Father sighed again and sat down heavily in the chair closest to where he stood. "I know this is not ideal. I know no matter what we do, there is potential for problems, for things going wrong. But I can't . . . I can't split my family up again, Sach. I can't. So please, don't ask me to. Even if it means our gryphons will be tired, even if it means the *jakla* will have more targets. I don't know what else to do."

Sachiel glanced at the trio standing together, watching her, then at me and Inara, then back to my parents. Finally she exhaled and ran her hands along the shaved sides of her head. "I'm sorry, Adelric. It's just such a risk. I understand why you don't want to be separated again. I . . . I wasn't prepared for all of this to happen." She gestured at the citadel. "To be trapped here."

"I don't think any of us were prepared for any of this," my father replied. "Nothing went how we expected." He glanced toward the window where the gravesite for Grandfather was visible below, across the courtyard.

"If this is what you think is best, then take your family with you. I will stay here with my battalion members and do our best to protect the gateway, should he get past you."

"I don't know if it's what is best, but it is what I *must* do." He turned to the three Paladin standing together. "Thank you for being willing to do this for me."

"And what about me?" Halvor asked again. "You can't leave me here. Please."

"That's up to Sharmaine." Father looked to her. "I won't force anyone to do something they're uncomfortable with."

There was a long pause. "Yes, sir," she finally agreed. "If that's what you wish, I will take him."

"Thank you. I know I'm asking a lot of you—and your gryphons."

"How soon will you be leaving?" Sami asked, eyes glistening. Her quiet question struck a shard of regret through my chest. Of course she couldn't come . . . she had no choice except to be left behind in a citadel full of strangers—unless she returned to Gateskeep after all of these years.

"The sooner the better," my father announced. "He has a head start on us right now, but with our gryphons, even weighed down, we will easily be able to catch up. And Sachiel is right—with that much power emanating from him, we should be able to sense him if we get close enough."

"*If* you can find him," Melia muttered, "may you have better luck than we did."

"Why not just let him go?" Cyrus suddenly burst out. "There are enough of us here—let's reopen the gateway and go home. Leave him here to rot."

"Cyrus!" Sachiel's eyes widened. "I didn't think *you* felt that way."

"He's right." Melia nodded at her husband. "Haven't we lost enough protecting these unthankful humans? Let the *jakla* do what he will."

I expected Sachiel to get mad at them, or at least scold them, but something akin to sorrow crossed her face as she crouched beside the grieving couple. "I know you have both endured far more than your fair share of sorrow, even before he murdered your gryphons and your friends. But I also know this isn't how you truly feel. With time, I think you would come to regret the choice to go back home, allowing him to murder innocent people, just as he took the lives of your innocent mounts."

"The humans figured out how to kill plenty of us last time. Let them deal with him. They'll stop him eventually."

"They've never faced anything like this before—not even the Five. He is unimaginably powerful now. Even if they *did* somehow succeed in stopping him, how many will die before then?" Sachiel reached out and gently rested her hand on top of theirs. I didn't know what to make of this side of her. "Even one more innocent life lost is too much. We took an oath to protect the lives of *all* those around us."

Melia and Cyrus shared a look, and then Melia shot a surreptitious glare at Loukas. "Can we have this conversation alone—another time?"

A muscle in Loukas's jaw ticked, but he kept his expression impassive. Did they think he was influencing Sachiel?

"As a *jakla,* his eyes might not even settle," Sachiel continued, ignoring their insinuation. "If they don't, the humans will have no warning of what he is—or what he can do to them. We *have* to find him and stop him. It's our duty." She stood back up. "You two can try to open the gateway on your own if you wish, but I am staying here."

Silence.

I continued to watch Loukas. As if he could sense my scrutiny, he met my gaze boldly, a challenge in his green-fire eyes.

"Well," my father said, "we'd best start preparing to go. Let's meet in the courtyard in an hour."

Everyone around us stood, but Inara and I remained sitting, holding hands. Raidyn looked like he wished to linger, but my father walked over to him and asked him something, and together they left the room, Loukas and Sharmaine trailing behind.

Once we were alone, Inara's icy fingers tightened on mine. "I'm scared, ZuZu."

I looked at my sister, my heart scraping like broken glass against my chest with every beat. I was being taken as live bait for someone "unimaginably powerful," according to Sachiel.

I am too, I thought. Out loud, I said, "It's going to be fine. Raidyn and I will be with you—we will heal you as many times as it takes."

She nodded, but I knew she could feel my fear as clearly as I felt hers.

"I won't let anything else happen to you, Nara. I promise," I vowed.

She laid her head on my shoulder, and I reached up to smooth her hair down. "I know you won't," she whispered. Her words were as hollow as mine, with our twin terror beating in our separate hearts.

SEVENTEEN

INARA

I took one last look at my room, everything inside me so tight, I wondered that I could keep breathing, keep moving at all. Would I ever return—ever see this bed, these walls, that window again? I'd never felt trapped here the way Zuhra did. The citadel was a comfort to me, the familiarity of the few rooms we lived in, the hallways I walked every day of my life, the lack of hatred here—that I knew awaited me outside the hedge.

But my eyes no longer glowed, my power no longer marked me as a target. I was nothing more than a normal girl to anyone I met now.

With a long, slow breath that chafed my throat, I made myself shut the door.

"Inara, good." A voice from down the hallway took me by surprise. "I'm glad I caught you."

Confused, I turned to see Sachiel striding toward me. For the first time in my life, I wore breeches like hers, after Zuhra explained how uncomfortable it would be to ride a gryphon in a dress. She halted in front of me, glancing around furtively.

"Is your sister in her room?"

"I don't think so," I replied, baffled by the fervency on her face, the low whisper of her voice.

"We don't have much time, so I will make this quick." She reached out for my arm and pulled me in closer to her, her voice dropping even further. "There *is* a way to get your power back."

Words could be so very powerful, and oh—the power that *those* words held. Everything stopped with them, even my heart stuttered to a painfully hopeful halt.

"But if they succeed in killing Barloc first, you will miss your chance." She glanced over her shoulder one last time before whispering, "You have to steal it back from him. The way he stole it from you. If you perform the same act, you can get it back. And then you shouldn't need to be healed anymore."

I stared at her. "Why are you telling me this now?"

She swallowed and glanced past me, urgency in every tense line of her body and the way she gripped my arm. "I thought you were healed—I thought that was the end of it. I didn't think it was worth the risk. But Adelric has already lost so much. And now . . ."

Now that we knew I would continue to need to be healed over and over, and that eventually it might not be enough to save me. Now it was worth the risk. "How do I it? Do I just have to . . . to drink his blood?" A shudder of ice-cold memory gripped me; Barloc crouched over me, his mouth stained crimson, my neck ripped open.

"Basically, yes."

"But . . . how would I ever get close enough to him to try—let alone actually succeed? This plan—*your* plan—hinges on Loukas being able to control him for only a few seconds. Just long enough to . . . to kill him." I couldn't bring myself to say *cut off his head.* It was no more than he deserved, but too gruesome to consider.

Sachiel glanced furtively down the hallway. "Well . . . I *do* have another idea." She beckoned me closer and began to whisper.

"I'm not sure about this."

I stared at the massive beast, heart racing, palms slick with sweat. It ruffled its feathers, as if my nervousness were agitating it.

"You'll be fine. Flying is the most amazing feeling in the world," Loukas said from beside me.

I wasn't sure what I was more scared of—getting on that thing, or having *him* get on behind me. I wanted to ride with my father or even Sharmaine, the other girl. But Father was taking Mother with him, Raidyn was taking Zuhra, of course, and Father said Halvor had to ride with Sharmaine to help keep the weight even.

That left Loukas for me.

I wasn't sure why, but he scared me. He was so big—tall and muscular—and so *quiet*; his strange green-fire eyes took everything in, but he rarely commented on anything or got involved in any of the discussions. I much preferred Halvor, his easy conversation and his warm brown eyes. But Zuhra didn't seem worried about me riding with Loukas, and Halvor didn't have a gryphon, so riding with him wasn't a choice.

I had no option except to lift my leg and let him help me swing into the saddle, the way Zuhra, Mother, and even Halvor already had, their Riders climbing on behind all of them. The breeches I wore were too revealing, too *tight*. Loukas grabbed my boot and easily hurtled me into the air. I had to grab onto a fistful of feathers to keep from launching right over the top of the gryphon and landing on the ground on the other side. I'd barely managed to right myself when he settled onto the saddle behind me, his arms coming round me to pick up the gryphon's reins. I stiffened.

"I'm sorry, but there's no other way to ride double. Maddok isn't used to it, so I need to have both hands on his reins," Loukas explained.

I glanced over to see Halvor scowling from where he sat in front of Sharmaine, her arms similarly wrapped around his thin waist to grip her gryphon's reins. I tried to summon an encouraging smile but was afraid it ended up being more of a grimace.

The only good thing about being paired with Loukas was that it gave me an opportunity to talk to him without being overheard.

If I could summon the courage to do it.

The other Paladin who were staying at the citadel stood on the steps, solemnly seeing us off. Father whistled loudly and the gryphons began to move. Sachiel lifted one hand, her burning gaze on me as Loukas's grip tightened even more and Maddok charged forward. Her words from earlier still rang in my ears as the gryphons leapt off the ground, their powerful wings spreading and catching the air, pushing us up into the sky. My stomach lurched into my throat as the ground fell away. I had to squeeze my eyes shut.

"Isn't it amazing?" Loukas was barely audible over the wind and the beating of Maddok's wings.

I didn't respond, too busy keeping my eyes closed and gripping the gryphon's feathers.

"You don't need to rip those out. I won't let you fall." It sounded like he was trying not to laugh.

It took conscious effort to relax my grip on Maddok, but somehow I managed to loosen my fingers—slightly.

"Don't you at least want to take one last look at your home?"

The finality of those words—the realization that I may never see the citadel again—was what finally jarred me enough to open my eyes and turn my head. We were already far enough away that the citadel and the hedge began to blend into the cliffside where it perched, the waterfall that ran underneath it entirely visible, plummeting to the valley floor a thousand feet below it. I'd seen bits and pieces of it before, from the courtyard, from the trail when I'd ventured to Gateskeep to try to heal those wounded by the rakasa . . . but I'd never seen it so entirely before. Not like *this*.

My home was . . . *breathtaking*.

I watched until the hedge was nothing more than a thin green line, the citadel a gray speck against the massive mountain.

"There," Loukas said when I finally twisted to face forward, "you see? It's not so bad."

I didn't respond.

After a few moments of nothing but the sound of Maddok's wings beating against the wind, I finally asked, "Where are we going?"

"I'm not sure. All I know is that we're following the river for now, since that's where Melia and Cyrus found him." Loukas released the reins with one hand to point at the earth far below, to a narrow, winding band of blue amidst the thick growth of trees and bushes.

"How will we see him from way up here?"

"We're flying this high because it's daylight and we're out of range of attacks up here. Once we switch to nighttime, we'll fly lower and probably a bit slower, too, to try to track him."

"Oh."

We fell into silence. Though Loukas was right—it wasn't so bad after all—I was still uncomfortable so far off the ground, being carried by the flying beast. If the Great God had intended for me to fly, he would have given me wings.

It took me quite a while to build up the courage to broach the subject Sachiel had talked to me about earlier that morning, but as the sun began slowly lowering in the sky, I realized our time without being overheard could be ending at any moment. Surely we had to stop to rest and eat at some point.

"Um, Loukas . . ." I began and felt him perk up immediately after the long stretch of silence. "I, um, have something to ask you."

He waited, but when I didn't continue, he finally prompted, "Yes?"

I cleared my throat, but no amount of effort could get my heart to go back into my chest where it belonged, instead of pounding in my throat. "After what happened last night . . . when Raidyn and Zuhra had to heal me again . . ."

"Yes?"

"Sachiel came to tell me an idea she had . . . a way to heal me. Permanently. So Raidyn and Zuhra don't have to keep risking their strength."

There was a long, weighted pause. "And what does her idea have to do with me?"

After what Sachiel had told me, I'd been even more terrified of riding with Loukas. But I didn't feel any different . . . surely if he'd wanted to use his power on me, he would have convinced me I loved flying . . . wouldn't he?

I swallowed. "I have to steal my power back. The way he stole it from me. But . . . I don't know how I'd ever get close enough to him. Especially when the plan is to kill him first."

He stiffened behind me, and Maddok, perhaps sensing his Rider's discomfort, made a sharp cawing noise, attracting the attention of some of the other Riders nearby. Raidyn and Zuhra were closest to us, and she looked over with eyebrows lifted. I tried to smile reassuringly at her, but my lips trembled.

"She told you about my ability, I presume." His voice was cold, all friendliness from earlier gone.

"Yes," I stammered.

"And you want me to use it to help you."

It wasn't a question. But I still repeated, "Yes," so softly, I didn't even know if he could hear me. "I don't know how else I could get close enough to him to try to get my power back."

"Did Sachiel happen to mention what using my ability does to me? What it requires of me?"

I shook my head.

Instead of telling me, he was silent for several minutes. Though I felt fine at the moment, I knew it was only a matter of time before whatever Raidyn and Zuhra had done would begin to unravel again, the hole within me tearing open once more. If Loukas refused to help me, soon we would track Barloc down and kill him. There would be no chance of getting my power back—of healing myself for good.

"And assuming I did this for you—am I honestly to believe you are willing to do back to him what he did to you? To *kill* him to regain your power?"

"*Kill* him?" I repeated.

"You are the only known survivor of such an attack. I doubt Raidyn and Zuhra would be willing to heal *him* over and over again."

"But . . . he didn't have the power to begin with. He won't have a hole inside when I take it back."

"If he survived the change—which it sounds like he did—then his body has changed with it, to accept your power as his own. Tearing it from him will have the same effect as it would on any Paladin."

I felt suddenly sick again, but this time it had nothing to do with flying. *Was* I willing to kill him? He was doomed to die either way as soon as we found him. But could *I* be the one to do it?

He'd stolen my power, had sentenced me to certain death that

Raidyn and Zuhra could only hold off for so long . . . but could I truly do it back? I thought of him crouched over me, the unbearable pain of having my power ripped out of me, leaving me a husk of who I'd always been, of Grandfather's body lying on the ground, dead, my grandmother injured on the other side of the gateway—all because of him. I thought of the triumphant joy he felt when he'd slaughtered those gryphons, that I'd experienced through the connection I had with him now, that I still hadn't found the courage to admit to anyone. The connection I was desperate to sever.

My gift had been to heal, but he would use it to kill and kill again and again and again.

"Yes," I finally answered, fierce and unforgiving. "I *am* willing to do it. And if you'll help me, I promise you I will succeed."

EIGHTEEN

Zuhra

We flew high above the trees for most of the first day. It was strange being on Naiki's back with Raidyn in *my* world, not his—and also surrounded by my family. Up there, the sky within reach, the ground so very far below, the air thin but his arms secure around me, it *felt* like we were alone . . . until I looked to the left or right and saw the other gryphons and Riders nearby. My father and mother. Loukas and Inara. Even Sharmaine and Halvor. There was so much to say, so much I wanted to do . . . but I was paralyzed by the worry of my parents looking over at us, my mouth sealed shut by fear of what the future held.

So I wrapped my arms over his and held on as tightly as he held me, and hours passed in silence, his chest and stomach pressed against my back, his fingers occasionally finding the tiny sliver of skin where my blouse had pulled free of my pants. Those delicious waves of sensation were the closest we got to reliving the kiss from last night.

Once the sun sank below the western horizon, the gryphons soared lower, barely above the treeline, following the river. The shadows changed the water to ink below us, and the trees to spectral sentinels marking our passage. The hot summer day turned cool as darkness stole the heat of the sun, the air above the river crisp and fresh, smelling of pine and damp soil.

"Do you think he means to fly all night?" I turned my head

so Raidyn could hear my question without raising my voice too much.

"I hope not," he said, his mouth brushing my ear, driving all thought from my mind other than his lips and wanting them on mine. His arm tightened around my waist. "Naiki is getting too tired to keep going much longer." He bent his head forward even more so that his lips were on my cheek.

Heat blossomed in my belly, chasing away the chill of night. Hoping the darkness hid us from view of the others, I tilted my face even farther back so that his mouth touched the corner of mine. He inhaled sharply, his fingers on the bare skin between my blouse and pants digging into my hip. "Yes, she needs to rest," I murmured, our lips brushing with each word. Achingly close to a kiss and yet so far away from what I truly wanted to do.

"Zuhra." My name was a raspy groan, deep in his throat, sending a hot shiver of need through me. His hand moved up my body, underneath my blouse, so that his fingers stroked the tender skin of the bottom of my ribcage. I sucked in a gasp at the astonishing feel of his callused fingers.

A sharp whistle ahead jerked me out of the languorous stupor of his touch; it felt like I'd taken some of Sami's sleeping herbs, making my body heavy and hot and my head fuzzy. Raidyn immediately pulled back, dropping his hand from my skin to grab Naiki's reins. I straightened as well, facing fully forward again just in time to see Taavi circling lower before landing on a large bank between the river and the forest. I caught the hint of a foul, acrid scent that turned my stomach.

The other gryphons had also landed by Taavi; Raidyn guided Naiki down beside them. The moment we reached the ground, Raidyn climbed off her back and helped me dismount as well.

"What is that smell?" Mother winced, squinting into the darkness.

"Are we stopping for the night?" Halvor asked with a yawn.

"Not here" was all Father said. And then he stalked forward into the forest.

Mother stared at his retreating back; Sharmaine and Loukas

looked to Raidyn at my side with eyebrows lifted in twin expressions of confusion.

"Should we follow him?" Halvor asked, walking over to Inara and taking her hand in his. She grasped it tightly, but her eyes were on the trees swaying in the brisk breeze that still carried that horrible stench, her eyes wide. I couldn't tell if it was the moonlight washing her skin pale, or if she was actually that wan.

"Maybe he just needed to relieve himself?" Loukas said.

Shar smacked his arm with a muttered "Louk!"

"What? We've been riding all day and half the night without a break. Surely I'm not the only one who needs to 'take a walk in the woods' and maybe find something to eat?"

I snorted back a laugh at the expression on my mother's face, a comical mix of shock and disbelief, with a hint of a sneer. But he was right; we had been on those gryphons for a *very* long time.

"Now that you mention it . . ." Sharmaine grimaced with a hand on her belly that grumbled as if on cue.

Even Inara laughed softly at that one. But the laughter and smiles died as quickly as they came when Father reemerged from the shadowed forest, deep grooves etched around his mouth and between his drawn eyebrows.

"I found them," he said softly. "It's as I feared. He burned the bodies."

Though we wanted to bury what was left of the remains, we had no tools. Instead, we gathered as many rocks as we could and piled them over what was left of the charred corpses in the small clearing where Father had found them—which was very little for four gryphons and two Paladin. The brief moment of levity was long gone, replaced by the sobering reminder of what we faced. There was a strange feel to the air, as if lightning had recently struck the earth and still left a lingering trace of its might all around us.

"Do you feel that?" I asked Inara as Raidyn, my father, Halvor, and Loukas finished putting the last few rocks on the pile. She'd been even more withdrawn than normal since we'd followed

Father back to this spot, a darkness deeper than night cloaked her. *What's wrong? What are you keeping from me?* The questions I *actually* wanted to ask my sister but didn't dare. A strange wall existed between us now. She was finally lucid, but I'd never felt more disconnected from her.

"That's *cotantem,*" Sharmaine answered quietly before Inara could. "It means 'lingering power.' A Paladin can feel it anywhere a massive amount of power has been used, sometimes for weeks afterward."

"If Paladin are the only ones who can sense it, I suppose that's why I can't feel anything." Inara's voice was as cold as I'd ever heard it.

"No—I didn't mean—"

But Inara had already walked away, over to where Mother stood with her arms crossed over her chest.

"I'm sorry," Sharmaine said to me, a blush creeping up her neck. "I wasn't trying to make her feel bad."

"I know." I could still feel Inara's pain, even from across the clearing. "I think it's going to take a while for her to come to terms with . . . what happened to her."

Sharmaine nodded, her eyes on the pile of rocks. All that was left of what Barloc had done.

Father straightened after setting the final stone on the gravesite and looked around at the somber group.

"Before we go, I'd like to say a few words, to send their souls to the Light for their eternal rest."

Father spoke for only a few minutes, about the sacrifice they had made, and their worthiness to ascend to a place of peace and rest, but with every word he said, a buzzing of fear spread in the blood that pounded through my body at the growing understanding of what I faced.

Raidyn gripped my hand in his, but even his touch couldn't warm the chill that had taken hold of me, the realization that this grisly end could be in the very near future for me.

I'd volunteered to do this. I'd known I was risking my life. But seeing that pile of ashes and bones had driven home the reality of what we faced more than any hypothetical scenario ever could have. No matter how hard I tried to control the fear surging through me, I couldn't keep my heart from racing, like a frightened animal trying to flee a snare.

Raidyn bent forward to press a brief kiss to my temple. "I won't let him hurt you," he promised.

I knew his promise, though fervent, was very likely impossible for him to keep. But I nodded regardless, hoping my agreement at least brought *him* some needed comfort. All it did for me was break my heart a little bit more.

What if by this time tomorrow I was gone—forever?

The trek back to the river was a silent one. The forest pressed in on us, dark leaves shuddered and twisted in the breeze that snarled through the shadowed branches. Inara walked a few feet ahead of me and Raidyn, with Halvor still at her side. I watched the back of her head and the rigid set of her shoulders, and tried to ignore the pang that nipped at the back of my throat, the feeling that she was avoiding me.

When she suddenly halted, her entire body stiffening, I seized Raidyn's hand and jerked to a stop. Then I let him go and rushed forward.

"Inara?" Halvor stared at her, eyebrows drawn. "What is it?"

She didn't respond. When I reached my sister's side, she was staring blankly forward again, unseeing and unresponsive, just as she had been in the garden—when she'd lied and claimed to merely be exhausted.

"What's going on?" Mother shouldered past Halvor and grabbed Inara's hand, squeezing it, Father right behind her. "Inara?"

She still didn't react, her face terrifyingly blank, eyes empty of recognition.

"What's happening? What is wrong with her? Is she . . . does she need to be healed again?" Mother looked to me, stricken.

"No," I said quietly, "this is something else. She did this before. But she wouldn't tell me what happened."

Everyone had gathered around us by then.

"This happened before? And you didn't tell us?" Mother's eyes narrowed.

Before I could respond, Inara gasped and, blinking a few times, returned to herself, stumbling back a step when she realized everyone was circled around her, watching.

"Inara!" Mother's focus was thankfully drawn away from me. "What *happened*?"

Inara's gaze swiveled from person to person until her eyes met mine and held; she was visibly trembling. "I . . . I . . ." Her voice quavered.

Her terror was so thick, it nearly choked *me*.

"Inara . . . what happened?" Father's voice was much more calm, but brooked no argument. She wouldn't be able to lie this time.

She continued to stare at me. I wasn't positive, but something like regret flashed across her face. Then Inara turned away.

"I see him," she admitted at last, her voice a mere whisper, her gaze dropping to the forest floor.

I hardly even noticed anyone else's reactions, I could only stare at Inara.

"You mean . . . the *jakla*?" Father took Inara's shoulders in his hands, still gentle but insistent. "You *see* him?"

She swallowed and nodded, her chest rising and falling. "I can't control it. It just . . . happens. When he uses my power." Her shaking increased. "I see flashes of his life, and then a glimpse of where he is when he uses the power."

Everyone was silent, staring at her. Worry warred with frustration that she had kept this to herself, that she'd been dealing with this alone. Why would she have kept this a secret—especially from *me*?

"Is that . . . normal?" Mother asked quietly, looking to Adelric.

"There is no record of such a thing happening before . . . but no one has ever survived what he did to her before." He studied Inara, his gaze gentle but concerned. "I know it might be hard, but can you tell us what you saw? Where is he right now?"

Inara still wouldn't look up. "I saw him with the Paladin again—his grandfather. And traveling here. And . . . and I saw him . . ." A shudder passed through her. She choked on the last few words; a tear slid down her cheek, nearly iridescent in the pale moonlight that had broken through the clouds overhead. "I saw him attack a home . . . with a family in it."

A ripple of shock ran through all of us, a shiver that started with Inara and spread out to all seven of us gathered around her. Father's eyes shut, his head dropping. My heart plummeted.

We were too late. He was already attacking humans.

"We have to keep going. He can't be too much farther ahead of us now," Father said grimly, releasing Inara and turning to us. "But we need to rest before we try to track him down and lay this trap. There is nothing we can do for that family now and the gryphons are exhausted. I say we fly a little bit farther away from here and find a spot to sleep for a few hours before we continue on."

No one argued with him. We were a morose group as we finished the brief trek to the river. I kept glancing at Inara, but she stared resolutely forward, refusing to meet anyone's gaze. She even shied away from Halvor when he reached for her; he let his hand drop back to his side, his shoulders slumping. A few tense minutes later, we'd all climbed back on the weary gryphons and taken off once more.

"We'll stop soon, girl," Raidyn murmured to Naiki before he swung onto the saddle behind me.

She hooted softly, as if she understood.

Raidyn held me tightly as we took off; I leaned back into the strength and comfort of his embrace and tried to focus on breathing slowly—in and out. In and out. I tried not to think about my sister seeing visions of Barloc . . . or the family he'd surely murdered. *Why?* What possible purpose could he have—

No. Don't think. Just breathe. In and out.

I tried not to think about the trap we had to lure him into—now more than ever. Or the pile of bones and ashes we'd buried, all that remained of the last group of Paladin and gryphon that had hoped to trap and stop him.

I tilted my chin up into the night-kissed wind, letting it whip the gathering tears out of my eyes before they could fall. Raidyn buried his face in my hair, pulling me as close to him as I could be. He didn't speak. There was nothing to say.

Thankfully, we didn't fly much farther before Father again guided Taavi back to the earth, this time to a small clearing a little way back from the river. We all followed, everyone quickly dismounting.

"We can sleep here for a few hours. Inara . . . if you have another . . . if you see him again, will you promise to tell us?"

She nodded, but I noticed she was still avoiding meeting anyone's gazes and keeping her distance from Halvor.

"We should circle together as tightly as possible with the gryphons on the outside to sound the alarm if . . . anything unexpected happens," Father instructed.

I swallowed hard, a lick of fire-laced fear racing over my skin—the fire that could turn me to ash and charred bone if he found us before we found him.

We quickly and quietly unrolled our bedrolls—which were nothing more than one thin blanket we'd each brought, not wanting to weigh down the gryphons any more than necessary—and ate the little bit of food Mother passed around that Sami had sent with us.

I found myself sandwiched between Mother and Raidyn. I longed to reach out for him, to ask him to hold me or even just tell me another story to help my mind stop spinning endlessly over everything that could—and probably would—go wrong, and allow me to sleep. But I didn't dare with my mother inches away. Instead, I lay on the hard ground, shivering and frightened, my eyes squeezed shut but nowhere near sleep.

A minute or two later, Raidyn's warm hand pressed against my back, solid and reassuring; soothing the sharp edges of my fear.

I wasn't sure how much time had passed, only that it felt like I had just barely managed to drift off, when Naiki, lying closest to us, clicked her beak once, twice, jerking me right back to full awareness. I opened my eyes to find myself facing Raidyn, our hands clasped in the small space between us. His blue-fire eyes glowed in the darkness, his body limned with a tense alertness that only exacerbated my own building nervousness. The milky light of the quarter-moon turned the grass to silver as we both sat up.

He glanced around the camp, but shook his head silently when I raised my eyebrows in concern.

Then Taavi's head suddenly rose and he did the same thing, clicking his beak once, twice. My father immediately snapped awake and also sat up. When he saw us both, with Naiki's head cocked and peering into the dark woods, alarm flashed across his face.

"Don't move—yet," Raidyn murmured to me before rising swiftly but soundlessly to his feet and joining my father in gently shaking the others awake, whispering to them, until we were all sitting up, alert and terrified.

All four gryphons had risen, and stood protectively around us, their heads turned the same direction. I could only think of the pile of rocks we'd left not too far behind. If it was Barloc out there, there was apparently little the gryphons could do to protect us—or themselves. My stomach clenched painfully at the unbearable thought of these majestic, intelligent creatures dying tonight.

And possibly the rest of us with them.

NINETEEN

Zuhra

"Is that—"

Father slashed one hand through the air, silencing Halvor's whisper at the same moment I saw it—bobbing lights moving through the trees. *Many* of them.

Many lights meant it wasn't Barloc—but there couldn't be any *good* reasons for a group of people to be wandering through the woods with torches in the middle of the night.

I noticed Mother reach for Father's hand, curling her fingers tightly around his.

"Is it a garrison?" Loukas leaned over and murmured to Father.

Inara stiffened at his question, her gaze flying to Halvor's then mine.

"Most likely," Father whispered back.

The night was so still and quiet; we strained for sounds of bootfalls on the ground, or voices coming near. At first there was nothing, just the flicker of firelight weaving through the trees. Then, the sound of a man's voice echoed through the forest, far too close for comfort, followed by a response. The words were indecipherable, but the tone was clear—they were definitely not just a band of travelers making up time at night.

Father lifted his hand, made a circular gesture, and pointed deeper into the forest. The other Paladin rose to their feet. The rest of us hurried to follow, grabbing our blankets and silently slinking through the trees, away from the torches.

Fear as thick as creeping fog spread among us as we all followed his lead, hurrying as quickly as we could without making noise. I was amazed at how quietly the gryphons were able to move through the foliage, tails raised and wings tucked in to avoid dead leaves on the ground or dry grass that would rustle as they marched next to their Riders.

We were far out of sight of the clearing when Father lifted his hand again and we all halted, breath held. No one dared speak. I glanced over at Inara. She had trailed behind Loukas and his gryphon but stayed ahead of Halvor, too, her face drawn and shadowed in the moonlight.

Though we were as far from the clearing as possible in such a short time, we could still hear the men's voices drawing closer and closer, until their words were audible as well.

". . . are we supposed to be able to stop him? He just destroyed an entire *village.*"

"He'll burn us all to death too," another voice responded.

"Using that amount of power should have drained him—that's why they're not letting us sleep," a third man said. "If we find him before he recharges or whatnot, then we have a chance of killing him."

"*Recharges?* What are you talking about?"

"You're clearly too young to remember the last war."

"You three—enough! Silence is paramount!" a third, commanding voice boomed, deep and oozing authority.

"Yes, sir!" they chanted back in unison.

Naiki dropped her head onto Raidyn's shoulder, lightly nipping at him. He patted her beak twice, and she exhaled softly. I reached out for his free hand, the warm strength of his grip helping to keep the rising panic within me from cresting.

There was no more talking, only the distant sound of boots marching over dry grass.

We waited until the sounds had all gone, and then waited even longer still.

"An entire *village,*" Inara finally whispered, breaking the silence.

Raidyn's hand flexed over mine. Horror flowed between us; it was impossible to separate his from my own.

Mother had gone so pale, the moonlight washed her face alabaster. "We have to find him and stop him."

"We need to find out what town he attacked and when," Halvor spoke up. His free hand was clenched into a fist, his eyebrows pulled down. "It will help us know which way to go to find him—and stop him before he can hurt anyone else."

"What possible reason could he have for attacking an entire *town*?" Sharmaine asked with a shudder. "He's by himself. He has no backup. Surely he doesn't think he's powerful enough to take on the might of the entire Vamalanian army?"

"He wields the power of three Paladin now." Father reached out one hand and buried it in the thick feathers on Taavi's neck. I wasn't sure if he was comforting his gryphon or steadying himself. "We don't know *what* he's capable of. But this . . . an entire village . . . Cinnia is right. We go after him right now. There's no time to lay a trap."

"With all due respect, sir," Raidyn spoke quietly but firmly, "if we act rashly, we will probably end up like that village and the others we buried earlier tonight. We have to follow the plan or we will have no hope of succeeding."

If it had been anyone besides Raidyn, I was certain my father would have snapped back, but though a muscle in his jaw tightened, Father held his tongue. After a long moment, he nodded, with a defeated exhale.

"You're right." He glanced around at us. "There are a few villages and towns nearby. We need to figure out which one he attacked. Inara"—he turned to my sister—"do you remember anything from what you saw—any detail that might help us figure out where he was?"

She shook her head. "No. I only saw the one home . . . not an entire village." The words were strained.

"That huge expenditure of power would definitely leave *cotantem* behind . . . Our only option is to trace any lingering power to figure out which way he went," Father said. "We track him down, lay our trap, and put an end to this."

"We have no idea which direction to start looking—and every hour we waste going the wrong direction could cost more lives," Halvor pointed out.

"What are you suggesting we do instead, then?" Father snapped.

"The main road we took to get to Gateskeep runs parallel to this river. There are plenty of small villages and towns sprinkled all along it. I'll go into the nearest town and buy some supplies and see what I can find out," Halvor offered. "Then we'll at least know which direction to go."

"By yourself?" The whites of Inara's eyes flashed in the moonlight.

"There's no one else," he replied, looking down at her. "I'm the only one without Paladin eyes."

"The only *male,*" she corrected. But she didn't volunteer to accompany him.

"No," Father responded before Halvor could. "It's too much of a risk. What if Barloc is nearby? He knows all of you by sight, with or without Paladin eyes."

"With garrisons out searching for Paladin? I doubt it. He's as big of a target now as the rest of you. We need information and we need it fast," Halvor insisted.

"And if you *do* run into him?"

"I won't."

"I'll go with you," I volunteered. Raidyn's grip on my hand tightened, but I continued. "I can keep a lookout for him while you act like you are merely buying supplies and see what you can find out. If I notice anything suspicious, I can alert you and we can leave. It would make sense for you to buy more food if there are two of us traveling together."

Halvor nodded but my parents exchanged a look of dismay. My mother was the one who said, "No. It's too dangerous."

"So is not knowing which direction Barloc is headed," I argued. "If we can find out where the attack took place, we will save ourselves a lot of possible wasted time."

It took some convincing, but finally Halvor and I prevailed, everyone agreeing to let us head to the nearest town with some of the money we'd brought so we could buy supplies as part of our cover. We were to pose as a married couple, traveling to visit family in Mercarum. Mother took off the slim gold band on her ring finger and gave it to me to wear.

"Please be careful." She closed my fingers around the ring, her hand lingering on mine.

"I will."

The sky above the treetops had lightened to pewter, softening the ominously dark trees from shadowy monsters into gentler giants, their arms and claws no longer menacing as dawn revealed them to be harmless leaves and branches.

While we waited for the sun to rise, Inara came over to where Halvor and I stood. I thought she was seeking him out, but instead, she came to me. "It should be me," she said quietly. "But . . . I was too frightened to volunteer. I-I can't face him. Not yet . . . not without everyone else."

"You'll be safe here," I said. "And we'll be fine. I promise."

"Don't make promises you can't keep."

I reached out and took her hands in mine. "He won't be there. And we'll be back before you know it."

Inara nodded, but worry swam in her eyes. I still wasn't used to seeing her without the Paladin glow. Her plain blue irises were even paler than normal in the gray light of predawn. I thought of the lie she had told me, but in that moment, with our future so uncertain, it didn't matter anymore. She was frightened and dealing with more than I could imagine. One lie was not enough to break what we shared. "Everything is going to be fine," I said again, forcing certainty into my voice, determined to help ease her fear, even if it was only a little bit.

Her fingers tightened around mine.

"Do you know where to go?" Father walked over to the three of us, and he and Halvor began discussing directions to get to the nearest town and then find our way back to the group where they would be waiting.

I glanced over at Raidyn, where he stood talking to Loukas and Sharmaine. I knew he wasn't happy about me going, but I didn't want to send Halvor alone. I didn't have Paladin eyes to mark me, and surely it would be safer to go together—to watch out for any sign of danger or Barloc. I wished I could take Raidyn aside, to talk to him—to kiss him, and let his touch melt away the fear of what lay ahead of us.

As if he could sense my thoughts, he finally looked over, his blue-fire eyes scorching through me. I had the sudden urge to tell him goodbye—just in case.

No, I told myself. *Nothing is going to happen.* I would see him again, very soon.

There was no reason for goodbyes.

It took about fifteen minutes to reach the main road Halvor told us about. We moved slowly through the forest, pausing frequently, listening for a sign of the garrison or anyone else—including Barloc—just to be safe.

But there was no sign of anyone.

We passed a second, smaller stream, tendrils of mist skulking along its banks as the earth warmed beneath the rising sun; I couldn't help but look at the clear water longingly, dreaming of dunking myself in it, and scrubbing the grime of travel from my skin and hair.

It didn't take long after reaching the main road before Halvor recognized where we were, having traveled through the area only a few weeks earlier.

"Over that crest is Dimalle. It's a bit bigger than Gateskeep so I can't imagine it's the village Barloc destroyed." He said it so matter-of-factly, but I didn't miss the shudder that shook his shoulders. We both carried knapsacks, and walked close together, like we truly were married. Mother's ring weighed my hand down, far more than such a small piece of jewelry should have, as if the farce of pretending to be Halvor's wife made it heavier. Though it had only been a few weeks, my hopes of having him want me were almost laughable now—after the feelings I'd discovered myself capable of with Raidyn. If only it could have been *him* at my side, pretending to be my husband. I would have felt so much safer . . . and the ring probably would have felt more like a hopeful promise, not an uncomfortable mockery of my former dreams.

"Are you sure you know where we are?" I asked, glancing around at the thick trees and bushes that lined the road.

"Yes," he said, "we stayed for a night on our journey to the citadel."

"Do you think they'll remember you, then? And wonder where your uncle is and how you got a wife so fast?"

"They had quite a few travelers that night. I doubt they would. They might remember my face as being familiar, but I can't imagine they would recall that much detail. We were a quiet pair; we kept to ourselves."

I swallowed past a sudden lump in my throat. He hadn't mentioned *that* to my father. I wonder if he would have let us go if Halvor had admitted he'd spent a night in this town a month earlier. Though the assumption he wouldn't be remembered *seemed* sound, my stomach still contracted at the unexpected potential snag.

The well-trod road was packed down, rutted from wagon wheels and grooved from horses' hooves. It was also empty this early in the morning. Dirt puffed up into tiny little clouds of protest at our intrusion with each step, cracked and dry after the heat of the previous day. We walked for a few minutes in silence as the road turned into a hill, enough of an incline to make me a little breathless. The trees began to thin as we got close to cresting the rise, and I spotted the first roofs in the unbroken sunlight. It was warm enough that sweat slid between my breasts and down my spine, making my blouse stick to my back and chest. I glanced down and suddenly halted.

"What? What is it?" Halvor glanced over at me in alarm.

I stared at my legs in dismay. "I'm wearing pants," I said.

"Yes?"

"Women don't wear pants here."

Halvor had the audacity to *laugh.* "Is that what your mother told you?"

I scowled at him. "Is it not true?"

"It's not *common,* I'll give her that. But there are enough women who do, that it won't be remarked on. I promise. Especially as a woman who is traveling a great distance."

"You better hope you're right," I muttered, storming ahead of him.

"Well, they're sure to believe we're married now." Halvor was still laughing. "Because you are obviously furious with me."

I wasn't sure if he was still mocking me or if he meant it. Regardless, I slowed my pace and schooled my face into a pleasantly benign half smile. "Do catch up, *dear.* I find myself quite famished after the long journey."

I ignored his snort and looked straight ahead as we reached the top of the incline, the town spreading out before us. It was much larger than I'd expected, building after building spreading far into the distance, the entirety of it surrounded by a large wall. *This* was "slightly bigger" than Gateskeep to Halvor?

"Is this . . ."

"Dimalle," Halvor supplied. "Yes. It is."

I swallowed. "It's . . . big." Though I'd flown over Soluselis, I'd never gone *into* the large city. I spent my whole time in Visimperum in the castle, the training ring, and the surrounding grounds.

"This place? It's bigger than Gateskeep, as I said." He looked at me sideways, one eyebrow lifted. "But it's small compared to Mercarum."

"Is it now?" A strange weakness, made of heat and trembling, stole the strength from my legs. Why hadn't I thought this through better? I had envisioned a small village, like Gateskeep, not a large town with hundreds of people in the market—if not more.

"Are you all right?" Halvor touched my elbow, his cold fingers jarring me back to myself.

"I'm fine."

"We better keep going, then, before the guards wonder why we're just standing here."

I nodded and forced my shaky legs to carry me forward, down the hill toward the large iron gate where a couple of exhausted-looking men stood together, gazing down at something one of them held—luckily not watching us. Halvor kept his hand on my elbow. Though I would have preferred to have Raidyn be the one beside me, I was grateful for the extra support and reminder that I wasn't alone.

As we approached the closed gate, the guards glanced up at us.

"Good morning," Halvor said.

"What brings you to Dimalle?" one asked, pocketing the dice he'd been holding.

"We're stopping for supplies. My wife and I are traveling to Mercarum."

The guard looked us over, then jerked his thumb to the man beside him. "Let 'em in."

"Thank you." Halvor tipped his head as we passed through the gate.

"See?" Halvor murmured to me as we entered Dimalle. "Nothing to worry about."

"Yet," I replied under my breath.

It was still early, but the town was already awake, men and women bustling here and there; some bent over gardens enclosed by whitewashed fences, some talking in small groups, some meandering from house to house on the side paths, and some pulling carts and wagons down the large, main road we walked on. The air was a maelstrom of scents—fresh bread that made my stomach growl, some sort of roasted meat, a waft of spice, a hint of floral perfume, a putrid undertone of waste. A few people looked at us as we walked by, but quickly moved on with their day, hardly taking notice of the dirty, travel-weary couple following the trail of goods and food converging on the town's market.

Regardless, I inched closer to Halvor, my heartbeat skittish. There were *so many* people.

"Are you all right?" Halvor glanced down at his forearm where I clutched him so tightly, my knuckles were as white as his shirt.

"Fine," I said, forcing myself to release him. There were little crescent marks in the fabric from my nails. "Sorry."

"I didn't think this would be overwhelming for you after your adventures in Visimperum."

The square was visible up ahead now. Brightly colored flags snapped in the breeze. Large groups of men and woman flowed around the carts and wagons, like a river made of bodies. The din of voices grew louder and louder as we approached. "That was a different kind of adventure."

"Follow my lead, then," he advised quietly, holding out his elbow for me to thread my hand through.

I nodded, all too happy to do just that.

We entered the market, Halvor guiding me through the crowds, our gait unhurried, perusing the wares for sale, but not drawing close to any cart or wagon yet. As we meandered, we caught snippets of conversations, very little of it useful—mostly neighbors and acquaintances chatting about crops, the weather, their children, and other everyday life happenings. I'd begun to lose hope, until we crossed near a trio of men, huddled together, their voices barely audible over the din in the square.

". . . completely destroyed, burned to the ground," one was saying, and Halvor immediately slowed his pace.

"They say there was nothing left," another man added. "Other than some charred bones. What Paladin can *do* that?"

I stiffened, causing Halvor to stumble, neatly covering it up by acting like there had been a stone on the ground. Instead of moving past the men, Halvor turned *toward* them, sending my already-beleaguered heart hammering into my ribcage.

"Pardon the interruption, but did I hear you say there was a *Paladin* attack somewhere?"

The trio spun to face us, and I shrank back from the force of their combined scrutiny.

When they didn't respond right away, Halvor continued, "My wife and I are traveling to Mercarum, and I don't want to risk her safety if those . . . those *monsters* are back in Vamala again."

The initial distrust on the townsmen's faces transformed into eagerness at Halvor's words. "You haven't heard?"

"No—we've been on the road. Is it true? Are they . . . *back*?" His voice lowered to a shocked—and terrified—hush.

"Yes," one of them affirmed. "The only survivor of the attack came through here yesterday and told us all about it."

I shuddered, thinking of so many dead—killed because Barloc

had escaped. What was his purpose in killing them? What possible reason could there be to slaughter innocent people?

"What did he say? Where was the attack?"

"He was from Ivra. He said the Paladin came during the night on their gryphons. The attack was unlike anything he'd ever seen before—they incinerated the entire village in a matter of minutes. No one escaped. Barloc only survived because they thought they'd killed him; he had to lay underneath his brother-in-law's body to protect himself from the fire." The man sounded equal parts horrified and fascinated.

At the sound of *that* name, my knees nearly gave out. Halvor jerked as if he'd been slapped.

"Barloc?" he managed to force out. Could they hear the way his voice shook?

"Yes, that was the survivor's name. Did you know him?"

"I . . . I don't think so. It sounded like someone I know, but I've never been to Ivra." Halvor managed to salvage his reaction.

My fingers dug into his arm to try to keep from collapsing. How was he still able to speak clearly—to not turn and sprint for the gate? "Is . . . is he still here? The survivor?" Halvor asked faintly, his arm beneath my hand trembling.

"No, he left last night. Said he was heading to Retrarum, to warn other towns along the way and try to reach the High Judges before those monsters do."

If only they'd known the true monster had been in their midst, had announced his plans directly to their faces. But . . . *why*?

"How he thinks he'll beat a horde of Paladin on their gryphons is beyond me," one of the other men piped up. "Crazy old man."

"Well, he did lose his whole family and village," the third one pointed out. "I'd probably be out of my mind too, if I'd just been through that."

The first man who had done most of the speaking rolled his eyes. His compassion was astounding. "Anyway, if what he said is true, the Paladin are headed for the capital, so you should be safe going to Mercarum."

Halvor put his hand over mine, covering the whiteness of my

knuckles where I gripped him too tightly again. "Crazy or not, I hope the warning reaches the judges in time."

The second man shrugged. "The garrison stationed here sent out emissaries to warn surrounding towns and runners on horseback to the capital. Perhaps they will have a chance of beating the gryphons—especially if a garrison succeeds in capturing and stopping them first. Soon all of Vamala will be on alert for their presence."

"Good," Halvor said, even though his skin flashed cold beneath his shirt. "Well, we won't take up any more of your morning."

"Good luck out there." The third man tipped his head at us as the trio turned away and moved on into market.

Halvor and I stood there, watching them merge into the flow of people, frozen with shock.

"We need to get the food and get back," he finally said, tugging me forward to the nearest cart. I hardly noticed what he purchased, my mind whirling over what they'd told us. None of it made sense. Why would Barloc murder an entire village, then come to the next town and announce his plans to travel to the capital? We were supposed to be trying to figure out how to set up a trap for him—but I had the sinking feeling he was doing the same thing for us. Now we not only had to track him down before he killed again and somehow make sure he found out I was an enhancer—we also had to avoid the garrisons that would all be looking for a supposedly murderous group of Paladin on their gryphons.

A fist of ice clenched my lungs, threatening to pull me under, drowning me in the rising tide of panic. We had to get back to my family—to warn them. I needed to get out of here . . . I needed to get back to Raidyn.

Halvor glanced over at me, a clear warning on his face. I was breathing too quickly, struggling to get enough air. How was he so calm? After what we had just learned—what we now faced?

"Is she—"

"She's fine; crowds make her nervous," Halvor answered for me, gathering up the rest of the food he'd purchased, shoving it in his knapsack and quickly guiding me away from the concerned merchant.

We weaved through the surging mass of men and women and children; most of the conversations we passed turned to the rumor of the Paladin returning to Vamala, and the village they'd destroyed. Crossing that square full of strangers was almost more than I could handle. But finally, we broke free of the current of people onto the less crowded main road we'd initially walked down, heading back to the gate.

It was already growing hot, and yet I still shivered, panic's cold grip growing stronger and stronger. By the time we reached the gateway and the guards who had nodded us through earlier, I was so light-headed I had to hold on to Halvor to keep forcing my legs to move forward.

"Going so soon?" one of them asked as we walked past, his hand resting on the hilt of his sword.

"We just needed supplies," Halvor said. "After hearing about the attack, we decided we'd better hurry on our way to warn our families."

The guard's knuckles whitened on the hilt of his sword, his eyes moving over our heads to the forest and sky—mercifully empty of gryphons—beyond. "Good luck out there. Hope you make it home."

"Thanks." Halvor pulled me forward as quickly as he could without breaking into a run. It was difficult to know if my lungs burned from the quick pace or from the fist of terror squeezing my oxygen away.

The moment we crested the hill and were out of sight of the guards on the other side, Halvor veered off the road, plunging us into the leaf-dappled shade of the forest. I gasped for air, my blood a rush of heat and fear in my veins, as he dragged me deeper and deeper into the woods, away from the road and Dimalle. Minutes, a lifetime, or seconds passed before he finally slowed and then stopped.

"Zuhra. Look at me. *Zuhra!*"

Instead, I stumbled to the nearest tree. The bark bit into the tender skin of my palms; strangely the pricks of pain forced the panic back enough for the roar in my ears to abate and my panting to slow.

Just in time to hear the sound of wings flapping overhead and a surge of terror that was separate from mine—one that I immediately recognized.

"*No.* What is he *doing*?" Halvor stared at the trees above us.

I followed his gaze and my legs nearly gave out. A familiar gryphon hovered low over the treetops, Raidyn scanning the area intently, the terror I felt—*his* terror—nearly choking me. Something was horribly wrong. The trees we stood beneath had branches heavy with thick, dark leaves, so that his gaze ran right over where we stood. Naiki continued on without stopping.

"Raidyn!" I shouted, heedless of the guards close enough to possibly hear. *"Raidyn!"*

Whether it was the flapping of Naiki's wings or the wind in his ears, he didn't pull back on the reins, didn't turn her toward us—flying straight for the road and the town beyond that would think he'd come to murder them all. The horror of the war stories I'd been told churned through my mind like flashes normally contained to nightmares—images of Paladin and their gryphons being killed by the humans, despite the Paladin's superior power, because of *their* sheer numbers.

There was only one of Raidyn and an entire town full of hundreds if not thousands of angry, upset, frightened humans.

"Raidyn!" I raced back through the trees. I had to stop him.

Halvor grabbed my arm, yanking me to a halt. "Zuhra, what do you think—"

I ripped free of his grip without a word and bolted, leaping over fallen tree trunks, crashing through undergrowth and bushes that tore at my pants and exposed skin with sharp thorns and tangled branches, my gaze on the sky above the entire time—tracking the progress of the gryphon that was easily outdistancing me even at such a slow speed for her.

I burst out onto the empty road, just in time to see Naiki swooping over the crest of the hill, toward Dimalle and the guards who had no doubt spotted them by now.

"No! Raidyn!"

The hard earth hurt the soles of my feet, even through the supple leather of the boots I wore, as I sprinted up that hill, desperation burning like acid in my lungs—his *and* mine. A low shout was followed by more yells and a shriek that had to come from Naiki. I pushed myself harder, but it wasn't enough—I wasn't fast enough and I knew it. Horror blossomed in my chest, spreading through my body like blood pouring from a wound—the exact scene I was terrified I would find when I finally made it to that wall where Raidyn had probably flown straight into his doom.

Why? Why had he done it?

I'd almost reached the top of the hill when I heard wingbeats—from *behind* me. I spun, praying it was somehow, miraculously, Raidyn and Naiki, but knowing it couldn't be when the ground trembled beneath my feet at the same moment the *boom* of an explosion detonated through the air on the other side of the hill.

"Zuhra! Where is he?" my father yelled from the back of Taavi, but his gryphon suddenly keened, pulling at his reins, his dark eyes wide and his beak lifted to the air.

I pointed at the hill, and he urged Taavi forward even faster. The gryphon needed no encouragement; he lowered his head and put on a burst of speed that lifted dirt from the packed earth as they passed me, driving it into my face. I followed as quickly as possible, but every painful step felt like I was moving *backward* not forward—the top of that cursed hill somehow getting farther and farther away.

Suddenly, Halvor was at my side. He grabbed my arm again, but before I could try to pull free, I realized he was dragging me *up* this time, not to a stop. He was trying to help me.

Finally, we reached the crest, only to stumble to a halt, my hands going to my mouth. My trembling legs collapsed, forcing me to my knees at the scene below us.

"Raidyn!" My throat was so raw, his name cracked halfway through my scream.

Taavi and my father were flying straight up into the air, out of range of the archers—archers that had shot Naiki down. She lay on her side, an arrow protruding from her left wing, blood pooling around her beautiful golden feathers, staining them garish red. Raidyn stood in front of her, but he faced at least twenty men wielding swords and spears. Every vein in his body glowed with his power—power that he had already expended to blast the gateway apart. It lay in a pile of melted iron and rubble, with more armed men clambering over it.

"I don't want to hurt you—but I will if you don't tell me where she is!" His words carried on the wind that blew my hair back from my wet cheeks.

Was he looking for *me*?

I scrambled back to my feet.

"Zuhra—what are you doing?" Halvor turned to me, his face pale and hazel eyes wide.

"We have to stop them!"

Halvor shook his head, his eyes widening further. "There's nothing we can do!"

There was no time to convince him. Instead, I sent a desperate prayer to the Great God and ran for the carnage below.

TWENTY

Inara

Mother stood next to me, gripping my hand tightly in hers. Sharmaine paced back and forth in front of her gryphon, Keko, while Loukas leaned against a tree, his arms crossed, eyebrows pulled down into a scowl, Maddok a short distance away, his feathers fluffed in agitation.

Father had left only a minute or two after Raidyn, despite Mother begging him not to leave her. Father and Taavi were still visible in the distance, but soon would disappear as Raidyn and Naiki had.

I wanted to pace like Sharmaine, or scowl like Loukas, or even climb onto one of those gryphons and take off after them. Instead, I remained motionless, while Raidyn's words echoed through my mind over and over. *Something's wrong. Something's very wrong. I can feel it. I can feel* her.

Father had argued with him, though he'd paled at Raidyn's words. *It's too dangerous. You can't go after her in full daylight. She's still alive—you can feel that, right? If you go after her, they will* kill *you.*

Raidyn had ignored him, climbing onto Naiki's back. *She's completely panicked—she's terrified. I can't just sit here and hope she's fine. I'm going to find her. I* have *to.*

"I can't believe he left me. I can't believe he's gone." Mother's hand was a vise on mine; my fingers tingled from the lack of blood.

"He didn't leave you," I assured her, though he had in fact done exactly that. "He's gone after Zuhra. There's a difference."

"I know . . . but . . . I'm scared." She stared at the speck that was all we could see of him in the distance with an intensity that frightened me. But not as much as the fear of what had happened to Zuhra. What if they'd run into Barloc? "I'm afraid none of them will come back."

I had felt it too. Not as strongly as Raidyn, but I'd felt it. The distant echo of terror that wasn't my own and panic that slicked my hands with cold sweat, making my heart flutter like a frightened bird's wings, rapid and quickly weakening.

"I don't know what I'll do if he doesn't come back again."

"Stop making everything about you." I yanked my hand free and stormed away—straight past Sharmaine, who had paused her pacing at my outburst, auburn eyebrows lifted. Disbelief? Dismay? It was hard to tell, and I wasn't sure I cared. I didn't know her, I didn't know Loukas, I didn't *want* to know them. I didn't want to be out here, lost in some forest deep in Vamala, with only my mother and two Paladin who were little more than strangers. I didn't want to have a connection with Barloc, or need to track him down and do what Sachiel had told me was required to regain my power.

But here we were, and there was nothing any of us could do to go back to how things once were. We could only go forward.

I was done waiting, always waiting. Stuck in cages all my life: cages made of poisonous green vines, of power that roared and drowned and saved all at once, of fear that bared bloody teeth, pressing me into the ground, shoving me into a corner, paralyzed. My sister was out there, and something was wrong. She was suffering; she needed help.

I would not stay in that clearing, holding Mother's hand, thinking I'd been left behind again when I could go and *do*.

What? I had no idea. But I would figure it out.

Twigs and branches cracked behind me from heavy footsteps; it had to be Loukas. Would he try to force me to change my mind? My face flushed hot at the immediate assumption. He'd never done anything to lead me to believe he'd used his ability on any of us yet . . . why would he start now? He would have been better to force Raidyn to stay if he were going to make anyone do anything. Though he'd been visibly angry at his friend's insistence on going in search of Zuhra despite the danger, he'd let him go.

"What do you want, Loukas?"

He came up beside me and reached for my arm, tugging me to a stop. "This won't help," was all he said.

I pulled free of his grip, though it took considerably less effort than breaking free of my mother's. "I have to do *something*."

"And if something *has* happened, what will you do? Raidyn made a reckless decision that is putting *all* of us in danger, and your father went to try to stop him. How do you think Adelric will react if he gets back and you're missing too?"

"He's trying to stop Raidyn? I thought he was going to help him find Zuhra."

Loukas ran a hand over his face. He had faint bruises beneath his brilliant green eyes and heavy stubble already darkened his entire jawline. Though he was a bit unkempt, he was still stunningly beautiful. Even more beautiful than the statues at home with their jeweled eyes and painted perfection.

And ten times more frightening.

"Have you ever loved anyone?" I asked.

He blinked. "Excuse me?"

"Because if you had, you would know that I can't keep being that person who sits back and waits while the people she loves are in danger—possibly hurt . . . or worse. I have to do *something*. *Please*."

A muscle in Loukas's jaw worked beneath his stubble. He glanced back to where we'd left poor Sharmaine alone with my mother and both gryphons. The trees pressed in so close, they nearly grew on top of one another, their branches tangling above us. We couldn't even see the small clearing anymore, and I knew I hadn't made it far before he'd caught up to me.

"Yes," he said at last, "I have loved someone. I love Raidyn like a brother, and I—" Loukas's mouth clamped shut and he turned back to me. "But even though I care about him, I will *not* go after him, because that would be foolish and only put more of us in danger. Your father went, and that is enough. The rest of us must wait—as hard as it is."

I was still new to deciphering facial expressions, the nuances to conversations, the hidden meanings of gestures and words said and *un*said. But there was *something* about the expression on his face when he'd turned away—when he'd looked back. A painful kind of *longing,* which had darkened his vibrant green-fire eyes. He was talking about Raidyn, but he was thinking of someone else. I was almost certain. And then it hit me.

"It's Sharmaine, isn't it?"

Loukas's eyebrows shot up and he took a step toward me. Though the shadow that crossed his face was as dark as his stubble, I held my ground.

"You don't know what you're talking about."

"Don't I? Have you ever told her?"

Loukas lips thinned. "How long have you been lucid now? Has it even been a *week*? And suddenly you think yourself an expert on interpreting relationships between people you've known for even less time than that?"

My infantile courage wavered and, though I hated myself for it, I flinched.

"I have trained for longer than you've been *alive* to know how to handle situations like this. But because you *love* someone, that means *you* must know what's right, not me." He flung a hand toward the forest. "Still determined to go after them? Then you know what? Be my guest. You'll probably just get lost and we'll have to come rescue you too. But by all means, go save your sister."

He spun on his heel and stormed back the way we'd come.

I stood there for several long moments, the sun-warmed air scraping through my lungs. *You'll probably just get lost and we'll have to come rescue you too.* The tangled, massive trees pressed in on me. It was an ancient forest, no place for us mere mortals to be trespassing; these trees weren't sentient in the way the *custovitan* hedge the Paladin had planted was . . . but there was a certain sense of *awareness* around them. An acrid tang to the air—like the aftermath of magic. Was it the *cotantem* they'd talked about, that I'd believed myself unable to sense any longer? My skin crawled, itchy with the feeling I was being watched. With a shiver, I turned in a slow circle. Did that feeling mean Barloc was nearby? Or something else?

Defeated by the fear that strangled any courage I might have possessed, I rushed back to the clearing to tell the others what I'd felt. To let them decide what to do while I waited and waited and waited some more.

Like I always did.

TWENTY-ONE

Zuhra

I ran down the hill. "Raidyn! I'm right here—*Raidyn*!"

At last, he jerked, and I knew he'd heard me—but he didn't turn. It took me a moment to realize he *couldn't*—if he did, the men with spears and swords and bows and arrows would attack. The only advantage he had right now was their fear of the power he wielded. They were waiting for more reinforcements to arrive, to defeat him through sheer numbers. But how many of them would die to kill Raidyn? How many had wives, children, families they would be leaving forever, sacrificing themselves on the altar of fear and mistrust? It was all such a colossal waste.

"Stop! He won't hurt you if you just stop!" I turned my focus to the guards as I continued to sprint to where Naiki still lay, though she kept trying to lift her head to look at Raidyn, with a low keen deep in her throat. A few of them glanced at the girl in men's pants with her hair halfway falling out of a braid, running toward them, waving her arms and shouting to get their attention, but most stayed intent on the Paladin and his glowing hands.

"Stop! He doesn't want to hurt you! No one has to die today! Please, stop!" I shouted and shouted until I tasted blood at the back of my throat, until a few more men looked at me. Fire ripped through my lungs when I finally reached Raidyn's side, gasping and trembling. I didn't dare touch him, knowing if I did, my power would surge up to meet his, and I would be lost in the grip of it all. I had some of the guards' attention—but more continued to join the ever-growing group facing us, and there was no mercy on their faces, only cold, deadly intent.

"He doesn't want to hurt you," I insisted. "Please—everyone just stop."

"He is a Paladin!" one man yelled back.

"They killed my uncle!"

"They murdered an entire *village*!"

I wasn't even sure where the shouts were coming from anymore; once they started, it turned into a cacophony of accusations and terror given voice. "It wasn't him!" I tried to be heard over them but it was futile.

"Zuhra, go. Now, before they attack." Raidyn's voice was low, mournful. His hopelessness was an empty pit of despair cracking open my chest, so that my heart caved in with the weight of his resignation.

My eyes burned. "I'm not leaving you."

"Yes. You are. *Now*."

"Killer!"

"Murderer!"

I'd never realized before how closely related fear was to fury, both spreading like poison through the mob, erasing all capacity for rational thought. Any hope I'd had of calming them and stopping the slaughter dimmed by the moment.

"Please—he won't hurt you!" I tried once more, but my voice cracked, utterly spent.

I sensed someone coming up behind us and spun, expecting a guard trying to attack from behind. Instead, I exhaled in relief to see Halvor.

"She's right. If you back down, he won't hurt you!" His voice was loud enough to carry, so loud, in fact, I couldn't believe it had come from the quiet-spoken scholar I'd always known. Loud enough to stun the bloodthirsty horde into momentary silence.

"This is not the Paladin who killed the villagers," Halvor continued, taking advantage of the pause in their shouts. "He is trying to find and stop him—them. If you attack him—if you kill this man—you will be letting the true murderers go."

The townspeople of Dimalle exchanged looks, a murmur going through them.

"I sold you food this morning! You were the one asking questions about the attacks!" One man pointed at Halvor.

"Because we're trying to find and stop the true murderer," Halvor repeated. "Please—let him go. He means you no harm."

"Then why did he destroy our wall?" one guard called out, his fingers white-knuckled on his still-raised sword.

"If he means us no harm, why is *he* ready to attack *us*?" another shouted.

Raidyn exhaled slowly and released his power; his veins returning to normal, the glow of his power pulling back into his body, visible once more only through his blue-fire eyes, which he turned to me, remorse etched into the deep grooves around his mouth. "I'm sorry. I thought something had happened to her. I thought she was hurt. I came for her." He spoke to them, but his gaze never left mine.

"Why would we hurt a *human* girl?" The older one, standing near the front of the guards, who had spoken the most and seemed to be in charge, now sounded affronted.

Confusion churned within me. Why had he thought me in trouble? Why had he—

Then it hit me. The panic. My blind charge into the forest. Had my emotions been so strong that he'd felt them from such a distance? That was the only answer for his behavior. He'd assumed it meant I was in trouble. He'd come—risking his life—because of *me.* And he wasn't out of danger yet. Though they were listening, the armed men hadn't lowered their weapons yet.

"He's a healer," I said when Raidyn didn't answer, probably not knowing how to explain why he'd known something was wrong—though he'd guessed incorrectly the *reason* for the turmoil he'd felt. He shook his head slightly, his eyes widening, but I continued, not knowing how else to get them to believe he wasn't intent on hurting them. "He saved my life by healing me once, and now he can sense my emotions. After we heard the details of the attack on the town by the other Paladin, I was so upset, he could feel it and wrongly assumed something had happened to me here."

Many of the guards stared outright at my explanation. One asked, "Paladin have the power to *heal*?"

"You're *friends* with this Paladin?" the leader accused before I could answer.

"Yes," I said.

"I am too," Halvor said. "He is trying to *help* Vamala. And so is the other Paladin flying up there. Please—let them go, so they can stop the dangerous ones."

"Don't listen to them!" someone cried from farther back in the crowd. "There is no such thing as a good Paladin—they'll kill us in our sleep!"

The crowd broke into a frenzy of yells and shouts again—some arguing for listening to us and some for attacking Raidyn, *and* us, if we didn't move.

"If he wanted to kill you, don't you think he would have by now?" Halvor roared with that same shockingly loud voice he'd used before.

The leader lifted his fist in the air and grudgingly the crowd eventually quieted. Naiki made a soft noise of pain behind us, but I didn't dare look at her, didn't dare turn my back on the volatile mob that was one wrong move from hurtling those spears and arrows at us.

Something had to be done to end this—*now*.

"If you choose to attack, you will eventually kill him," I admitted, the truth of my words like hot coals in my belly, scalding terror that turned my insides to ash. "But if you force him to defend himself, you know he can and will kill *many* more of you before you succeed. Do you truly want that?" I paused and pointed to a young man, standing in the front line of guards. "Do you want to die today?" He blanched and his sword lowered infinitesimally. "How about you?" I moved my finger to the man beside him who looked to be my father's age. "Do you have a wife? Children? Do you wish to never see them again because you've been told all Paladin are evil and must be killed?" I let my words sink in for just a moment before continuing, forcing myself to ignore the morass of emotions pulsing from Raidyn, who stood stiffly beside me. "My friend is right—if Raidyn had wanted to kill you, as you've been taught to believe, don't you think he would have by now?"

The leader appraised me with narrowed—but considering—eyes. "And what assurance of our safety do we have if we *do* let you go?"

It was a temptation to exhale, to believe the battle was ending before it truly began . . . but I didn't dare relax. Not yet.

"I give you my word, on the Great God, who rules over all—we mean you no harm," Raidyn swore. "We are trying to *stop* the one who is hurting your people."

"I don't trust the word of a Paladin." The man next to the leader spat on the dirt, sealing our fate with that small wet speck of hatred in the dust. Before any of us could blink, let alone speak, he jerked his arm back and with the speed and malice of a viper, hurtled his spear directly at Raidyn's heart—Raidyn, who had released his power in a show of good faith.

Time reduced to a crawl and still it wasn't slow enough for me to stop the sharpened point flying through the air directly at Raidyn's heart. His power exploded out from his eyes, down his veins, but it wasn't fast enough—he would never be able to defend himself in time—

I could only watch, paralyzed by inevitability—by powerlessness; my entire being carved out with the visceral knowledge that we had come *so close* to escaping, only to die now, like this, without taking a single one of them with him—

And then, inches from impaling Raidyn, the spear ricocheted off of seemingly nothing but air and bounced harmlessly at our feet.

Raidyn immediately dropped to his knees, spinning to face his gryphon and placing his glowing hands on her wounded wing.

It took my mind an extra few moments to catch up—and only after more spears and arrows were loosed at us, only to also ricochet off the same empty air inches from where Halvor and I still stood. But this time, I noticed the slight ripple of iridescent blue when the sharpened points hit it.

I whirled to the hill behind us to see Sharmaine seated on her gryphon, her entire body lit with her power, her hands extended toward us, Loukas on his gryphon beside her, Inara clinging to him from behind. He, too, glowed, but his veins pulsed bright green, not blue.

"Let them go. Retreat, immediately!" the leader suddenly barked from behind me.

I spun back as shock flared over the mutinous faces of his guards.

"I said retreat—*now*!" he snarled this time and began physically shoving his men backward, toward the ruined gateway. Finally, they relented, doing as commanded, more and more of their expressions changing from angry to complacently obedient.

Loukas.

Here, at last, was what his power could do.

It could buy Raidyn time to heal Naiki.

It could save us from a horde of frightened, angry townspeople.

And for the first time, I felt a surge of hope. If he could control *that* many men at once, perhaps he truly *could* give us a chance against Barloc after all.

TWENTY-TWO

Inara

I still wasn't sure what changed Loukas's mind, though I had a suspicion it was Sharmaine that had convinced him to suddenly agree we needed to go after the others. I only knew that when I'd reentered the clearing, before I could warn them I hadn't felt alone in the forest, they'd both been climbing on their gryphons, Mother hovering near a tree, her face chalky. *Well, do you want to go after them or not?* Loukas had asked, holding out a hand to me. I didn't question his change of heart, merely ran to his side, grabbed his hand, and let him yank me onto the back of Maddok. I'd expected Mother to get on behind Sharmaine, but when we took off and I glanced back to see her still huddled against the tree, it was too late to make them turn around for her.

When we'd crested that hill and come upon the standoff below, my stomach had plummeted, all thoughts of my mother fleeing. We made it with seconds to spare, Sharmaine had barely succeeded in getting the shield of her power up in time to block the spear aimed for Raidyn's heart. I muffled a cry of relief to see Halvor and Zuhra standing beside him—well and whole. At least from what I could tell.

Father, high up in the sky, wheeled Taavi around and dove toward us, behind the protection of Sharmaine's shield.

"What happened?" Sharmaine had to shout to be heard over the beating of the gryphons' wings, her voice strained with the effort of holding her shield up.

"I'm still not sure—but Zuhra wasn't there," Father called back. "She showed up *after* Raidyn."

I looked to my sister, who hovered protectively over Raidyn as he healed Naiki. It appeared that his gryphon had been shot down by the guard's archers; she lay in a pool of blood, Raidyn's hands pressed to her wing, up high, near the joint where it met her body. The giant, beautiful beast shuddered beneath his touch.

Every minute that passed increased the tightness at the base of my throat. Loukas began to tremble from the effort of using his power to buy them time. How long could he hold an entire town's consciousness in his control? It was sprawled far beyond the crumbled wall at the base of the hill. Would Sharmaine's shield withstand another assault if they came back, confused or perhaps even angrier, to realize their minds had been altered? *Would* they realize that was what had happened?

Finally, Raidyn sat back on his heels, the glow in his veins dissipating and then disappearing altogether. Naiki tested out her wing, lifting it from the ground and flapping it once. Then she quickly clambered to her giant back paws. Raidyn helped Zuhra get on first then launched himself onto the saddle behind her. Halvor turned and rushed back to where the rest of us waited. Sharmaine let her shield go, her veins returning to normal as she guided her gryphon to land and helped pull Halvor on behind her. Within seconds, we were all airborne and winging away from the town and the near tragedy.

Loukas finally released his power with a loud exhale. I held on to him tightly, afraid of falling off, so it was impossible to miss the way his shoulders slumped forward and his unsteady grip on the reins.

"Where is Cinnia?" Father shouted, swooping closer to me and Loukas.

"She wouldn't come!" Sharmaine yelled back from the other side of us. "She's in the clearing!"

His gaze turned sharply to the side, to where his wife was waiting, alone. I couldn't understand why she would have refused to come, but at least now I knew why Sharmaine had left her. Father whistled to Taavi and the dark-feathered gryphon shot forward over the treetops, a streak of night against the bright sun glaring overhead. The other two hurried to catch up, but Loukas didn't signal Maddok and his gryphon maintained the same pace, turning his head to peer at his Rider with one bright orange eye.

His hands began to shake, a tremor that quickly traveled up his arms and then spread out through his body. I clutched his waist, terrified to feel him shivering beneath my grip as though it were midwinter, not midmorning on an already sweltering summer day.

"Loukas!" I shouted over the wind and beating of Maddok's wings. "What's wrong?"

He didn't respond.

"Loukas!" My heart was frantic beneath my ribs when he began to slump farther forward in the saddle in front of me.

He was far too big and heavy for me to be able to hold him in place. If he lost consciousness, we would both fall from Maddok's back, plummeting through the forest below to our possible deaths. I wasn't sure how high of a fall could kill a person, but I definitely didn't want to find out today.

I scooted even closer to him in the saddle, pressing my entire body up against his, keeping one arm clenched around his waist. I let go with the other and stretched forward to grab the reins in front of his loose grip. Then, with a deep breath, I repeated the same motion with my other hand, so that I was clasping both reins, my hands completely white-knuckled, my arms stretched over both of his, creating a barrier of sorts to keep him upright—though a pitifully weak one.

"Go, Maddok!" I cried, slapping the reins on his neck, praying the gryphon had sharp enough ears to hear my words before the wind whipped them away. "Get us to the clearing *now*!"

The gryphon needed no further urging—his wings redoubled in speed, and we lurched forward, quickly gaining on the rest of the group. But I was afraid no matter how fast Maddok flew, it wouldn't be enough as Loukas continued to tremble, his entire body quaking. He started to lurch to the side, and I bit down on my lip as I squeezed even tighter, trying to keep us both from falling off the side of the gryphon.

"Loukas!" I shouted in his ear. "I can't lift you up—you have to hold on!"

He moaned something unintelligible but managed to straighten back up once more.

The ride to the town had seemed painfully long, when I'd feared for my sister's life; but the ride back was merciless. Within minutes, my arms ached from squeezing Loukas, trying to do what I could to help support him. It didn't take long for the ache to escalate, my underused muscles on fire from the strain. If we didn't land soon, there was no way I'd be able to continue holding on to Maddok's reins, let alone keep Loukas in the saddle.

Just when I didn't think I could bear any more and that we would surely fall to our deaths at any moment, the trees broke apart and we soared over the river. The clearing was mere moments away.

Hold on, hold on, hold on.

Maddok followed the other gryphons toward the small clearing, tucking his wings in to land, but we were still at least two stories off the ground when Loukas finally crumpled forward. It was more than I could handle. His deadweight yanked my hands off the reins, and before I even realized what had happened, we both plummeted to the earth.

A scream ripped out of my throat.

I squeezed my eyes shut, waiting for the impact.

TWENTY-THREE

Zuhra

Raidyn's arms around me with Naiki's newly healed wings beating us away from Damille back to the clearing felt like a miracle, like magic—like *rebirth.* I'd been certain that spear was going to impale him. I thrummed with the pure shock and joy of being *alive,* after believing death was upon us. Naiki chased after Taavi, who flew faster than I'd ever seen at Father's urging. I didn't understand why Mother was the only one who'd stayed behind, but I couldn't bring myself to worry about it—not when Raidyn transferred the reins to one hand so he could wrap his other arm all the way around my waist, pulling me even closer so the entire length of his hard, muscled chest and abdomen pressed against my back. His lips brushed my ear, featherlight, the sweep of a hummingbird's wings against the tender lobe, still somehow sending a bolt of heat to my chest and then lower. My belly tightened. If only it were safe to turn around and do what I *truly* longed to in celebration of our narrow escape.

"Zuhra," he murmured, his voice low, almost guttural. "Oh, Zuhra." His hand on my hip flexed, his arm tightening so I could hardly draw breath. But I didn't care—he was *alive* and holding me and not lying on the ground, cold and gone forever. As if the same thought had transferred from me to him, he shuddered and buried his face in my neck. I tilted my chin toward him, so my cheek rested against the top of his head. Longing, my constant companion on this journey, swelled, rising above the tumult of emotions that crashed over me at all times.

Every moment together felt stolen, snatched from the uncertainty of our future on this quest that I feared was futile and possibly fatal. Now, more than ever, I realized just how valid those fears were.

After several minutes of holding each other as best we could while Naiki winged her way back to the clearing, Raidyn lifted his head so his mouth was near my ear again.

"What *happened* to you?" he finally asked. "I felt your terror . . . your *panic* . . . I thought . . ."

Hot shame flashed over my skin, rising up my neck to heat my face. It was as I'd feared; the panic I'd been unable to subdue had been strong enough to reach him, even over such a distance, and had driven him to risk his life to attempt to rescue me.

I didn't know how to answer him, to tell him that nothing had *happened* to me, that I'd merely been unable to control my fear after we learned Barloc had been in that very town last night, that now all the garrisons would be searching for a group of Paladin riding gryphons.

If not for Sharmaine, he would have died because I was a coward.

I murmured, "I'm so sorry," the only thing I could think to say.

He didn't push me—yet—and we fell silent. He sat up a little taller, but kept his cheek resting against my hair. I watched the dark speck of Taavi in the distance. Raidyn didn't urge Naiki to go as fast, most likely wishing to save her strength for whatever lay ahead, rather than wasting it on a useless sprint to my mother, when Father was already almost there. When I glanced over my shoulder, Sharmaine and Halvor were right behind us, but Loukas and Inara were quite a bit farther back—I could barely see them in the distance.

I thought about asking Raidyn if we should slow down, but I was afraid if I started talking, he would ask me what had happened to me again, so I stayed quiet.

Flying back was much quicker than walking and soon, up

ahead, Taavi swooped lower and then disappeared out of sight below the trees. As Naiki closed in on the clearing, a brush of fear tickled at my mind, gentle at first, but steadily increasing. The trees separated below us, revealing the small grassy patch where Father, Mother, and Taavi stood together, my parents' arms wrapped around each other.

"Do you feel that?" Raidyn asked, releasing me to take both reins in his hands again, tightening his grip on them as Naiki began to descend toward the ground. "I think it's—"

"Inara," I breathed, realization dawning in a rush of guilt. I should have recognized immediately that I was sensing *her* fear, not my own.

I twisted around to look for Loukas and my sister, but couldn't see them through the trees as we descended. Because I was looking backward, I wasn't prepared for the landing and it jolted me forward, nearly unseating me. Raidyn grabbed my waist to hold me onto the gryphon. Keko landed lightly beside us, but I barely even glanced at Sharmaine and Halvor, all my focus on that patch of empty blue sky.

When the last gryphon came into view, the fear I'd sensed escalated into sheer panic. Loukas's face was ghastly pale, even from where I stood, my hands covering my mouth. He listed to one side, his arms hanging limp below my sister's, where she clutched the reins. Was she trying to *hold him up*?

As I watched in growing horror, Loukas crumpled forward, breaking Inara's hold. He tumbled off the side, dragging Inara with him. A scream built inside me, but I couldn't catch my breath to release it as my sister and Loukas plummeted toward the ground.

"Shar!" my father cried, but she was already glowing, her hands extended. A few feet before they would have hit the ground, Inara and Loukas sank into her shield and then slowly lowered to the earth.

Inara immediately scrambled to her feet, her face and lips bloodless, eyes wild. But Loukas remained unmoving on the ground.

"What *happened*?" Father rushed forward and dropped to his knees next to Loukas.

“I don’t know!” Inara crossed her arms, squeezing herself tightly. “He was shaking . . . and he . . . he just *collapsed*!”

Halvor clambered off Sharmaine’s gryphon, all long limbs and urgency, and rushed to Inara’s side, taking her in his arms.

“He pushed himself too hard,” Raidyn muttered beside me.

“What’s happening—what’s wrong with him?” Mother hadn’t moved from where Father left her, her hand on Taavi’s sleek feathered neck.

“He tried to control too many minds for too long,” Sharmaine said, coming over to kneel on his other side across from my father. She took Loukas’s hand in hers and the look on her face was unbearable—sadness and worry and something else, something deeper all wrapped into her downturned lips and drawn eyebrows.

“I can heal him,” Raidyn offered.

“No.” Father didn’t even consider before refusing. “What happened today already used up too much power for far too many of us. We must rest now anyway. He will have to regain his energy on his own. We need you at full power as soon as possible.”

Raidyn’s gaze dropped to the ground, hot shame flashing through him—and me. It was my fault he’d come—because he had, Sharmaine and Loukas were drained, and Raidyn had to use his power to heal Naiki.

“I’m afraid it might not be safe to stay here.” Halvor still stood beside Inara, holding her hand in his. His sandy-brown hair was windswept and his cheeks were showing the first sign of a sunburn again, as they had been when he first showed up at the citadel.

“Why not?” Father glanced up.

“We learned a few things in town.”

Raidyn’s hand tightened on mine. “What kind of things?”

I waited for Halvor to tell them, not sure I could do it.

“Barloc was there last night,” Halvor admitted. He continued over the gasps of horror, “He told this town that it was a group of Paladin on gryphons that attacked the village of Ivra, burning it and all of its inhabitants to the ground—all except him. He claimed to be a survivor, trying to reach the capital to warn the judges of what happened. And the local garrison has sent runners to all the nearby towns and villages to warn them to watch out for a group of murderous Paladin."

The only sound in the clearing was the rustle of leaves as a light breeze danced through the nearby trees.

Sharmaine was the first to speak up, her fingers still clutched around Loukas's limp hand. "Why would he do this?"

"*Why* he did it is far less important than the fact that now all the nearby garrisons will be searching for a group of Paladin on gryphons—which puts us in even more danger." Halvor shoved his free hand through his already-untidy hair.

"Actually, Sharmaine has a point," I disagreed, something itching at my mind, just out of reach, like a flash of movement from the corner of my eye, the type that no matter how fast I turned my head, it was faster, dashing out of sight. Was the amount of power surging through his body, changing him to the most powerful Paladin ever known, also turning him into a madman? Or was there a method behind his lunacy?

"You think that trying to figure out why he did all of this is more important than the fact that soon every garrison in Vamala will know there is a group of Paladin on gryphons here again? He just succeeded in signing our death warrant."

Inara blanched beside Halvor at his sharp retort.

"Perhaps you should let her finish speaking." Raidyn's voice was low—not quite *menacing*, but laced with enough of a threat that Halvor's mouth snapped shut.

All eyes turned to me, even Father's. Their gazes had weight to them, heavy with fear and worry and an unexpected twinge of hope—looking to me to say something that could help us still succeed in our quest to stop and kill Barloc. "I keep trying to think of why he would have attacked the village then pretended to be a survivor—even giving them his true name," I began slowly, trying to pull my disjointed thoughts together. "And then announced where he was planning on going next. It's almost as if he *wants* us to know where he is. But if that's the case, why would he say it was a group of Paladin on gryphons that attacked Ivra—making it so that every garrison will be searching for a group that matches *our* description?"

"Those men said he was not in his right mind because of grief," Halvor pointed out with a frown. "Perhaps they were partially right. Maybe stealing the power from three Paladin has made him lose his mind."

I flushed, wishing I hadn't spoken up. "I don't think that's it."

Loukas moaned and everyone turned to him, thankfully looking away from me. Sharmaine's eyes brightened, her irises flashing with hope, but when he fell still and silent once more, her shoulders sloped forward and she gripped his hand tighter, pulling it into her lap.

"What if he's trying to lay a trap for us?" Mother's unexpected question took me off guard.

"What?" Adelric looked up at her. She stood a few feet away, her dark hair falling out of the braid she'd been forced to adopt rather than her normal bun, dark circles under her eyes and her cheeks drawn.

"What if he's *trying* to get us to follow him—but he'll have a garrison waiting for us if we catch him?"

I stared at my mother.

"If that's the case, how will we ever take him off guard now?" Inara was still pale, staring down at Loukas's unmoving body on the ground.

"The goal was never to take him off guard. It was to get him to come to us," Raidyn pointed out.

"The plan stays the same," Father said. "At least we know which direction he's heading. We get ahead of him, lay the trap the way we planned, and proceed. Now, more than ever, he *must* be stopped."

Sharmaine looked down at Loukas's hand clutched in hers on her lap, then at his face, his eyes still shut and his skin wan. "We won't have a chance of succeeding until Loukas is back to full strength."

Father rocked back on his heels, his expression calculating rather than concerned. "True—*if* Barloc were at full strength. But it would have taken a tremendous expenditure of power to destroy an entire village by himself. He is drained right now too. Weakened. We must track him down as soon as possible."

He looked around at each of us in turn. It suddenly dawned on me that I couldn't remember the last time I'd seen him smile, the last time his eyes had crinkled at the corners like they had so often in Visimperum. The lines around his downturned mouth were etched deeper than ever into his skin.

"Everyone try to get some rest. As soon as Loukas wakes up, we don't stop until we find and kill Barloc."

Though we were supposed to be resting, and I was exhausted, I couldn't sleep. Too frightened that a garrison would stumble upon us and we'd wake up only to die. Too scared of what lay ahead if—*when*—we found Barloc. There were so many variables to the plan that could go wrong. And most of them resulted in me—and everyone I loved—dying.

Would Loukas even recover enough to be able to control Barloc?

"The weaker the mind, the easier it is for him to use his ability," Raidyn had quietly murmured to me, when he'd caught my worried glance at his unconscious friend as we spread out our meager bedrolls to try to sleep on for the rest of the afternoon, beneath the cover of some of the trees on the edge of the clearing, before the undergrowth became too thick. "So though he did push himself by spreading it across so many minds, at least it wasn't a large group of Paladin who knew an onslaught was possible. After a few hours of sleep, he should be much better."

I lay on my side, the slow hum of insects buzzing in the midday summer heat overhead, the occasional susurration of a breeze brushing my cheeks. It was futile to even close my eyes; when I did, there were too many images and near-misses to flood my mind, shoving my exhaustion below the surface of my panic, drowning any hopes of sleeping. Instead, I watched the rise and fall of Raidyn's chest beside me, almost close enough to touch—but not quite. And beyond him, Loukas, who still hadn't moved, except for another moan when the men had moved him out of the middle of the clearing into the shade of the trees.

The gryphons surrounded us as best they could, though there

were inevitable gaps. Naiki and Taavi were on the far sides, majestic golden and night-black endcaps to our little band of travelers. Maddok took a spot in the middle, closest to Loukas, while Keko, Sharmaine's gryphon, prowled through the trees behind us. I wasn't sure how long it had been, but it felt like at least an hour, when Keko nudged Taavi, and the two gryphons switched spots—Keko lowering herself to the earth and resting her head on her talons, while Taavi took up the vigil through the trees. I marveled at their intelligence.

The sun moved steadily overhead, the leaf-speckled light growing weaker as the afternoon slowly passed through the trees. Birds coasted drowsily between the branches, unhurried and utterly free. I thought back to the day everything had changed, the afternoon when I'd felt so trapped in the drawing room, watching the birds outside the window so easily escape the hedge, flying off into freedom without even realizing the gift they possessed. Now I, too, had escaped, but I still wasn't free. We were hemmed in by unseen threats, by Barloc, by the garrisons, by the terror that still drove the people of Vamala to fear and hate the Paladin.

It felt like far longer than a few hours before my father stirred and then slowly sat up. I'd hoped Raidyn would be the first to wake, and possibly steal a moment alone, but he was still sleeping as my father gently shook Mother's shoulder, rousing her and then moving on to the others. The sun had already dropped below the trees, casting the forest into deep shadow, dark and unsettling. It gave us cover, but it also hid our enemies as well.

My eyes burned and my head swam with exhaustion when I sat up, but the panic that was never far enough away for rest, let alone peace, crowded my chest, squeezing my lungs and heart.

"Zuhra." My father crouched beside me, his eyebrows knitted together. "Did you rest at all?"

I shrugged. "How long do you think it will take to catch up to Barloc?" I asked, knowing turning his mind to the plan at hand would distract him.

"Hopefully not much more than a night. He is on foot, after all—and weakened. Even he will have to stop to sleep at some point."

"I hope so."

He reached one hand up to cup my face briefly. "We're asking too much of you, my sweet girl. But I promise. I won't let anything happen to you."

Don't make any promises you can't keep. I swallowed the words and forced myself to smile instead. "I know you won't."

TWENTY-FOUR

INARA

I woke up when my father gently shook my shoulder, jerking back to alertness with a surge of adrenaline that sent my heart racing, until I realized we weren't under attack, merely packing up to leave.

It was a shock that I'd actually fallen asleep. I'd lain on the hard ground for quite some time, my mind racing over and around everything that had happened that morning. I'd willed myself to keep my eyes shut, to force my breathing to stay even, terrified I would sink into that awful place where fear overtook everything else and humiliate myself in front of everyone. It was a testament to how truly exhausted I was that I'd eventually managed to drift off.

Everyone was quiet as Halvor passed out some of the dried fruit and cheese he'd purchased in the town before . . . everything that had happened. I glanced over at Loukas, who still lay on the ground.

"Has anyone tried to wake him up yet?" Halvor asked, following the direction of my gaze.

"No," Father said. "I suppose we can't wait any longer."

"I'll do it," Sharmaine offered, handing the little bit of cheese she hadn't eaten yet to Zuhra, who stood beside her. The dried apple wedge I chewed lost all its flavor. My sister looked so fragile, like a slight breeze would tip her over, with deep purple bruises beneath her eyes. As if she felt the weight of my worry, she glanced up and offered me a brief, unconvincing smile.

Sharmaine knelt beside Loukas and shook his shoulder. He moaned but then fell still again.

"Loukas." She shook him again. "You have to wake up now."

He groaned, his eyelids fluttered—but then he suddenly jerked and sat up so fast, Sharmaine had to jump back to avoid having their foreheads smash together. His green-fire eyes flashed, wide and wild. "What happened? Where is Raidyn? Is he safe?"

"He's fine. We're all fine. You did it, Louk. We all got away." Sharmaine took his hand in hers, her voice low and soothing.

Did he not remember the flight back to the clearing?

At Sharmaine's assurances, Loukas's shoulders relaxed slightly.

"How do you feel?" Raidyn stepped forward, toward his friend.

"Beat," he confessed. "I didn't expect it to take that much out of me."

Sharmaine and Raidyn exchanged a look of exasperation. "You didn't think controlling at least fifty men's minds at once would take it out of you?"

Loukas shrugged and glanced around at the rest of us, watching the exchange silently. It was difficult to tell in the dimness, but it looked like his neck flushed. "You didn't have to wait because of me, did you?"

"No," my father lied without pause, "we all needed a little bit more rest. It's time to go now, though. Are you up for flying?"

"Of course." Loukas climbed shakily to his feet, but once he was standing, he threw his shoulders back, his normal cocksure grin back in place. "See? Good as new."

The look my father gave him made it obvious he didn't quite believe the bravado, but he didn't question Loukas. "Then we take off in the next few minutes. There's no time to waste. Barloc is weakened right now, so there is no better time to track him down."

I bent to finish rolling up the thin blanket that counted as a "bed" ever since we'd left the citadel.

"Nara?" Zuhra's hesitant voice took me by surprise. "How are you holding up?"

I almost retorted that I should be asking *her* that, when I realized she meant the *other* thing—the hole inside me—not my exhaustion. "I haven't felt any change yet."

Relief washed over her face, so deep and profound, she swayed on her feet. Or perhaps that was the exhaustion that hung off her narrow frame like an oversized cloak, dragging her down. "You'll let me know if anything changes?"

"Yes," I agreed, even though I had no idea how she expected to be able to heal me again with the condition she was in. I needed to get to Barloc before my father—and I still had to convince Loukas to help me. If the others got to him first and killed him before I had the chance to steal my power back . . .

Whatever Raidyn and Zuhra had done the second time was lasting longer, yes. But it wasn't a forever fix, as we all knew. My time was limited, and I wasn't sure if they'd even be able to continue to "fix" me. There would come a point when I wouldn't survive it, even with their help. Though the emptiness hadn't broken free yet, I still felt the wrongness inside me, like a wound that wouldn't heal, scabbed and itchy and waiting for me to move wrong and tear it wide open once more.

Someone's hand closed over mine, warm and comforting, fingertips callused from hours and hours of writing. I squeezed Halvor's hand back, but I wondered if he could sense my agitation. He didn't know the turmoil that gnawed at me, growing sharper and more insistent with every passing day. We'd had no chance to talk, for me to confess the terror that lived with every stolen heartbeat, every *whoosh* of blood through my veins that held no Paladin power.

"What's wrong? Have you seen him again?" He bent to whisper in my ear. The movement wasn't missed; my father's sharp, glowing eyes were on us. At night the blue-fire that wreathed the Paladin's irises was even more striking, burning through the darkness.

There *had* to be a way to reach Barloc first, to take back what belonged to me before they killed him.

But . . . how?

"No, I haven't. He hasn't used his power again. I'm fine, just tired," I finally said with a plastered-on smile.

With one last searching look, Father lifted his hand and rotated it through the air. "Everyone saddle up. We've lingered here far too long."

Ice-coated fear slithered from the crown of my head down my spine. I'd assumed we were safe after what Loukas had done—but perhaps I was wrong. Was the mind control he used permanent? Or did it wear off? Would those guards change their minds and come looking for us?

Everyone dispersed quickly, heading in pairs to their gryphons—except Halvor wouldn't release my hand when I tried to break free. "Are you sure you're fine?" He peered down at me, as if he could somehow stare hard enough to know if I was lying or not.

Did I tell him about Barloc and why I needed to find him? I *wanted* to confide in him, but something kept the words stuck low in my throat, choking me. "I really am—for now," I managed to force out. It was enough of a half truth that I hoped he wouldn't sense the ping of guilt.

He lifted his other hand to smooth my hair back from my face. I could only imagine how I must have appeared after the long hours on the back of a gryphon and sleeping on the ground. Halvor didn't seem to mind as he cupped my jaw, staring down at me.

"Are you two finished yet?"

Halvor flinched at Loukas's question, but let his hand drop and stepped back. "We better get going," he said, and I nodded, though I wished we could somehow make everyone disappear, even for just a few moments alone.

"It's not like our lives depend on not getting caught or anything," Loukas added.

"Louk!" Sharmaine snapped at him.

I flushed and spun away from Halvor, stalking over to where Loukas waited by Maddok, glowering at him darkly. "You think I don't know that?"

"Apparently not, if you think staring into each other's eyes while the rest of us wait is a good use of time right now." He didn't even pause for me to lift my leg, grabbing me beneath my armpits and hefting me up into the saddle, then immediately climbing on behind me.

"That is *enough,* Loukas." My father's voice brooked no argument. "I know we are all frightened right now, but you will treat my daughter with respect."

"With all due *respect,* sir," Loukas retorted, reaching around me to grab the reins, "the guards from that town are confused and upset about letting us go. They're preparing to come searching for us as we speak. So forgive me for being rude to your daughter, but we really do need to go. *Now.*"

My anger dissolved into alarm.

"How does he know that?" Zuhra asked at the same time I twisted in the saddle to look at him and said, "How do you know that?"

"There's a cost for what I can do," was all he said.

Even Father had paled at his words. "Everyone follow my lead—we will fly higher tonight. Even though we might be more easily seen, it will keep us out of range of archers. Let's go!"

Taavi leapt forward and took off, soaring into the sky. The other gryphons and Riders quickly did the same. My stomach lurched as Maddok went airborne. Naiki flew next to us; the whites around Zuhra's eyes flashed in the darkness. I stared back at my sister, the word "archers" echoing over and over in my mind.

Please, keep her safe, I pleaded silently with the Great God.

The first few hours of the flight passed mercifully without incident. The farther away from Dimalle we got, the more Loukas relaxed, even though every wingbeat brought us closer to Barloc and the far greater test of his ability. We were quiet for most of that time, silent but alert.

Father had claimed we would catch up to Barloc sometime in the morning. So, though I was terrified to broach the subject, as the first blush of light warmed the horizon, I knew I was running out of time to convince Loukas to help me. During the hours of silence, I'd thought of at least two dozen ways to bring it up. I didn't want to dive right in after going for so long without speaking. So, instead, I started by asking him about something that had been bothering me since he'd left me in the forest.

"Loukas . . ."

He made a noise to indicate he was listening.

"When I was alone in the forest—after you told me to go after my sister if I wanted to—I sensed something strange. It reminded me of when I did have Paladin power . . . of how the air felt after I'd used it, how it smelled, even. I thought maybe it was *cotantem*, but no one had used any power anywhere nearby and definitely not a large amount of it. What else could it have been?"

Loukas was quiet for so long, I wasn't sure he'd heard me. Finally, he said, "I'm not sure what it was. Maybe you were imagining things."

"I was *not* imagining it!" I had to exhale twice to wrangle my temper back under control. I hadn't known very many people in my life, it was true, but I'd never met anyone who could anger me as quickly as he could. "There isn't any other explanation or reason I might have felt that?"

"Nothing comes to mind, no."

So much for getting him talking first. Acidic frustration pooled in my belly, making it burn. We were short on time, and I was short on patience. "Do you remember what I talked to you about yesterday—what Sachiel told me?"

He grunted, which I took as agreement.

A haunting shriek from underneath the cover of the trees far below us, the sound of some animal dying, sent a shiver scraping down my back. Loukas shortened Maddok's reins when the gryphon tossed his head in agitation.

I clutched the front of the saddle, digging my nails into the supple leather. "We can't let them kill him before I get my power back. We have to get to Barloc first, somehow. If we don't . . ."

"Your father said we're not stopping until we find him, so there's nothing we can do about that anymore."

"There has to be a way to get to him first!" I couldn't give up hope. Maybe I should have told everyone what Sachiel had told me. But I was afraid of what my parents would do if they knew what I was planning.

Then an idea—albeit a dangerous one—began to take shape in my mind.

"What if . . . what if we *forced* them to stop?"

"Have you *met* your father?" Loukas snorted. "Once he has his mind made up, nothing will change it. You're not going to convince him to take another break."

"You're right, *I* probably can't. But *you* could."

There was a long pause with only Maddok's wings beating to fill the silence. Thankfully whatever animal had met its end below us had fallen quiet.

"I have a feeling I'm going to regret asking what in the world you're talking about."

I grinned, even though he couldn't see me, and told him my idea.

TWENTY-FIVE

Zuhra

We rode and rode, through the cover of darkness and on into the first flush of dawn. Father pushed Taavi into a faster pace than he had on our previous flight, forcing the other gryphons to work harder to keep up. Raidyn didn't comment on it, but I sensed his frustration. He spent much of the ride telling me stories of his childhood and growing up in Soluselis. He never brought up what had happened at Dimalle, and I didn't either. Neither did we broach the topic of what would happen when we did find Barloc. The soft, musical cadence of his voice, the warmth of his memories, wove a peaceful spell around me, chasing away my fear. Encircled by his arms, his lips moving by my ear, I finally felt as if I could have dozed off—even this far off the ground, on Naiki's back. I couldn't remember ever being so tired in my life. Only the bite of the cold night wind kept me from falling asleep.

The sun slowly began to rise, the horizon brushed amber with the first light of dawn that gradually melted into gold. When the sun broke over the horizon, the air quickly warmed, even as high off the ground as we were.

"Did you feel that?" Raidyn tensed, sitting up taller.

"Feel what?"

"A hint of *cotantem*. You don't feel anything?"

I strained to stretch my awareness out, to catch that flicker of lingering magic that we had hoped would trail Barloc with how much power he had absorbed, claiming as his own. At first there was nothing—only the clean, clear wind, the warmth of Raidyn's arms around me, and my own exhaustion. But then . . . a flicker of heat that had nothing to do with the sun, a hint of bitterness on the breeze that wasn't the loamy scent of earth or the crisp smell of evergreen and leaves. *Cotantem.*

"Yes," I breathed. "I think I do."

"We might be catching up to Barloc." Raidyn's arms tightened around me.

Perhaps it was because I was so intent on trying to feel the *cotantem* that I didn't sense my sister's emotions until it was too late.

A scream ripped through the air, even over the wind and wings—one I would have known anywhere.

Inara.

Raidyn and I both twisted around in Naiki's saddle, to see Loukas slumped over on top of her, crushing her into Maddok's neck. At any sharp movement, he would fall from the gryphon—*again*—possibly taking Inara with him. Another scream tore through the air.

"Do something!" I yelled at Raidyn, grabbing his arm with one hand and shaking it.

"Shar!" he shouted, and when that didn't get her attention, he let go of the reins with one hand and pushed his fingers against his tongue, giving off an ear-shattering whistle.

Both Shar and my parents looked back at us. Raidyn pointed at Maddok. Shar blanched and my mother's mouth opened in a cry that I couldn't hear over the wind. Father immediately yanked on Taavi's reins, wheeling him around, shouting something to Sharmaine as he passed her, rushing toward us.

Taavi came even with Naiki and my father gestured toward Maddok's left side. "Raidyn—take Naiki and help me create a blockade so they don't fall. Then we all land together!"

I glanced down at the thick foliage beneath us, wondering where we could possibly land, as Raidyn pulled Naiki's reins, following after Taavi. Each gryphon came up on either side of Maddok, only a few feet lower so their wings didn't entangle. I looked up at Loukas's arms dangling over Inara's, and gulped. Were we supposed to catch him if he fell? He was even bigger than Raidyn. He'd crush us both.

"Where are we going to land?" There was still no break in the trees below us. From what I understood, Father had chosen a route that kept us away from the main road and as many towns as possible to avoid the garrisons, but that meant there were few breaks in the forest.

"I don't know." Raidyn's arms were stiff around me, his entire body tensed.

Sweat slipped down the back of my neck.

"Nara, are you all right?" I called up to her.

"I've been better," came her muffled response. "He's really heavy!"

"What happened?" Raidyn asked.

"I don't know! He said he still wasn't feeling well and that he needed a break a while ago!" Her voice was strained, each word accentuated by a puff of air from Loukas's weight pressing down on her.

I looked over at my parents, curious if they'd heard. I'd wondered if we'd pushed Loukas too hard too fast—if *Father* had pushed him too hard. Loukas had been unconscious for a considerable amount of time, after all. And Father had immediately expected him to be recovered enough to fly for hours on end?

Father was looking up, his lips pressed into a thin line, eyebrows drawn together. Mother's spine was as straight as the trees beneath us, her face pale and drawn.

"Look—we could land there!" Raidyn shouted, pointing to a small clearing up ahead.

Father nodded, and then looked up again. "Inara—you're going to have to guide Maddok down there!" he shouted.

"How?" was her breathless response. "I can't move!"

"Do you have the reins?" Raidyn asked.

"Yes . . ."

"Pull them tighter, get Maddok to drop his head down. Hold on and we'll help lead him down!"

Her response was too muffled to understand. But a few seconds later, Maddok's head dropped, as if she had done exactly what Raidyn had told her to.

"Maddok!" Father yelled at the gryphon, then gave two short whistles through his teeth, and Taavi began flying lower, toward the clearing below, Raidyn guiding Naiki to do the same. I glanced backward, to see Maddok following, but Loukas's deadweight began to list to one side.

"Shar!" Raidyn shouted.

"On it!" Her voice was barely audible.

I looked over my shoulder to see her and Halvor right behind Maddok, on Keko. Her veins glowed with power. When I looked back to Loukas, he hadn't straightened up at all, but he hadn't fallen any farther either. He seemed to be trapped, halfway on, halfway off the gryphon as we all soared lower and lower, Sharmaine's power holding him in place.

When we finally touched down in the small field, I heaved a sigh of relief.

"Stay here," Raidyn said, vaulting from Naiki's back and rushing over to help catch Loukas the moment Maddok landed. Together, with my father, they carefully lowered him to the ground while Inara sat back up with a grimace. Once he was safely on the ground, Father helped Inara climb down as well. She seemed shaken but unharmed.

Raidyn hurried back over to assist me, reaching up to encircle my waist with his strong hands. My body ached from sitting that long; my legs were so stiff when I tried to stand, my knees almost buckled.

We all gathered around Loukas, staring down at his unmoving form.

"What happened?" Sharmaine asked, glancing at Inara, who had wrapped her arms around herself. Halvor stood beside her, his hands hanging at his side, as though he *wanted* to comfort her, but didn't dare.

"I don't know. He said he still didn't feel very well. He seemed exhausted. Maybe . . . maybe he wasn't recovered enough." Inara shifted on her feet, rubbing at her arms.

"I can't believe it took this much out of him," Sharmaine said softly, her face flushed from the use of her power yet again. "He must have been controlling even more minds than we realized."

"What do we do now?" I looked to my father.

He pushed a hand through his hair. "I don't know. I guess we have to rest again. We can't do anything without Loukas."

"How long do you think it'll take?" Inara asked without looking up.

Father shook his head, impatience flashing across his face, but he quickly smothered it. "As long as it takes, I suppose."

There was a pause and then Raidyn spoke up. "Sir, right before this all happened, Zuhra and I both felt a hint of *cotantem*."

"Do you think it was him?" Father's eyebrows shot up.

"I'm not sure. But I think so . . . I don't know what else it would have been." Raidyn looked to me for confirmation.

"Was it strong?"

"No, it was pretty faint. We barely felt it."

"If it wasn't very strong, it may have just been a pocket."

"A pocket," Raidyn repeated.

"We didn't know what else to call it." Father glanced out at the forest surrounding us. "When we were here before . . . I felt a few of them myself. They were these small spots in Vamala where there was a hint of Paladin power for some reason. As if the barrier between our two worlds was thinner in those areas." He looked back to us. "So it's possible that's all you felt. If we'd been able to keep going and follow it to see if it got stronger, then we would have known for certain, but . . ."

We all looked back down at Loukas. My legs trembled. It felt like I had sand in my eyes when I blinked, my eyelids scratchy and painful from fatigue.

"If he's going to be out for a while . . . could we rest a little bit too?" I hesitantly asked. I wasn't even sure I *could* sleep, but I really wanted to try.

Mother's gaze immediately snapped to me, her hazel eyes bloodshot and her hair as disheveled as I'd ever seen it. Father looked about to protest, but she put her hand on his arm and said,

"Of course we can rest. I think everyone could use a little more sleep before we face . . . whatever is ahead," she said.

He swallowed whatever he'd been about to say and nodded instead. "Yes, of course. We will catch him—and soon. But it will be better if we're all at full strength."

Which of course meant that Barloc would have more time to regain his strength as well. But if Loukas was going to remain unconscious, there was nothing we could do. And I really hoped I'd be able to sleep.

"I have some more food, if anyone is hungry," Halvor offered. We took the fruit and cheese quietly, eating it while we spread our blankets out yet again.

"Everyone stay closer together today," Father instructed, his voice little more than a whisper. "Then the gryphons can circle around us. Just in case."

We settled down on our blankets. I was almost getting accustomed to lying on the hard earth with weeds, branches, and rocks for both pillow and mattress. Almost.

Raidyn lay on one side of me and Inara on my other. We were close enough together that I could feel the warmth of his body in the small space between us. He turned his head toward me; our gazes met and held. When his eyes dropped to my mouth, my stomach tightened, all thoughts of sleep fleeing. If only I could steal a few minutes alone with him, even just a few *moments,* to lose myself in the heat and power of his touch, to take me away from the fear and exhaustion and worry of this potentially fatal journey.

"Zu?"

Inara's soft whisper jarred me back to reality—and the fact that Raidyn wasn't the only one lying right beside me. His mouth crooked into a fleeting half smile.

I rolled over to face her, tamping down my reluctance to turn my back on Raidyn. Though the cost of her lucidity was immense, I could never begrudge the chance to speak with my sister, after the countless hours I'd spent for most of her life trying to accomplish that very thing.

Her dark hair fanned out beneath her head, a thick, tangled

pillow on her thin blanket. Her pale blue eyes were bloodshot. What a sight we all were.

"Yes? Are you all right?"

She nodded. "I just . . . I wanted to tell you thank you."

"For what?"

Inara reached out and took my hand in hers, pulling it into the space between our bodies. "For always being there for me—no matter what. For saving me over and over again. From the roar, from what Barloc did . . ."

"You don't have to thank me for any of that. I'm your sister. I love you. I would do it all again and more if I needed to, happily."

Inara's eyes glistened in the ever-brightening light of day. She blinked a few times rapidly. "I don't know what I ever did to deserve a sister like you." She took our clasped hands and lifted them so she could press a kiss to the top of my knuckles.

A wave of sadness crashed into me . . . familiar and foreign all at once. Were they Inara's emotions or my own? Sometimes the *sanaulus* was more confusing than helpful. "I am the lucky one," I said at last, blinking back tears of my own. What had brought this on? "Are you sure you're all right?"

Inara laughed and sniffled. "Yes, I promise. I'm sorry. I didn't mean to worry you. I just wanted you to know how grateful I am for you and how much I look up to you and your strength."

If she only knew how weak I truly was—how frightened and easily beset by panic—but I squeezed her hand back and smiled. "I think *you* are the strong one."

"Rest well, Zuzu."

"You too, Nara."

We remained facing each other, hands clasped in the small space between us. She closed her eyes and I made myself do the same, praying I was finally tired enough to sleep without any more panic. A few moments later, Raidyn's warm, heavy hand came to rest on the top of my hip. Ensconced between the two of them, the warm sunlight enveloping us like a blanket, I finally, mercifully dozed off.

* * *

"Where are they?"

The shout jerked me awake.

It took a moment to orient myself and realize Father was the one yelling—a distinct lack of concern for being found that showed just how distraught he was.

Then I noticed the space next to me where Inara had slept was empty, the blanket gone. I scrambled to my feet, and turned in a circle, horror blooming in my chest. Not only was Inara gone, but so was Loukas—and Maddok.

My stomach plummeted, as if I'd been soaring above the trees, only to drop from the sky, much as they both had done yesterday when they'd fallen off Loukas's gryphon.

"Where is she? Where is Inara?" Mother stood beside my father, her lips bloodless and jaw clenched. "Did he take her? Did he take my daughter? Why would he take her?"

"He wouldn't do that," Raidyn tried to comfort her, even as he shot me a look of utter shock, his blue-fire eyes flashing. His alarm pulsed alongside my own.

"Well, apparently he would. Because he *did*," Mother insisted as Sharmaine climbed to her feet, staring at the spot where Loukas had been lying.

"What's going on?" Halvor sat up, blinking blearily. He glanced around the clearing and then blanched. "Where's Inara?"

Father paced back and forth in front of Taavi, who fluffed his feathers, his beak snapping in agitation. Naiki sat on her haunches, her golden eyes flicking back and forth, watching us carefully, but remaining still. "Something woke me up, and when I looked around, they were already gone. Why would they do this—why would they leave?"

A sudden nausea seized my stomach, clenching it like a fist. "She left all the healers behind," I said, trembling all over.

Father's eyes widened.

If she started to fail again—if the emptiness inside her broke open—there was no one there to save her.

I didn't even realize how hard I was shaking until Raidyn hurried to my side and pulled me into his arms for support.

"*He* did this. It was that boy Loukas that forced all the soldiers back, isn't it? He made her leave with him!" I hadn't seen Mother this mad since before I was sucked through the portal into Visimperum. Having us all returned to her—including her husband—had softened the bitterness that held her captive for most of my life. But now she seethed, hazel eyes bright and fierce, her tiny body humming with a familiar fury.

"We need to leave immediately."

Raidyn wrapped his arm around my shoulders, pulling me in even closer to the solid strength of his body. But I sensed the underlying turmoil behind his calm mien.

"We have no idea where they've gone," Mother said.

"Perhaps their departure is what woke me up. If we hurry, we might still be able to see and follow them."

The next few minutes were a blur of frenzied activity as we rushed to roll up our blankets, climbed onto the gryphons that were left, and took off. My heart thundered in my chest as Naiki flapped hard to get us high in the air fast enough to clear the treetops.

Taavi was in the lead and reached the open sky first.

"There!" Father's cry was barely audible over the wind and pounding of the gryphon's wings.

We were right behind them. I followed where he pointed and could barely make out a speck in the distance. My breath caught in my throat.

Inara.

"What is he *thinking*?" Raidyn's low murmur thrummed through me, echoing my own thoughts.

Taavi surged forward, Father urging him to fly as quickly as he was capable with two people on his back. Raidyn slapped the reins against Naiki's neck with a sharp whistle, and she, too, put on a burst of speed.

I had no idea why they had left. I could only pray to the Great God that we hadn't all misplaced our trust in Loukas.

TWENTY-SIX

Inara

I glanced over my shoulder again. "I think they're gaining on us!"

"He's going as fast as he can," Loukas responded, his voice tight. But he whistled to Maddok and kneaded his hands along the gryphon's neck, urging him to give us a little bit more.

"Can you still feel it?" I asked. "Is it getting stronger?"

"Yes," was all Loukas said. This plan hinged entirely on us following the *cotantem* and reaching Barloc first, before the others. If they caught us before we caught him . . .

No, I cut the thought off. *We'll make it. We have enough of a head start. This will work.*

It had to.

I glanced back again.

"You're just going to make yourself even more upset if you keep doing that. Focus on what's ahead of us—on what *you* have to do if we catch him."

He'd done a masterful job of acting like he'd passed out again, making it so convincing, *I* nearly believed him. Especially when he almost fell off Maddok. We'd waited until we were sure everyone was asleep, and then waited a little bit longer, just to be certain. It couldn't have worked out better for Zuhra to ask if we could rest again, saving me from having to do it and possibly raise any suspicion.

But now came the even harder part—tracking Barloc down, taking him by surprise before he could attack us, and then . . .

I'd take back what he'd stolen from me.

Though the air above the trees was much cooler than on the ground, the sun still beat down on us, relentless and nearly unbearable, as we rushed away from my family and the other Paladin, chasing the elusive *cotantem* that Loukas had also felt before he'd pretended to lose consciousness. My body kept flashing hot then cold then hot.

You can do this. You can do this.

"You're sure it's him and not a pocket?" I asked.

Loukas groaned and I remembered too late that I'd already asked him that. "I told you, it wouldn't be getting stronger."

"Right."

"Are you *sure* you can do this?"

I didn't hesitate. "Of course!"

"You seem very . . . nervous."

"Just because I'm nervous doesn't mean I'm incapable. You keep him from attacking us, and I will do what I have to do."

We both fell silent after that. I resisted the urge to look back to see if the others were still gaining on us. We'd hoped they'd stay asleep longer. At least we had a significant head start . . . but would it be enough? We would have very little time to act.

Loukas suddenly tensed, his arms stiffening around me.

"What? What is it?"

"I felt—"

Before he could finish, darkness closed in on me.

I saw Barloc sitting alone at his desk at the library, Paladin books open in front of him, but he stared forward unseeingly. Loneliness pressed in on him like the darkness that swelled beyond the reach of the solitary candle he had lit. Loneliness and a longing that burned hotter than any fire, hidden away deep within him—a longing to go to the world his grandfather had told him about. A longing to claim the power he'd witnessed but never wielded—power that was his birthright—and use it to prove his superiority to all those who had ever mocked him for his assertions of being part Paladin or berated him for his fascination with them.

Then I saw him standing in a forest, spinning toward the sound of wingbeats, the immense power he now wielded flooding his veins as he summoned it forth and waited until a gryphon came into view—with a girl who looked like Zuhra and Loukas on its back—a jolt of disbelief, of recognition—

I slammed back into my body, a scream of warning building too late in my throat, just as the blast of Paladin fire exploded out of the trees beneath us. Maddok banked so sharply, it nearly unseated us both. The fireball passed by close enough to singe the edge of Maddok's wing. The scent of burning feathers and acrid power made my eyes sting as Loukas pulled on Maddok's reins, sending him into a nosedive, straight into the trees. Branches and leaves tore at our legs and arms, but the pain hardly registered as I caught sight of Barloc standing below us, his body glowing so brightly with power that I almost couldn't look directly at him.

His hand filled with more Paladin fire, but before he could release it, his blindingly bright eyes widened and then he froze, the fire flickering and then fading.

There was barely room for Maddok to land. His back paws slammed into the ground with such a thud, it jarred every bone in my body. Loukas immediately vaulted off his back, his glowing hands stretched out to Barloc.

"Go—now—" The words were so strained, I could barely understand what Loukas had said. His arms shook, every vein lit bright green with his power. His entire body trembled with the effort of controlling Barloc. I slid off Maddok's back, landing on the hard ground with a sharp ping in one of my ankles. Ignoring the pain, I rushed forward, pulling the knife from the sheath that Loukas had strapped to my thigh before we'd taken off. Though I was willing to drink his blood to get my power back, I didn't think I could tear his throat open with just my teeth.

As I watched, the painfully bright glow of Barloc's veins slowly faded until he stood before me as I'd known him, as Halvor's scholarly uncle, except for the unsettling half grimace on his face as he tried to fight Loukas's control on his mind. His body was stiff with resistance, but slowly, painfully, his knees bent until he knelt, then lay down on the ground, each movement like watching a broken puppet being coerced into submission.

The Paladin blade shook in my hand as I forced myself to kneel beside him. Though his body was completely still, his eyes still moved, turning on me with such loathing, searing panic burned in my gut. If I didn't succeed—and *fast*—he would kill me.

I gripped the hilt of the dagger in my sweaty hand and lifted it over his neck. *Just enough pressure to cut, not kill. He has to be alive while you drink the blood for you to absorb his power.* Loukas's instructions rang through my fevered mind. Sunlight flashed off the blade. The shaking in my hand spread up my arm and out to my entire body.

I lifted my other hand up to grasp the handle too, and swallowed once, hard. Memories of Barloc's attack assailed me. Sweat gathered at my temples.

You can do this, Inara. You have *to do this!*

And still, I hesitated.

"Inara!"

The shout was distant, barely more than a whisper through the rustling leaves around us. My mother's voice.

I clenched my teeth and lowered the blade.

Paladin steel was unbelievably sharp; it slid into his skin like a hot knife through butter. Blood spurted out around the blade and I quickly pulled it back with a cry of shock. Though he still couldn't move, there was no missing the agony and terror that replaced the fury in Barloc's eyes.

I'd believed myself capable of doing this, but now that the moment had come, the reality of *actually* drinking his blood made my stomach roil.

"Inara!"

"Loukas!"

The shouts were louder, closer.

I was out of time.

With a half-swallowed sob, I forced myself to bend over him and cover the wound I'd given him with my lips. His blood, hot and metallic and awful, trickled into my mouth. I gagged, barely managing to choke down a tiny mouthful. But the second the vile blood hit my stomach, the emptiness inside where my power had once resided pulsed, greedy and desperate. I clamped my eyes shut and forced myself to swallow again, this time a full mouthful of Barloc's power-laced blood.

"Inara—*no*!"

The scream was so close, *too* close. Other shouts sounded as well, along with gryphons screeching. I didn't dare open my eyes. A hint of power warmed my body, trickling back into my veins. Though my stomach heaved, threatening to rebel, I made myself swallow yet again.

"What are you *doing*?"

I thought my father's shout was aimed at me, but oh, how wrong I was.

"No—"

It took a split second for me to realize it was Loukas who had yelled. Less than a heartbeat later, Barloc broke free of Loukas's control and grabbed my arms, yanking me so hard it made my head snap back. Two heartbeats and somehow he had the knife in his hand, angled at my throat, while he dragged me to my feet in front of him.

"You are a *mentirum*!" he crowed hungrily.

I stared at Loukas, who swayed on his feet, his face deathly pale. The other gryphons circled overhead, trying to find a break in the trees to land. There were more shouts, but I couldn't understand their words over the thundering of blood in my head.

Then Loukas's eyes rolled back and he crumpled to the earth.

Barloc tried to drag me over to Loukas, but Maddok jumped in front of his Rider with a shriek that stunned Barloc into stillness.

Three simultaneous blasts exploded around us; the ground shook so hard, I stumbled and nearly fell. Barloc shoved me forward, at Maddok. The gryphon cawed when I crashed into its feathered chest, as Barloc summoned his power and dashed around us to where Loukas lay unconscious—for real this time.

Instead of ripping his neck open to drink his power, like I thought he would, Barloc merely grabbed his arm with one glowing hand and lifted the knife with his other. For some reason, the knife also glowed with his power, so brightly I had to squint.

Maddok cawed again and grabbed at the back of my shirt with his beak, pulling me out of his way.

"Inara!"

My sister's shout was a dull echo through the roar in my head as Barloc lifted the glowing knife and uttered a phrase in Paladin then slashed it through the air. Another explosion ripped through the forest, but this time, it knocked me *and* Maddok backward. I slammed into the ground and lay there stunned for a beat.

"NO!"

The gut-wrenching scream shocked me back into action; I scuttled over onto my hands and knees just in time to see Barloc drag Loukas *through* a glowing tear in the air—

And disappear.

Maddok screeched beside me. Hardly even knowing what I was doing, I sprang to my feet and barely managed to grab his reins and swing my leg over his back before he lunged to his paws and talons and charged forward after his Rider.

"Inara—*no*—"

Zuhra's shout echoed after me as Maddok leapt into the blinding slash of light and everything went silent.

PART 2

WARRIORS OF FLAME

TWENTY-SEVEN

Zuhra

Naiki landed with a thud. Raidyn launched himself off her back before she'd even completely stopped and hurtled toward the slash of light, seconds after Maddok and my sister—her mouth and neck covered in half-dried blood—charged through it and also disappeared.

But an instant before Raidyn reached it, the light exploded out again with a deafening boom, knocking Raidyn backward to land flat on the ground, then vanished.

I stared at the now-empty air.

An inhuman cry rent the air, and it took a moment for me to realize it had come from my mother.

They were gone.

My sister was gone.

"Where are they? Where did they go? Where is *Inara*?" Mother's shrieks barely penetrated the growing buzz in my ears.

There'd been nowhere to land, no break in the trees to reach them. The Paladin each had to use a blast of power to create a narrow strip of space. Too little, too late. Always, always, too little, too late.

What had Barloc *done*? Where had they gone?

Twin fists of icy panic clutched my heart and belly.

Raidyn climbed shakily to his feet as my father and Sharmaine rushed forward, Halvor and my mother not far behind. I was the only one who remained on a gryphon, too numb with shock to move. Carved out with disbelief.

Sharmaine's cheeks were tear-streaked as she ran straight to Raidyn and threw her arms around him, her shoulders shaking uncontrollably. I felt nothing but a detached sense of disbelief as he hugged her back, his gaze going to mine over her head. I stared back at him, shaking so hard, I was afraid I might fall off of Naiki.

"I've never . . . I don't understand . . ." Father faltered. I'd never seen him so defeated, not even when his father died, not when we'd nearly lost Inara the first time. Taavi let out a low keen behind him, stepping forward to nudge his beak into his Rider's back, as if he could sense Adelric's devastation.

Halvor was as white as the benign clouds that passed overhead, heedless of the horrors taking place below. "What . . . what do we do now?"

"We have to go after them, right?" Mother clutched Adelric's arm. "We have to go get my daughter!"

"*Our* daughter," he said softly. "And we can't. At least, not here."

Sharmaine pulled back from Raidyn. "What do you mean 'not here'?"

My father put his arm around Mother's shoulders. "The only place they could have gone is Visimperum . . . somehow. I've never seen anything like it, but I think he might have created a temporary gateway with all the power he has."

"Is that *possible*?" Sharmaine gaped.

"It must be. It's the only explanation I can think of."

"So do it!" Mother's lips were bloodless.

"I can't!" It was the sharpest tone I'd ever heard my father take with her. "Don't you think I *would* have already if I could?"

She flinched, but he didn't even seem to notice.

"We have to get back to the citadel. Our only hope is to open that gateway and go back to Vamala. And pray we find them in time."

Before Barloc killed them both.

Raidyn's bleak, grief-stricken expression matched my own—because the horrific reality was that he probably already had.

What chance did an unconscious Loukas and powerless Inara have against him—a Paladin so powerful, he could rip gateways between worlds?

Bile burned its way up my throat. My chest caved in as though someone had reached in and wrenched my heart out. After everything we'd done, after everything that had happened to save her life over and over, I had to resign myself to the fact that Inara was gone. And Barloc most likely had claimed Loukas's power for himself now too.

"Everyone saddle up. Now!" My father barked out the command, startling us into action—everyone besides me, who still sat on Naiki's back, the forest blurring. Even Raidyn, hurrying back to his gryphon, was wavy and unfocused. His burning blue-fire eyes glistened with his own unshed tears. Naiki swung her head around when he reached her side and climbed on behind me, nipping at his boot softly with a low hoot.

"Thanks, girl," he murmured as he stretched his arms around me and picked up the reins.

"There's no point," I said, despondent. "They're gone."

"I know." His voice broke as he squeezed Naiki's sides. She stretched her wings in the small space and jumped up into the air, flapping as hard as she could to rise back up into the sky.

No telling me I would know if my sister were gone, no attempt to seek solace from his mother's words as he had in Visimperum. Any lingering hope I may have clung to shattered.

The three gryphons cleared the forest once more, turning back the way we'd come, leaving the empty thicket where the only sign that Loukas, Barloc, and my sister had ever been there was some blood-stained bushes. The air was still thick with *cotantem*; the acrid after-scent of magic even coated my tongue, bitter and sharp.

"But," Raidyn continued, low and uneven, "even if they are both gone, we have to at least *try* to get to Vamala and warn everyone that he's there—and how powerful he is. If he can rip gateways into either world using just his own power, who knows what else he's capable of now."

I nodded, unable to bring myself to speak, my grief choking me. *Inara. Oh, Inara.*

What had she been *thinking*? Why, *why* had she and Loukas gone after him alone? And why had *she* been trying to drink *his* blood?

Questions that I would never get any answers for.

Only endless, all-encompassing grief.

We only stopped twice that day. None of us was able to sleep, so after letting the gryphons eat and drink and rest for a bit, we pressed on, but with every passing hour, the gryphons grew slower and slower, their heads drooping.

Raidyn finally pulled up even with my father and shouted, "Sir, I know you're in a rush to get home, but we have to let the gryphons rest longer!"

Father looked ready to argue, but Taavi let out a low keen, as though he'd understood Raidyn's words. Adelric's shoulders caved forward in defeat and he nodded. "You're right."

We landed in the next small clearing we found near a stream, the gryphons eagerly rushing over to the clear, cool water.

"We need to find them something to eat," Shar said, watching Keko noisily slurp up water in great, heaving gulps.

"I'll go hunting," Raidyn immediately volunteered. "Keep them here so they can rest. I'll bring back what I can find."

I watched in silence as he stalked off into the forest, his entire being humming with a volatile mix of grief and anger. We'd barely spoken during the flight back; the journey passed in a haze of anguish. It all blurred together into a kaleidoscope of sun and wind and tears and helpless fury.

"I have a little food left," Halvor offered, his voice as lifeless as his eyes. "If anyone is hungry."

I turned away from him, unable to bear his grief on top of my own. My stomach was too much of a riotous mess to eat anyway. There was a large tree stump near the stream bank; I walked over and dropped down on it. My body felt far heavier than normal, weighed down under the crushing reality that I'd lost my sister *again*—and this time, I couldn't fathom a way she had survived.

I went over and over the conversation I'd had with her lying on the hard ground before she'd left with Loukas—when it had seemed like she was saying goodbye. Was there anything I could have done to stop her? To prevent what had happened? Why had Raidyn and I succeeded in healing her—twice—only to lose her like this now, to Barloc yet again?

I stared at the water, watching it flow over rock and stone, so clear I could see weeds and moss beneath its crystalline surface. It burbled softly, sweet and calming, but nothing could soften the knife-sharp pain that cut deeper and deeper with every beat of my heart, every shallow breath I took, flaying me apart from the inside out.

I was gutted with guilt, so sick with it, I couldn't eat, and sleep was out of the question. While the others spread out their blankets and lay down, trying to rest a little bit, I sat on the trunk and watched the stream. The gryphons curled up around the rest of the group, though Naiki kept lifting her head, looking toward the forest where Raidyn had disappeared quite some time ago, or peering at me, her bright orange eyes concerned. She'd settle back down for a few minutes, then lift her head again. Until she suddenly jumped up to her haunches, her front talons pressing her chest up off the ground and her head perked toward the trees.

Father sat up as well, his face gaunt underneath the thick stubble covering his jaw and lower half of his cheeks. Mother stirred beside him but didn't wake. Sharmaine also opened her eyes, but stayed lying down.

Moments later, Raidyn strode back out of the woods, a trio of limp rabbits gripped in one fist. He tossed one to Naiki first, who eagerly gulped it down with only one bone-crunching snap of her beak. Then he gave the remaining two to the other gryphons.

"Thank you, Raid." My father's voice was barely above a whisper.

Raidyn nodded in return. Without a word, he walked around the diminished group lying on the ground and came over to where I sat. He crouched in front of me, his eyes traveling over my face. I wondered what he saw—what he felt. The maelstrom of his emotions was a tidal wave that threatened to crash over me and pull me under, the force of his suffering combined with mine more than I could bear.

"Why aren't you lying down?" he murmured, low and concerned.

"I don't dare close my eyes," I answered honestly.

Raidyn reached up and put one of his hands on top of mine. "I'll sit up with you then."

As much as I would have preferred to have him do exactly that, I said, "If you can rest, you should try to get some sleep."

"I doubt I can either." He glanced at the group, where my father had lain back down, and Sharmaine had closed her eyes again. I wondered if they were actually sleeping or just trying.

Now that Raidyn had returned, all three gryphons were asleep as well.

"Besides, someone needs to stay up and listen for any patrols."

"I can do that," I said. "I'm already sitting here anyway. Lie down, see if you can get some sleep."

His mouth twisted, but he finally relented. "Fine, but I'll lie down right here. And we can switch off in a little bit, so you can try to rest too." His gaze softened. "I can tell you stories if that will help."

I nodded as he pulled his blanket out and spread it over the dirt right in front of my feet. He lay down facing me, his head pillowed on his arm. He closed his eyes, but the intensity of his emotions didn't relent one bit; he was having as much trouble sleeping as me, it seemed.

He eventually did doze off, and I didn't have the heart to wake him. I wasn't sure, but it felt like two or three hours before my father sat up and gently shook my mother's shoulder. Within a minute or two, everyone was sitting up, blinking and stretching. The gryphons also stirred, climbing to their feet and shaking their feathers and tails out.

I bent over to softly touch Raidyn's cheek; his eyes immediately shot open.

"I think we're getting ready to go," I said.

“You didn’t wake me,” he accused.

I stood, my legs stiff. One of my feet prickled like I’d stepped on a hundred tiny sewing needles. “You need the sleep. I’ll be fine. Maybe I can doze off during the ride.”

The sun had begun to set. Color bled across the wide expanse visible above the treetops, day leeching into night; crimson streaked across the fading blue, like blood staining the sky. Almost a whole day since we’d lost Inara, Loukas, and Maddok.

Everyone quickly packed up their blankets and headed over to their gryphons. Raidyn helped me get on, but right before he climbed behind me, all three gryphons’ heads simultaneously snapped to the woods across the stream from us.

We turned to follow their gazes, my heart jumping to my throat.

“Everyone, quick—”

Before Father could finish whatever order he’d been about to give, an arrow whizzed out of the woods, imbedding in Halvor’s shoulder, too fast for anyone to react. He tumbled off Keko’s back with a cry of agony.

“Halvor!” My scream was drowned out by the sudden shouts of at least fifty men who sprinted out of the woods, straight for us.

TWENTY-EIGHT

INARA

I was momentarily blinded, clutching a handful of Maddok's feathers and the reins with all of my strength. Then the flash of light was gone and we burst out of the suffocating silence into the air above a sharp cliff.

Maddok screeched as our momentum sent him tumbling over the edge. I barely clung to his neck, my legs clamping onto his sides as he spread his wings, caught an updraft, and leveled out. But then, with another cry, he suddenly nosedived, plummeting once more. I barely caught sight of Barloc lying unconscious on the edge of the cliff, his gore-covered neck and face pressed to the rock face as we dove past him.

"Maddok! Maddok, *stop*!" I shrieked, flattening myself onto his neck, barely able to cling on to him without tumbling over his head to the earth far, far below.

But the gryphon ignored me.

The wind screamed past my ears, whipping my hair back and lashing at my eyes and face. What was *wrong* with him?

And then I spotted Loukas—tumbling through the air beneath us.

"Loukas!"

The gryphon was diving as fast as he could, but I wasn't sure if we could reach him before he smashed onto the rocks below.

"Go, Maddok, *go*!"

The rocks surged closer and closer, growing larger and more

deadly by the second—until I began to fear that we, too, would shatter onto them. Then somehow we soared past him and Maddok immediately twisted in midair, spreading his wings to level out, a split second before Loukas slammed onto the gryphon's back, crushing me. All the air was forced from my lungs, silencing the scream that had built in my throat.

This time, he wasn't faking being unconscious—and there was no Sharmaine to hold him onto the gryphon with her power. When he nearly tumbled off one side again, Maddok lowered the opposite wing to force him to slide back on. It worked, but only for a moment. He was complete deadweight; it was only a matter of time before he slid off of the gryphon. We needed to land, and soon. I twisted around, squeezing Maddok's sides as tightly as I could with my knees, and wrapped an arm around Loukas, pulling him forward to collapse onto my back. I hoped I could keep him at least level until Maddok found somewhere to land.

The gryphon soared away from the cliff and the sharp rocks, while I clung to Loukas and the saddle. I'd dropped the reins entirely, hoping Maddok knew where to go—and that he needed to hurry. Already my arms shook from the effort of holding on to Loukas's heavy body, my muscles burning from disuse. Below us the rocky outcroppings gave way to rolling hills with thick copses of trees and stretches of swaying grasses.

"Land, Maddok! We need to land!" I shouted, praying the gryphon could understand me.

The creature twisted his head back and squawked at me, with an agitated snap of his beak.

"I can't hold on to him any longer!"

Part of me recognized the ridiculousness of arguing with a gryphon, but my desperation was stronger than any logic.

Maddok bobbed his head twice, his beak lowering, almost as if he were telling me to look down. Though I felt even more silly, I did, my eyes roaming over the seemingly perfect landing spots once more. The grass moved peculiarly beneath us; I squinted as I strained to look down without losing my balance and my grip on Loukas.

And then I noticed them—the strange-looking animals scuttling across the field. Their narrow backs were the exact same shade of green as the grass, which was why I hadn't noticed them at first. There were so many, they covered the entire field, which was why the grass had looked like it was moving. There had to be hundreds of them. They were like nothing I'd ever seen before.

What *were* they?

And where were we?

"Hurry, Maddok. I really can't hold him any longer," I shouted against the wind as he hurried away from the horde of creatures all rushing the way we'd come.

The burning in my arms turned into sharp pain that shot up into my back.

"Now would be a really good time to wake up!" I yelled at Loukas, though I knew he couldn't hear me. If only I'd succeeded in getting my power back, I could have tried to heal him. I'd been *so* close—if the others hadn't followed us and ruined it. I still wasn't entirely sure what had happened; I only knew I hadn't drunk enough blood to make the change back to Paladin. The hole within me that Raidyn and Zuhra had patched up was still there. I remembered what it felt like to have my power inside me, and I didn't feel that way now. There was a slight warmth within, the softest brush of power stroking at that emptiness, but it was only a ghost of what I'd once possessed—a pale shadow of what I'd needed to take back before everything had gone wrong.

"Loukas! Please!" I shook him as best as I could without unseating both of us.

He moaned something unintelligible.

"Louk! Wake up! *Now!*" I shook him again, even though I barely had the strength to hold on to him, let alone try to move his body without both of us falling to our deaths. Maddok screeched, as if he understood what I was trying to do and wanted to help.

A shudder went through Loukas's body, and he mumbled something.

"Louk! You have to wake up, or we're both going to fall off this gryphon!"

"Fall?" His voice was thick, the word nearly unintelligible, but with a huge grunt, he managed to push himself off me to sit up.

I nearly cried in relief. My arm cramped the moment I was sure he was alert enough to remain in his seat and let it drop. Overhead, the sky was an endless expanse of thin slate clouds, the sun barely visible, its warmth weak at best. Without Loukas sprawled over me, the chill swooped in, raking over my skin, making me shiver.

"W-what happened?" His voice was a scratchy whisper, but his mouth was still close enough to my head for me to hear his quiet question.

How did I answer it when I honestly had no idea?

"I don't know . . . you lost control of Barloc, and he used your knife to make this glowing cut in the air and dragged you through and—"

He suddenly stiffened, cutting me off. "Are we . . . is this *Visimperum*?"

"No . . . that's not possible." But even as I denied it, an icy cascade of terror washed over me. It *wasn't* possible—was it? Could we really be in the world where the Paladin and rakasa lived?

"It is," he said, his disbelief palpable. "How . . . how did we get *here*?"

I explained what Barloc had done, how Maddok and I dove through the narrow strip of glowing light after him and Barloc—and how Barloc had been lying on the cliff that Loukas had fallen off, that Maddok had barely managed to save him from smashing on those rocks.

Loukas twisted behind me; I glanced over my shoulder to see him looking backward, then to the side. "I know that mountain. I know where we are. We've patrolled here before. It's not too far from the gateway . . . maybe a day's flight or less."

"Then let's go there—we have to get back." Hope, delicate as a tiny sprout pushing through the soil, sprang up.

"I can't open the gateway by myself, and I'm guessing you didn't succeed at getting your power back."

My silence spoke volumes.

"We have to go to Soluselis and warn them about Barloc. I've never heard of anyone being able to rip portals to our world through thin air before. If he can do that now, that means he can do it back to Vamala—and take others with him."

"But . . . what about my family? What if I . . . if I need to be healed again?"

"Soluselis is where the most powerful Paladin are . . . If you need to be healed again soon, going there is our best bet at keeping you alive."

He picked up the reins and pulled Maddok to the right. "It looks like midday. We should be there by tomorrow evening, if we don't stop much. But first we have to get away from here. We're in rakasa land, and they'll be drawn to the amount of power Barloc used to rip a gateway out of thin air." That was what those green creatures had been—rakasa, a whole herd of them, rushing toward the explosion of power.

I lapsed into silence. There was no convincing Loukas to go to the gateway—and it sounded like even if we did go there, we wouldn't be able to get back to my home and my family anyway. If only I'd had more time to talk to Zuhra about her experiences when she'd been here—and how she'd convinced them to open the gateway for her to come home. Would they do it again for me?

We only stopped once until we were clear of the rakasa lands, to relieve ourselves and get some water, but Loukas was determined to continue onward until we were back in the safety of the Paladin lands, despite his obvious exhaustion—and Maddok's as well. I tried to distract myself by looking at the scenery of Visimperum—in a few short weeks, I'd gone from being lost in the roar most of my life, to healing multiple people who were near death, including myself, losing my power, leaving the citadel, and now I was in a whole *other world*—but my mind kept circling back to what had happened, how it had all gone so horribly wrong. I replayed it over and over, each time more awful than the last. My stomach twisted into knots. I made myself breathe slowly in through my nose, afraid if I didn't calm down, I would vomit the blood I'd swallowed all over Maddok and Loukas. I shuddered at the thought of what I'd done, of the disgusting heat of it, the metallic taste still in my mouth if I let myself think about it. And for what? Nothing.

I'd failed.

So, even though I should have been full of wonder at the chance to see this whole other world, instead, I glared at the rolling hills and grassy fields and mountains that grew and grew, until they towered over us, monstrous in the darkness, the moon hidden by the same clouds that had obstructed the sun.

"We should be safe now," Loukas finally murmured, after hours that seemed to have stretched into eternities. "We have to stop. Maddok must rest or he won't make it through the pass."

I didn't even bother asking him what "the pass" was as he angled the gryphon toward a small pond and the clearing around it. In the far distance, a glimmer of lights shimmered, hazy and indistinct. A small village or town, the first sign of habitation I'd seen in this world.

As soon as we landed, Loukas climbed off Maddok's back. I didn't realize just how exhausted he still was until I felt his arms tremble from the effort of helping me down. It had never fazed him before. Once we were on the ground, Maddok hurried to the pond, dropping his beak into the water and slurping it up in great gulps. Ripples spread across the surface, marring the reflection of the dark sky above us.

I stood still, arms wrapped around my waist, watching as Loukas walked over to the edge of the pond and knelt in the muddy banks, dropping his hands into the water and lifting it to his mouth. Once he'd drank his fill, he turned to look at me. His green-fire eyes were dulled from the expenditure of his power trying to control Barloc, but they still glowed, a beacon in the night. Vivid and beautiful and intense. Our gazes met and held, and for the first time since we'd left the rest of our group behind to track down Barloc, it hit me that I was *completely* alone with a boy I barely knew.

"Are you thirsty?"

His voice was deep and melodic, with that Paladin accent that made all the words in our language sound so much more lovely than they had any right to sound. I didn't respond, even though my tongue was swollen from dehydration, scratchy and thick in my mouth. I was too afraid to move for some reason. I'd chosen to rely on Loukas, to ask for his help, but now that we were stranded together in the Paladin world, the reality of our situation sent my heart racing. Could I trust him? He'd done what he'd promised to do, with no benefit to himself, and had nearly died because of it—because of *me.* I wasn't sure I had a choice at this point, other than put my faith in him and hope I wasn't making yet another terrible mistake.

"Yes," I finally croaked, embarrassed at the strain I couldn't hide from my voice.

He gestured me forward, but when I moved, my legs buckled and nearly gave out. I caught myself before I fell, but my overused muscles trembled, rebelling against my need to remain standing and move to the life-sustaining water.

Loukas was there at my side before I'd taken more than a few unsteady steps. He took my arm, more gently than I might have expected, and helped support me as I staggered toward the pond.

"I'm sorry," I mumbled, cheeks hot, even though the night was cool and a breeze that danced over the ripples still spreading across the surface of the pond lifted the hair from my neck.

"You aren't used to riding for days on end—or having to support my deadweight for part of the ride," Loukas said as he guided me to the bank where he'd knelt. "There's nothing to be embarrassed about. It takes time to build up muscle. Especially if you've never been particularly active before."

I wasn't sure why, but his words made me bristle. Halvor had never made me feel ashamed of my secluded life, knowing the limitations the roar had forced upon me. Yet somehow, with only a few words, Loukas made my stomach burn with embarrassment.

"I didn't really have a choice," I said.

"I know you didn't."

We stopped at the edge of the water, but he didn't kneel yet. I felt the weight of his focus on me and reluctantly turned to look up at him. Our gazes met and held. I swallowed once, hard, almost involuntarily. We were so close, *too* close. His hand was on my arm, his body within inches of mine. His eyes searched mine, so intent, so piercing, my heart thumped against my ribcage and a flash of heat skittered over my skin when his fingers tightened around my arm.

He's in love with Sharmaine. And I have Halvor, I reminded myself, shocked by my unexpected reaction to Loukas—and more than a little mortified. It reminded me far too much of what Zuhra had described feeling with Raidyn.

As if I'd spoken out loud, he suddenly released me and stepped back. "Let me know if you need help."

I was grateful for the cover of night to hopefully hide my blazing cheeks as I nodded and dropped to my knees, cupping my hands to scoop up some of the cool, clear water. Though it was dark, I still caught sight of my reflection—of the blood crusted around my mouth and chin—and nearly heaved up the one mouthful of water I'd swallowed. There was nothing to be done for the stains on my clothes, but I splashed the water on my face and did the best I could to rub away the gore. My stomach roiled, and I reluctantly gave up on drinking any more.

"We can sleep for a few hours and then push on to Soluselis," Loukas announced as I forced myself to stand and turn away from the pond. Maddok had already curled up near where Loukas had spread out both of our blankets, side by side, close to the shore.

"You don't want to get back to Sharmaine as quickly as possible?" I didn't look at him when I spoke, but I felt the change in the air between us—the tension that surged up, the spark of . . . *something*. I wasn't sure what.

There was a pause before he said, "I know there's no time to waste, but it won't do us or the others any good if Maddok collapses or if I'm not back at full power before we push on."

I nodded silently, not trusting myself to speak, eyeing the lack of space between the two blankets.

Loukas must have followed the direction of my gaze. "We need to stay close together so I can protect you. Just in case," he added when my eyes widened. "We're far enough from the rakasa lands that we should be safe here."

My legs began to tremble again, but I was afraid it wasn't merely from my exhausted muscles anymore. *Be brave, Inara. You can do this. It's only for a few hours. Halvor would understand.*

I forced myself to kneel and then stretch out on the blanket, facing away from Loukas, toward the pond.

I felt him do the same, the heat of his body filling the small space between us. A shiver of awareness started at my scalp and slinked down my spine to my belly. *Stop it,* I commanded myself, determined to control the disconcerting reaction to his proximity.

"How long have you loved Sharmaine?" I asked, staring at the water that had gone still once more, as smooth as glass, determined to build a barrier between us—emotionally if physically wasn't an option.

Loukas made a choking noise as though I'd startled him in mid-swallow.

"How did you know it was love?" I pressed on, determined to keep his mind on her—and get some answers all at once.

When he finally answered, it wasn't what I was expecting. "I don't," was all he said, his voice low and gruff in the darkness, some of the melodiousness cut away by the sharpness of his tone.

Still, I refused to be deterred. "You don't love her, or you don't know if it is love?"

He exhaled, so hard, his warm breath brushed the back of my neck; goose bumps flashed over my skin. "Do you love that scholar? The *jakla*'s nephew?" he countered.

I wanted to be able to say *yes* without hesitation—but for some reason, I couldn't. *Did* I love him? I enjoyed speaking with him, I'd healed him and we shared a bond from that, and his touch, his kiss, helped erase my pain. I cared for him—deeply. But that was why I insisted on asking Loukas how *he'd* known . . . because *I* didn't. "He's kind to me . . . he understands me." It wasn't an answer, and we both knew it.

"Does he, though? How can he *truly* understand you when he can never know what it feels like to be hated for what you are? When he can never imagine what it felt like to be trapped in your own mind? Is it possible to love someone who can only know parts of you—the parts that make sense to them?"

His words raced like poison beneath my skin, hot and uncomfortable, bringing too many things left buried too close to the surface. Memories of my mother, memories of the townspeople of Gateskeep, memories of the prison I'd spent only one night in—but had believed would be my last. "You don't know what you're talking about."

"Don't I?"

"No, you don't." Was it my imagination, or had he shifted ever so slightly closer to me? Why could I feel the length of him behind me, the heat of his body, even though we weren't touching?

"I'm a *mentirum,*" he said, as if that proved his point.

After a long pause, I finally said, "And?"

He laughed, a short burst of sound that held no humor. "*And* if you think growing up as the only Paladin surrounded by family was hard, imagine growing up among thousands of Paladin who all know you could control their minds without their consent at any time, should you choose to."

"Oh." I was tempted to turn over—to read the emotions on his face, because I couldn't understand the tone of his voice. He sounded . . . strangely indifferent about what he was saying, but there was an undercurrent of something else, something deeper that pierced at the hidden pain in my own heart.

"So I know how kindness, especially when it's rare, can be . . . confusing."

"Are you claiming to understand me better than Halvor?"

He laughed again, but this time, he had the audacity to sound amused. "I wouldn't be surprised."

"Well, you're wrong," I insisted. But, yet again, his claims writhed beneath my skin, forcing doubts I hadn't wanted to admit existed to become more clear. Halvor was kind, and he tried to be there for me—to understand me. But there was so much he couldn't, that he never would. I didn't know why—if it was the darkness, or the having barely escaped death together more than once in a day, or just his proximity, but I had a sudden urge to admit the truth to Loukas—to this man I hardly knew, but feared might understand me better than anyone else in my life. Even Zuhra. "I don't know," I finally whispered.

There was a pause, and then, "I agree, there are a great many things you don't know, but you will have to be a bit more specific for me to follow."

"I don't know if I love him," I clarified, part annoyed at his continual mocking and part horrified to realize I'd admitted to him what I hadn't even dared admit to myself until that moment.

Loukas exhaled, his warm breath brushing over my exposed skin and making me shiver. "I have to admit I'm surprised you can be that honest with yourself."

"Excuse me?" Before I could think better of it, I rolled over to face him, indignation burning in my chest. But my heart stuttered when I realized he was even closer than I thought—his face only a few feet from mine, pillowed on his arm, watching me, his expression inscrutable in the darkness. "What is *that* supposed to mean?" I forced out past the sudden pounding of my heart.

"You've been trapped in a roar most of your life," he said. "You've met only one boy—until now—but you also healed him and created *sanaulus* between the two of you. So even though you've known him less than a month, I was fully expecting you to believe yourself to be madly in love with him. I'm impressed that you can be objective enough not to be certain."

I stared at him, at a complete loss for words. He'd somehow managed to make me annoyed *and* proud all at once with his summation of the last few dizzying weeks of my life. "I think having known a girl for most of your life and still not being certain that you love her is far worse than if I had believed myself to be in love with a boy I've only known for a month."

Louk's eyes widened, but before he could respond, I added, "Don't you think it's possible to fall in love with someone in a few weeks? Especially if you're together all the time? I've seen Zuhra and Raidyn together—I am certain he loves her. Don't you think he does?"

A shadow crossed Loukas's face, a muscle in his jaw tightened. "I don't know why you insist on talking about this. We need to rest." And with that, he rolled away from me, leaving me to stare at the wide expanse of his back, my mind racing and my heart a jumbled mess of uncertainty.

It took me an eternity to get to sleep, but I must have eventually dozed off, because I woke to Loukas shaking my shoulder and the sun rising above the trees to the east of us.

"Time to go," he said, not meeting my eyes. "I found some wildberries if you're hungry." He pointed at a pile on his blanket that was folded near my head, and then walked away to where Maddok sat on his haunches, saddled and ready to go.

I blinked the lingering fuzziness of sleep away and sat up, grabbing a few berries and shoving them in my mouth before scrambling to my feet. I picked up both blankets, the rest of the berries plopping on the ground, and hurried to Maddok's side, ignoring the stiffness in my legs.

Loukas wordlessly grasped me around the waist and lifted me up into the saddle. I ignored the heat of his touch through the thin material of my blouse. Why was I reacting to him this way? Why did he have any effect on me at all?

I didn't know anything about boys or what it felt like to be in love—but I was pretty certain that if I *was* in love with Halvor, I wouldn't have felt anything when Loukas was near, when he touched me, or when his eyes met mine. Would I?

But if that was true . . . then what did it mean?

I was miserable and confused and achy and still exhausted. *Focus on getting back to Zuhra and your family. Focus on stopping Barloc. None of this matters right now.* The terror of what might lay ahead finally forced away everything else, so when Loukas swung onto the saddle behind me, his arms encircling my waist, I *almost* didn't notice the muscles in his forearms flexing, or the strength of his body pressed up against mine.

"We're about to go through the pass," Loukas said, the first words he'd spoken in what felt like hours. We'd flown most of the day without a break, and the sun had already set again, hours ago. "It's a tight squeeze, so you're going to need to hold on to Maddok's neck while I hold on to you."

"I don't understand."

"You will."

Maddok soared up higher and higher, toward what looked a lot like insurmountable peaks to me. "Are we going *over* those?"

"Not over. Through."

"*Through?*" I repeated weakly.

"Get ready to lean forward," Loukas warned, pushing me down onto Maddok's flank.

Uncertain of what was happening, I wrapped my arms around the gryphon's muscled neck, as Loukas pressed his body over mine, his arms going around me and Maddok. My heart raced—from fear and his closeness. Before I could ask what he thought he was doing, the gryphon suddenly banked, tipping his entire body so he was nearly perpendicular to the ground far, far below.

A scream built in my throat as we soared straight toward the hulking mass of the mountains. Right when I was certain we would smash into the rocky face of the cliffs, the gryphon slipped into a narrow gap between the two peaks. I slammed my eyes shut. The loamy scent of earth and rock filled my nose; I could feel the cold rock faces as we soared past them.

And then, suddenly, Maddok straightened back out and the air turned sweet and clear once more.

"There it is. Soluselis. I never thought I'd see it again."

My muscles trembled with the surge of adrenaline; I was certain we'd narrowly escaped death. When I finally forced my eyes open, the sight that greeted me took my breath away. A massive city spread out across the valley nestled among all those colossal peaks. It was mostly dark, its inhabitants sleeping, only a few homes glowed with light. But ahead, on a hill in the center of the valley, the most beautiful building I'd ever seen, in life or book, towered over the city below. It was entirely white and seemed to glow, even in the darkness of a moonless night.

This was where Zuhra had been? Where my father was from?

It was magic given shape, in the form of a castle.

We were silent as we soared across the valley, but I sensed a building tension in Loukas. His arms tightened infinitesimally around me the closer we got. Finally, we glided over the hedge—so similar to the one surrounding the citadel—and landed in a huge, empty field near the castle. Before we'd even had a chance to dismount, a handful of Paladin rushed out of the castle, jogging over to us.

"*Loukas?* Is that really you?" one of them shouted.

"It's really me, Teron."

"We heard you were trapped in Vamala!"

Loukas climbed off Maddok's back and faced the group of Paladin now standing a few feet away. "I was. Did Ederra . . . is she . . ."

"They healed her. She's here."

Loukas's shoulders sagged in relief. "I need to speak with her—immediately."

"Of course." Teron, the man in front who had recognized Loukas first, glanced up at me. "But what about her?"

Loukas turned back and reached up to help me get down. "She comes with me."

"Are you sure Ederra will—"

"Yes," he cut him off. "This is her granddaughter."

I froze. "What?"

"*What?*" Teron said at the same time. "The one everyone risked so much to get back home?"

"No. This is her *other* granddaughter."

With that, Loukas grabbed my hand and pulled me forward. I stumbled past the Paladin, my legs still partially numb from the long flight.

"Where are we going?" I was afraid I already knew.

"To talk to your grandmother."

TWENTY-NINE

Zuhra

A dozen more arrows followed the first from unseen archers in the trees around us, but this time they bounced off Sharmaine's shield. The men wielding swords and spears charged across the stream, their boots churning the previously pristine water into a morass of mud and uprooted moss.

Raidyn vaulted onto Naiki's back, his veins lit with power. It gathered in his hand and he launched the fireball at the oncoming soldiers. It exploded into the first few, blasting them off their feet, toppling over several men behind them. Another blast from my father took out at least a dozen more.

"Take off! Take off now!" Father shouted, digging his heels into Taavi's side, even as he sent another blast at the garrison.

"But Halvor!" I screamed, my eyes going to where he lay on the ground in a puddle of blood, his eyes only half-open.

Sharmaine still sat on Keko, her arms shaking from the effort of holding her shield up against the continued onslaught of arrows. Raidyn sent another blast of Paladin fire at the seemingly endless tide of men, barely keeping them from reaching us as they clambered over their fallen comrades, heedless of the danger. I stared at the carnage in horror, the scent of burnt flesh caustic in my nose.

Though I knew it would mean even more death, I also knew this *had* to end—and now—or else Halvor and possibly the rest of us would all die.

The gut-wrenching truth was I would rather all these men died than any of us.

"Stop them. Stop *all* of them!" I cried, as I reached out and clamped my hands onto Raidyn's arm.

My body filled with fire, my veins exploded with the heat and power of it. Dimly I realized my back had arched, my mouth falling open in a silent scream. Unlike the other times when I'd enhanced his ability to heal, I didn't see any flashes of Raidyn's life. There was only endless, all-encompassing fire consuming every cell of my body. Even my vision was full of blue flame, the world washed cobalt.

And then it was sucked out of me, rushing down my arms, out my hands, and into Raidyn. He bellowed, a nearly inhuman sound, as the entirety of it surged into his body. My vision returned to normal, but I still panted, my power continuing to fuel his as it gathered in his hands, so bright, it was nearly blinding. When it exploded out, it erupted not as a fireball, but a continuous stream of blue flames that he aimed at the men. It blasted through the onslaught of soldiers like they were nothing more than kindling. One second they were running at us, weapons lifted, and the next instant they were gone, incinerated into ash.

Though the flames came from Raidyn, it felt as though *I* were the one being ravaged, my muscles and veins liquefied by fire and then draining, draining, draining out of me into him and on to destroy an entire battalion of men—until I was nothing more than a dried-out husk, barely aware of anything beyond all-consuming, devouring, death-delivering fire.

Within moments, they were all gone. Dozens and dozens of men made of flesh and bone and life obliterated by our combined power. Those far enough away to avoid the blast finally turned and fled.

There were a few shouts from the trees above, but no more arrows came.

Raidyn finally cut the fire off. My fingers unclamped, but remained curled like claws, sliding limply off his arm; the outlines remained on his skin—burns in the shape of my hands. Darkness hedged the outer edges of my sight, tunneling in faster and faster as my entire body began to shake violently.

"Zuhra?" Raidyn's soft voice sounded as if he were far, far away, not sitting right next to me.

"Don't ever let Barloc see you do that, unless it's two seconds before you do it to him."

I couldn't even tell who had said it, as the darkness closed in on me, swallowing up my desiccated body.

The darkness was sweet, and so, so soft. It was rest, and it was release. It was temptation and ease. It was a gentle drifting away. But there was something . . . a *tug* . . . just beneath my ribcage, as though there were a hook lodged in the tender flesh of my heart, attached to a cord that kept *tug, tug, tugging* with just enough force to send a twinge of pain through the lovely dark, refusing to let me entirely submerge and lose myself in it. Each sharp pull was accompanied by a glimpse of something other than the neverending blackness surrounding me.

Tug.

A shock of blond hair falling forward into devastatingly blue eyes.

Tug.

A rare, cherished smile on a girl's face whose name I should know.

Tug.

A tiny woman who somehow reminded me of a mountain made flesh.

Tug.

A mouth lined by grief and eyes that were permanently crinkled by laughter, who should have been dear to me but had been taken away for far too long.

Tug.

A hand, reaching out to me in the darkness—the key to unlock the only true home I'd ever known.

Part of me wanted to reach for it, but I was *tired.* So very, very tired.

And the darkness was so sweet and gentle.

Tug, tug, tug.

Lips that taught my mouth to love without words, eyes that burned into my soul when they met mine, a heart that had already broken into too many pieces and would shatter completely if I stayed here.

Something else entered the darkness, a flickering of light that I recognized, but only vaguely. It beckoned to me, trying to coax me out of the shadows.

Who or *what* was it? I wasn't sure I wanted to find out. But something inside me told me I needed to reach out to it . . . or it would be too late.

Though I didn't truly *want* to, I forced myself to stretch toward the light . . . reaching and reaching as the pain intensified, until my entire body burned with it, as though *I* were the one incinerated by fire, not those men.

All those men . . .

Lives snuffed out in an instant because of *me.*

The flames scorched. I burned, but there was no relief; I writhed, but I couldn't move; I screamed, but there was no sound.

Until the darkness, ever caring, ever gentle, swooped in and soothed away the pain, the struggle, the scream. It swallowed up the light, and the *tug,* until there was nothing but velvety night and oblivion.

THIRTY

INARA

I trailed half a step behind Loukas as he stormed into the beautiful castle, his hand still around mine, forcing me to follow. I barely had a chance to take in the thick wooden doors, the gleaming floor and soaring ceilings, as he marched us through a maze of hallways that all looked the same—polished and perfectly white, glittering as if magic was imbued into the very floors and walls.

My heart pounded harder than our feet with every step that carried us closer to my grandmother. I hadn't heard much about her, except that she had been formidable, not very happy Zuhra had been there, and had almost died when Barloc came through the gateway and blasted her with the full brunt of his power.

I was glad, in a detached, unknowing kind of way, that she'd survived. Because Adelric—my father—would have been devastated if she, too, had died, after losing his father.

My stomach sank as I realized *she* didn't know her husband was gone.

The world was upside down and wrong—*I was in the wrong world*—and my sister was the one left behind this time, and I was going to meet my grandmother and be the one to tell her that her husband had died and I didn't know if I *could*.

The emptiness inside me had receded in the face of the little bit of power I'd managed to take from Barloc, but it wasn't enough. Already, I could feel the hole inside absorbing that trace of power, refusing to let it take root. It felt like I'd eaten something bad, but instead of my belly rebelling, it was the space where my power had once resided that was cramping and clenching, fighting against the emptiness.

"She'll probably be asleep," Loukas warned me, the first thing he'd said since we'd entered the castle.

"Couldn't we wait until she wakes up, then?" My voice trembled.

"No."

I didn't argue with him. I knew Barloc was out there, wielding the power of *three* Paladin, with the ability to tear temporary gateways between worlds. We didn't have time to let her sleep in. But I dreaded waking her up to give her all the terrible news we brought.

He stopped before a door and dropped my hand to knock once, loud and hard. I sucked in a breath, waiting . . . and waiting.

When nothing happened, I exhaled slowly.

Rather than knocking again, Loukas turned the knob. I opened my mouth to protest, but before I could, he spat out a word in Paladin under his breath and then turned to me. "It's empty. She's not here."

I couldn't help the relief that washed over me. There would never be enough time to prepare myself for meeting her, but every extra minute I got felt like a reprieve. I wasn't sure why, but some part of me knew that once I met her and told her everything that had happened, the course of my life would change irrevocably—and *she* would be the one who decided what direction it would go.

"Come on." Loukas grabbed my hand and pulled me forward again. "We have to find her."

I wanted to resist, but knowing he wouldn't be deterred, I let myself get dragged back the way we'd come. At least, I *thought* we were going back. I really had no concept of direction in this building. All the hallways curved slightly, as though they were circling something in the center of the castle.

We stopped at two more doors, but both rooms were also empty. I didn't need *sanaulus* to sense Loukas's building frustration. His hand tightened on mine, the temperature of his skin rising a degree every time he failed to find her.

We'd only passed a couple of other Paladin, but before I'd been able to get a good look at any of them, they'd taken one glance at the thunderous expression on Loukas's face and scurried away like mice who had been spotted by a cat.

"Maybe if you'd stop scaring everyone away, we could ask one of them where she is," I pointed out quietly after another Paladin, a girl with a basket full of laundry, had turned on her heel and rushed back the way she'd come the second she spotted us.

"Why do you assume it's me? Have you seen the way *you* look?"

I glanced down at my shirt, at the blood splatters there. Was it still on my face too? I'd tried to wipe it off with the pond water, but maybe I'd failed. I flushed but doggedly refused to back down. "They aren't looking at me when they run away—so you must be even scarier than I am."

"You think I'm *trying* to scare them?" Loukas growled. "Even if I walked around with a smile on my face, carrying a basket of cookies, they'd still turn tail the minute they saw me."

I snorted indelicately, trying to imagine Loukas carrying a basket full of cookies with a big, goofy grin on his normally saturnine face. "You might be surprised. I've never had a cookie, but I hear they're amazing."

He shot me a scowl. "They are afraid of *me,* not the expression on my face. But I'll be sure to give it a try some other time, when every minute we waste isn't the difference between life or death."

"You always did have a flair for the melodramatic, Loukas," a woman said from behind us. "But I'm afraid it might be warranted in this case. How are the two of you back—and where is everyone else?"

We both spun around. My heart skipped up into my throat, where it thrummed like a hummingbird's wings—something I'd only seen once when I was lucid on a beautiful spring day, its wings beating so quickly they were nearly invisible.

The woman wore breeches, boots to her knees, and a blouse, her fiery red hair liberally laced with white pulled back in a tight bun, her blue-fire eyes sharp and unwavering. One side of her neck had a spiderweb of silvery lines on it that delved below her blouse.

She stared right back at me. "You aren't Zuhra."

I swallowed. I knew I should say something—*anything*—but I could only stand there with my mouth intractably clamped shut.

"This is your *other* granddaughter, Inara. Inara, this is your grandmother, Ederra."

I didn't need Loukas's introduction. I'd known there was no one else it could have been. But, after hearing the little bit Zuhra had told me about her, I hadn't expected to see disappointment cross her face when she realized the granddaughter who had come to her castle was the *other* one.

"I thought you had immense Paladin power," Ederra said, her gaze raking over me with a hint of distaste, reminding me once again of the gore I most likely still had on my neck and clothes, and then moving on to Loukas.

"She did."

"*Did?*" Ederra repeated coldly.

"Before Barloc ripped it out of her. She's the one who made him a *jakla*."

I'd only known her for less than two minutes, but I already guessed that the shock that crossed her face was not something many people saw. "Then how are you . . . *here*?"

I knew she didn't mean in the castle, though that was certainly another question she would no doubt want answered soon. "I . . . I was healed," I finally managed to squeak out.

"No one can heal that."

"Raidyn and Zuhra did. Together."

Ederra's eyebrows shot up. "Raidyn and *Zuhra*? She *does* have power?"

"She's an enhancer," Loukas confirmed.

"An enhancer," Ederra repeated with a tone bordering on astonishment. "Then Alkimos was right after all."

"But none of this matters anymore. Well, except for the fact that the healing doesn't last forever. She keeps having to be rehealed." Before Ederra could ask him to explain himself, he barreled on. "We have bigger problems right now." He quickly told her what Barloc had done—how he'd stolen the power from two more Paladin, how we'd tracked him down and I'd almost succeeded in stealing my power back ("Well, that explains all of this," she'd said with a gesture at me, making my cheeks burn with embarrassment), before he'd broken free of Loukas's power, and then ripped the portal open to Visimperum.

With each revelation, Ederra paled, until she was nearly as white as the hair on her head. "I knew such a thing was possible in theory," she admitted softly, almost to herself, "but I've never heard of anyone *actually* succeeding in doing it by themselves." She reached up and pressed three fingertips to one of her temples. "I need to sit down." She turned on her heel and walked away.

I wasn't sure she wished to be followed, but Loukas gave me no choice when he hurried after her; leaving me to either follow or stand there in that hallway until someone remembered to come back and find me.

As she walked, she peppered him with questions about Barloc, what we knew about him, what he'd done so far, and what condition he'd been in when we'd left him. As Loukas had been unconscious for that part, he glanced over his shoulder at me, trailing slightly behind them.

"You'll have to ask Inara," he said.

Ederra also glanced back. "Well?"

"He was lying unconscious on the edge of a cliff. I didn't get a good look at him—Maddok and I flew right past him to try to catch Loukas before he . . ."

"Met an untimely end on the rocks at the bottom of that cliff," Loukas supplied.

"Now is not the time for your caustic sense of humor." Ederra cut a glare at him.

"I assure you I am being entirely earnest."

She looked back at me again, and I nodded.

"Let me get this straight—*you* rode *his* gryphon *off the side of a cliff* and saved him before he hit the bottom?"

I nodded again.

Something akin to admiration crossed her face, but only momentarily. Still, it warmed me as nothing had since Loukas and I had snuck away from the rest of my family on our ill-fated attempt to save my life.

"So we must assume he's out there somewhere, temporarily weakened but alive. And once he regains his strength, he can track down other members of the sect, possibly even distant family members, and rip open a gateway to Vamala anywhere he wishes." Ederra stopped before a door and pushed it open. She and Loukas walked in first, me trailing behind. Inside was a massive table, with flickering blue light—much like the Paladin fire in their eyes—burning in lanterns hung at intervals along the walls, casting the whole room in an otherworldly shade of cerulean.

"We must convene an emergency meeting of the council right away."

"With all due respect, there's no time to wait for them to all come here," Loukas said as Ederra sat heavily on one of the chairs.

"I agree. We won't wait for those not in attendance. We will have to make a decision with those who are and act immediately. He is a threat to our world too—especially if he tries to steal power from any other Paladin he comes across, or convinces other members of the *Infinitium* sect to do it as well. If we can track him down before he regains full strength, perhaps we can stop him before he hurts anyone else." She glanced up at Loukas. "Will you please go find Yemaya and tell her to bring every council member in residence here immediately?"

Loukas glanced at me, the first hint of concern I'd seen crossing his face.

"She'll be fine with me, Loukas. I won't bite her. You may go."

I gulped, somehow less encouraged by this statement than if she'd said nothing at all. But he did as she commanded and left, the door shutting behind him with a resounding *thunk*.

I stood halfway between the door and the table, my hands hanging awkwardly at my sides, not able to bring myself to meet her piercing gaze.

"You're different than your sister," she said after several moments of silence.

Zuhra. The distance between us was as painful as it was insurmountable. At least I knew *she* was safe; Barloc was here in Visimperum. He couldn't hurt her or anyone else that I loved. At least . . . not until he went back, if the Paladin here couldn't find him before he did.

"She and Raidyn really healed you," she continued, "which is truly remarkable." There was a pause. "But it doesn't last?"

"No." I barely managed to make the word audible.

Something in her gaze, a hard edge, softened infinitesimally. "Are you frightened of me?"

Yes.

"No," I repeated, only a tiny bit louder than the first time.

"Zuhra never showed any fear toward me. She was angry with me—and hurt. But never *afraid.* It was a mistake for me to refuse to get to know her. Alkimos was right about that too. He was probably thrilled to be there with both of you girls." Her mouth curved up slightly, as though she were trying to smile, but had forgotten how to do it quite right. "I will try to do better with you."

I couldn't return her smile. Alkimos . . . that was her husband's name. My grandfather. She didn't know he was gone. And Loukas had left. Which meant *I* had to tell her.

"It will take a bit of time before they all show up—most of them are sleeping, I'm sure. I'm the only one who hasn't been able to sleep for more than an hour or two since . . . everything that happened. We could go get you a change of clothes and something to wash off your face, so that—"

"He's gone," I burst out before I lost my nerve.

She paused, her eyebrows lifting. "Excuse me?"

I winced, my heart thundering in my chest. "Alkimos . . . your husband . . . he . . . when Barloc came back through, he tried to stop him . . ." I couldn't go on, but I didn't have to. It was one of the worst things I'd ever seen—the way she froze as if time had stopped in that instant, and then her face crumpled as an inhuman noise escaped her throat, a cry of unadulterated anguish. Then her body folded in on itself.

And I just stood there, helpless, *useless,* a stranger with blood in my veins that made us family, but nothing more to give me the right to walk to her side and offer any comfort that might be unwanted and unwarranted—especially when, technically, *I* was the reason her husband had died. It was *my* power Barloc had stolen, my power he'd used to injure her and kill my grandfather.

"I'm so sorry," I whispered.

She didn't even seem to hear me. Ederra's sobs ripped through her as if she'd bottled up a lifetime of grief and losing her husband was what finally broke her, letting all of her pain escape in this awful, uncontrolled flood of tears that made her entire body quake.

Whether she wanted me to or not, whether I *should* or not, I couldn't handle standing there watching her cry. With a deep breath to fortify my flagging courage, I slowly shuffled toward her, prepared for her to yell at me to stop—or *go away*—at any moment.

She never looked up.

I paused at her side, unaccountably terrified to put my hand out and rest it on her shoulder.

Are you frightened of me?

Yes.

But I made myself do it anyway.

She jerked at the contact, her sobs pausing for a moment. But then she leaned into my touch, just slightly, her entire body trembling with the weight of grief known and unknown.

She only cried for a minute or two longer, and then with a suddenness that took me completely off guard, she cut off the sobs as abruptly as they'd started. Her body still trembled beneath my hand, but she sat up taller, until I had to either curl my fingers over her shoulder to remain holding on or let them slide away.

I let them slide away.

She wiped at one cheek, then the other, and glanced over at me, her eyes burning and bloodshot. "Now we both need to go get cleaned up before this meeting."

With that, Ederra pushed her chair back, stood, and strode to the door, obviously expecting me to follow.

I did exactly that, watching her brush past Loukas, who had to sidestep to avoid getting plowed over by her. He looked to me with lifted eyebrows and mouthed, "Alkimos?"

I nodded, rushing after my grandmother.

"Everyone is coming," he called after us.

"Tell them we'll be back in five minutes or less," Ederra said, redoubling her speed, until she was nearly jogging.

I followed in her wake, wondering how I'd traded one indomitable woman in my mother for another in my grandmother. Apparently my father had really liked strong-willed women in his life. Perhaps, I realized, I needed to be more like them. Even Zuhra, much as she was loath to admit it, was more similar to both of them than me. She was strong and determined and courageous, and I . . . I was weak and frightened with only rare bursts of anything even remotely akin to bravery. The only claim to power I'd ever had was gone.

But Zuhra had been strong before she'd ever known she possessed any power beyond that of her own will.

Could I be like her? Could I find strength in new ways?

If I had any hope of getting back to her, I had a feeling I would have to.

If I could stay alive that long.

Even as we rushed down the hallway, a shudder passed through me, a chill I recognized all too well.

The hole inside me was cracking apart once more.

THIRTY-ONE

Zuhra

The darkness was thicker, heavier. Still velvet and soft and soothing, but also dense and clinging. I was cocooned in it, unable to move even if I'd wanted to.

Why would I want to leave it?

There is only pain for you up there, it told me. *Pain and loss and guilt. Terrible guilt, for you did a terrible thing.*

The *tug* was softer now, barely even noticeable unless I focused.

Blue-fire eyes.

Hands that had held mine.

Lips that had spoken stories that softened panic into sleep.

But the darkness pressed me down; it suffocated the fire that scorched if I tried to fight my way back above it.

So I succumbed, sinking deeper and deeper into its embrace.

And the blue-fire eyes grew dimmer and dimmer, until they were barely even a flicker of memory.

The musical voice that had once spoken the words that comforted me so often faded until it was a mere echo, distant and growing weaker every minute.

But the darkness was there to fill the void, to soothe away any memory of pain.

THIRTY-TWO

INARA

When Ederra said "five minutes or less," she'd meant it.

She burst into a room not far from the one with the large table, where she rushed to a nightstand, yanked open a drawer, and tossed me a clean white shirt. "Put that on and wipe your face off." She pointed to a cloth on top of the dresser, next to a wide, low bowl. She bent over it and splashed some water on her face.

I held the buttery-soft shirt, staring down at the brilliant white fibers with awe. I'd never seen a piece of clothing so beautiful. I hadn't realized before how worn and aged everything we used in the citadel was until I saw the difference, how unbelievably white fabric could be—as white as clouds, as white as fresh snow.

"Inara! Hurry!"

Startled by her vehemence, I quickly stripped off my filthy, blood-stained top, humiliated by the difference in the two pieces of clothing when I held one in each hand. I dropped the used one on the floor so I could put the clean one on. It smelled of sunshine and lemons and slid over my body like water gliding over my skin.

"We might as well just burn this . . . um . . ."

I pulled my head through the neck to see her gingerly pick up the soiled shirt with only her pointer finger and thumb and toss it into her dormant hearth. I flushed but hid my embarrassment by busying myself tucking the clean shirt into my equally dirty and used trousers.

"Your face," Ederra reminded me, as she pinned back the few

errant hairs that had managed to escape the bun in her emotional outburst. There was hardly a trace of it left visible; she had transformed herself back as though she'd never cried once in her life, let alone the torrential flood of grief I'd been witness to.

I hurried to the washstand, catching a glimpse of myself in her mirror. Though I'd tried to clean it off, dried blood still coated the edges of my lips and was smeared in streaks over my cheeks, chin, and even my neck. I shuddered at the sight, my stomach heaving. I barely managed to swallow the bile rising up my throat at the memory of Barloc's blood in my mouth, of the effort it had taken to swallow the few gulps I'd managed to drink before it had all gone so wrong.

And for what? *Nothing.*

I shivered again as I hurried to dip the cloth in the water and wiped furiously at my skin, wishing I could scrub away my memories along with the dried blood.

How long would it take this time before the chasm cracked wide open, forcing me to need to be healed or else truly die?

"It's gone, dear."

It was the gentleness in her voice, the use of the word "dear" that startled me into stillness, to realize I was still scouring my skin though the blood was long gone, my skin red and agitated from the vehemence of my scrubbing.

"Right," I murmured, crossing the room to toss the stained rag in the fireplace beside my shirt.

Ederra watched without comment.

We were both silent on the short walk back to the room with the table where the council would be meeting, but right before we walked in, she paused and turned to me. "You're not going to try to convince me to open the gateway for you?"

I shook my head, confused.

"To get back to your sister?" she added.

"I want to go back home to her as soon as I can, but I know that you have to do what is best for everyone right now." I glanced down at my feet, not wanting her to see the weakness in my eyes. I was afraid if I truly started crying, I wouldn't be able to stop. Certainly not the way she had.

"Hmm," was all she said, and with that, she opened the door and strode in to the room, where a handful of other Paladin and Loukas all waited.

I slunk in behind her, not sure if I was welcome or not, but not knowing where else to go. I stood in the corner, hoping to make myself as inconspicuous as possible, but every eye in the room turned to me immediately—except for Loukas's.

"As you can see," Ederra said, taking her same seat, "things in Vamala haven't gone as we'd hoped. This is my other granddaughter, Inara." And with that, she launched into the entire story we'd told her.

As she spoke, I tried to force myself to focus on her, not to let my mind wander to Vamala and wonder what *had* happened to Zuhra, my family, and Halvor after we'd disappeared. Would they be able to figure out where we'd gone? Would Halvor and my sister know I was alive—that Loukas and I had both survived? For the first time since we'd gone through that tear into Visimperum, it occurred to me they might assume we were dead—that they would have believed Barloc might have killed us both.

Don't give up on me, Zuhra. I'm still here.

Halvor . . . please know I'm still alive.

For now.

The hedge surrounded me on all sides; it had grown, lengthening to hide the citadel from view, trapping me in the gardens I had once tended that were now sun-scorched, brown, and dead.

My family stood across from me, all three of them with arms crossed, scowls on their faces.

Halvor stood beside me. I wanted him to take me in his arms, to kiss away my guilt and pain, but he kept his hands shoved into the pockets of his trousers. He didn't glare at me, but the love I'd once seen when he looked at me was gone, his normally warm brown eyes changed to the color of frozen soil.

"You have to do *something*, Inara." Zuhra had never spoken to me in that tone before, harsh as a winter wind.

"You were supposed to *save* us, not *doom* us," Mother added, her lip curled in disgust.

"That *jakla* exists because of *you*. Now no one can stop him." My father's eyes flashed with burning fury.

"My uncle is gone forever—because of *you*. If you hadn't given him your power, none of this would have happened," Halvor spat. "And now I'll never get him back."

I tried to speak, to tell them it wasn't my fault, to apologize, to beg for their forgiveness, but when I opened my mouth, their accusations, their hatred and spite, filled it and choked the words away.

"Do you know how many have died—because of *you*?"

The hedge loomed closer, inching forward as they spoke, leaves peeled back, exposing the deadly barbs beneath, like an animal snarling.

I shook my head, tears gathering in my eyes.

I'm sorry, I'm so sorry . . .

But the words wouldn't come out. I couldn't breathe and—

A touch on my shoulder jerked me awake with a stifled gasp. My heart slammed against my ribcage; sweat slipped down my spine. I blinked several times, disoriented and confused. I was sitting on the ground, my knees pulled up to my chest, my head tipped back against a wall.

"You fell asleep," Loukas whispered. He crouched beside me. "I would have let you keep resting, but it seemed like you were having a nightmare."

I stared at him, the horrific dream still fresh and painful. Did my family really feel that way? Did Halvor?

"I'll send out two patrols right away. If he's still here, we'll find him."

Slowly, I remembered where I was—and what was happening. The meeting to decide what to do about Barloc and the threat he posed to the Paladin and human worlds.

"Thank you, Yemaya," Ederra responded. "If we can't find him within the next twelve hours, we will implement the contingency plan."

With a few low murmurs, everyone around the table stood, and within moments, the room had emptied out—all except for Loukas and my grandmother.

"I'm sorry I fell asleep." I flushed, humiliated that I'd missed such an important meeting—one that had been called because of me. Though I hoped the hatred I'd felt in my dream had been just a projection of my own fears and not reality, the truth remained: Barloc *was* a *jakla* now because of me. If it weren't for my power, he never would have been able to head down this path.

"I should have offered to let you rest. You've been through a terrible ordeal."

"No, I wanted to be—"

A sharp stab of pain suddenly pierced my chest, so intense, it doubled me over.

"Inara? What is it?"

I dimly heard Loukas's question as I clutched at the clean shirt right over my heart, pushing my fist into my breastbone, trying to drive the pain away. The intensity of it stole my breath; I searched for the little bit of power I'd taken back from Barloc, but it flickered feebly and went out, leaving only the expanding emptiness.

No, no, *no*.

I fought back, tried to calm my racing heart, to force the fissure cracking through Raidyn and Zuhra's healing back together, refusing to let it crumble apart. *Not here. Not now.* I wasn't sure how long it took before it finally passed, somehow, mercifully holding—for a little longer—leaving me panting and shaken.

I slowly straightened. Loukas and Ederra both watched me, Loukas with eyes hooded and Ederra with thinly veiled apprehension.

"What was *that*?" I wasn't sure if she was asking me or Loukas, but thankfully he saved me the effort by answering.

"I believe that was the healing beginning to fail. Again."

I wasn't positive—it was there and gone again so fast—but it looked like fear flickered across his face.

Ederra's brows furrowed. "You said it took Raidyn and Zuhra to heal her—a healer *and* an enhancer?"

Loukas nodded. "Are there any enhancers here at the castle

right now? I'm afraid she's going to need to be healed again sooner than later."

Ederra pressed her fingers against her temples. "Yes, Zeph is here. But I'm trying to think of which healer is strong enough to be able to do this with him. If *he's* even strong enough to do this—to save her."

My heart finally slowed, my breathing returned to normal, and the shakiness abated. But I was still unsettled, frightened by the suddenness and severity of the attack. And Ederra's words turned me cold with alarm.

What if the Paladin here weren't strong enough to heal me?

How long did I have before whatever Zuhra and Raidyn had done the second time failed completely—and all of it, all the effort to save me, was for nothing?

THIRTY-THREE

Zuhra

The darkness was no longer sweet, as it once had been. It was heavy and pulsing and insistent. It filled every thought . . .

Every feeling . . .

Every piece of me.

I was lost and falling deeper. There was only this abyss—

This unrelenting oblivion.

Tug.

I wasn't even sure what the curious sensation was, it was so far removed from my memory.

Tug.

A flicker of something, so faint, I almost missed it. I couldn't remember what it was, only that I had once known it.

Flicker.

Tug.

Flicker.

Light.

That was what it was, I recalled sluggishly. It was a flicker of light, trying to push the darkness aside.

But the blackness was *everywhere.*

So strong, so complete . . . in my nose, in my eyes, in my ears, in my heart and blood and soul.

Tug.

A flash of blue-fire eyes.

Tug.

A flush of heat from a kiss.

Tug.

A soul that recognized me, that had intwined itself indelibly into mine.

Raidyn.

The moment I remembered his name, the light, though small, surged forward, driving through the inky black until it reached me. The once-familiar brush of his soul against mine made me shudder. He spoke without words, a feeling given meaning, as his light tangled with the darkness inside me, battling to unravel its immovable grasp, its inky claws trying to drag me away from him and light and anything but everlasting darkness.

Come back to me.

Fight it.

Fight for me.

I was weak and frightened, and I knew there were reasons I should stay in the dark; pain and guilt and horror that awaited me if I let him pull me back into the light.

But Raidyn was also there.

And my family.

Inara.

No. Not Inara.

The darkness pulsed. Pain, too dark and deep to bear, bared its teeth.

But Raidyn's light, his gentle, beautiful soul, refused to let go. I felt him wrap that healing light around me, filling me with it. Softly at first—careful, so careful . . . but as the darkness slowly, angrily receded, the light grew stronger, brighter, warmer, until it filled me as completely as the black oblivion had.

Together. We'll face whatever comes together.

Soul to soul, he spoke to me without sound.

Come back to me.

I love you.

A radiant beam, of light and hope and *knowing,* as warm and powerful as anything I'd ever experienced, pierced through the darkness, a straight shot to my heart. Words spoken without sound, soul to soul, left no room for doubt or disbelief. There was only wonder, that *he* truly could love *me.*

And finally, *finally,* I turned to him fully, embracing his light, letting him pull me back, up, up, up, through dark, through pain, through oblivion, back to life.

Back to him.

Sound returned first, but it was distant, a buzz of voices that I couldn't separate from the sluggish beat of my heart. All except for one.

"Zuhra," Raidyn said, soft and achingly gentle. "Open your eyes."

Though it took an enormous effort, I did as he asked, forcing them to peel open. My eyelids were scratchy and remarkably heavy, as if they'd been *sealed* shut, not just closed. The sun was bright overhead, *too* bright. I winced at the onslaught. But Raidyn was there, bending over me, his veins lit with power, though it was quickly receding back. His eyes were dulled, hardly any fire left in them.

"Raidyn?" His name was a mere croak, my voice gravelly from disuse.

He smiled at me, a tilt of his lips that was full of both relief and pain. He cupped my face with one hand, the other still rested on my sternum, just above my breasts. Everything was muddled; he'd healed me—that much was clear. But . . . from what?

"Zuhra?"

At the sound of Mother's voice, Raidyn finally sat back, withdrawing both of his hands. The sun was hot overhead, the air thick, heavy with humidity, as if a storm had recently passed by, but I shivered, chilled.

I tried to sit up, but my head swam.

"Whoa . . . take it slow." It was my father who spoke this time. "You will probably need to rest for a bit before you can do much."

He knelt next to Raidyn, and Mother did the same on my other side, taking one of my hands in hers. Her fingers were warm on mine, a testament to how cold I was, as she was usually much colder than me.

"What happened?" I made myself ask, though I was afraid to find out. My memory was hazy; I vaguely recalled losing Inara and Loukas—but my mind darted away, shying from that recollection as soon as it arose, like a skittish horse—straight into flashes of a clearing, of Halvor being shot, of men rushing at us with weapons lifted, of fire that consumed, of bodies there and then gone—

"Zuhra, *ssshhh,* just breathe, sweetheart. You need to rest. We can talk about what happened later."

I didn't even realize I was wheezing, fighting a rush of panic, until my mother spoke, stroking a piece of hair back from my forehead. I looked to her; she'd never been so gentle with me before. But her touch wasn't what I needed. I turned for him, but found my father instead. The only person I truly wanted to see was Raidyn. I *needed* him to hold me—to hold me *together.*

I needed to know what I'd felt when he'd healed me was true.

"Raidyn."

The trembling whisper sent a flash of hurt across my mother's face, but my father quickly moved, his face a mask, letting Raidyn scoot back up by my head.

"It's the *sanaulus,* my heart. Don't take it personally."

I barely registered my father's murmur, as Raidyn took my hand in his, his eyes on mine. He looked as exhausted as I felt, but he was *real* and he was *there.* And because of him, so was I.

"You can close your eyes and rest. It's going to take a little bit before you regain your strength." He stroked my hair back, over and over, methodical and soothing. A small corner of my mind that was working a bit better than the rest wondered why I needed rest when he'd healed me—I'd never needed to rest after any other time.

But the majority of me, that felt as though I might never have the strength to move from this spot on the ground, succumbed to the exhaustion and his touch and with a helpless flutter, my eyes shut and I drifted off once more.

* * *

When I woke again, the sun was gone, all light erased, there was only darkness, inky black and never-ending. For a brief moment of suffocating terror, I thought I had sunk back into the abyss—that Raidyn saving me, dragging me from its endless hold, had been nothing more than a feverish, desperate dream.

"Zuhra, it's all right. I'm here." Raidyn's actual voice—*real,* and right beside me, *not* a memory—was the only thing that cut through the building panic. I turned toward it instinctually, though I still couldn't see anything. "You're safe. I'm here."

I blinked a few times and slowly, my eyes adjusted to nighttime in the forest. Not the darkness where I'd been caught for . . . I wasn't sure how long.

Raidyn lay beside me, less than a foot away. He reached out for my hand, curling his fingers over mine. I was still so tired, the exhaustion delved deep into my bones, but unlike the first surfacing, memories came flooding back all at once, an agonizing barrage of reality—and stark horror. Barloc and my sister on the ground . . . both of them disappearing through that tear of light . . . the horrible hours that followed . . . the attack by the river . . .

What I'd done to save us.

All those men I'd killed.

My stomach heaved, but there was nothing but bile to rise up into my throat. Guilt coated my skin like ice. I shivered and squeezed my eyes shut, but when I did, I was assaulted by images of the stream of fire blasting out of Raidyn's hands, incinerating an entire garrison of men in mere seconds.

"Zuhra." Raidyn's voice was a low murmur, soft but insistent. "You saved us. None of us had enough power to stop that many men. Many of them would have still died, but *all* of us would have died with them."

I nodded, even as tears slipped over the bridge of my nose and down my temple to soak into my hair and the soil beneath my head. I'd known that when I'd chosen to put my hands on Raidyn's arms. I'd known I was choosing our lives over theirs. But the reality of so much death—*because of me*—was something I didn't know how to live with.

"Don't cry, *meaula amarre.*" Raidyn tenderly wiped the tears from my face, scooting closer so he could gather me into his arms. I curved into his embrace, burying my face in his shoulder. But instead of stopping, my tears turned into sobs that wrenched through me. He held me as I shook, soaking his shirt. When the torrent finally passed, leaving me rung out and weaker than ever, he still didn't let me go.

We were silent for a long time; the only sound the steady beat of his heart beneath my ear, and the whisper of the wind brushing the leaves overhead. He waited for me, let me gather my thoughts.

"It drained me entirely," I said at last, a statement, but he still said, "Yes."

"How long was I . . ."

There was a pause, and then he said, "Two days."

I stiffened. I'd known it must have been a while, but . . . *two days*? I'd thought I had no tears left, but to realize I'd lost two whole days was such a shock they leaked out the corners of my eyes once more. I didn't even realize that I'd still managed to cling to a tiny shred of hope that Inara had survived, until the realization that we'd lost so much time when we could have been in Visimperum searching for her tore me apart once more.

"It drained me as well. Your father had to use what power he still retained after that attack to heal Halvor—though only enough to save his life. They had no choice but to wait for me to wake up on my own, and it took half a day," Raidyn explained quietly. Halvor was alive then, I realized with relief. At least he had survived. "Your father tried to heal you too, when I was still too weak. But he couldn't reach you. It was . . ." His arms tightened around me. "I have never been so frightened in my entire life."

He didn't have to tell me any more—I knew the rest. On the second day—today—he'd finally succeeded in bringing me back. I shuddered when I thought of the darkness that had held me captive, how close I'd come to giving in to it entirely, letting it take me away from him.

From *everyone* I loved, that I'd sacrificed so much to save.

And though it hurt to even let myself cling to any hope, I couldn't give up on Inara either. Not until I knew for certain she was gone. We'd both defied death before, more than once; was it possible she could have done it again?

If not, then what had it all been for?

I opened my eyes again, but this time, though it was still dark, I could see the shape of the trees above us, and the stars overhead, like glitter spilled across velvet, distant but brilliant. And Raidyn, his blue-fire eyes glowing in the night, looking down at me.

"Thank you," I whispered.

"For what?"

"Everything," I said. "For saving me. For giving me a reason to come back. For always being there for me." I paused, gathering my courage. But if there was anything I'd learned over the last few weeks, it was that there were no guarantees of how much time we'd have together. And I couldn't face whatever was ahead without telling him, out loud, how I truly felt. "Did you mean it . . . what I felt when you healed me?"

He stared down at me, the fire in his eyes intensifying. "Yes, all of it." His voice was husky, low in his throat.

Heat blossomed in my heart—and pooled in my belly at the burning hunger in his gaze.

He lifted one hand to cup my jaw, his thumb brushing my lower lip, sending a wave of need through my body.

"I've never been more scared than when I thought we might have lost you forever. When I reached you today, with barely a flicker of life left . . ." His voice grew hoarse and he stopped. His head dipped, his lips found mine, brushing a soft kiss to my mouth as if he couldn't wait one moment longer to do it. Before I could even react, he'd pulled away again. "But you came back to me, *meaula amarre.* You came back to me, and I realized I'd *hoped* you would know how I felt about you, because of the *sanaulus.* I didn't want to say it out loud and risk having you not say it back. But I don't care anymore. I am not risking another day going by when I don't tell you how much I love you, Zuhra. Because I do. I love you. My heart, my life, my soul are yours."

I stared up at him, my heart so full, it felt too big to be contained in the confines of my body. "I love you too, Raidyn. With every—"

He cut off my words with his mouth, our lips crashing together. Where the first kiss had been soft and brief, a question more than anything, this kiss was the answer, and it was urgency and love and an all-too-painful awareness of the risk that it might be our last. His hands closed into fists around my shirt, his knuckles kneading my spine as his lips moved on mine. I pressed closer to him, my own hands roaming over his back, pulling his shirt until it tugged free of his pants, so I could run my fingers against his bare skin. He shivered beneath my touch, with a low groan deep in his throat. I felt at once powerful at my effect on him and weak from his on me.

Raidyn reached up with one hand, plunging it into my hair, to tilt my head back, his lips insistent on mine, parting them beneath his, so his tongue could sweep forward, claiming my mouth. I gasped, hot with a nameless ache that begged me to somehow get closer to him, to—

He broke away suddenly, breathing heavily, his eyes burning in the darkness. "If we do much more of that, I can't make any promises that your parents won't wake up and find us in a compromised position."

There was a soft hoot nearby; I was almost certain it was Naiki, offering us her approval or a warning, I wasn't sure. A soft giggle escaped my lips—a *giggle.* I hadn't even realized I was capable of such a noise.

"Maybe I don't care if they do."

"Don't tempt me," Raidyn growled, bending forward to take my bottom lip between his teeth, with just enough pressure to turn my legs liquid and make my heart slam against my ribs.

I moaned, pressing into his body again, and he immediately pulled back.

"And no more noises like that either!"

I wanted to protest, but with the little bit of space between us—enough for the the night air to swoop in and cool my heated cheeks—a hint of reason returned, and with it, a rush of guilt that turned the languorous heat in my limbs to acid in my stomach.

"Is everyone healthy now?"

Raidyn blinked at the sudden change in topic.

"Healthy enough to fly?" I clarified.

"Yes." He pushed up onto his forearm. "Halvor is healed, and everyone else has recovered. We haven't moved—we didn't dare with the condition you were in. But there haven't been any more attacks."

I nodded. "Then wake everyone up. We should go. Now."

"Now?"

"I've rested long enough—we've wasted *days* because of me. And if there's any chance my sister is still alive, we need to get to her as fast as possible."

"Zuhra . . ."

I could hear the caution in his voice, but I ignored it with a sharp shake of my head. "A *chance,* Raidyn. That's all I said. And I know it's small. But I have to believe it still exists. As long as you're breathing, there's still hope, right?"

He winced at the reminder of his mother's words.

"Well, here I am, breathing against all odds—again. Perhaps she is too."

He reached up with his free hand to cup my cheek. There was no passion behind this touch, only a bone-deep sadness that transferred to me even more strongly through the press of his fingers against my jaw, and a regretful sigh. But he said, "You're right. Of course we can hope there's still a chance. For Loukas too."

I nodded, fierce and desperate. "And no matter what, we have to stop Barloc," I added. "Before he brings an army here and kills even more innocent people. Before he destroys this whole world."

Raidyn's eyes flashed in the darkness. "We will stop him. We *will,*" he repeated, a fierce promise under the distant stars.

THIRTY-FOUR

INARA

I trailed a foot or two behind Loukas. Ederra had asked him to take me to a room where I could lie down and rest. But my steps were heavy and slow, forcing him to glance over his shoulder more than once to see if I still followed.

"Are you all right?" He paused and turned to me after the third time looking back. "Is it happening again?"

"No, not yet."

Loukas waited, his green-fire eyes even brighter than normal in the night-shadowed hallway. So different, so unique, marking him as *other*. Making fellow Paladin afraid of him. I'd noticed the way even the council—supposedly some of the most powerful Paladin in Visimperum—gave him a wide berth in that room, casting sidelong glances toward him with narrowed eyes and stiffened shoulders. He didn't give any indication that he noticed or cared . . . but I wondered.

It struck me in that moment, standing alone in the hallway together, that the last person I'd ever expected to be able to understand me was the one staring at me, hands shoved into his pockets, broad shoulders thrown back in his usual self-assured stance. His comments near the river that I'd brushed off, tried to ignore, rose back up, forcing my heart into my throat.

Was that why he'd finally agreed to help me go after Barloc alone? Because he, of all people, could understand what it had been like to grow up with a mother who couldn't stand to be in the same room as me? We both knew what it was like to have those who should have cared for us fear and avoid us. And perhaps he knew how the power he wielded, that caused that divide, had become his comfort—how, if it had been torn from him, he would have felt far more than just a hole inside. He would have felt as if he himself—what made him *Loukas*—had been ripped asunder, leaving him a husk.

"I don't know if I dare go to sleep," I finally admitted. "I'm afraid it's going to happen again. And maybe this time I won't wake up."

He flinched.

There was a long pause of silence. And then, "Well, your grandmother wants you to rest."

My faltering hope that maybe he did understand me, or even cared for me—at least a little—snuffed out. Of course I had been dreaming up a connection that didn't exist; I'd assumed because the first boy I'd ever met had been kind, that maybe *most* people were kind, deep down. Or deep, *deep* down, in Loukas's case. And maybe they didn't show it the same way, leading me to ignore all the signs that Loukas *didn't*—

"But I'm going to go check on Maddok, so if you want to follow me, I can't really stop you," he added, turning on his heel and heading back the way we'd come, leaving me standing in the same spot, baffled.

Why would he leave me there—with no idea where the room I didn't even want to go to was located—and tell me he'd decided to do something else, and with such a strange warning about not being able to stop me if I—

Oh.

Loukas had already turned the corner when I lurched forward, stumbling in my effort to follow him. I caught sight of him heading down a flight of stairs and managed to catch up to him as he hit the bottom step.

He didn't look over at me, but I swear one corner of his mouth twitched as I panted at his side, my hand pressed into the stitch below my lungs from having to nearly run. Even now, his long legs ate up the floor so I had to take two quick steps for every one of his.

"Why didn't you just say I could come with you if I didn't want to lie down? Are you afraid of upsetting my grandmother by going against her wishes?"

Loukas finally glanced over at me, his eyebrows lifted. "You're very direct, aren't you?"

"Is that bad?" My neck flushed. Of course it was. Yet another social mistake, because no one had ever had the time to teach me how to act or what to say or how *not* to make a fool of myself when I was only lucid for such brief periods of time.

"No," he said. "It's . . . different. Much like you, I suppose."

The flush crept up higher, warming my cheeks. In my experience, different wasn't a good thing. My mother had avoided me most of my life because of it; the townspeople in Gateskeep had tried to have me killed. Now the thing that had made me different in Vamala was gone, but I was here in the Paladin world, different once again. The only person who had always treated me the same, no matter what, was Zuhra.

And not only had I lied to her and hidden the truth of what I was enduring from her, I'd lost her, yet again.

Regret, sharp as needles, barbed my heart. Grandmother had seemed surprised I hadn't pushed to get back to Zuhra. I wanted to—oh, how I did. But I knew that I wasn't the priority. Stopping Barloc was.

"Do you ever wish you *weren't* different?" I asked.

"Excuse me?"

"You're a Paladin . . . but not like the others. I've seen how they look at you. Have you ever wished you were the same as the rest of them?"

He didn't answer, his strides growing even longer. I had to break into a jog to keep up.

Maybe I'd been wrong to think we had anything in common—or to dare ask him about it.

We came to a large, heavy door, and Loukas reached for the handle, but then paused and turned back to me.

"Yes," he said at last, his green eyes unflinching on mine, fire-bright and intense, and for some reason my breath hitched in my throat.

Say something . . . an*ything* . . . but I couldn't make my mouth open. And he just looked and *looked,* fierce and haunted and exposed.

"I'm sorry," I finally managed, my voice high and tight.

A shadow flickered over his face, there and gone again. "When your sister was here I heard her say that your mother was afraid of you, that she didn't even want to be around you."

I winced, his words digging into an old wound that I had buried over the last few weeks. She'd changed, even before I'd lost my power. She'd spoken to me, had been attentive—loving, even. But a lifetime of hurt still festered, underneath the hasty patch of her recent kindnesses I'd forced over it.

"My parents were both afraid of me," he continued, his eyes still on mine. "When I was born with green eyes . . . when I could force them to do what I wanted as a child." A muscle in his jaw clenched and unclenched. "I didn't do it on purpose; it was before I learned how to control my ability. But they were so scared, they would try to lock me in my room—until I'd get upset and shout for them to let me out, inadvertently using my power on them to *make* them do it. I never had any friends. Not until I met Raidyn and Sharmaine. So, yes, I spent a lot of hours wishing I wasn't different. But, you know what? It's who I am, whether it means people are frightened of me or not. Even if I *could,* I wouldn't change anything." The fire in Loukas's eyes burned even brighter. "And neither would you."

I stared up at him, horrified to think of what his parents had done to him. "You don't know that."

"Yes, I do. Why else were you willing to risk so much to get your power back? Even though it made you different and caused you pain, without it, you don't know who you are anymore."

"It's because I'll die without it," I insisted, not wanting to admit that he was right. This connection, this understanding, was exactly what I'd been searching for, but for some reason, I was frightened. Frightened of what it meant for him to read me so well, so quickly—and frightened of how his understanding made me feel. Exposed and raw and strangely out of control, as though we were back on Maddok, spinning, diving headlong through a blinding fog to a destination I couldn't see.

He turned away as if he hadn't heard me, opened the door, and stepped outside.

After a pause, I followed Loukas into the cool night air. A freezing wave crashed over me, as cold as the water trapped beneath a layer of ice in the winter, but it came from *within.* From the emptiness that grew stronger every hour.

I'd begged him to help me go after Barloc to *save my life,* to rescue Zuhra and Raidyn from that terrible day when they would use every ounce of power they both possessed and still watch me die.

But his words burrowed beneath my skin, itchy and insistent. How had he known the truth—that without my power, I wasn't sure I *wanted* to fight against that emptiness?

I stayed half a step back from him as we crossed the dark field, the sky above an endless black expanse, the stars swallowed up by thick, heavy clouds.

Loukas glanced over his shoulder at me. "When we go in the stable, make sure you stay right by me. Gryphons can sense if you are a Paladin or not, and since your power is gone, they might think you're an enemy and attack."

"What?" I grabbed his arm, yanking him to a stop. "Why are you only telling me this *now*? After one of the gryphons I've been around for days could have attacked me at any time?"

He stared down at me solemnly. It was that same little twitch at the corner of his mouth that gave him away.

"Oh." I released his arm, my stomach clenching, hot and angry. "You are disparaging my ignorance."

He glanced down at the wrinkled sleeve my grip had left behind and then back up at me, with eyebrows lifted. "I'm not *disparaging* anything. I was *teasing* you."

I glared at him. "I'm not certain I understand."

"You don't know what it means to tease?"

I shook my head, forcing down my embarrassment. *I don't care what you think*. I didn't dare say the words, but I did stand a little straighter.

"It's usually an attempt to make someone laugh."

"You thought to make me laugh by *frightening* me?"

Loukas's mouth turned down. "I assumed you would know I wasn't being serious, since you have been around Maddok for days without a problem." He began walking toward the stables again, more slowly this time. "They won't harm you—even if you aren't a Paladin."

"I don't know if I should believe you or not."

He shot me a wordless glance.

When we reached the stables, he pulled the door open and gestured for me to go in first. Inside, the wide walkways were dimly lit by glowing blue orbs hung in glass containers at even intervals on the walls. There was rustling and the occasional huff of air from the massive stalls we passed. I stayed in the center of the aisle, as far away from the openings on either side of me where the gryphons could push their heads out if they wanted to. They all stayed empty, their occupants most likely sleeping, except for down the row, where one gryphon stretched his neck out as far as it could go and let out a little caw.

"He's happy to see you," I remarked.

Loukas didn't respond, but his strides lengthened again, so he reached Maddok in a matter of moments. I stayed back, afraid to interrupt their reunion. Loukas was so often aloof, gruff, or ill-tempered; but with his gryphon, he was softer, gentle even. He reached up and ruffled the dark feathers along Maddok's neck. Maddok butted his beak into Loukas's chest, eliciting a low laugh from him. He said something in Paladin to the gryphon, his tone similar to what he had explained as "teasing."

Rider and gryphon shared a bond that was real. Watching them together twisted something inside me, knife-hot and painful.

It made me miss my sister.

She was the only one I knew who loved me for me, just as I was, whether I had Paladin power or not, with no magical bonds to influence her.

A soft, sad keen came from behind me, and I turned to see a gryphon two stalls away, looking at me with gentle umber eyes. I wasn't sure why or how, but I knew, in some visceral way, that this creature was grieving. Sorrow clung to her, bowing her head low where it hung heavily over the doorway.

I moved toward her, hesitant and unsure; but something about her called me to her side. I wasn't even certain why I knew it was a she—I just *did*. The closer I got, the harder my heart thrummed in my chest. But she merely lifted her head a bit, a spark of what I could only describe as hope gleaming in her eyes when I got close enough for her to stretch her neck out and gently bump her beak into my sternum, as I'd seen other gryphons do to their Riders. Somehow nervous and certain all at once, I reached up and ran my hand over her soft neck feathers that were the color of wheat. She hooted softly and lifted her head up to look straight into my eyes.

Then she bent forward and bit my shoulder, so hard it drew blood.

"Ouch!" I cried, jumping back, shocked and dismayed. I grabbed my throbbing shoulder and glared at her accusingly. She hooted softly again, but she seemed excited, her feathers ruffled and her eyes twice as bright as when I'd first noticed her.

"Well, *that's* unexpected."

I jumped again and spun to see Loukas standing only a few feet away, hands back in his pockets, but his eyes wide, eyebrows raised.

"Why did she *hurt* me? I was just trying to comfort her."

"She wasn't hurting you," Loukas said, continuing before I could show him the blood on my hand as proof, "she was *marking* you."

My protest died on my lips. "Marking me?" I asked instead, baffled.

"Yes." Loukas stared at the gryphon, not me. "She just chose you as her Rider."

THIRTY-FIVE

Zuhra

It only took a few minutes to wake everyone up and convince them I was healed enough to continue on. Though no one spoke of it, the ghosts of my sister and Loukas hovered over us all. Mother and Father both had dark circles beneath their eyes, visible even at night as they quietly rolled up their blankets and tied them on the back of Taavi's saddle. Though Halvor was technically healed, he looked terrible as he climbed back on Keko, in front of Sharmaine. He'd always been thin, but now he looked hollowed out, his cheeks sunken in, his eyes lifeless, the color of dust. Even Sharmaine was worse for the wear, her normally porcelain skin sallow and her hair tied back in a limp braid.

We took off, the three remaining gryphons well rested after having to wait for me to heal. Their wings beat strong and fast; flying as quickly as they were able, back the way we'd come only a few days ago, so full of hope that we would succeed in stopping Barloc.

I still couldn't let myself fully think about what had happened. If I tried to face it straight on, the pain would have consumed me, so my mind skipped over the edges of those memories, blurring them, darting across the horror of it, like a stone skipping over water, barely touching the surface of those awful few minutes when we'd tried to reach Inara and Loukas in time—

And failed.

Raidyn's arms were secure around me, his body warm and

solid behind my back. I leaned into him, forced myself to focus on the living, breathing reality of him, or staring at the horizon—*anything* to keep myself from falling apart.

When the citadel finally came into view, a few hours after another shorter stop, my lungs constricted. We were returning home—but it would never feel like home again. Not without Inara. I could barely stand the thought of facing her gardens and orchards without her.

Or telling Sami what had happened.

My eyes stung as the gryphons wearily winged their way up the mountain, the hedge growing ever larger. But the closer we got, the clearer it became that something was terribly wrong.

"Is that smoke?" I squinted, not sure I could trust my eyes.

Raidyn tensed behind me. "I think so."

I couldn't tell if the thin, black tendril winding lazily up toward the cloudless sky was from the grounds or the citadel itself. It was either the very end of a fire or the beginnings of one. Part of me wanted to tell Raidyn to turn around, to go somewhere else—*anywhere* else. I wasn't sure I could handle any more tragedy. But I kept my mouth closed, my heart in my throat, choking me with fear.

Those last few minutes to reach the hedge seemed longer than the entire flight combined, somehow. Why did such dread fill me? Surely nothing that awaited us could be worse than what we'd just gone through.

We soared over the hedge, and I realized the smoke was coming from *within* the citadel—through the broken window in the Hall of Miracles.

Perhaps the horrors were just beginning.

The gryphons tossed their heads in agitation, their beaks clacking as they touched down in the courtyard. It was eerily silent. I hadn't expected Sachiel and the others to be watching for us and come out and greet us . . . but there was a quality to the silence, a *heaviness,* that pressed in, making the absence of sound ominous and *wrong.*

"You all stay here. I'm going to go—"

Before Father could finish his sentence, a soul-rending shriek rent the air. Naiki shuddered, straining against the reins, but stayed still when Raidyn pulled them back, forcing her head down.

I twisted in the direction of the scream and wished I hadn't.

A body dangled from the broken window of the Hall of Miracles, barely visible from where we had landed. Bloodied and torn, the only way to recognize her was the long braid down the back of her shaved head.

"Sachiel!" My father's shout was thunderous.

He grabbed my mother around the waist, roughly set her down, kicked his heels into Taavi's side, and took off.

Sachiel turned her head toward us, and even from this distance, sorrow was visible on her gore-splattered face. She hung on to the edge of the broken window, her body twisting over the thousand-foot drop to the bottom of the waterfall far, far below.

Every beat of Taavi's wings was matched by the thudding of my heart, slamming against my ribcage. The gryphon shot through the sky, with an ear-splitting shriek.

A bellow sounded from within the citadel, and Sachiel's head snapped back up.

Father bent over Taavi's neck, urging the gryphon even faster.

But it wasn't enough.

A monster—a rakasa—appeared in the broken window, and slashed at Sachiel's already-battered body. Claws ripped through flesh and bone, and seconds before Father would have reached her, she fell.

Her scream echoed across the peaks that stood as silent witness to the horrors that had happened here. Her arms flailed, her braid floated up into the air, above her head, and then she dropped out of sight.

Father yanked back on Taavi's reins, barely stopping him from soaring within range of the monster's reach, and instead sent him into a nosedive, plummeting after Sachiel.

My heart pounded once, twice, and then they also disappeared from sight.

The monster loosed a horrific roar, so loud it reverberated through my body. Naiki shuddered beneath us.

Before I even realized what he was doing, Raidyn had pressed a kiss to my forehead, and then grabbed me around the waist and yanked me from Naiki's back, setting me on the ground beside my mother. I stumbled and barely caught my balance as Naiki took off, Raidyn's veins already filling with the glow of his power—power that was most likely still depleted from healing me the day before.

"No! *Raidyn!*"

But my cry was whipped away by the wind from Naiki's beating wings.

"Shar—help him!" I shouted, spinning to face the last gryphon.

Halvor was already climbing off Keko's back. Shar's veins lit with her power. Her fire-bright eyes met mine and she nodded. Then Keko leapt forward, her wings spreading as she chased after Naiki, the two Paladin going to face down the rakasa in the Hall of Miracles.

"Where are the rest of them?"

I barely heard Mother's question, as I stared at Raidyn and Sharmaine, waiting to make sure they were able to kill the rakasa and return to us safely.

"Zuhra"—she grabbed my arm, yanking me around to face her—"where are the other Paladin? And the gryphons?" Her face was winter-snow white beneath the sunburnt cheeks and nose, her lips bloodless.

Another growl sounded, not nearly as loud as the first, but much, *much* closer.

We both whirled to the citadel.

Something moved in the shadowed entryway visible through the still-ruined front door, where Barloc had blasted his way out.

Panic, hot as boiling water, surged into my blood, scalding and useless. *I* was useless. An enhancer, with no true power of my own.

We were weaponless, defenseless, easy prey for whatever stalked forward with another throaty growl.

I tried to open my mouth to scream for help, but my jaw refused to obey, clamped shut. Every muscle in my body clenched; the terror coursing through me had turned my muscles into stone, except for where Mother's hand, still on my bicep, trembled so badly, it made my whole arm shake.

When the monster stalked forward into the light, even my heart seized with horror.

My brain supplied the name from that forbidden book I'd hoarded for so long, as if it were detached completely from the terror coursing through the rest of my body.

Chimera. Head of a lion, body of a goat, tail of a serpent. Breathes fire.

Mother's nails dug so deep into my arm, pain shot down into my hand before my fingers began to go numb.

The beast moved toward us slowly, purposefully, its yellow eyes vicious, intelligent. It knew we were two little mice, caught by a very, *very* large cat.

We would not escape.

A black tongue darted out, curling over fangs so long, they were visible even with its mouth closed.

Mother slowly began to back up, somehow mustering the strength in her small body to drag me with her. The beast made no move to speed up, enjoying our terror, licking our fear out of the air and savoring it as an appetizer.

My gaze darted to the sky, where Raidyn and Sharmaine's gryphons hovered, their backs to us, barely out of reach of the rakasa in the hall, sending blasts of Paladin fire at it.

They wouldn't see us, couldn't save us.

The Chimera watched as we continued to scramble away—desperate, *hopeless*—its massive clawed paws sending little puffs of dust up into the air with each deliberate step. Soon we would run into the hedge and there would be nowhere else to go—nothing else to do except await our doom. I hoped it would burn us to death, praying that was a faster way to go than if it decided to truly treat us like a cat with mice and play with its food before devouring it.

Mother and I reached the fat, heavy leaves of the hedge at the same moment, both of us slamming to a halt when our arms brushed the vines. It fluttered behind us, but didn't open. Even if it had, I didn't think we were anywhere near the gate.

There was no escape.

The Chimera's throat vibrated with another rumbling snarl. An eager, hungry noise that sent a shiver of dread through me.

"I'm sorry, Mama," I whispered, reaching for her hand and clutching it in mine.

"I am the one who should apologize, my sweet girl." She squeezed back, so hard, as if she were trying to force the truth of her words into me through the strength of her grip.

The Chimera's serpentine tail swished back and forth. It was close enough now that I could smell it, the reek of putrid meat. Its maw was stained with blood—wet, fresh blood. It had already feasted somewhere inside this citadel.

"I love you, Zuhra. I hope you know that."

"I love you too."

Fingers intertwined, shoulder to shoulder, we faced our doom together, words that should have been said so long ago, at last given voice, here at the end.

A bellow—a *human* roar—sounded from our right, shocking all three of us, including the Chimera, into swiveling toward it.

Halvor.

In my terror, I'd forgotten about him. He held a large branch like a sword, wielding it like it could possibly do *anything* to stop the beast that had halted, its head cocked, inspecting this new prospect for prey.

No. No. *No!*

But the words stuck in my throat, turning to ash in my mouth. I was a coward, too afraid to draw the Chimera's focus back to me and my mother.

"Go!" Halvor shouted, his eyes never wavering from the Chimera's, though tears rolled down his cheeks. "Get away while you can!"

Something in my chest caved in when the beast changed course, swinging its leonine head toward Halvor, a feral roar rumbling up from its throat.

"Go!" he shouted again. "And if you ever do find Inara—if she survived—tell her I love her!"

Then he charged at the monster.

My scream was drowned out by the horrific roar the Chimera loosed, making the earth shake beneath our feet. Mother took the hand I still gripped and yanked me the opposite direction of the Chimera. I let her force my feet to break into a run, but I looked over my shoulder as the Chimera leapt forward, its jaw opening and a stream of flames erupting out, enveloping Halvor in fire.

"NO!" I stumbled, my knees slamming into the earth.

"Get up, Zuhra! Don't let his sacrifice be for nothing!"

The world blurred as she dragged me back to my feet, jerking my arm so hard, something in my shoulder popped. I couldn't look back again, couldn't bear to see the Chimera slaughter my friend.

Mother cut through Inara's garden, toward the citadel. Where did she think we could go? We were trapped, surrounded on all sides by death and hopelessness. Each step was only prolonging the inevitable. Any moment now the Chimera would come for us, after it finished with Halvor.

He'd bought us a few precious seconds, but for what?

"Raidyn! Sharmaine!" Mother's yell rose above the carnage in the courtyard.

I glanced up, not even daring to hope they'd hear—or have enough power left to save us.

But neither of them responded as another roar echoed above us from the hall, and behind us, halfway across the courtyard, an answering one sounded.

Mother shouted for them again.

I turned to see the Chimera facing us once more. But this time, it didn't stalk forward—it *charged* toward us, tendrils of smoke curling up from its bloody maw.

THIRTY-SIX

Inara

The gryphon, whose name I didn't even know, ducked her head, as if she were a little bit bashful after "marking" me.

"Why did you walk over to her?" Loukas asked, his gaze moving to me.

"I . . . I'm not sure." I rubbed the wound on my shoulder; I could feel my heartbeat pulsing in the cut she'd given me through my blouse. "She seemed . . . sad. I felt like I needed to comfort her. Like she needed me." Even as I said it, I realized how ridiculous I sounded.

When Loukas just continued to look at me, without responding, my cheeks grew warm.

The wide door at the end of the hallway slid open and we both turned to see Ederra striding toward us.

"I thought I told you to take my granddaughter to a room where she could rest," she said without preamble.

"He tried, but I—"

"What happened to your shoulder?" She cut me off, her eyes going to the bloody, torn shirt.

"Er . . ."

"This gryphon marked her," Loukas supplied, as though he were commenting on the weather. But there was a tenseness to his stance, a tightness in the way he held his shoulders, that led me to believe he wasn't as nonchalant as he seemed.

"You must be mistaken." Ederra looked sharply at the gryphon. "Sukhi's Rider only died two days ago. For her to choose a new one so fast . . . and a *powerless* one, at that . . . It's unheard of."

"And yet, she has both chosen a new Rider two days later, and a *powerless* one at that." Loukas lifted one eyebrow, his voice a tad sharper.

Sukhi. My gryphon's name was Sukhi.

It took half a heartbeat to realize I already thought of her as mine.

Ederra turned her burning gaze on Loukas, her eyes narrowing.

Sukhi suddenly cawed, drawing all of our attention before Ederra could deliver whatever scalding statement she'd been about to make. The gryphon lifted her head up and down twice, short, jerky motions, visibly agitated.

"Sukhi, what is it?" I stepped forward, lifted my arm to try to calm her, and—

Pain exploded in the patched-up void beneath my heart.

I staggered backward, hands clutched to my sternum. Distant voices echoed dully, murky and indecipherable through the pounding of my heart and the darkness that spilled out from within me, like blood pouring from a wound. This time was different; it was sudden and vicious. I dropped to my knees, barely able to draw breath.

Hands grasped my shoulders before I collapsed. An arm slid beneath my knees, and another behind my back. The ground fell away.

Sukhi's agonized keen cut through the chaos in my head, clearing my mind enough to find her umber eyes in the dim stables as Loukas lifted me into his arms, cradling me against his chest, as though I were a child . . . or something precious and fragile.

"She needs healers—immediately."

Loukas's voice was a low rumble against my cheek where it rested on his soft shirt. I bounced in his arms; it took two laborious breaths to realize he was running. The pain came in waves that broke over me, pulling me under the darkness, sweeping away all awareness of my surroundings, until it ebbed away again.

The respites lasted in small spurts of cognizance; flashes of sensation and sight—the sound of Loukas's boots slapping against the floor of the castle, a glimpse of the green-fire in his eyes darkened to burning moss, the tendon in his jaw flexed from clenching his teeth, Ederra's voice shouting for a name I didn't recognize, the softness of a bed but a sudden chill replacing the warm security of Loukas's arms.

And in between it all was the roiling, starving darkness, eagerly shredding the healing my sister and Raidyn had sacrificed so much to accomplish, desperate to devour . . . to destroy. And pain. Endless, everlasting pain. It writhed, it clawed, it shredded. Hands pressed against me, pushed me into the soft embrace of the mattress, but everything *hurt* and I needed to escape, I needed it to end.

I needed to end.

More hands, grasping my arms, pushed against my sternum, burning hands—heavy and hot and powerful. But not powerful enough. I felt them try, I felt a presence enter the darkness, but there was too much and not enough; the pulsing black emptiness tore right through the Paladin flame, dousing it as it hemorrhaged out into my body, my mind, my heart.

I tumbled into the bottomless abyss, falling and falling and falling, where no Paladin power on earth could find me.

THIRTY-SEVEN

Zuhra

Mother's screams grew even more desperate.

The Chimera's paws pounded against the ground as it leapt forward.

Time slowed, narrowing those last few seconds before inevitable death reached us into a strange montage of details:

The scent of Inara's orchard, crisp apples and green leaves and the musk of earth.

The beating of my pulse against the too-thin skin of my neck.

The softness of my mother's hand that still gripped mine.

The heat as the Chimera's jaws gaped open, wider than should have been physically possible, so wide, I could *see* the flames gathering in the back of its throat.

My final exhale, my chest collapsing as the last air I would ever breathe escaped.

The flames exploded out of its mouth. The heat hit me before they did—

Something crashed into me, slamming me and my mother into the ground, sending us rolling in a tangle of legs and arms and heads slamming hard, dry dirt as the stream of fire soared overhead, so close, the pungent scent of singed skin and hair burned my nose.

A shriek split the air, simultaneous to a roar that made the earth tremble beneath my body. Instinctually, I curled into a ball, pulling my knees into my chest and covering my head with my arms.

"Zuhra—get up!" a voice I'd believed I'd never hear again shouted, and then his hand closed over my bicep, pulling my arms away from my face, yanking me to my feet. I stared at Raidyn's sweaty, dirt-streaked face for a split second before he shoved me toward the hedge. "Go! *Run!*" He spun away from me, lifting his still-glowing arms, though the fire in his veins was so weak, it barely lit them up at all.

Mother dashed back the way we'd come, toward the hedge.

Naiki hovered above the Chimera, talons bloody; the beast's back was ripped into shreds. But it spun toward her, its mouth glowing orange once more. Sharmaine sent a blast of Paladin fire from Keko's back, but it barely even made the monster flinch. She was too weak. They were both too weak.

I didn't run away.

I ran *to* Raidyn and clamped my hands onto his raised arm once more.

Just as it had at the river, fire exploded through my veins, scalding its way through my body before draining out of me into Raidyn. But unlike at the river, I felt him trembling beneath my touch, his lack of strength struck a frigid bolt into the core of my power, almost extinguishing it. Instead, I pushed my strength forward, willing my energy to fill his body with the ability to stop the Chimera before it killed Naiki, Sharmaine, Keko—and us.

With a bellow that scraped at the dredges of his very soul, Raidyn gathered my power into his and sent one final blast at the Chimera the same instant it released its own fire at Naiki.

The gryphon dodged the attack as our stream of fire exploded into the rakasa. The monster loosed an unearthly howl, but it cut off as our combined power tore through its body, obliterating the beast in seconds, turning it to harmless smoke and ash.

The instant the threat was gone, Raidyn yanked his arm away from me, breaking our contact. My power reeled back, slamming into me with such force, I was knocked to the ground, stars spotting my vision.

I lay on my back for a long moment, forcing myself to breathe, pushing away the whirling abyss that darkened the edges of my sight. But I didn't black out. Dirt and rocks cut into my skin as I rose to my elbows. Raidyn staggered toward Naiki, who landed and bounded for her Rider, her normally bright eyes wild. She cawed at him when he collided with her breast, his arms rising up to encircle her torso. The gryphon dropped her head, tucking him under her neck.

Though the air was still sticky with heat, a shiver scraped down my spine as I watched their reunion—one they'd come far too close to losing. If I'd listened to him—if I'd run away . . . My mind darted away from the horrors that would have occurred.

My entire body ached with exhaustion. It felt as though I had been yanked apart, every drop of energy rung out of me.

Keko landed beside them, but Sharmaine didn't dismount; she bent forward and buried her face in her gryphon's neck, her entire body shaking with sobs the feathers couldn't quite muffle.

Raidyn pulled back from Naiki and immediately turned to me. I wanted to go to him, but when I tried to stand, my legs buckled, forcing me to my knees. He half ran, half stumbled to where I waited, dropping so he knelt in front of me and gathered me into his arms.

"You stubborn, frustrating, amazing girl," he mumbled into my hair, one hand cupping the back of my head and the other wrapped around my body, clutching me to him.

I clung to him with any last bit of strength I possessed, but there was so little, he had to hold me up. I sagged into his embrace, hot tears streaking down my cheeks. Tears of relief, of lingering terror, of grief . . . and guilt.

I hadn't dared look to where I'd last seen Halvor. I didn't know if I could bear to face whatever awaited us there. I'd thought his sacrifice worthless—that it had only delayed the inevitable. But he'd ended up saving our lives by giving his. And now, if my sister miraculously still lived and if we somehow got her back . . . she would return to find out he was gone.

But if she, too, was gone, perhaps they were reunited now, in the Light.

I didn't know it was possible to feel sorrow in such an acute, horrific way—as though the very fibers of my body were compressed by my grief, my tears wrung out from muscle and bone and my feeble heart.

"It's all right, Zuhra. We're safe, for now." Raidyn stroked my hair with one hand.

I tried to catch my breath long enough to explain, but the sobs ravaged through me. Tears for Halvor *and* for Inara, who I hadn't let myself grieve for yet.

Then a half-choked cry came from behind us. I twisted in Raidyn's arms, scanning the courtyard. Mother hovered halfway between the hedge and where we knelt together, eyes wide and hands on her mouth, staring at a spot just over our heads.

We both turned as one and gasped when Taavi laboriously flew over the hedge, struggling beneath the weight of two full-grown adults—one of whom was lying across Father's lap, her mutilated arms swinging limply beside her blood-streaked braid.

Sachiel.

Father shouted, "She's still alive—but just barely! We need to heal her right away!"

But, as Taavi landed and he took in the scene in the courtyard—including my mother running toward him—his urgency transmuted into fear.

"What happened here?" His eyes widened at the charred earth where ashes still fluttered up into the air, lifted by the breeze, and then his gaze flickered over all of us. "Where's Halvor?"

Raidyn stiffened and pulled back, glancing around sharply as if just realizing the other young man was missing. And then he looked to me, a terrible understanding darkening his face.

I couldn't speak.

Mother was the one who finally said, "He's gone."

THIRTY-EIGHT

Inara

Inara.

Inara.

Inara.

I was pain. I was lost. I was darkness.

That's what I was.

What I was.

What was I?

Inara.

Daughter.

Inara.

Sister.

Inara.

Monster.

Inara.

Healer.

Inara.

Ray of Light.

Inara.

The night I was born, the stars died and were reborn in my eyes.

Inara.

The night I was born, a power entered the world strong enough to steal my father, to steal my mother, to open a gateway.

Inara.

I was no longer light.

I was darkness and darkness was me.

Empty, void, barren, and bereft.

The stars giveth and the stars taketh away.

You are not darkness.

In the abyss, a quiet but beautiful voice, sound made entirely of light.

You are *light, Inara. You are brave and true, Daughter.*

The light was so pure, so powerful, it banished the darkness entirely; it completely filled the void, until I couldn't even remember what emptiness had felt like.

From this place I came into the world—the first, the Mother of all Paladin. And from this place you shall be reborn, Daughter. Darkness threatens the world of man and Paladin alike. Use the light well. Fulfill the purpose of this gift given to you, pure of heart and soul.

The light expanded and expanded, not only filling the void, but filling *me*. Every bone, every muscle, every fiber and cell. An endless, eternal light that was only partially power and fire and healing and minds. This light was far greater than anything I had ever imagined; it connected every life form, no matter how big or small, in this world and every other—extending even beyond this existence into the afterlife.

I saw the brightness and shape of the souls closest to me first: my grandmother, so full of pain and grief, but also an aching hope and wish for another chance; Loukas, who had hardened himself against all those who had hurt him repeatedly, who loved fiercely but with fear, whose heart was shattered beneath the veneer of indifference he presented to the world; and others, *so many,* my awareness traveling out, out, *out,* flying over land and sea and barriers between worlds, thinner than I'd ever dreamed possible, the light carrying me on its wings. Taking me to my sister, to my parents, and Halvor—even to Barloc, who burned with the power of too many, whose mind had been shaped into anger and hatred and vengeance—and loneliness—by others who'd carried those things with them from one world into the next. I felt acutely his desire to belong somewhere; to use the power he had amassed to find those he believed to be his real family, here in Visimperum, and then, with them, bring suffering to the humans who had scorned and eventually murdered his grandfather. Who had shunned *him*.

Instead of disgust or hatred, I felt only pity and sorrow for him.

I saw as she did, I felt as she felt, as her light went far beyond *filling* me—it encompassed and enlightened and connected. I realized for the first time the finite fragility of our lives, how easily they could be severed—but also the joy of reunion in the life to come, the peace of release and rest. Such peace that I longed to be taken there, to my *true* home, rather than sent back to the broken one I inhabited, so full of pain and sorrow. The feeling that came in response was no longer words, but I understood it the same as if it had been.

Not yet.

And then the light began to recede, reeling me back into my body, unspooling from my soul. But it left a kernel behind, a bright, pulsing thing that more than healed the hole inside me.

Who am I?

I am Inara.

I will *be a Ray of Light.*

I woke in a bed, softer than anything I'd ever slept on. I let my eyes remain shut, relishing sensation. Silken sheets on my skin. A cool, fresh breeze drifting across my face. A warm hand holding mine. And inside my breast, beneath the stunning joy of a beating heart, that pulsing, beautiful light. The gift from the Mother of all Paladin. Warmth and wholeness and *rightness*—again and at last.

I inhaled soft and slow, noticing a hint of lemon and mint, and opened my eyes.

A head was bent over the hand that clasped mine, his dark hair damp; when I turned toward him, the scent of lemons and mint grew stronger.

Though a part of me was surprised Loukas sat at my bedside, another part wasn't. When I was in the light and felt his pain, I'd been given the sacred chance to see his heart—his *true* heart. In that moment, I'd felt *something*—unlike anything I'd ever felt before, except for my sister. Something so encompassing and deep, it frightened me now in the stark light of day.

I didn't know what the tenderness that flooded me for Loukas meant for me and Halvor. How could my heart contain such hope and such confusion and pain all at once?

"Louk," I said, quiet, hesitant.

He startled and looked up, his hand flexing on mine, his green-fire eyes flaring bright, despite the shadows that bruised the tender skin beneath them. When our gazes met and held, his eyes widened.

"Inara . . . *your eyes* . . . they're . . ."

I didn't have to look in a mirror to see that they glowed with Paladin fire again. I already knew my power had been returned to me. I couldn't keep from smiling. "It's back. I can feel it. *All* of it."

I hoped he'd smile back, but instead, his jaw clenched, his eyes flashing. Oh, how I longed for the ability to sense him in that moment, to understand why he looked like he was in pain when I'd expected happiness, or at the very least relief.

"It was a desperate attempt to save your life . . . we hoped it would *heal* you . . . but *this* . . ." He jumped to his feet, pulling his hand from mine, and stalked across the room, his long legs eating up the floor, until he reached the empty hearth, pushing one hand against it as though he wished to crumble the stones, shoving the other through his damp hair repeatedly.

"I don't understand." I sat up in the bed, still in the same clothes as last night. "You seem . . . upset."

He spun to face me, his hair in disarray, his eyes flashing wildly. "You were *dying*, Inara. I failed you. I helped you go after him, but you didn't get your power back and you were dying *right there* in my arms . . . and it was *my* fault. And now you're not only alive, you're . . ." He gestured at me. "You're *Paladin* again somehow. I'm not *upset*, I'm . . . I'm . . ." His teeth snapped shut, and he turned away once more. "We need to get you back home as soon as possible. To your sister and your parents . . . and Halvor."

The name dropped like a boulder catapulted into the room. I didn't know what to say. I didn't know what to do. If we somehow made it back to Vamala, and I saw Halvor again, what would I feel?

Especially after what I'd experienced in the light—what I'd perceived in Loukas. The hurt he held so close, a constant companion, so familiar, I wasn't sure he knew how to survive without the pain imbedded in every beat of his heart. I'd felt the most overpowering desire to help heal Loukas's broken heart . . . Was it because it had hurt *me* so much to feel his pain, to know intimately the suffering he hid so masterfully? Or was it something more?

Fissures of doubt crackled through the certainty I'd felt upon waking.

When Loukas turned back again, he was completely composed, no hint of distress in his demeanor, not even a flicker of emotion in his eyes beyond indifference. "Now that you're apparently healed—better than new, even—you might be interested in knowing there was news last night, before your . . . episode."

"News," I repeated, chilled by the swiftness with which he shut off one of the only true reactions I'd ever witnessed—though he still hadn't been honest with me.

"Not the good kind either, unfortunately."

Before he could expound, the door opened and my grandmother strode into the room, wearing a fresh white blouse, a leather vest, fitted breeches, and leather boots up to her knees. Her hair was scraped back in its familiar bun, her mouth pursed, creating deep grooves around her lips. But when she saw me sitting up, her face lit up.

Then her eyes met mine.

Her eyebrows shot up, her mouth dropping open into a small *O* of shock.

"Y-your eyes . . ." she stammered. I had a feeling she *never* stammered.

"Have you ever heard of the *luxem magnam* doing *that*?" Loukas sauntered over to my grandmother, his head cocked to the side as though he found the return of my power amusing—not life-altering.

I wanted to shout at him, to stand and beat my fists against his chest, to elicit any sort of *genuine* response from him, not this terrible mask he wore with such ease.

Instead, I pulled the sheets back and slid off the bed, facing them both, the stone floor cool on the bottoms of my feet.

"No," Grandmother breathed. "I didn't know such a thing was possible. I knew it could heal if someone was chosen to receive that gift by the light . . . but *this*? To return her power?" She stared and stared. Before what happened in the light, it would have made me uncomfortable, nervous even.

Now, I straightened my shoulders and said, "She spoke to me," keeping my eyes on my grandmother, but I could see Loukas in the periphery of my vision.

Grandmother hesitated before asking. "Who spoke to you?"

"The Mother of all Paladin. In the light."

Grandmother reeled back, going white as the wall behind her.

Louk froze, the carefully curated insouciance on his face slipping into incredulity before he could smother it.

"She is the one who healed me and gave me my power back."

"That . . . that's not . . ." Louk's mouth opened and shut several times, the fire in his eyes flaring as bright as I'd ever seen it.

"The *Mother of all Paladin*?" Grandmother repeated when words failed him. "As in the *First Paladin,* who was born from the *luxem magnam* a thousand generations ago?"

"Yes," I confirmed. "She said she was the First, the Mother of all Paladin. I heard her voice in my head. And I felt her light. It . . . it was indescribable."

Grandmother pressed her hands to her mouth, eyes gleaming. Then she rushed forward, opening her arms to me and taking me in them, squeezing so tight, the air was forced from my lungs. I held on to her just as tightly, having experienced the sorrow she also held so close, the cracks in her heart that had never healed. When she released me, it was only to draw back enough to lift one hand to press against my cheek.

"Inara . . . my beautiful Ray of Light." When she smiled it was a soft, wistful thing; an expression of awe, but also regret and sorrow. "You must truly have a pure heart to have been given such a gift. I can see now why Zuhra fought so hard to get back to you."

Zuhra. Who probably thought she'd lost me—yet again. Her life force had been very far away, but I'd sensed turmoil, grief, even agony in the brief glimpse I'd been given of her in the light.

"She is the one with a pure heart," I said, thinking of how I'd lied to her, how I'd deceived my whole family to try to steal my power back. I wasn't sure why the light had chosen to give me this gift when I certainly didn't deserve it. "I know you must do what needs to be done for the good of all. But I do hope to get back to her . . . someday."

"Speaking of that," Loukas said. "Has there been any further word on the murders?"

Grandmother winced. I pulled back from her touch, turning to Loukas.

"What murders?"

He leaned against the wall, his expression shuttered once more, his arms folded across his chest. "Five Paladin, all found with their throats ripped out—like wild animals had attacked them."

Ice slicked my veins, turning my blood cold. *"Barloc."*

Five more Paladin? Could his body truly have withstood that much power?

"We don't know it was him for sure," Grandmother protested. "There's still the chance it was a rakasa attack. They were all found in a town that borders their lands. Attacks there are common enough not to rule out."

"You know it was him. And if it's true—if he now wields the power of *eight* Paladin—there is no one who will be able to stop him."

Grandmother ran a weary hand over her face, pressing her fingers to her temples, a gesture I was beginning to recognize as one she used when she was under great stress. "No one could survive that much power."

Though my stomach roiled, and I was nervous to admit it after their reaction to knowing the Mother of all Paladin had spoken to me, I didn't dare withhold the information that could lead us to him in time to stop him from hurting others. "I felt him," I admitted quietly.

"What was that?" Grandmother sputtered.

"When I was in the light . . . I could sense . . . *everyone.*" Trying to explain it out loud made me realize how ridiculous, how *impossible* it sounded. But it had happened, and though I didn't know this world well, I knew the direction of where I'd sensed him. "I recognized him. If you show me a map, I can give you a general idea of where he is. At least, where he was when I was in the light."

Loukas stared at me, a muscle in his jaw tightening. "You felt . . . *everyone*?"

Grandmother's eyebrows lifted again, uncertainty crossing her face, but she only said, "There's a map in the council room. We can go there right now."

I followed her into the hallway, Loukas falling into step behind me.

"What do you mean you *felt* everyone?" he asked again, but I didn't respond, choosing to let him mull that one over for a bit.

Grandmother led us to the same room where the meeting had taken place the night before, though the table and chairs were all empty once more. She marched over to the far wall, where a large map hung.

I came up beside her, examining the drawing, trying to orient myself.

"This is Soluselis," she said, pointing at a large city on the map. "That's where we are."

I stared at the spot she'd pointed at, trying to figure out how to pinpoint where I'd felt Barloc's presence.

"Well?" Loukas prompted from behind us, all impatience and doubt.

"I'm not sure," I admitted, heat creeping up my neck, into my cheeks. "Perhaps if you could take me back to where I was last night when I was in the light, I can point the direction I felt his presence."

"You can *point*?" Loukas scoffed, but Grandmother cut him off.

"That would be helpful—it's better than trying to guess."

We all headed back out into the hallway, but this time we used the connecting hallways that led us into the center of the castle.

As we walked, I felt a *pull,* a presence of sorts, drawing me toward it. So familiar and powerful, even if Grandmother hadn't been walking the direction it came from, I wasn't sure I would have been able to resist it.

Then, up ahead at the end of the hall, I noticed a glow. The pull grew even stronger; it attached to the kernel of light and power inside me, filling me with warmth and a need to hurry, to get to the source of that glow faster. It took all of my willpower to force my feet to walk, not to dash ahead of Grandmother.

When we entered the room, I faltered to a stunned halt. I'd never seen anything so beautiful in my life. Glittering diamond balustrades encircled the center of the room, refracting the light that filled every inch of space with its glow and power. Slowly, reverently, I moved toward the origin of the light, held back from walking straight into it by the diamond railing.

"This is the *luxem magnam.* The birthplace of all Paladin power, where the First Paladin—a male and a female—were born out of the light, each with three gifts of power, thousands of years ago," Grandmother said, her voice hushed. "This is where we brought you last night, in supplication to heal you, when no one else could succeed in saving your life."

Tears welled in my eyes as I stared down at the beautiful, undulating light. The power she'd gifted me pulsed beneath my heart, filling my body with warmth and life. The *luxem magnam* glimmered brighter, as if it recognized me.

"We laid you in the light and prayed for you to be saved. The healers all failed . . . and you were dying. There was nothing else we could do. I never dreamed . . ." Grandmother's glowing Paladin eyes met my own.

"Thank you," I whispered—to her, to Loukas, to the *luxem magnam.* It was insignificant, impossibly inadequate, but it was all I could offer in gratitude for the gift I'd been given.

I held on to the banister, the diamonds cool beneath my hands, and let the light wash over and around me. Grandmother fell quiet, and even Louk stayed silent, as I stood there.

Finally, I forced myself to turn back to her and said, "Where was I when you brought me here?"

"When we laid you in the light, your head was back there, and your feet were here." Grandmother pointed.

"How did you lay me in there, with the banister in the way?"

"Loukas held you and climbed over it."

I noticed a shudder go through Louk out of the corner of my eye.

"Thank you," I repeated, turning to him.

He didn't respond. His face was a mask, but his green eyes gleamed in the rippling light of the *luxem magnam*, searing through me with their intensity. Heat unfurled in my chest, quickly dropping to settle low in my belly, completely different than the warmth from the *luxem magnam* or the power I finally had back; it somehow ached inside me, sending my heart slamming against my ribs.

Unsettled and flustered, I faced the banister once more, willing the coolness from the diamonds to send the unfamiliar sensation away.

"Can you tell us where you felt him?" Grandmother prompted.

I nodded, with a slow exhale to calm my still-pounding heartbeat, unsure why it was continuing to race—or why it had started to in the first place.

"If I was lying that way, then I felt his presence that direction." I pointed across the room.

Grandmother followed where I pointed and her hopeful expression fell.

"That's the direction of Folten," Loukas said, the first words he'd spoken since we'd come to the *luxem magnam*. "Where the bodies were found."

"Yes," Grandmother confirmed, defeated. "It was him, then. As we suspected." She turned to me. "Loukas told us last night that ever since Barloc stole your power, you have a connection with him—that you see flashes of where he is when he uses it. Have you seen anything? Any hint of what he's doing or where he's going?"

My eyes narrowed on him. Why had he shared that without asking if I wished for the Paladin here to know it? He refused to meet my gaze. "No, I haven't seen anything. I'm sorry. I'll tell you if I do."

There was a pause, then Loukas pointed out, "Folten is one of the closest cities to the gateway. It can't be a coincidence that he's there."

Tension rolled off Grandmother in waves, disconcerting and out of place for such a sacred place—a room where peace should have held supreme. "If he can tear portals between our worlds with a Paladin knife and his power, I don't know that it matters where he is in relation to the gateway anymore."

"Unless he's trying to bring others with him. The portal he made only lasted for a few seconds—and the expenditure of the power to do it left him unconscious."

They shared a dark glance, and then without a word, Grandmother strode out of the room. Loukas quickly followed. Though I wished to linger, to absorb more of the healing, comforting light of the *luxem magnam,* I reluctantly hurried after them.

"Didn't a battalion already leave to investigate the bodies?" Loukas was asking.

"Yes, but I'm afraid one battalion won't be enough after all. We need to send as many of our forces as we can spare. He must be stopped."

While Grandmother called together the members of the High Council once more, I asked Loukas if he would take me to see Sukhi. He agreed, but did so with a scowl. I tried not to let his obvious irritation sting.

"What does it mean to be marked by a gryphon?" I asked as we walked back to the stables. It was hard to believe it had only been six or seven hours since I'd collapsed in front of her stall. How could someone change so entirely in such a short time? I'd gone from empty, weak, frightened, and alone, to healed, full of power and hope, even purpose.

He took a few more steps before deigning to respond. "It's how a gryphon picks their Rider. It is an unbreakable bond between the gryphon and the Paladin they choose—one only death can sever. And even then, the survivor will feel the loss tremendously. I've heard it described as having a piece of your soul rent apart."

I thought of how I'd sensed the sorrow within Sukhi last night, how I'd been drawn to her—how I'd felt prompted to comfort her. Had it been because I was meant to be her new Rider? Was that why she'd chosen me so quickly after losing her previous Rider, something Grandmother had been shocked by? The wound she'd given me was healed, presumably by the *luxem magnam,* but a scar remained—a reminder of the bond she'd sealed upon us when she marked me.

"Will you teach me how to be a Rider?"

Loukas stiffened. "I don't know if that's a good idea."

Another unexpected sting. I tried to ignore it. "Why not?"

"It just isn't, all right?"

He lengthened his strides, storming ahead of me.

The fissure of doubt from earlier that morning cracked even wider. I thought we had started to become friends, but it seemed I was mistaken. Though I was afraid I was only inviting him to inflict more hurt upon me, I forced myself to hurry and catch up.

"Louk . . . wait . . ." I managed to reach his side and put my hand on his arm. I'd only been trying to slow him down, but he slammed to a halt and spun to face me, glaring at my fingers on his sleeve. "Are . . . are you mad at me?" I managed, despite the obvious anger on his face.

"What are you playing at, Inara?" he bit out, yanking his arm away, so sharply it startled me.

"I . . . I don't understand . . ."

"I didn't think it possible, but you are even more naïve than your sister was," he spat, and turned to storm up to the stable door, pulling it open with so much force, I was afraid he might rip it clean off its hinges.

I stood there, staring at his retreating back, baffled and embarrassed, unsure if I dared press forward and continue to reach out to him. He obviously wanted nothing to do with me.

A flicker of memory rose unbidden, the pain I'd felt in the light—*his* pain.

Nervous and uncertain, I forced myself to go after him—one last time.

The stable was a different place in the morning. Other Paladin bustled about, leading gryphons from their stalls, or bringing armfuls of dead rodents to them. Loukas was easy to spot, taller than nearly all of them, his dark hair a beacon in the sunshine that gleamed through the skylights and windows—that and the way everyone avoided him, turning their faces away, moving to the other side of the path, creating a wide berth around him. He was surrounded by activity but had never looked so lost and alone as he did standing in front of Maddok's stall, resolutely ignoring them all.

I moved slowly toward him. When I passed Sukhi's stall, she had already pushed her head over the door and clacked her beak at me eagerly.

"Just a second, girl," I murmured, continuing on past her.

I was certain Loukas knew when I walked up to him—I was the only one willing to stand by his side, it seemed—but he refused to acknowledge me, continuing to rub Maddok's neck methodically.

"I'm sorry I upset you," I said.

He ignored me, but a muscle in his jaw jumped as if he'd clenched his teeth.

"Thank you for saving my life," I continued, refusing to be cowed. The old Inara would have been too scared to press on. But something had happened to me in the light, a newfound courage pumped through my veins along with the Paladin power. It wasn't infallible. But it was there, and I clung to it as his fingers curled into fists in Maddok's feathers.

"You want to learn how to be a Rider? Go get a saddle and put it on Sukhi. Meet me out front of the stable."

With that, he opened the door to Maddok's stall, walked in, and slammed it shut on me.

I stood there for a moment before spinning on my heel, in search of a saddle. Perhaps, if we got away from all the other Paladin—if he really was willing to teach me how to ride—I could figure out what I'd done to make him so angry.

* * *

I had to ask another Paladin to help me put the saddle on Sukhi. She'd seemed concerned and a little bit suspicious when I tried to convince her the gryphon had marked me.

"You aren't a Rider," she'd accused. "I've never seen you before."

"She's telling the truth," Loukas had said as he stomped past, Maddok on his heels.

The unknown Paladin had jumped back, out of his path, her eyes widening. But she'd retrieved a saddle for me without another word and told me how to hook the straps around Sukhi's torso. Luckily the gryphon held perfectly still for me. Once I'd double-checked every strap, she followed me out of her stall, then down the pathway to the open doors out of the stable.

"I don't really know what I'm doing," I admitted to her in a whisper, "so try to make this easy for me, all right?"

She hooted softly, butting her beak into my arm as if she actually understood and meant to reassure me.

Loukas stood by Maddok's side, a tall, dark thundercloud waiting to break in the middle of all that lush green grass and brilliant sunshine.

"You managed to do it. I'm impressed." His tone said otherwise, but I smiled sweetly at him as Sukhi and I stopped a few feet away.

"I'm a fast learner. I've had to be."

Something crossed his face, a wisp of some emotion far less caustic than those he'd exhibited so far, but before I could pinpoint what, it was gone.

"If you're going to be a true Rider, you will have to get on and off your gryphon by yourself. No more help from me."

But in typical fashion, he didn't tell me how exactly I was supposed to do that. He merely turned to Maddok, easily climbed into the saddle, and sat there, waiting for me.

I faced Sukhi and whispered, "How do I get on your back?"

She gave me a nudge with her beak. I swallowed and walked around her folded wing to her flank. There was no stirrup, like I'd seen illustrated on a horse, something I'd never thought to miss before now—when Loukas had always given me a boost into the saddle before climbing on behind me. And though Sukhi was a bit smaller than Maddok, she was still enormous, far too tall for me to yank myself up and over her back. Perhaps, if I'd been practicing all my life and had built up the muscle necessary to do it . . .

But I hadn't. So instead, I stood there, staring up at the impossibly high saddle, defeated but refusing to admit it.

Then Sukhi bent her front legs, lowering her body much closer to the earth—and to me.

"Thank you, girl," I murmured, as I easily grabbed onto the edge of the saddle and jumped, so that my stomach landed on the top of the saddle. From there, I pushed myself up and swung my leg over her other side. Once I was seated, I gathered the reins in my hands and held on tightly as she stood back up fully.

"I did it," I announced unnecessarily.

"Cheater." Loukas shook his head, glowering at my gryphon.

But I didn't care. I grinned like a fool at my victory—at *our* victory. We were already working together as a team.

"Now we fly."

"*Now?* You don't have any instructions to give me? There's nothing I should know before we just—"

"Nope," Loukas cut me off. "Experience is the best teacher. At least, that's what my parents told me."

With that, he pushed his heels into Maddok's sides, and the gryphon leapt forward, taking off after just a few bounds across the field, quickly gaining height to miss the hedge that was even bigger than the one at home.

"Well, Sukhi . . . here we go."

I clutched the reins in hands that were suddenly damp, squeezed my legs as tightly as I could, and imitated what he'd done, pushing my heels into her sides.

When she jumped forward, it nearly unseated me, but I managed to cling to her back as she took two more bounds and then leapt into the sky, her wings unfurling and catching the updraft, carrying us off the ground with a swoop in my stomach and a lurch of my heart into my throat.

As the world fell away, and Sukhi's wingbeats turned rhythmic, smoothing out the jerkiness of takeoff, my stomach settled back down where it belonged. My heart still raced—but now it was with exhilaration, with the realization that I was flying *by myself* on *my* gryphon's back. I felt as though I could reach up and brush the sun with my fingertips, letting sunshine drip down my arm and coat my body with its warmth.

I felt invincible.

Loukas and Maddok soared away, over the gleaming rooftops of the city surrounding the castle. I tugged on Sukhi's reins to guide her in the same direction. Once the homes and bustling streets gave way to fields and then forest, he glanced over his shoulder and lifted one eyebrow, his mouth curving into a sly smile.

Then he yanked Maddok's reins and the gryphon cut sharply to the right, so we soared on past them, now heading the wrong direction.

I quickly followed suit, and Sukhi dipped her wing, cutting back to follow after the other pair. The suddenness of the movement took me by surprise, and I slid partially off the saddle with a half-swallowed scream. But I squeezed my legs harder and managed to stay on the gryphon. Pride and irritation beat in equal parts through my blood.

He'd done that on purpose—to test me? Or to lose me?

As soon as he saw us behind him once more, he repeated the maneuver, but to the left—and this time I was prepared for him. I immediately signaled Sukhi, and we chased after them for the next several minutes, as Maddok cut and dove, twisted and then climbed nearly straight up into the sky. I had to press myself flat onto Sukhi's neck, gripping my saddle with every ounce of strength I could muster in my legs to avoid slipping off her back and plummeting to my death in the forest far, far below.

But no matter how badly my muscles trembled, or how slick the sweat on my hands made the reins in my grip, I refused to fail at whatever test this was.

Finally, after yet another nosedive—where Loukas only signaled Maddok to level out mere feet above the treeline, barely giving us a chance to do the same or crash through them—he pulled back on the reins and let the gryphons slow, coasting on the wind that whipped my hair back and stung my eyes.

"Is that all you've got?" I shouted, hoping he couldn't see the way my legs shook, my muscles quaking from strain.

He threw back his head and laughed. A sound of such abandonment, it took me completely by surprise. And despite my irritation with him, I couldn't resist the deep tenor of his laughter and found myself joining in. Sukhi released a piercing caw of triumph.

I'd done it. I'd managed to succeed at every curve and challenge he'd thrown at me.

We'd done it, I corrected myself, reaching down to pat Sukhi's neck.

"There's a stream up ahead where we can let them get a drink," Louk called out to me, pointing.

We followed Maddok, soaring over the treetops until they thinned and then opened into a small clearing where there was indeed a narrow stream, just as he'd promised.

Sukhi landed right after Maddok, but Loukas had already climbed off and stood there, arms folded as Sukhi bent her haunches down once more, so I could get off without having to jump as far. When I landed, my legs wobbled and nearly gave out.

I threw out my arms, but before I could catch myself on Sukhi's body as I'd intended, Loukas was there—just as he'd been that first night in Visimperum by the pond. He grabbed me with both hands, his fingers encircling my waist, so we stood mere inches apart.

A shadow crossed his face. "I pushed you too hard. You're not going to be able to walk tonight—let alone tomorrow."

I stared up at him, the heat of his hands scalding through the thin material of the pants and tunic I wore. Louk's green-fire eyes met mine and held. His fingers flexed against my waist and my breath caught in my throat. Fire raced beneath my skin, hot and heady. My legs trembled, but I wasn't certain if it was still muscle fatigue or something else entirely.

His eyes raked over my face, pausing on my mouth. My heart slammed against my ribs. I'd never felt anything like I did in that moment, as though I were drowning, but in a way that made me never want to surface again, sinking into a forbidden pool of heat and want and need.

"Do you have any idea what it was like?" He finally spoke, low and sharp, his gaze moving back to my eyes. "To think you were going to die in my arms—*knowing* it was my fault?"

"It wasn't—"

"I was *terrified*," he cut right over me, his hands moving farther around my body, to clutch my back, drawing us even closer together. "And *that* scared me more than I've ever been in my entire life. Why did I care so much?" Louk's eyes blazed, one hand stroking up my spine to my neck, before plunging into my hair, tilting my head even farther back. "*Why* do I care *so damn* much?"

I swallowed, staring up at him, unable to speak, hardly even able to breathe. My body burned with a nameless need that was at once foreign and achingly familiar.

"Inara," he murmured, his gaze dropping to my lips again, sending the heat in my limbs pooling in my belly. "Ray of Light. You weren't supposed to happen. *None* of this was supposed to happen."

My mouth parted, but before I could summon the will to speak, his head dropped and his lips crashed down on mine.

My arms had been limp at my side the entire time, but as his mouth moved in ways I hadn't even known were possible, I reached up to grasp onto him, clinging to him as urgently as he gripped me.

When he parted my lips and his tongue delved into my mouth, I moaned, my already-trembling legs almost giving out entirely. Louk's arm tightened around me, crushing my body into his, partially lifting me from the ground so only my toes brushed the earth.

Where the few kisses I'd shared with Halvor had been sweet, tender even, this kiss was as similar to those as the moon's light to that of the sun. Louk's kiss was desperation and need and *demanding,* but also seeking and asking and surrender and *flame,* and it burned through me, searing my soul in a way I hadn't even known was possible.

Fire raced beneath my skin; it coursed through my blood. In his arms, I *was* fire.

A distant corner of my heart whispered that I should end this, that it wasn't fair to Halvor, but then Louk was pulling my shirt from my pants so his hand could skim the bare skin of my back, and any drop of reason left burned away with his heated fingers stroking my spine.

His mouth left mine, moving across my jaw to the sensitive groove just below my ear. He brushed his teeth against the tender skin along my neck, eliciting an involuntary gasp. Louk's fingers skimmed my ribcage, sending a fiery shudder of need through me.

Encouraged by his actions, I imitated what he'd done, tugging at his shirt so I could run my hands up his muscled back. A shiver went through him, his arms impossibly tightening even more around me. An entirely different kind of power rushed through my veins, intoxicating, heady. The power I held to make him respond to *my* touch—to *me.*

I dragged my nails across his skin, and he growled, deep in his throat, moving back up to recapture my lips. I met him kiss for kiss, our mouths crashing and moving together in a dance as urgent as it was insufficient. I wanted more, I never wanted this moment to end—

He suddenly broke away, setting me down and backing up so quickly, I staggered forward a few steps before I managed to regain my balance, my legs still quivering from the flight—and what had just happened between us.

Loukas stared at me, his eyes darkened to evergreen flame, his chest rising and falling.

The breeze from the stream where our gryphons both had laid down to drink and rest cooled the heated rush of my blood, sending a chill skittering over my skin.

"I shouldn't have done that," he said at last, low and gruff.

"Don't," I said. "Don't do this." I took a step toward him, but he backed up, a muscle in his jaw tensing. I halted but refused to look away or back down. "I've never experienced anything like that before in my life—and I would bet you haven't either."

Louk winced, but said, "You mean Halvor never made you moan like that? I can't imagine why not."

"Stop it," I bit out, stalking toward him. He kept backing up as I advanced, but when he reached the bank of the stream, he had to stop or step into the water and soak his boots. "Don't you *dare* do that. Not now, not after *that,* not with me."

"It was just a kiss, Inara. It didn't mean anything."

"Like hell it didn't," I said, repeating a phrase I was pretty sure I wasn't supposed to know, but it felt like the right thing to say in that moment. His eyebrows rose. It struck me as funny that hearing me *curse* was what surprised him after everything else I'd—*we'd*—done.

I stopped mere inches away from him. His chest rose and fell, his muscled shoulders tense, defensive; his shirt was damp, sticking to his sculpted abdomen. Though his expression was guarded, there was a flash of true fear in his eyes, a vulnerability that sank like a hook into my heart, yanking on it—yanking on *me*—until his pain became my own. "When I said I felt everyone . . . I meant it," I said, more softly. "I felt *you,* Louk. I felt *everything.*"

He shook his head, the vulnerability in his eyes chipping away at the mask he wore as if it were truly him—and not what hid *beneath* his façade of indifference. "You . . . you don't know what you're talking about."

I reached up to his face. He flinched, but I persisted, stroking a piece of his dark hair back from his forehead.

"I'm so sorry for the way you've been treated. I'm sorry for the hurt you've had to endure, because of a power you didn't ask for and often wished would go away."

"Stop it." The words scraped out brokenly. *"Please."*

But when I cupped his jaw, he closed his eyes, leaning in to my touch. "I don't know what is between you and Sharmaine"—his eyes flew open again at that—"but if she hasn't been able to see past the façade you present to the world to the amazing heart you have beneath all of that, then she is a fool."

Louk's jaw tightened beneath my hand and his eyes gleamed in the dappled sunlight of the clearing. He stared down at me, his beautiful, haunted gaze raking over my face, his mask stripped away, his pain laid bare.

"I see *you,* Loukas," I whispered, my own vision blurring at the emotion that filled my heart, so unexpected and so powerful, it hurt. "I will *always* see you."

He shook his head again, but instead of arguing, he closed the distance between us—not to kiss me this time, but to wrap his arms around my waist, pulling me against his body, to bury his face in my hair. I clung to him as he shook, a lifetime of hurt and pain breaking free of the iron grasp he'd had to learn to wield against it.

I held him as tightly as I could, as Loukas, the strongest person I'd ever known, broke down into sobs.

THIRTY-NINE

Zuhra

"What do you mean he's gone? What happened to him?" Sharmaine glanced around the courtyard, as if hoping those two words had a different meaning in our language—that he might appear, well and whole, at any moment.

Tell her I love her. His last words before the Chimera attacked him. Before he'd saved us with his sacrifice. The memory was a stab of pain, the knife formed of regret, the blade twisted by guilt. That *I* had survived because *he'd* died.

If she'd been given the choice—which one would Inara have chosen?

I gritted my teeth together, willing the storm of emotions to still.

"That monster . . . it was going to attack us . . ." Mother spoke when I couldn't, her voice thick, her words halting. "He . . . he saved us."

Sharmaine's eyes met mine and the truth she saw in my face was enough; her shoulders sagged as she squeezed her eyes shut with a rough shake of her head.

Raidyn's arm around me tightened, his fingers digging into my shoulder; I wasn't even sure he was aware of doing it, but I didn't say anything. I'd finally managed to stop crying, but I was ravaged by the death and carnage that had taken place, hollowed out by the sudden loss of Halvor.

“Where is everyone else? Where are all the other Paladin? And Sami?” Mother stared at Sachiel’s body still hanging over Father’s lap, her lips bloodless.

A shiver of dread scraped down my spine when no one answered. Surely, if any of the others had survived whatever had happened here, they would have come out by now. I could only pray Sami had gone back to the village.

Mother’s question spurred Father back into action. “I don’t know. But we have to heal Sachiel now—or she isn’t going to make it.”

“I should go help him,” Raidyn said at last, his voice as hollow as my chest.

“You have nothing left to give,” I protested, but he ignored me and hurried to Taavi’s side. Together, he and Father gently lowered Sachiel’s battered body to the ground.

Her wounds were even more horrific up close. Her chest barely moved. My father looked to Raidyn. When their eyes met—and Father noticed how dim the fire in Raidyn’s irises was—his expression fell. “You’re nearly drained.” A comment, not a question, but Raidyn still nodded, miserable and ashamed.

“He stopped the rakasa that attacked Sachiel and saved us from the Chimera,” I defended, walking to where they stood beside Sachiel. “I can help whichever of you has enough left to try.”

Father swiped a hand over his face, leaving a streak of blood on his cheek—Sachiel’s blood. “I’ll do it. But only enough to keep her alive. And”—he looked to me—“you will not help me. We need you to save your stores.”

He didn’t have to explain why. We all glanced to the citadel, where more unknown horrors could await us.

Father knelt beside Sachiel, placed his hands over the worst of her wounds, and closed his eyes. His veins lit, his power racing toward the dying general. Within seconds, his hands began to tremble. The shaking rapidly moved up his arms, until, with a ragged gasp, he yanked his hands away from her, his eyes flying open. Her wounds had stopped bleeding, and some of the more minor ones had closed, but the largest ones remained open and unhealed. "It's the best I could do," he said, panting slightly. "She was almost gone. Anything more would have drained me too."

"It's enough for now." Raidyn placed one steadying hand on Adelric's shoulder.

We all stared at her for several long moments, watching her chest rise and fall.

Then Father shook off Raidyn's hand and stood, his expression grim. "We need to search the citadel, make sure there aren't any more rakasa." He sounded as weary as I felt, like a rope pulled too tight, fraying and about to break.

"I'll go with you," Raidyn said.

I shook my head. If they *did* find anything else inside there, I wasn't sure they would be able to stop the beast. Raidyn was nearly drained, and I wasn't sure my father was much better off after saving Sachiel. "Not unless I go with you too," I said.

When I looked back at Raidyn, he was shirtless, his tanned, muscular body a shock. I glanced past him and my heart constricted at his thoughtfulness; Sachiel's torso and shredded arms were hidden by his shirt, giving her the courtesy of being covered, the severity of her gruesome wounds hidden underneath the soft material.

"No," Father said before Raidyn could respond. "I am not risking losing you too."

"He's nearly drained," I argued. "And so are you. If you *do* find something in there, how do you expect to be able to stop it? It'll kill you both. I'm useless on my own, but if I can add my power to either of yours—then at least we'd have a *chance.*"

"Or no one goes in," Sharmaine interjected. "We stay together and wait. If anything else is in there, it will come out soon enough."

Father and Raidyn shared a glance. I sensed the relief course through Raidyn's body at her suggestion, proof of just how drained he really was.

"What about the gateway?" Father looked up to the ruined window. "We need to find out if it's still open or not. And if anyone else . . ." His voice cracked. "If there are any survivors," he finally managed.

"There's nothing any of us can do about the gateway. Not until we rest and regain our strength," Shar said quietly. "And if there are survivors, let's hope they come out to us. It's not worth risking our lives too."

Sharmaine had a point, but I also understood Father's need to know; if the gateway was shut, then whatever had come through was it. But if it was still open . . . what we'd faced so far was just the beginning.

"Take Taavi and fly up there. If the room is empty, fly in—just long enough to see if the gateway is open or shut. Then come right back."

Father considered my suggestion and then nodded. "All right. I'll hurry."

Mother hurried to his side before he could go to Taavi and grabbed his hand.

"Be careful."

He pressed a swift kiss to her forehead. "I will."

We watched as he climbed on Taavi's back and the gryphon took off once more.

Within seconds, they hovered near the shattered window to the Hall of Miracles, and then they swooped through it, disappearing inside the citadel.

Mother came over to stand next to me and Raidyn, reaching out to clasp my hand. Sharmaine stayed on Keko, tense and alert. We were silent, frozen with dread, waiting . . . and waiting.

This is taking too long.

I didn't dare speak the words out loud, but Mother's hand tightened around mine as though I had.

After another breath-stealing minute passed without any sign of my father, Raidyn shook his head.

"Something's wrong. I'm going to go up there."

I grabbed his arm before he could walk away, our eyes meeting and holding. "Please—don't go. Stay here. If something *did* happen to him—"

"There he is!" Sharmaine shouted.

We both spun to see Taavi emerging through the broken window, Father seemingly unharmed on his back.

Mother sagged with relief beside me, her fingers going slack on mine.

Taavi dove for the ground and landed with a thud only a few feet away. Father was pale but otherwise safe. Mother rushed to Taavi's side, but Father merely sat there, staring at the ground.

"Adelric?" Mother gently touched his knee; he startled as if he'd forgotten the rest of us were there.

When Father looked up, his cheeks were streaked with tears, cutting tracks through the dust and grime on his face. I reached for Raidyn's hand, his fingers flexed back around mine.

"The gateway is closed," he said, his words toneless, no hint of relief on his face, his normally bright eyes dulled. "But it was too late." His voice cracked; he stopped, his gaze dropping back to the ground.

I wanted to slam my hands over my ears, to keep him from continuing, wishing I could stop him from saying anything else.

But I already knew wishes were as useless as I was beginning to believe hope to be. With a strangled noise that I realized was his attempt to keep himself from crying, he finally said, "They're all dead."

The shovels we'd used to bury my grandfather were still leaning against the side of the citadel where we'd abandoned them in the storm. Though we were all exhausted, broken, and losing hope, we still took turns digging a huge pit in the courtyard, big enough to bury all the bodies, including Halvor . . . or what was left of him. I'd gone with Raidyn to get the shovels and had finally forced myself to look to where I'd last seen Halvor. The horror of what the Chimera had done to his poor body would forever be branded into my memory, certain to haunt my nightmares for the rest of my life. The monster had only partially burned him, choosing to slash and tear him apart, rather than incinerate him. I'd spun away from the remains, acid surging up from my throat while tears burned in my eyes once more. Raidyn had immediately pulled me into his arms, burying my head in his bare chest, holding me close as I shook and tried to keep from retching.

He stroked my hair and waited, as patient as ever, even though he had also suffered a huge loss.

Every single Paladin we'd left behind had been massacred. Some appeared to have been attacked by the rakasa, but others looked like they'd been attacked by other Paladin.

Which could only mean Barloc was back. And if that many Paladin had been unable to stop him, I was afraid he'd brought others with him.

The only two pieces of consolation we had were that Father hadn't found Sami among the dead—giving us hope that she'd somehow survived—and that the gateway had closed behind them. There was no way to know how many Paladin had come through, or if other rakasa were now loose in Vamala, but at least it wasn't an unleashed stream of them.

Yet.

There were no gryphons in the citadel, however, which led us to believe the Paladin had been taken completely unaware—without even time to call for their mounts. Father had gone to the stables, hopeful, but he'd returned even more shattered.

Every single magnificent beast had been slaughtered in their stalls.

"It must have happened right before we arrived," Father had said, his shoulders bowed under the weight of so much loss. "Since Sachiel . . ." He'd broken off, unable to finish, but I understood.

She'd been horrifically wounded but alive when we'd landed—barely in time to save her, but too late for all the others.

If only we hadn't had to stop again . . . if only I hadn't caused a two-day delay. If not for me, we would have been here—we would have been able to stop the massacre.

Or become part of it.

Tears mingled with our sweat as we took turns digging. My muscles burned from the strain—the pain a welcome distraction from the overwhelming grief and rage.

The sun had begun to set when we finally finished. It was shallow, but sufficient. And none of us had any strength left to make it any deeper. Raidyn and my father could barely manage carrying the bodies down, one at a time, on the backs of their gryphons—none of us dared go through the citadel yet.

We laid them out in the shallow grave, side by side. Somehow, in the hours since those first ghastly moments when I'd been too upset to look at Halvor'r remains, I'd grown numb to the horror of what had happened to their bodies. I stood between Sharmaine and Raidyn, my parents next to him, and stared down at my friends. Some I'd known better than others, but every single one of them had been willing to come here to Vamala, to risk injury and death to help protect our world.

And they'd all paid the ultimate price.

All except Sachiel, who lay just beyond the grave, unconscious but breathing, thanks to my father.

I hadn't had a drink of water since our last stop. I was devastated but also dehydrated. So though my eyes burned with my grief, no more tears fell as Father brokenly attempted to sing the same song Raidyn had at Grandfather's burial.

Raidyn and Sharmaine joined with him, their voices only slightly stronger than his.

Past the hedge, the sunset streaked across the sky in fiery bursts of tangerine, honey, and even shots of crimson. It was breathtaking and terrible, as though the sky itself wept tears of blood for the lives that had been lost.

When they finished the Paladin burial ritual, we again took turns with the shovels, covering the bodies with the heavy, dank soil we'd just dug up.

Each low *thud* of the earth landing on the lifeless bodies made me flinch.

When it was my turn, the blisters on my hands from digging the grave burned, some of them breaking open, but I ignored the pain, falling into a rhythm of dig, heft, twist, turn, and drop. *Thud.* Dig, heft, twist, turn, and drop. *Plop.*

With each shovelful I thought, *I'm sorry.*

Dig, heft, twist, turn, drop. *Thud.*

I'm sorry.

Dig, heft, twist, turn, drop. *Thud.*

I'm sorry.

But no matter how sorry I was, it would do nothing to bring any of them back. It couldn't save Halvor or spare my sister the grief his death would cause her.

If she had managed to survive whatever had happened on the other side of the tear between worlds.

The plan was to sleep outside the citadel. No one wanted to go in at night, even though no other rakasa had made themselves known yet. We were to take turns keeping watch so the others could rest, but I was pretty certain I wasn't the only one who couldn't sleep. When it wasn't our turn to sit up, I lay next to Raidyn, hands clasped between our bodies. But whenever I closed my eyes, a barrage of images assaulted me—Inara bent over Barloc, drinking his blood; the moment she disappeared through that rip in the air; Halvor disappearing beneath the onslaught of Chimera fire; the Chimera lunging toward us and Raidyn shoving me away, also prepared to die for us; Halvor's destroyed body; Sachiel swinging in the air from the edge of the shattered window, her arms shredded . . .

I would open them again, staring at Raidyn's face instead, drinking in great gulps of air, desperate to calm myself and wishing I could somehow erase sections of my brain entirely.

More often than not, his eyes were also open. And so we lay there, silently seeking solace in each other's gaze, side by side, hand in hand, exhausted but not sleeping, broken but alive, until dawn finally brushed the onyx sky navy, then ashy gray, desultory and nowhere near daylight yet, but it was enough to claim night had ended. I sat up, giving up the pretense.

Raidyn sat up as well. In that faltering first light of a new day, his burning blue eyes met mine and his arm came round my shoulders. He murmured, "What's wrong?" Because somehow, he knew—he felt—the extra layer of sadness upon all the other sadness. Like the worst kind of cake—something I'd seen in the fairy-tale book I'd read Inara so many times.

It had been a slice on a plate with delicate layers of pink and white. I'd asked Sami about it once—if she'd ever eaten cake.

She'd tried to describe it to me, the way it melted on your tongue, the sweetness of sugar and cream and flour—almost too good to be real. She'd told us it was usually for celebrations: weddings or birthdays or anniversaries.

I'd never had true cake, but we'd tried to make something similar for Inara's birthday one year, layering bread—a delicacy for us—with fruit from her orchard and a drizzle of honey that Sami had hoarded from one of her visits to Gateskeep to procure more food during winter. But Inara hadn't emerged from the roar to even recognize it was her birthday, and so we'd had to eat it, and instead of being sweet, it had tasted like heartache and frustration, and I'd never asked Sami to make it again.

As I sat there in Raidyn's arms, marveling that he'd noticed a different sadness, I couldn't help but think of cake. Layer after layer of sorrow. And the bitter frosting on top—the extra layer he'd sensed.

"It's midsummer," I whispered, soft and defeated. "It's Inara's birthday. She would have been sixteen today."

"She *is* sixteen today," he whispered back with a squeeze of his arm around my shoulders.

I was the one who had told him to hold on to hope, but after a long, sleepless night, wondering if we'd managed to survive again only to die today . . . after the waking nightmare of what we'd already endured . . . I'd lost that kernel of belief. We didn't know where they'd gone; we couldn't fathom how she and Loukas could have had any chance against Barloc. I'd failed her, I'd *lost* her, and I couldn't bring myself to cling to any more hope only to have it turn to ash in my mouth as all the others had.

A tear slipped down my cheek as I turned into Raidyn's embrace. The little bit of fruit and vegetables we'd managed to force down last night had apparently been enough to enable me to cry again, but not much. Not enough for my sister, who deserved far more than one measly tear.

I wondered if my parents would even realize what day it was—if I should tell them if they didn't.

"Maybe we should go find some breakfast for—"

Raidyn's suggestion cut off at the exact moment I stiffened, both of our heads going to the shattered window in the Hall of Miracles.

"Did you feel—" Sharmaine, who was sitting up on watch, turned to us.

"The *gateway,*" I cried out, terror slicking over my skin like ice despite the flash of heat we'd all felt—the rush of power emanating from that cursed, death-filled room.

FORTY

Inara

When Sukhi touched down in the field next to the gryphons' stables beside Maddok, the last thing I expected was for Louk to come to my side and help me down, or make any show of what had happened between us.

But I also hadn't expected him to practically throw himself off his gryphon and storm back to the stable, ignoring me entirely.

Sukhi bent so I could dismount, which I did, slowly, my legs shaky and stiff, my heart only slightly less so. Something had happened between us in that clearing—something far deeper than a kiss. I knew it . . . and I knew *he* knew it. But what would he do now? Now that we were back to the reality of what lay ahead, so many unknowns, so much potential devastation and struggle—the chance to return to Sharmaine . . .

Sukhi stood and bumped her beak against my stomach, a soft tap, as if letting me know she understood my turmoil and was there for me. I reached up to rub her feathers, the downy softness of her neck striking me as fascinating—that a creature so giant, so powerful, so *deadly,* could also be so soft, so gentle, so thoughtful.

Much like Loukas, except reversed. He was all deadly, powerful, angry intent, but underneath that hardened shell, he was softer and kinder than he was ever willing to admit.

Perhaps that was why he had fled, rushing away from me as fast as he was able. The neck of my shirt was still damp from his tears, and my arms ached from holding him. I was a witness to his suffering now, a potential threat of exposure—or a potential threat of further harm.

"Come on, girl," I murmured, leading Sukhi to the stable, unsure if I should try to find Loukas or make sure to give him enough time to flee. I was awash with indecision, embarrassment even. In the clearing I had felt so strong, so *right.* Being with *Loukas* had felt right.

But now, with him gone, doubt swooped in where there had been certainty.

Doubt . . . and guilt.

I'd never kissed Halvor like that, as I'd admitted to Loukas. I'd never *felt* like that with Halvor. He had always been sweet to me, caring and gentle and kind, and *there* for me. He'd never fled, had never abandoned me. And what had I done? I'd hurt him by falling for the boy who couldn't even *look* at me after we kissed, after I'd held him while he cried.

That was the bigger problem, I knew. Not the kissing—not even the fact that if we made it back and they'd all survived, that I could tell Sharmaine that we'd kissed, when perhaps he wished to keep it a secret.

It was the fact that he'd broken down with me, that he'd shown me his heart.

Somehow, I knew he'd never allowed anyone else to see him so vulnerable before. And *that*, more than anything, was why he'd bolted.

When the storm raging within him had finally finished, leaving him shaking and drained in my arms, we hadn't said a word. We hadn't even kissed again. He'd merely pulled back and I'd let him go.

We'd mounted our gryphons in silence and flown back without speaking. Not even once.

It had been a mistake.

I knew that now, but I'd been nervous . . . and afraid. Afraid of what he'd say to me—what he *thought* of me. Afraid that, despite what I'd said, he probably viewed me—and what had happened—as a mistake.

I'd used up all my bravery in that moment when I'd refused

to let him shut me out, leaving me gutless when I'd needed it most.

"Inara!"

We'd almost reached the stable door when the shout took me by surprise. A woman's voice, slowly becoming familiar—though not the panic it held.

I turned to my grandmother, who wasn't quite running across the field, but walking as fast as legs could move *without* running.

"Where have you been? Where is Loukas?"

"He took me flying—on Sukhi."

"For the entire *day*?" She reached me and my gryphon, anger spitting from her eyes.

I flushed. "I'm sorry. I didn't know we'd be gone for so long." There was no plausible way to explain how long we'd been absent without admitting what had happened, so I fell silent and waited.

"You have no idea where you are, so I didn't expect *you* to be able to make sure you were back sooner than this. But Loukas . . ." She shook her head, her mouth downturned in displeasure. "There's nothing for it now. And there's been more news."

My embarrassment drained into dread at the way she said "news"—the way someone might say "death" or "tragedy," both of which were probably part of what she had come to tell us about.

"What's happened now?"

Louk's deep baritone from behind us made me jump. I spun around to see him leaning against the open door of the stable, hands shoved into his pockets, any lingering traces of his breakdown erased, his imperturbable mask back in place. Our eyes met and held; a tremor from the hook still wound around my heart shivered down my spine to the bottom of my belly. I refused to be the first to look away. With a slight lift of one eyebrow, he turned to Grandmother. For some reason that tiny triumph of willpower—*you will not ignore me, you will not push me away*—felt like victory enmeshed with failure. As if his willingness to give up so easily was his way of saying *I don't care.*

Grandmother exhaled, a push of air out her pursed lips redolent with weariness and worry. "Another patrol arrived over an hour ago. There have been more murders . . . and every single one of them had their throats ripped out," she said, and all thoughts of Loukas and kisses and tiny triumphs fled. "There's no possible way Barloc is acting alone—not with this many dead. We must assume he's found members of the *Infinitium* sect and is having them steal power as well. For what purpose, we can only imagine. And with his ability to rip tears between worlds, they could leave at any moment. We no longer can hope to keep them from your world by only *guarding* the gateway." Her eyes lifted to mine, an apology in their depths.

My breath came fast and hard, my blood a spinning rush in my veins. "What can we do?"

Grandmother's eyes dropped to the earth, her hands clasped in front of her. "I know what Alkimos would have had me do."

My grandfather. Her husband, who had died in Vamala.

When she looked back up, her eyes flared with determination. "We will take an army and go to the gateway. We'll find Barloc and stop him and whoever else he has brought with him. No more innocent lives will be lost—not on my watch."

I couldn't help but stare. After everything I'd heard about her, the magnitude of such a declaration wasn't lost on me. "When?"

"As soon as possible. We'll fly through the night if we must." She turned on her heel and marched back the way she'd come. "Loukas," she called over her shoulder, "gather whatever members of my son's battalion are here and willing to go. You will lead them until we reach Adelric."

There was a shocked moment of silence, and then he said, "Yes, madam," but I wasn't sure if she even heard him—or the gratitude he couldn't quite conceal from his voice—as she was already halfway across the field.

"We're going back," I said, a relieved smile lifting my lips.

"You can't ride on Maddok with me if I'm to lead the battalion." Loukas glared at me, as if I'd asked him and he was refusing me.

My smile turned into a scowl. "I don't need to. I have my own gryphon now," I reminded him.

"You think you're qualified to ride in a battalion because you managed to endure one easy flight?" he scoffed.

I stalked forward, until I was close enough to shove a finger into his chest. "That is *enough.* First, you know that was not an 'easy flight'—and I kept up with every twist and nosedive and climb you threw at me. And second, I don't know why you're acting like this. You can try to pretend like nothing has changed between us, but you *know* it has and so do I."

The fire in Louk's eyes flared brighter, a muscle in his jaw jumped. "I told you then and I'll tell you now—it was a mistake. You think you know me, you think you *understand* me, but you're wrong. You are too young . . . and naïve . . . and you have Halvor. I'll agree not to tell him what happened by that river, but only if you agree to keep it to yourself as well."

I stared at him, my lungs caving in, the hook in my heart ripping right through it. After that kiss—after the way he'd cried in my arms—the way he'd held me as if he were drowning in his own pain and I was his only chance at ever reaching the surface . . . *this* was it came down to? He wouldn't tell Halvor if I didn't tell anyone either?

Sukhi cawed, a sharp warning at my side. Loukas backed up a step.

"If you're determined to ride her to the gateway, I can't stop you. But hopefully you can survive the pass through those cliffs. I won't be there to catch you if you fall."

With that, he turned on his heel and strode away, leaving me standing beside Sukhi in stunned silence. Alone—and somehow furious and devastated all at once.

Grandmother was true to her word. By the time I finished finding Sukhi water and a meal—I had to ask another Paladin where they kept the stash of rodents—and went in search of food for myself, she had already gathered two dozen Paladin willing to go through the gateway, with twice that many more saying they would also come. All of them, plus the members of the council who were needed to open it, made for a much larger force than I'd even dared hope for.

I hadn't seen Loukas again, but part of me didn't want to. I just wanted to go *home*—to my sister, to Sami . . . even my mother and father. And Halvor. If he survived whatever lay ahead and still cared for me, I couldn't lie to him. I would have to admit what had happened with Loukas and how it had changed me.

Could I build a life with Halvor—if that was even what he wanted—now that I'd had my world and heart turned upside down and torn apart by Louk?

Focus on seeing Zuhra again. Focus on finding and stopping Barloc. None of this matters unless we all survive. You have a gryphon and your power back—you can help. That's the most important thing to remember.

Though I'd yet to figure out if my power was the same—if I was still a healer or not—somehow I knew it was even stronger than it had been before Barloc had ripped it from me. I knew I could help . . . one way or another.

After rushing through a small meal of fruit, some sort of roasted fowl, and fresh juice—one of the best meals I'd ever been given, but that I hardly even tasted—I hurried back out to the stables, to Sukhi. I wanted to be sure I wasn't left behind . . . and I wasn't certain I could trust Loukas to wait for me if everyone gathered and was ready to leave before I got there.

When I walked through the open door into the fading light of evening, nearly a *hundred* Paladin and their gryphons filled the field outside the stable.

It was stunning and overwhelming; it was hope reincarnated in the form of more than a hundred pairs of glowing Paladin eyes turning to me and then away again when they realized I wasn't Ederra, the leader of the council and the one who had, inexplicably, had such a massive change of heart and orchestrated this mission.

To rescue the humans—who had taken so much from her, and from them—but who were, for the most part, innocent and not worthy of dying at the hands of a murderous, power-hungry sect of *jaklas* with the ability at last to do as they'd long dreamed—to take over the human world and become their rulers.

I looked out over the army of Paladin and my heart swelled, my eyes burning.

I was going *home,* and I was bringing hope and a chance at victory with me.

It only took a few minutes for me to weave through the assembled crowd, go into the stables, resaddle Sukhi, and head back out with her in tow. By the time I did, my grandmother was there, standing on the steps in front of the massive door that led into the castle.

"I know I am asking a lot of many of you. I am not the only one who has lost loved ones at the hands of humans in Vamala. But, as my late husband often pointed out"—a murmur rippled through the crowd at her words: *Alkimos is gone? Alkimos died?*—"most of them are innocent and afraid. And they are in need of our protection once more. The *jakla* who attacked me found a way back to Visimperum. He has recruited other members of the *Infinitium* sect to his cause—and has made them into *jaklas* as well, through the murder of at least fifteen Paladin that we know of so far." Another surge of shock went through the assembled Paladin, the combined horror of such a large group palpable in the air. "So you see, this no longer only affects Vamala. If we let them go unchecked, who knows how many more Paladin will also die, feeding these true monsters their power and enabling them to grow so strong, we will have very little hope of stopping them."

She paused, letting her words sink in. It was in that moment I realized she was speaking in Paladin—and I still understood her. Had that been part of the gift the Mother of all Paladin had given me? Before I could make sense of such a phenomenon, she continued.

"I know we are all risking our lives by following after them and trying to stop them. Especially when they are capable of absorbing our power for at least the next few days until the change is completed. But we have to try. Before they slaughter anyone else. I asked you to bring your Paladin steel because even a *jakla* can't survive a beheading."

With that last, gruesome word, Grandmother lifted her fist. "To the skies! And may the Light hold us and keep us safe in our quest!"

A responding cry went up from the crowd, echoing up to the

stars that had begun to emerge as velvet night spread across the world. Then everyone climbed on their gryphons, weapons strapped onto backs and legs, faces set in determination.

My heart beat rapid-fire in my chest, part thrill and part terror. Only now did Louk's meaning become clear, about surviving the cliffs . . . I'd forgotten about that tiny strip between two peaks that was the difference between life and a swift, painful death, and was also the only way in or out of the bowl of sky-high mountains surrounding Soluselis, a natural defense that had never been breached.

The mountains encircled us, distant right now, but all too close soon enough. Those jagged peaks split the night into shards of starlight and flayed my already-flagging courage.

"Having second thoughts?"

I spun at his voice, torn between snapping something ill-tempered and begging him to let me ride on Maddok in front of him—just until we made it through that thin little gap far, far above the earth. Sukhi could follow behind and I would ride her the rest of the way—in the open air.

All I ended up saying was, "No."

In the sea of blue-fire eyes, mine included, his green ones flashed like a beacon, announcing to everyone that he was different. Even there, in that field crowded with Paladin and gryphons, they gave him as wide a berth as possible. I wondered how many members of my father's battalion were there—if any had refused to fly under Loukas's leadership, out of misplaced fear.

We stood there, several feet apart, surrounded by organized chaos, for the span of three heartbeats that somehow felt like thirty and none all at once—time slowing and speeding past, in a tangle of emotion and regret and fear and longing. I looked up into his shadowed face, his dark hair falling forward into his brilliant emerald eyes—jewellike, stunning . . . and *sad.*

It finally struck me—never once had he said: *We shouldn't have done that.* It was only ever: *I shouldn't have done that.*

I stared at him, my heart thudding against my ribs. "Do you think you somehow *influenced* me? Do you think it was *your* doing—what happened by the stream?"

Louk stiffened, his lips thinning, but he didn't deny it.

"That had *nothing* to do with you. Well, it *did,*" I amended when his eyebrows lifted, "but not because of *that.* Not because of your . . . ability. *I* chose to kiss you, because *I wanted* to."

"You can't know that for sure." His voice was low and a little hoarse. "Sometimes . . . if I'm feeling something *very* strongly, it happens when I don't intend to use it. It's more subtle, but it's still there—it's still *me.* Not them . . . Not *you.*"

I stepped toward him, but Louk backed up, a warning flashing across his eyes. There was no time—or space—to push him. Not right now. So I stopped, miserable and frustrated, that hook around my heart pulling me to him no matter how much he resisted. *Was* that his power? Or was it my own true feelings?

"You're too young and naïve to know your own mind and heart enough to decipher the difference."

My cheeks burned; I could only hope the darkness hid my embarrassment. "I don't know if you keep saying that to convince me or yourself."

He had the decency to flinch.

"And yes, thanks to the roar that consumed me for most of my life, I suppose I am naïve. And yes, I'm younger than you, it's true. But I am not *that* young—and I am fully capable of knowing my own heart and mind. In fact," I continued in a rush, knowing the signal to take off would be given any minute, with neither of us on our gryphons yet, "if anything, I know my own heart and mind even *better* because of it. When I recognize something real—something true and powerful—I embrace it fully because I have no idea how long I will be allowed to experience it." I blinked hard a few times to force the sting in my eyes to go away—at least until I was safely away from his burning gaze, which raked over my face with such intensity, it chased away the chill of night and sent my breath crashing through my lungs. "The truth is that the only person who doesn't know their own heart or mind is *you.*"

Louk's mouth opened and then shut, his eyes flaring in the darkness.

Before he could respond, I turned away, to Sukhi, who immediately knelt on her front knees to let me climb on her back.

"Inara."

I refused to look down, though his voice came from right beside where my left leg hung at her side.

"Inara, please."

When his hand came to rest on my calf, still noticeable even through the supple leather of the boots my grandmother had found for me, a shiver slipped up my leg, and I relented, looking down at him. He was tall enough that his face was level with my hip, even on the back of a gryphon. His fingers tightened on my leg when our gazes met.

"I'm sorry," he said, so softly, I might not have believed I'd heard him correctly, except I'd seen his lips form those two words that made all the difference. "I've never . . ." He trailed off and shook his head. His shoulders tensed and his gaze dropped.

Before he could say anything else, there was a piercing whistle from the steps. Silence fell over the crowd of assembled warriors—which had grown even larger—so immediate and absolute it was a little chilling.

Loukas squeezed my leg again and then let go, shooting one last haunted glance up at me, before turning and rushing to Maddok and swinging himself onto his gryphon's back.

Within seconds, the first group of Paladin Riders had taken to the skies, with the next group right behind them. Loukas's battalion—my father's battalion—were second to last, but it only took another minute or so before it was our turn. I tightened Sukhi's reins, squeezed my already-fatigued legs against her sides, and prayed that I would somehow find the energy to stay on her back—especially through those cliffs—and make it back to my sister.

Then finish the conversation with Loukas.

Preferably *before* I came face to face with Halvor again.

FORTY-ONE

Zuhra

I'd only ever experienced something like it once in my life, when the Paladin High Council had opened the gateway in Visimperum—the *pull,* the *need* to get closer to all that power, drawing me to my feet.

Raidyn grabbed my hand, stopping me before I would have begun walking toward it, bewitched out of common sense. The call to *come,* to join my power with it, still coursed through me, but his touch brought me back to myself enough to resist it.

"What is it—what's going on?" My mother's groggy voice came from behind us, followed by my father's response, "The gateway has been opened again."

I glanced back to see her rubbing her eyes, pushing herself to her feet. Perhaps she had managed to fall asleep after all, and I was glad for it. She was worn too thin around the edges, so much of her indomitable fire doused from exhaustion and loss. "How do you know?" she asked, looking from him to me.

"We can feel it," he said, the edges of his eyes tight as his gaze moved to the shattered window. "But we can't tell what's about to come through it."

"Nothing good, I'm afraid." Raidyn spoke under his breath, so I wasn't sure anyone heard him beside me.

"Do you think it's Barloc?" Mother blanched, her eyes also going to the side of the citadel, so high up in the air.

"If it is, then who came through it yesterday?"

There was no answer.

"What do we do, sir?" Sharmaine turned to my father, pale but determined, the dawn breaking bleak overhead, the sky washed gray by thin, low-lying clouds.

His gaze dropped to my mother at his side. I had so many memories of her in this courtyard—how I'd always imagined her a tiny mountain made flesh, immovable and unstoppable. But faced with the possibility of a frighteningly powerful *jakla* and more rakasa, she'd never seemed more fragile—more mortal and breakable. We all had power to at least give us *hope* of fighting and surviving, but she . . . she had nothing but her will and a temper, neither of which would save her from this kind of enemy.

"We prepare to fight," he said, his eyes meeting mine, the bleakness in his echoing the cavernous fear inside me.

Mother swallowed but nodded, squaring her shoulders, as if she could possibly hope to face what was to come.

Naiki suddenly rose to her feet, hackles raised, with a sharp caw, Taavi and Keko right behind her.

"How touching."

We whirled to face the hedge where the voice had come from.

Barloc.

Flanked by at least a dozen other Paladin.

Behind them, the hedge was pulled back, the gate open.

Had they come from *outside* the hedge? Then who—or *what*—was coming through the gateway?

"I don't want to kill all of you," he continued, slowly strolling forward, as if he were commenting on the weather, not our lives, "but I will, if you force me to."

Raidyn's hand tightened on mine, his veins lighting with power. My father and Sharmaine's did as well; their gryphons rushed to our sides.

"I'm disappointed in you." Barloc shook his head, his eyes and body filled with so much Paladin power, almost every inch of his skin glowed, not just his veins. "You know that's useless against me. Unless you intend to donate your gifts to my cause." He flashed his teeth at us, an expression of vindictive greed, more like an animal baring its fangs as a threat than anything resembling a human smile.

"What do you want?" Father spat, pushing my mother behind him, toward Taavi.

The gryphons' wings were all partially lifted, prepared to take flight the moment their Riders climbed on. But we all stood there, frozen in fear—at an impasse, knowing the power we wielded would just be absorbed by the *jakla*. I wondered if the fire Raidyn and I could create together—strong enough to incinerate a Chimera—could destroy him before he could absorb it. Our hands were still clasped, but though his power filled his veins, ready to explode out, he hadn't summoned it fully yet, so there was nothing I could do, except cling to him, ready and willing to lend my power to his if he chose to use it.

"I appreciate you taking the time to ask, rather than wasting any more lives needlessly. I'm not completely unreasonable." His laugh did little to convince me of his sincerity—or sanity—but Father remained still, tensed, ready to fight or flee, but not moving—yet. "All I want is your daughter's power. And the rest of you walk away, unharmed."

"No." Father's response was so immediate, I'd barely had time to assimilate the meaning of Barloc's words before he spat his answer back at the monster that had once been Halvor's uncle. I'd thought for a moment he meant Inara—the one I was used to thinking of having power, even now. Even with her gone. "You already took hers."

"You know I'm not talking about that one." His gaze lifted to mine, and I barely kept from flinching at the fathomless malice in his blinding eyes. "I want *her* power."

"She has no power," Raidyn burst out, his fingers digging into my hand to the point of pain. I squeezed back just as hard, every muscle in my body taut, strung too tight and ready to snap. There were fifteen Paladin men and women plus Barloc against the four of us and my mother. If this turned into a fight, there was no chance we would survive.

"*Liar.*" The word was low and sinuous and spoken so calmly it was almost worse than if he'd yelled. "I watched you all. While

I waited for my strength to return from opening that gateway, I watched and learned. Oh, she *has* power. Yes, she does. I *did* warn you . . . do you know what I do to liars?"

Sharmaine threw up her shield, but it wasn't fast enough. The blast came with so little movement on his part, none of us were able to react quickly enough.

Time slowed, as viscous as the blood sludging through my veins, so that one blinding blast of power seemed to travel at half speed, but I was still unable to move or do anything to stop it. I could only watch as it shot past my father and mother, past Sharmaine, past me—and exploded into Raidyn, ripping his hand from mine, throwing him backward.

FORTY-TWO

Zuhra

A scream built inside me, cleaving through muscle and lung and heart, shredding its way out my throat, until I was nothing but that scream, nothing but horror and anguish given voice.

Naiki threw herself down on the ground, so that Raidyn landed splayed across her back, his arms open wide, his bare chest a mass of bloody, torn, charred flesh. His eyes met mine, the fire in them flickering weakly. His mouth moved but no sound emerged except the wet, sucking sound of each slow, laborious breath.

"Zuhra, take him and go! *Now!* She can't hold them off any longer!"

My father's shout echoed dully through the roar in my head, as if he were in a remote corner of the courtyard. But then he was there, dragging me over to Naiki and Raidyn. The ground trembled beneath my feet. Detonations sent waves vibrating through the air. Father turned Raidyn so he hung over Naiki's front haunches on his mutilated stomach, the same way he'd brought Sachiel back to us.

"Take him and go! I will come as soon as possible to try to heal him!"

Then he grabbed me underneath my armpits and hefted me onto Naiki's saddle behind Raidyn.

The numbness drained away when Father slapped her haunches and the gryphon launched herself forward, immediately taking off. Sound and awareness returned. I grabbed Raidyn's shoulders, wincing at his low moan of agony, but couldn't let go, even when his blood began to soak my pants, afraid he would slip off and fall. When I glanced back, Sharmaine sat on Keko's back, hands lifted, her arms visibly shaking as she struggled to maintain a shield against the onslaught from Barloc and his fifteen Paladin who were spreading out to the side, searching for the edges of her power. Father was lifting my mother onto Taavi's saddle and climbing on behind her.

Terror slicked my hands with sweat and throbbed behind my temples.

Then Raidyn's body went completely limp; it wasn't until he slipped into unconsciousness that I realized I'd been absorbing his agony and fear alongside my own.

"*No!* Don't you dare leave me! Don't you *dare*!" I shouted, my fingers digging into his shoulders as we soared higher and higher. I prayed we were out of reach—and that the other three would somehow escape too.

But part of me knew there was no way they would. I didn't even know if *we* would.

Then—as if from a dream, conjured straight from wishes and prayers and hopes that had all seemed pointlessly futile—gryphons and Riders began pouring from the broken window of the Hall of Miracles.

Naiki cawed in welcome—in *recognition*—perhaps even in warning. Without a signal from me, she turned and headed for that window. I clutched Raidyn and scanned for anyone that looked even remotely familiar.

"A healer," I croaked, my voice thick with unshed tears and strangling terror that still hadn't abated. "I need a healer!" I tried again, louder this time as Naiki soared through the Paladin—so many, *so many*!—into the Hall of Miracles.

The gateway glowed with power and a constant stream of gryphons, their Riders pulling swords and knives out and following their comrades out to battle the *jaklas*.

Naiki landed as gently as possible, but it still made Raidyn slip to the side. I tried to hold on to him, but he was deadweight—far too much for me to manage. He toppled off, pulling me with him. He crumpled into a disjointed heap beneath me, breaking my fall, but, I was afraid, injuring him even more severely. Quickly scrambling off of him, I strained to roll him over. I nearly crumpled at the sight of his ruined body and ashen face.

"Help! Please, I need a healer!" I cried out, desperate and terrified he was already too far gone.

"Zuhra?"

I froze. My heart slammed against my ribs. *It couldn't be—*

Hope shot through my body like lightning. I looked to the gateway where it had come from and everything went completely still and silent.

She sat atop a beautiful, golden gryphon, soaring into the Hall of Miracles, her eyes brilliant with Paladin fire as I'd always remembered them—powerful and poised and *alive.*

My sister was alive.

The gryphon swooped over to us and landed, crouching down on its front haunches, and then Inara was there, rushing to my side, her eyes moving over Raidyn with a dawning horror.

"Barloc," she said, low and fierce. Then she looked up at me. "We can heal him, Zu. Together."

I nodded, almost blinded by the tears swimming in my eyes.

Another gryphon landed nearby, and I barely registered that Loukas was also alive.

"No—Raidyn—*no*!" His guttural cry caused Inara to glance up at him.

"I will heal him," was all she said.

"You don't even know if that's what power you have anymore!" Loukas cried, eyes wild, dropping to his knees with a thud on the other side of Raidyn's inert body.

Instead of responding, Inara pressed her hands to Raidyn's charred, bloody skin, her veins exploding with light, her power gathering and then flowing out into his ravaged body. He was barely even drawing breath anymore, his lips the bloodless white of a corpse.

Please. Please. Please.

With every painfully normal beat of my heart, that one word became my mantra, my prayer.

Then I put my hands on top of my sister's.

I'd shared my sister's power once before, to open the gateway; I'd joined my power to Raidyn's multiple times, to heal *and* to kill. I'd felt the magnitude of both of their gifts in those moments. They had both been blessed with incredible amounts of power.

But nothing compared to what I felt when my power joined with Inara's as we knelt beside Raidyn on the floor of the Hall of Miracles.

Whatever power she had once possessed had been a stream, beautiful and capable of bringing life to many, but so very small compared to what she now wielded—the roaring might of a waterfall, of a river, of an *ocean*, endless and incomprehensible in scope.

I was almost certain she didn't need me at all, but I clung to her anyway, as images filled my mind—some I knew, from her childhood, but many were completely new and shocking in their unexpectedness. Saving Loukas on the back of Maddok; nearly dying; a voice telling her of her gift—a voice that the core of me knew somehow, though I couldn't put a name to her; a light that was endless and eternal and powerful beyond imagination; a gift of power from that same voice that even now was pressing forward into Raidyn's body; a kiss with *Loukas* that was so full of passion and need and love it took *my* breath away; and finally a bond with a gryphon that had carried her here.

Then we pressed on, together, her power interweaving with mine, letting me join my soul with hers as we saw flashes of Raidyn's life together. But, even as images of his parents, of Naiki, and moments with me flew past, I felt . . . *different.* Inara wasn't using my power at all; if anything, I felt *stronger,* more revitalized than I had in days—maybe even weeks.

Somehow I was still with her as her power infiltrated Raidyn's wounds, healing with a speed and perfection that left me in utter awe. What had happened to my sister? She'd always been powerful but *this* . . . this was something else entirely. Where had it come from? Whose voice had I heard in her memories?

Always when I'd helped heal before, it had caused me pain and exhaustion—I'd felt myself being pulled out and into the person I was healing; and I'd lost consciousness nearly every time after reeling back into myself. But as Inara swiftly but gently finished her work and then pulled us both back out, turning her hands over to squeeze mine for a moment before releasing me, I felt . . . fine. More than fine. I felt as though she'd somehow healed and strengthened *me* at the same time as Raidyn, curing my exhaustion, erasing the strain of all the trauma and travel and lack of sleep and anguish.

My eyes flew open to meet hers.

Her smile was so full of joy and satisfaction—and peace. So much peace. Somehow, in that moment, I felt as though I were the *younger* sister. Whatever had happened to her in Visimperum had changed her, but in remarkable, breathtaking ways.

Then I looked down at Raidyn. His exposed skin was smooth, unmarred—not as though he'd been healed, but as if the injury had never occurred in the first place.

His eyes were still shut, but he looked as though he were just resting now. The color had returned to his lips and face.

"You did it." Loukas's murmur held all the relief and awe that coursed through me.

When I looked up, he was staring at my sister with a look so heavy with emotion, complex and full of meaning, it felt as though I were intruding on a private conversation taking place without words.

Then I remembered what I'd seen in her memories—the kiss they'd shared.

Eyes wide, I looked to her and was shocked to see just as much emotion in *her* gaze as she smiled that same peaceful, confident smile at Loukas.

"I told you I would."

The citadel rumbled beneath us, a reminder that a battle was being waged outside. I wondered how much time had passed while she'd healed him. It had felt so fast . . .

I looked to the gateway. It was dark, closed once more.

But standing at the base of it was a handful of Paladin and

gryphons—and one indomitable woman, well and whole and staring at me.

"Zuhra," my grandmother said, soft, hesitant—but still audible even from across the hall. As different from the woman I'd left at the gateway a week ago as a person could be in such a short time.

Though I wanted to stay by Raidyn's side, waiting for him to wake, I stood, my gaze never leaving hers.

She didn't *run*, but she did hurry forward, and when she was only a foot away, she opened her arms. Before I even knew what was happening, my grandmother wrapped me in a hug as tight as it was shocking. I stiffened in disbelief for half a heartbeat. Ederra—my implacable, emotionless grandmother—was *hugging* me?

But then I quickly wrapped my arms around her narrow waist.

"I'm sorry," was all she said, but it was enough.

I squeezed her tighter, until Inara said, "Zuhra, he's waking up."

Grandmother released me and stepped back. There was too much to say, and no time for it. She was already rushing back to her gryphon, to join the battle, a sword strapped to her back.

I turned to Raidyn to see his eyelids fluttering and then opening, his eyes as bright as I'd ever seen them. I dropped to my knees beside him as he struggled to sit up, his gaze roaming wildly over the room, until they landed on me, and then he exhaled and stilled.

"You're *alive,*" I managed to choke out, through the emotion that rose up as he lifted one arm to wrap around me, pulling me into him with a fierceness that warmed every remaining inch of ice that Barloc's attack had—

I stiffened so suddenly, he jerked back.

"What is it? What's wrong?" His gaze roamed over me.

"My parents . . . Sharmaine . . . they were out there, with *him*—"

"We have to go help," Loukas said, standing.

Raidyn startled at the sound of his voice. "*Loukas?*" he said in disbelief. Then he noticed my sister, who had also risen to her feet, moving to stand by Loukas. "*Inara!* You're both alive!"

"Thanks to Inara, yes, we are," Loukas said, shooting her

another one of those meaningful looks that almost brought heat to *my* cheeks.

Raidyn's eyebrows furrowed, but with a slight shake of his head, he climbed to his feet. Naiki stepped forward, butting her beak into his back, with a low hoot.

"Zuhra? *Inara!*"

The tiny cry came from the doorway behind us, across the large hall.

I spun to see Sami, white-faced and trembling, staring at us.

"Sami!"

She hurried as quickly as she could across the wide expanse, tears streaking down her face. "I thought for sure you were all lost," she said and pulled me into a hug.

"Where have you been? I thought you went back to Gateskeep!"

"I hid in the library," she said into my hair as she squeezed me tight. "Why would I go back there when my family is here? I was waiting for you to come home. *Praying* that you would."

Another explosion outside rattled the citadel, and my heart lurched up into my throat. Sami released me, and I turned to see Grandmother flying back through the shattered window, the blood drained from her face. She waved her arms with a shout. "Make room! Hurry—they're bringing the wounded up!"

We rushed to obey, clearing the center of the room, just as a handful of Paladin soared through the broken window, carrying broken, bloodied bodies with them.

Everyone was covered in soot and grime and blood, so it took me a moment to realize one of the wounded was Sharmaine, being carried by a Paladin I didn't recognize.

"Shar!" Loukas's eyes widened. He ran to the gryphon carrying her, Inara right behind him. Raidyn sucked in a gasp when they gently laid her body down, exposing the extent of her wounds.

The other Paladin who stood by the gateway dashed forward and began helping to pull the other wounded down. *Healers,* I realized. Waiting here for this very moment, rather than joining the fight.

But there were too many for them, with more continuing to

come through the window. Another Paladin I didn't know even brought Sachiel and laid her body down near Shar's.

I stood beside Raidyn, Naiki behind us, and stared at the carnage in horror. There had to have been at least a hundred Paladin that had come through the gateway—against *sixteen.* How were we losing this battle?

FORTY-THREE

INARA

I made myself focus on Sharmaine, too afraid to look at Loukas, to see what his face—what his *eyes*—would reveal as he stared down at her battered body. She was alive, but not for long. I'd thought myself prepared for this, for when we returned to the ones we had believed ourselves to love before the light, before the stream. But it turned out I wasn't.

So I did what I knew I had been given this amazing gift to do.

I healed her.

As quickly and completely as I'd healed Raidyn. And even though her wounds were horrific, when I finished, pulling my hands away from her newly mended skin, I was a little tired, but not even remotely close to drained.

What had the Mother of all Paladin given me? What had I ever done to deserve a gift of such magnitude?

When Sharmaine's eyes fluttered and opened, her chest expanding with a life-sustaining gasp of air, Loukas visibly sagged beside me, even on the periphery of my vision. I stood and turned away, unable to bear witnessing whatever reunion was about to take place.

"Thank you," I heard him murmur as I walked away as quickly as I dared without making it too obvious that I was being a coward and fleeing.

My sister watched me, her eyes searching, mouth twisted with concern.

"What is happening out there?" I heard another healer question one of the Paladin who had brought a wounded comrade up.

"They're *all jaklas,*" she responded, winded. "They've formed a circle around him. We can't get close enough to do anything. Every time a battalion tries, we lose four times as many of ours as they do. We've only managed to slay five of them."

"How many dead?"

I paused, afraid to know, but also unable to move away, to block the unknown Paladin's answer.

"At least twenty," she said, soft and defeated.

Grandmother, who had just walked over, made a noise that took a moment for me to realize was a strangled sob. "Call them back. All of them. We have to try something else."

"What else can we do? We can't use our power. The only hope we have of stopping them is to keep trying to get within range of using our knives and swords."

"I will not allow our people to be slaughtered by them. Call them back. That's an order!"

The younger Paladin finally nodded. "Yes, madam." She wheeled her gryphon back toward the window and began shouting in Paladin as they soared out to the carnage below.

Grandmother's eyes met mine, and I swallowed at the bleakness in her face.

Within a minute, dozens and dozens of Paladin and gryphons surged back into the Hall of Miracles, until there wasn't room for any more. The last one to make it in, before the others had to hover outside the window and wait, was a familiar gryphon with two riders. They were both filthy, bloody and battered, but alive.

She saw me first, her eyes widening and then filling with tears. "Inara!" she screamed, struggling to dismount before Taavi had even landed. At her shout, Father's head whipped to the direction she looked, and when he saw me, his face crumpled, his shoulders sagging forward. Taavi quickly landed and they both clambered off his back, running to where I stood, their arms coming round me in a hug so tight, I could barely breathe.

"You're *alive,*" Father said, his voice thick with tears. Mother couldn't speak at all, her whole body shook with sobs. "And your eyes," he added, pulling back enough to look into my face. "How is this possible? What happened?"

I smiled through my own tears. "It's a story for another time. Right now, we have to end this."

"Right. *Right,*" he repeated, more forcefully, letting his arms drop with a sharp nod. He turned and I could see the general in him assessing the situation, his gaze traveling over those in the Hall of Miracles. When he noticed Loukas standing beside Sharmaine, he paused, his eyes widening. "Loukas!" he shouted.

Louk looked up to where we stood. I quickly glanced away, to the floor.

Outside the window, a gryphon screeched, a horrific sound, followed by more shouts and screams.

"They're coming closer!"

"What do we do?"

There was no way to fit any more of the gryphons and Riders in the hall, but the ones left outside were sitting targets.

"Fly over the hedge—get out of range!" someone shouted back from within the hall.

An explosion boomed below us and the citadel trembled from the impact. It was only a matter of time before Barloc began to attack us as well—either storming the citadel or bringing it down over our heads.

For the first time, I realized I wasn't having any blackouts—I wasn't seeing anything when Barloc used his power. Either he was letting all of the other *jaklas* do the fighting for him, or we were no longer connected now that I had been healed in the light.

"What do we do, Ederra?" someone shouted, and all eyes turned to my grandmother.

My father stiffened and spun. "*Mother?* You're *alive*!" And then he was running to her, weaving through the small spaces between all those smashed together in the hall.

"General Adelric!"

"It's the general!"

The murmur grew louder, spreading across the hall . . . voices rising and rising, a swell of something that sounded like hope.

"General! What do we do?" The cries turned to focus on him as he grabbed his mother into a swift, bone-crushing hug.

He quickly released her and turned to face his battalion and the others who had been willing to come, knowing they were risking their lives—as so many had already lost.

"We have to make them separate," he said, in the language of Vamala for the benefit of my mother and sister. I hadn't even realized everything else had been spoken in the Paladin language until that moment—another reminder that I somehow understood both languages now. "We can't reach them when they're huddled in a circle like this. But if we can get them to split into groups, then we would have a chance to take more of them out."

"How do we do that?"

While my father and the others traded ideas, I felt *him* walking over to where I still stood, resolutely staring forward. I sensed Sharmaine behind him, the *sanaulus* from healing her now allowing me to recognize her emotions. I'd seen flashes of her life, as I always did when healing someone, had recognized how truly kind and *good* she was . . . and it had made me realize, if he truly did love her, I shouldn't interfere. No matter what I felt for him.

"I can't believe we're all here together again. I really didn't think it would happen," Raidyn said from the other side of where I stood.

That's when it hit me. I turned to face Raidyn and Zuhra, suddenly hardly able to draw breath. "Wait . . . where's Halvor?"

Zuhra stared at me, stricken, and I knew, even before Raidyn spoke, hesitant and low, his words buzzing through my brain, barely decipherable through the roar of blood in my ears. Something about a Chimera and sacrificing himself . . . but all that mattered were the words he *couldn't* bring himself to speak.

Halvor was gone.

I'd never even had the chance to say goodbye.

I'd healed two potentially fatal wounds in less than ten minutes without getting drained, but I'd been too late to save Halvor. The realization that I would never again see him, never again look into his eyes, or have the chance to speak with him, stole the strength from my legs. I staggered forward, my hand going to my chest, clutching my shirt over my sternum. I knew the peace that awaited us all when we crossed into the next life—I'd wanted to go there myself after feeling a mere moment of it; I knew the joy of reunion he was experiencing with his parents, whose deaths had been the source of so much anguish in his life . . . but in that moment, it didn't matter. The only thing I could think was that the sweet, kind boy who had cared for me when nearly no one else had, was gone.

"Inara, I'm so sorry. Truly, I am."

The gentle, sorrowful murmur wasn't from my sister, or even Raidyn.

It was Louk, stepping forward and tenderly taking me into his arms, holding me as tears—so much loss, so much pain, *would we ever escape it?*—streaked down my face and shook my shoulders. I didn't let myself relax into his touch, but he held on, refusing to let me go. Both of us stubborn and confused and hurting, but ultimately unable to resist the pull to one another.

I sensed Sharmaine's bewilderment, even over the tumult of my own emotions—bewilderment and concern and even a cautious gladness . . . but no anger, no jealousy.

That was when I finally curved into his body, letting his arms tighten around me. When I realized she didn't love him after all. As a friend, yes. But there was nothing else there for him—nothing like what I felt.

Loukas's heart beat beneath my cheek, steady and true, and his arms were strong and secure around me. Halvor's death hurt in ways it would probably take weeks, months, even years to unravel. I'd never felt so confused as I did in that moment, sinking into the comfort of Loukas's touch while being ripped apart inside with grief.

Another explosion shook the citadel, and this time, a few pieces of the ceiling broke loose, falling down on us like hail made of plaster and stone. I pulled back from Louk. Just as I'd told my father, now was not the time for stories, it was also not the time for mourning. That would have to come later—if we survived this.

Father and a handful of Paladin were still arguing over different possible plans, oblivious to our small circle of shared grief.

Then Zuhra stepped forward.

"Use me," she said. When only a few Paladin turned to her, she repeated in a shout, "Use me!"

Silence fell across the crowd, as more plaster from the ceiling rained down on us and the stones beneath our feet trembled from the onslaught below.

"He wants my power," she continued, her voice still near a yell. "So use me as bait. Draw him out. Make his forces split by offering him what he wants!"

"No." Raidyn's eyes were wild. He shook his head as if my father had already agreed to her madness. "It will never work—you'll sacrifice yourself for nothing!"

"What about what you did with the Chimera?" My mother spoke up in the brief silence that followed Raidyn's outburst. "I know they are *jaklas,* and can absorb power, but there has to be a point when it's too much, isn't there? When their bodies literally can't contain any more?"

The look on Zuhra's face, part terror and part determination, melted into sagging relief. She glanced at Raidyn and he nodded.

Though I'd pulled away, Loukas reached for my hand, taking it in his and holding it tightly. And then he spoke up. "I can help," he said. "I can control the other *jaklas* so you will have a chance to stop them and reach Barloc. I don't know how long I will be able to hold their minds in my control with as much power as they all wield, but I can at least give you all a few seconds."

A few seconds. Those words burned through my skull, echoing into a dark space where terror still lived, far beyond the reach of the light that had gifted me with more than just unbelievable power.

What happened after a few seconds?

"No," my father said. "It's too big of a risk. There are too many, with too much power. You will lose yourself."

"I won't," Loukas insisted. "And if I do . . ." His hand flexed on mine and that terror turned to dread. "It will be worth it if it saves everyone else."

"I can help him," Zuhra offered. "I can—"

"No," Louk cut her off. "*You* have to help Raidyn. You two are our only hope to stop Barloc. Your combined power might be enough to kill him before he can absorb it all."

I listened as they all made suggestions, as they took turns volunteering to risk their lives to save others. Even Sharmaine offered, saying her shield could be used to protect a battalion long enough to slay at least some of the *jaklas*.

And the entire time, the explosions increased in frequency and intensity, until everyone had a fine coating of plaster and dust on the tops of their heads and cracks had begun to form on the walls around us. If we didn't make a decision and act soon, the citadel would fall down around us, crushing any hope of stopping Barloc and allowing him to reign in Vamala unchecked with blood and horror at his right hand.

"This is our only chance," Father's voice finally boomed out, silencing the din. "We form our battalions, and do what we've trained our whole lives to do." He went on to explain his plan, to draw out as many *jaklas* as possible, clearing the way to get to Barloc.

Grandmother's eyes met his across the hall and the sea of gryphons and Paladin. "I agree."

"That's settled then," Father bellowed as more explosions rocked the citadel. "We break into four battalions with as many as are healed enough to fight. We each attack a side of Barloc's defenders. Each of you know what you are supposed to do. May the Light hold us and keep us safe."

"Are you sure you can do this?" Loukas turned to me as all the Paladin hurried to mount their gryphons one last time.

"Are you sure *you* can?" I retorted, trying to make my voice sound like what he'd called "teasing," but staring up at him in desperation, drinking in every feature, every nuance of emotion that crossed his face, the flicker of green flame flaring brighter in his eyes as his gaze roamed over my face as hungrily as mine did over his. I'd already lost Halvor . . . was I destined to lose Louk today as well?

"This will work," he said at last, low and fervent. "It *has* to."

"It will," I promised, though I knew it wasn't mine to make.

With one last look that burned like a caress but that fell far short of actual touch, he released my hand and we both turned to our gryphons.

Zuhra already sat behind Raidyn, her face set into a determined mask, but I sensed the cataclysm of emotions in her.

Our eyes met—hazel and blue-fire—and I realized suddenly that I hadn't given her one last hug, hadn't said any last words to her . . . just in case.

But then my father whistled and there was no more time as we all surged forward, out the shattered window, into the wind that battered a storm toward us and the battle that loomed below.

FORTY-FOUR

Zuhra

The plan was complex and simple all at once. Four groups of Paladin, each with a "secret weapon" to help make it possible to attack as many of the *jaklas* surrounding Barloc as possible, hopefully without risking any of the secret weapons' lives any more than necessary as it would have been to try to use them against all ten of the surviving *jaklas.*

Raidyn and I would wait until Barloc was exposed. Then it was our turn.

For the first time since they'd been reunited, my father had convinced Mother to remain behind. *I can't bear to watch you ride away from me, not knowing if you'll ever come back again,* she'd said, but he'd kissed her and whispered something and she'd finally nodded and stepped back, her eyes flickering to where Inara and I had stood.

Now I clung to Raidyn, trying to peer over his shoulder, hating having to wait while others risked their lives to give us our chance to kill Barloc. Including Sharmaine and Loukas, who were two of the secret weapons for their groups—Sharmaine using her shield to protect them long enough to attack the *jaklas* without their blasts reaching the Paladin, and Loukas using his mind control to force the *jaklas* his group was targeting to stand still and withhold their power until the Paladin could behead them. Gruesome but effective.

The interaction between Sharmaine, Loukas, and my sister

had been baffling . . . and touching. To see Loukas treat Inara with such tenderness, to witness the emotion that had softened his face when she'd learned of Halvor's death—I'd already started to step toward her, to comfort her as I always had, when he'd done it instead. And Sharmaine had watched, surprised, but looking almost . . . relieved. As if she were *happy* for him. For *them*.

Now, she was flying away, in the center of a group of Paladin I didn't know, and I could only pray she survived. Inara had already saved her life once today. My sister's power was immense but it couldn't be *truly* limitless. Surely, she would reach the end of it and soon, if she had to keep doing such intense healings.

There was another shielder, like Sharmaine, in another group, and the final secret weapon was the entire group, including my grandmother, aiming all of their firepower at once on three or four *jaklas,* hopefully overwhelming their bodies with the sheer amount of combined power, and with any luck, killing them.

There were so many variables, and so much potential loss.

I glanced over at Inara, whose gryphon treaded air beside Naiki, her sharp blue-fire eyes watching as the groups split off and dove toward the *jaklas* below. Those who'd had to fly away over the hedge to get out of reach came back, but we gestured for them to wait—or go back into the Hall of Miracles. A final backup plan if we all failed.

I still couldn't believe my sister was alive, her power restored, and riding her own gryphon, no less. How had so much changed in only a couple of days? I should have been used to it by now, and yet I was continually shocked by how quickly life could shift course and people could be altered.

Raidyn stiffened and I focused back on the scene ahead of us, my heart in my throat. The first two groups surged slightly ahead of the last two, so that when the other Paladin who could form a shield threw it up to protect his group, the *jaklas* to the left of their targets were able to send a volley of fireballs at the outer flank of their group, past the reach of his shield. Several gryphons plummeted to the earth, their Riders dead or dying.

Inara gave a tiny cry; I glanced at her to see her face contorted with grief, her knuckles white on the reins she clenched, but she didn't signal her gryphon to move forward—not yet. The other groups got into place and soon all the *jaklas* were busy contending with each of the joint attacks.

I stared as Sharmaine's group surged forward, under protection of her shield, while the *jaklas* in Loukas's froze in the act of lifting their hands, veins lit but their ability and will to act stolen by his power. The Paladin in both groups surged forward, gryphons swooping low, so their Riders could leap from their backs, swords lifted. One *jakla* fell, two, three . . . four . . . and then a stream of fire to rival what Raidyn and I could produce blasted through the hole where the three jaklas from Loukas's group had fallen, incinerating the front row of Paladin who had succeeded in killing them.

A scream echoed in my ears, and it took a minute for me to realize it was my own.

Below us, the battle turned into chaos. The Paladin, including my grandmother, had all sent their fire at once at three *jaklas,* but only forced one into falling. The other two fought back, absorbing power and sending their own blasts, killing a handful of gryphons and Paladin, and forcing the others to retreat. One blast was aimed directly at my grandmother; her gryphon twisted in midair to let it shoot past them and explode against the side of the citadel, but the creature screeched in pain when the edge of the fire singed its wing.

When a guttural cry erupted from my sister, my gaze flew to Loukas in time to see him collapsing forward onto his gryphon's neck, as the fourth and final *jakla* in their section shook free of his hold and sent a blast of fire toward the group. Maddok retreated, swerving back and forth to keep Loukas on his back as his Rider dipped and swayed, nearly falling more than once as Inara kicked her heels into her gryphon's side and dove for them.

"No! *Inara!*"

But she was already gone.

Raidyn stiffened but didn't say anything. He didn't have to.

Though six of the ten *jaklas* had fallen, many more Paladin had died or were dying, and four *jaklas* remained, closing in around

Barloc. The male shielder fell back with what remained of his fellow Paladin, along with the decimated group that had tried to fight fire with fire. Loukas's group was also fleeing the onslaught of fire from the *jaklas,* while Inara's gryphon turned alongside Maddok, so she could reach out and grasp his arm, her veins already lit with power.

I saw the moment Barloc recognized her, the fury and hunger that twisted his face when he saw the power lighting her veins—power he had already stolen once.

"No!" The wind whipped my shout from my mouth. I bent forward and yelled, "He's going to go after Inara!" pointing over Raidyn's shoulder to where Barloc was pushing the four remaining *jaklas* forward in front of him, to where Maddok and Inara's gryphon hovered in midair as she tried to heal him, her eyes shut, unaware of the danger rushing for them.

Raidyn didn't hesitate, though we'd all agreed that we couldn't risk the plan to save others, even those we cared about. He kicked his heels into Naiki's side and she surged forward.

But as we watched in amazement, Inara pulled her hand away and Loukas stirred, and then sat up.

"Inara! Loukas! *Go—now!*" Raidyn shouted and they both glanced where he pointed, to where Barloc and the *jaklas* rushed across the destroyed grounds, dodging bodies, to try to reach them, already throwing blasts of fire at their gryphons.

"Don't kill them! Just the mounts!" Barloc was shouting, his words barely audible over the ever-increasing wind.

But Inara and Loukas's gryphons burst into action, racing away from them toward us.

What could we do now?

Our plan had *almost* succeeded. We'd come so close.

But the only way the fire Raidyn and I could produce together would have any chance of being enough to kill Barloc was if it was used on him—and *only* him. And four remained, barring our way.

"What do we do?" Raidyn shouted over his shoulder.

Before I could answer, I noticed someone sneaking around the corner of the citadel, a butcher knife clutched in one hand and a mallet in the other. My heart plummeted, dread as cold as the bitter winds that stole through the citadel in the depths of midwinter chilling me to the bone.

No. No, no, *no*! But I didn't dare shout, or point, or do anything to alert Barloc to Sami's presence as she tried valiantly to sneak up on him from behind. One small, aged, powerless human woman against a monster.

Raidyn's stomach clenched beneath my hands, his shoulders stiffening, and I knew he had seen her as well.

All the remaining gryphons and Riders had fled, even Grandmother because her gryphon was injured and could barely fly straight; all except two who circled back to hover beside us. I didn't dare look away from Sami, but I recognized Taavi and Keko out of the corner of my eye.

Inara and Loukas reached us and turned their gryphons around.

The six of us against the five of them . . . and Sami.

"You'll never win this," Barloc shouted, still urging his *jaklas* toward us, though, for some reason, they'd stopped their attacks at our mounts. I could only hope they were running out of power. They were *jaklas,* yes, but surely even they would eventually lose their strength like all Paladin. Even Barloc had admitted to needing to rest, spying on us while he regained his strength after the strain of opening the gateway. "Surrender now and I'll let you live. Or I can end you all. It doesn't matter to me. The rest of my family is joining me later today, so I have time to kill." His laughter was cruel, bordering on maniacal. I could hardly remember the blustering but scholarly man Halvor had called uncle, the façade he'd created to hide his true desires and intentions, even from his nephew.

"You killed the only family you have left!" I shouted back, so full of fury and desperation and grief, I couldn't hold it back. "The monsters you unleashed here murdered Halvor!"

There was a brief moment, a twitch of his lip, a drawing down of his eyebrows, when I thought my words had struck something within him, some small corner of his heart that still remembered what it was to be human, to have a nephew. But then the tiny flicker of humanity twisted into a sneer. "He was no family of mine—he was weak, like his mother. Good riddance!"

Rage at his callousness, his *depthless* cruelty, flashed beneath my skin on Halvor's behalf, the memory of his sacrifice fresh and awful.

"Hold your ground," Father said, before any of us could react, barely loud enough for us to hear him. "There has been enough death today. The six of us will finish this. Now."

Before anyone could ask what he intended for us to do, Sami suddenly broke into a run, lifting the butcher knife in the air.

For a breathless, hope-filled moment, I believed she might actually succeed. Barloc still faced us and she was close—*so close*—and then with a twist of his lips that looked like a grin, if a grin could be full of malice, he spun to face her, as if he'd known she was there all along and had intentionally allowed us a moment of hope so he could delight in tearing it away.

She veered to the left, toward one of his *jaklas* as he lifted his arm. The knife swooped down . . . the fire that exploded out of Barloc's hand flashed on the sharpened blade, like the last ray of sunlight in a sunset, breaking across the sky—

The fire consumed her at the exact moment her knife imbedded in the back of the neck of one of the *jaklas.*

"Nooo!" The scream was guttural, wrenching up from the deepest depths of my heart, met and matched by a similar cry of despair from Inara, as the only woman who had ever been motherly to us for the majority of our lives fell to the ground, convulsing, burned but not dead—yet.

The *jakla* she'd managed to attack dropped to his knees, blood pouring from the wound in his neck. Barloc jumped forward, mouth parted, as though he would drink it and try to absorb his power before he died too, but Father sent a blast of his fire at the *jakla,* finishing what Sami had started. The *jakla* dropped, eyes unseeing, veins flickering and then going cold as his stolen power died with him.

Three remained, two men and a woman, and Barloc.

But I could only stare at Sami as her convulsing slowed and then stilled.

My screams turned into sobs.

"No more," I choked out, half-blinded by tears, but fate-altering wrath igniting in my belly and spreading, a fire of fury. "We end this *now*! Loukas—stop them! Sharmaine—shield us if he fails! Father, kill them and give us access to Barloc! Inara, be ready to heal us if we need it!"

I barked out the commands as if I had any clue what I was doing and shockingly, everyone obeyed.

For the first time, when his eyes met mine, I saw true fear flicker across Barloc's face. He quickly smothered it, shouting out commands at his *jaklas*. "Attack them! *Now!*" he bellowed.

But they didn't respond. They couldn't.

Loukas's hands were lifted, his veins glowing.

Father and Sharmaine sent blasts of Paladin fire at the *jaklas,* killing one and injuring the other two as they stood frozen by Loukas's power, only their eyes giving away their terror in the instant before the fire blasted into their bodies, knocking them to the ground, leaving Barloc unprotected for the first time.

His hands were lifted, but Sharmaine had already thrown out her shield as Loukas reeled back his power. The blast Barloc sent at us was so intense, so massive, that when it hit her shield, it exploded, sending our gryphons reeling backward. Shar jolted as if she'd been struck, barely managing to stay seated.

Raidyn and I were already prepared, my hands clamped into his arms, his veins lit with power, fire racing through us both, building, fueled by rage and grief and a fierce determination. My power surged out of me into him and then the stream of flames blasted out of his hands, exploding into Barloc.

Whenever we'd done this before, our enemy had been incinerated, turning to ash within seconds, even the Chimera.

But Barloc didn't.

Smoke filled the air as his hair and clothes burned away, but somehow he remained standing, his arms splayed open, his eyes turning from blue to brightest, glowing red, like the heart of a fire. Even the blue glow of his veins changed, cutting through his flesh like red rivers of blood turned to *true* flame, rather than Paladin flame.

Impossibly—terrifyingly—he was *surviving* our onslaught—absorbing our power and becoming something else entirely. Not human, not Paladin, not *jakla,* but something *other.* He took a step forward, *into* the stream of flames, the ground trembling beneath that one step, and then the next. And still we blasted him, though Raidyn's arms shook beneath my hands and I could feel myself draining.

We would never prevail against him. We were all going to die, just as he'd promised.

Our last chance. This is our last chance. I willed myself to stay conscious, to pull the last dregs of power I possessed out of every cell of my body, even if it killed me, even if—

A hand closed over mine, cool and soft, and the relief was instantaneous. It took every ounce of strength I managed to summon to turn my face to my sister, on her gryphon beside us. Her arms were stretched out to both sides, one hand on mine and the other on Loukas's where he hovered on the other side of her. Her veins were brilliant with power, brighter than all the stars in the sky, brighter than the moon; Paladin fire without end, power without limits.

The night Inara was born, they said the stars died and were reborn in her eyes.

In that moment, Inara *was* a star. She was light made into flesh.

That power entered my body, and with it came energy and healing and more fire. My heart calmed, and my mind cleared. Raidyn's arms quit shaking, his body settling deeper into the saddle. The stream of fire cut off, but only momentarily.

I looked to Barloc—or to the horrific creature that *used* to be Barloc. The movement was free of strain now, even though I felt more power coursing through me than I'd ever experienced. His flesh began to blacken, but his destroyed face cracked into a triumphant sneer, his teeth glared white against his charred skin. His hands lifted, his entire body flared with crimson fire, his red irises flashed—

Then he froze, his face contorted.

Loukas, I knew with calm security. Able to easily control him with Inara's help.

When the stream of flames exploded out of Raidyn's hands this time, it was so strong, it nearly knocked both of us off of Naiki. I was dimly aware of my fingers digging into Raidyn's arms and his legs tightening around Naiki, barely holding us in place as the continuous fire slammed into Barloc.

For the space of two terrified heartbeats, I thought it wasn't going to work. He still stood in the stream of flames, his body mutating even more, every bit of his flesh turning red, like the glowing embers at the base of a flame, the hottest part of a fire.

But Inara's hand tightened over mine, and with a cry that started with me and ended with Raidyn, reverberating off the walls of the citadel and the mountains that surrounded us, our Paladin fire intensified beyond all comprehension.

Barloc's eyes widened, that one tiny movement all he could muster under Loukas's control, as finally, *finally,* the flames consumed him.

The thing that had once been Barloc crumpled to the earth. When his body hit the ground, it turned to ash.

I nearly collapsed when Raidyn cut the stream of flames off, but Inara kept her hand on mine; her healing presence restoring not only my strength and my power, but Raidyn's as well, *through* me. The wind howled around us, blowing the ashes off the earth, lifting Barloc's remains and taking them away. The storm was nearly upon the citadel. The first few raindrops began to fall when Inara finally released my hand.

We'd done it. Somehow, together, we'd really, truly done it.

I turned to my sister, a heady mix of triumph and relief making me dizzy.

But she wasn't looking at me. Or Loukas. Or Father or Sharmaine, who were racing back to where we all hovered. She stared down at her hands, her veins flickering blue and then white and then blue again.

"Inara?"

She tried to look up then, when I spoke her name, but the

effort—the visible strain—hit me like a punch in the gut. Her eyes, when they finally met mine, were dull and glazed. And then they rolled back in her head and she crumpled, falling off the side of her gryphon, plummeting through the ash-strewn wind to the earth below.

FORTY-FIVE

Zuhra

An hour could pass like a dream, speeding by, blurry and unreal. And a minute could stretch for an hour, chokingly slow, painful in its passing. I'd experienced both in my life. Hours with Inara when she was lucid racing by as though someone were pushing the hands of a clock faster and faster, until the hour was gone and so was she. Or the minutes in the drawing room when I wanted to be anywhere but there, plying needles, dreaming of the freedom of birds, minutes creeping by like those same hands of a clock trying to sludge through a mud bog, weighted down and impossibly slow.

But as my sister's body dropped, as her gryphon and Loukas's and my father's all dove after her, as her hair pooled out around her head, and her arms waved as though she were floating in water and not falling through air and sky, my heart slowed, my breathing stopped, and seconds turned into hours that passed like a lifetime of nightmares.

I saw Sharmaine try and fail to create a shield, too drained—and the only one who Inara hadn't healed.

I saw Loukas stretch for her, his fingers almost brushing hers, but missing.

I saw my father's mouth open in a scream, but Loukas had edged him out and he couldn't reach her.

I saw where she would land, on what remained of her gardens, her plants charred and trampled.

I saw her gryphon pin her wings to her sides, zooming for the ground so quickly, there was no way she would be able to catch Inara and break her own headlong descent in time to keep from breaking her neck.

Those seconds drew out, as death closed in, and my heartbeats were an eternity.

Then, somehow, impossibly, as impossible as so many other things that had happened—miracles and tragedies, both—her gryphon opened her wings, mere feet before Inara slammed into the raised garden beds, before the gryphon herself would have broken herself on the ground, and caught an updraft, her talons extending out and—

Snatched my sister out of the jaws of death, inches before her head would have cracked open on the wooden edge of the only place that had ever brought her joy for the first fifteen years of her life.

In the seconds it took for that gryphon to carry my sister back up, away from the earth, away from death, time raced forward again, along with my heart.

After she'd saved all of us—over and over again—the gryphon had saved her.

I sagged forward into Raidyn, let my eyes close, and sobbed.

FORTY-SIX

INARA

Darkness.

Light.

Both had their places in life and both had worked their way through me.

I lay there, at the crossroads of both, struggling to find my direction—my way home.

Darkness: when I had felt empty, broken, reduced to a shell of my former self.

Light: when I had been saved, when I had saved others.

Who was I now?

I was Inara, Ray of Light, and I was Inara, daughter, sister, friend, healer.

You have done well, my daughter.

Her voice was unexpected here, at the crossroads, where the light existed, but was nowhere near as strong as the *luxem magnam.*

You used your gift well, as I'd hoped. And so we will leave a piece of it with you, to keep. To heal, not only others, but yourself.

I wanted to thank her, but somehow I knew she was already gone.

Someday . . . when I went into the light for good. Then I could.

But for now—

When I opened my eyes, I was lying on the ground, dark clouds roiling overhead. Raindrops fell, landing wet and cool on my face.

Someone held my hand, fingers tightening around mine when I turned to meet his worried green-fire eyes.

"She's awake!" Louk called out, his gaze never leaving mine.

I blinked against the rain. My body ached in a way it hadn't since I'd emerged from the light—like I'd been drained and was still recovering. I still sensed power within me, but it felt like my *old* power, the one I'd been born with, not the unspeakable gift I'd been given that had saved us all.

And, even though it had gone beyond description to wield that kind of power, I was actually *glad* for it to have been taken back. I'd never wanted more than I'd been born with; I'd only ever wanted what had been stolen from me.

"Inara!" Zuhra crashed to her knees beside me, streaks running through the dirt on her face, as though she'd been crying, though her eyes were clear for the moment. "I was so scared . . . I thought . . ."

I squeezed Louk's hand back and then let go to push myself up until I was sitting on the dirt, tiny splotches of wet surrounding us. The rain was growing more insistent by the minute, but when I glanced around, I saw Paladin rushing across the grounds, some kneeling beside other Paladin, treating wounds or attempting to heal them, while others were digging a large pit.

I quickly looked away from it—and the far-too-large row of bodies near it.

"What happened after we stopped him? How did I end up here?"

Zuhra quickly filled me in on how I'd lost consciousness and fallen from Sukhi's back and how, though others tried, she'd managed to save me—at the last second, in the instant before we both would have died or been gravely injured.

"Where is she?" I glanced around, but didn't see my gryphon anywhere.

"She hit her wing on the garden box when she caught you. One of the other Paladin took her over by the stables to tape it up for now. We have to use the healers for the Paladin."

I climbed shakily to my feet. "I need to go see her—and then I can help heal the injured."

"No, you've been through too much," Louk protested. "You need to rest."

"I can rest later."

"You really shouldn't go over there," he insisted, sharing a dark glance with Zuhra.

"He might be right . . ." she agreed hesitantly.

But I refused to be swayed, even though the look they'd shared sent a chill skittering down my spine. "I need to see her." Before either of them could try to convince me otherwise, I strode away, pretending to be stronger than I felt.

Louk grumbled something under his breath in Paladin—something I apparently could no longer understand—but I ignored him, rushing toward the stables, on the other end of the grounds, all the way around the citadel.

I sensed Louk shadowing my steps, but staying far enough back that I couldn't hear his boots on the dirt over the other sounds that filled the air. I had to weave between Paladin and gryphons, many moaning or crying in pain. Burns, exposed bones, bloody gashes . . . so many wounds, so many injured. Gryphons and Paladin alike. The air was a potent mix of charred flesh and the crisp hint of evergreen carried on the wind and rain. They needed my help—and soon. There were far too many injured and only a handful of healers who already looked exhausted, on the brink of being drained.

But Sukhi had saved my life and I needed to see her, at least for a moment.

When I reached the stables, I saw a dozen gryphons with various injuries being treated by their Riders, but Sukhi wasn't among them. The door was wide open, so I hurried past the unfamiliar mounts to duck inside, but stopped short. It was dim, shadowed from the clouds blocking out the sun, but it was silent—*too* silent—and there was a fetid stench heavy on the humid air, something I instinctually recognized as the smell of death. Though they'd assured me Sukhi had only injured her wing, fear gripped my heart, squeezing it as I rushed to the nearest stall and then slammed to a halt, my stomach lurching, caustic acid rising in my throat.

A gryphon lay in the stall, dead, a hole burned through its breast.

"Inara—stop!"

Loukas's shout echoed dully through the roar in my head. I backed away and then hurried to the next stall, only to find another dead gryphon. My blood was a rush through my body; dizziness struck me and I stumbled away from the corpse.

Strong hands closed over my shoulders, spinning me around and pulling me into a warm, strong, living body. "I tried to warn you," Loukas murmured, but there was only sorrow in his voice, not censure.

"Where is she? Did she really survive or are you all lying to me?" I pulled back, though part of me wanted to bury my head in his chest and let him hold me until all of this somehow went away—the death, the pain and suffering. We'd stopped Barloc, but not before he'd taken far too many lives—human, Paladin, and gryphon alike.

"She's alive," he said, gently guiding me back to the doorway and out into the rain. "They must be treating her somewhere else nearby. I promise, she's alive," he repeated as I began to tremble, a delayed reaction to the horror we'd endured.

"Are there more injured gryphons nearby?" Louk called out, and a couple of Paladin looked up from their work bandaging and treating their mounts.

"There's one or two more around the side," one said, pointing. "We ran out of space over here."

Loukas nodded and turned me toward the other side of the stables, walking around the outside of it. When we turned the corner, relief coursed through me, so powerful it was heavy somehow, draining my strength so that, even though I wanted to run to her, I could barely lift my legs to walk to where Sukhi lay on her side, her leonine hind legs tucked in and her left wing extended. An unfamiliar Paladin was wrapping it, holding a thick piece of wood in place to splint her wing with a long length of bandage that looked a lot like a sheet that had been torn into strips.

She lifted her head when I hurried to her side, and gave a soft hoot. I dropped to my knees by her beak and pulled it into my lap, stroking the soft feathers back from her eyes. She closed them with another soft noise in her throat.

"Thank you," I murmured. "Thank you for saving my life."

"I'm almost done here," the Paladin wrapping her wing said. "She won't be able to fly for a few weeks, unless someone heals her before then."

I longed to heal her, but I knew there were other more life-threatening injuries I had to save my strength for . . . but soon. Once the Paladin who still lived had been healed and I'd regained my strength fully.

"Thank you for helping her," I said to the Paladin securing the bandage with a knot.

He looked to me and there was something akin to awe in his expression. "Thank *you* for saving all of us."

My neck flushed. "It wasn't just me. We all did it. Together."

Loukas crouched down beside me and Sukhi, and the look he gave me filled me with warmth even as the rain sluiced down my hair and face, slowly soaking my clothes. "He's right. Without you, we would have failed."

Our gaze met and held, and everything else faded away. There was only Louk and the heat in his green-fire eyes, and a sudden realization that we had survived. That we were *alive.* So very alive. Hearts beating and lungs breathing and lips speaking. I suddenly wished we were alone so our lips could be doing something very different. His eyes dropped to my mouth, as if he knew exactly what I was thinking. Heat unfurled in my stomach, and I suddenly became very aware of my skin, of the current that rushed over it, like lightning had distilled into the rain and coated my body with sparks, just waiting for him to close the space between us and touch me, igniting the fire he'd awoken in me by the stream.

Had that only been one day ago? How was it possible that only one night and one day had passed, when it seemed an entire lifetime had been encompassed in those hours?

Louk's eyes burned, his body tensed as though the pull between us was just as strong for him as it was for me. But wishes weren't easily fulfilled; we weren't alone and there was too much to do, too many people suffering who needed me, to indulge in something as miraculous but untimely as another kiss. And alongside the wonder of having survived was also the blistering guilt of it . . . because so many hadn't. Including Halvor.

I looked down first, ripping my gaze from his as though tearing our souls apart. *Later.* There would be all the time in the world because, whether we deserved it or not, we'd survived and we were alive. But for now, I was needed elsewhere.

Hours passed in a blur of rain, mud, blood, and summoning my power again and again, until my hands shook and my muscles trembled with exhaustion. I couldn't fully heal the worst of the injuries, knowing it would drain too much of my power. It was much more finite now that the Mother of all Paladin had taken back the endless well I'd wielded for such a short time—but at the most crucial moment I ever could have needed it. So I did just enough to save their lives, to minimize their suffering, and had to fight the urge to keep going to finish what I started, pulling back instead and moving on to the next injury. Six, seven, eight . . . ten, eleven, twelve Paladin before I glanced around and there were no more to work on. The other healers' gazes met mine and I saw my own exhaustion echoed in their dull eyes, their Paladin fire barely flickering after the massive drain on all of our power.

My legs barely held me up, I was covered in mud, my clothes were soaked from the rain that remained a steady drizzle while we worked. Some of those who weren't injured as badly were moved inside the citadel, but the worst ones remained where they were until we got to them, and then were taken inside after we stabilized them. I was cold, exhausted, and on the verge of collapsing.

Somehow, we'd done it. We'd saved everyone that we possibly were capable of saving.

But there were far too many that we'd lost.

Now that the work had ended, I stood there in the middle of the nearly empty grounds, shaking and wet and overcome. As I'd healed and healed and healed, I hadn't been able to think about the ones I'd lost—hadn't *allowed* myself to think of them. I'd forced myself to stay focused, to do what had to be done.

But there was nothing left for me to do, and with that nothingness came a tidal wave of grief.

Zuhra had taken me aside at one point and told me Halvor's last words—how he'd asked them to tell me he loved me. His loss was sharp and terrible. It knifed through my heart, a blade formed of grief, serrated with guilt—that we hadn't come back in time to save him, that he had sacrificed his life to save my family. Zuhra had held me as I sobbed, tears of despair and shame and *relief*—because of him my sister and mother lived.

I would never be able to thank him for caring about me—for loving me. For being my first kiss, and my first . . . *everything*. He had changed our lives, and mine in particular, forever.

Around me the other Paladin hurried to finish carrying the survivors in, but I stood in middle of the courtyard in the rain, my body and mind completely drained, my defenses weakened so that I could no longer avoid the one death my mind had darted away from, like a skittish deer through all the hours of healing.

Sami.

The pain of her loss nearly doubed me over. The only death that could have hurt worse would have been if I'd lost Zuhra. Next to my sister, Sami was the one who had always been there for me—the mother my mother hadn't been capable of being for either of us. She'd taken down one of the *jaklas* with her death, but the cost was far too high. If only she would have stayed in the citadel. My eyes burned and I tilted my face up to the sky, letting my tears mingle with the rain slipping down my cheeks.

"You are truly remarkable, do you know that?"

I spun at the sound of Louk's voice. He stood a few feet away in the rain, his dark hair dripping, his brilliant green eyes a stark contrast to the charcoal clouds above and the mud below. When our gazes met, his brow furrowed, his smile slipping.

"What is it?"

I shook my head, unable to speak, the tears coming faster and harder.

Without another word, Louk opened his arms, and I let him

envelop me in his strength and warmth, holding me as I sobbed, grief slamming into me like waves, over and over. I would surface just long enough to suck in a breath of air before another one pulled me under again.

I wasn't sure how much time had passed before my sorrow spent itself—for now—and the tears slowed and then finally stopped. The rain had petered out sometime while I'd cried, soaking his shirt even more.

"I'm so sorry," he said, his voice low, and a little hoarse. "I know what he meant to you."

I pulled back to peer up into his face. His face was shuttered once more, revealing none of the hurt I sensed coursing through his veins from the *sanaulus* we now shared after healing him during the battle. He thought all of this was because of Halvor. And it *was*; it was confusion because I *had* cared for Halvor and instead of coming back to have the heart-rending conversation with him I'd been preparing for, I'd never seen him again, to tell him anything. Not *thank you for being there for me* or *I'm sorry* or *please forgive me* or any of the other inadequate words I'd tried to come up with to explain myself and my actions with Louk. Halvor was just . . . gone. And I didn't know how to handle that—yet. On top of all of that was losing Sami. Her death gutted me in a way I didn't know how to heal from. There was no magic fix for the pain both of their losses left inside me.

But . . . I didn't want all of that to push Loukas away. I *needed* him, now more than ever. I reached up and cupped his jaw as I had by the stream. He winced at the touch, a tiny prick of hope sparking but met and overcome by doubt. It amazed me, the way I could read his emotions so clearly. It almost made me feel guilty . . . except that it gave me hope—that perhaps he *did* care for me. Naïve and young as I might be, as he'd pointed out more than once.

"I'm not going to lie to you—you're right. Halvor's death . . . hurts. A lot. I cared for him . . . deeply," I began.

Louk stiffened, his jaw clenching beneath my hand; I pressed on before he could withdraw or shut me out again.

"And he . . . he sacrificed himself to save my sister and my mother. If he were here, it would mean they were gone." My voice broke, but I forced myself to continue. "So yes, I will always have a special place in my heart for Halvor, for being there for me and for what we shared, for helping me find hope when I wasn't sure I could . . . and for saving my family. But also because without him coming into our lives, Zuhra never would have met Raidyn, we wouldn't have ever seen our father again, and . . . I never would have met *you*. I . . . I never would have learned what I was capable of feeling . . . of what I do with you." My words were woefully insufficient, but it was all I dared say—as much as I could bring myself to admit.

Louk's mask slipped, his face softening, filling his eyes with a warmth I'd never seen before. "Inara, I—"

I barreled right over him. "And I was also crying because of Sami." Even saying her name made my eyes sting again. My arm began to shake and I had to let my hand drop. "She was like a mother to me, when my own mother was incapable of showing me love. She didn't need to die. I don't understand why she did that—why she thought she could stop him." My throat tightened and I finally stopped.

He cupped *my* face this time, with both hands, gently stroking my damp hair back. He opened his mouth, but when no words came out, he merely bent down and pressed his lips to mine. His kiss was soft, gentle even, speaking what he couldn't say. One of his hands wove through my hair, while his other arm dropped to encircle me, carefully pulling me into his body. I sank into his embrace, heedless of where we were, of who might be watching, losing myself in the warmth and strength of his arms.

Our first kiss had been desperation and heat and need, a crashing of wills and hearts; this kiss was softer, his lips moving tenderly on mine, a meeting of souls, a celebration of survival, a surrendering that was like falling and being caught all at once. I felt his walls crumbling as our mouths slowly moved together, the rush of pure emotion that filled his heart and body flowing into mine through his hands, his kiss—the connection that had begun that day I climbed onto a gryphon for the first time in front of him and culminating there in the courtyard, where everything had begun all those weeks ago when the hedge had let a young man through the gate.

Though I was a mess inside, grief and relief, sorrow and joy, guilt and wonder, all twisted up in each other—a tangle of memories and wishes—in that moment, in Louk's arms, I could relinquish it all, and just *be.* Even if it was *only* for that moment, for the length of a breathtaking, soul-healing, heart-stopping kiss.

For now, that was enough.

FORTY-SEVEN

Zuhra

I stood in the shadows of the great entryway, watching the final few healers outside finishing up, including my sister and father. I was too tired to move, even though the numb oblivion of work was wearing away in that stillness, leaving too much space for grief to surge up in its place—exactly what I'd been trying to avoid.

The floor behind me was full of wounded Paladin, those who were only partially mended because their injuries had been too severe to completely heal without risking draining the healers themselves. I'd spent hours working side by side with my mother, grandmother, and other Paladin, finding blankets and pillows that weren't ruined with age or by mice, making poultices, fetching water, trying to find food, and anything else I could do to help make them more comfortable—and stay as busy as possible, trying to force my mind away from the horror of the last day and night. Any pause in activity allowed a rush of memory too painful to delve into; the Chimera, Halvor's sacrifice, nearly losing Raidyn, all the Paladin who had been slaughtered by the *jaklas* . . . *Sami*. I'd volunteered to go out into the rain to pick any ripe vegetables or fruit to eat, unable to bear facing the kitchen, when I knew I would never again find her there, her cheeks dusted with flour; I'd never again stand side by side with her washing dishes, talking about everything and nothing.

I sensed Raidyn coming up behind me moments before his

arms slid around my waist, pulling me back into his chest, the warmth of his body chasing away some of the chill that slithered over my skin, delving deep into muscle and bone. I wrapped my arms over his, holding him tightly, all too aware of how close he'd come to dying. Only the inordinate power Inara wielded had been capable of saving him. But after she'd lost consciousness and then woken again, she'd been different, worn out, more easily drained; whatever bottomless well of power she'd been allowed to tap into had closed, leaving her with a gift to be reckoned with, but nothing like what she'd been capable of during the battle.

A gift that had been our salvation.

Without her endless store of energy and power, we wouldn't have succeeded, and many more would have died. Including Raidyn and Sharmaine. Possibly *all* of us, ultimately.

So I stood still and held on to him, because he was *real,* and solid, and warm with life, and so was I. Though my body ached with fatigue, my eyes burning with suppressed grief, more than anything I was just *grateful*—that I was alive to feel that exhaustion and sorrow, that we were able to cling to each other there in that empty doorway.

We were silent, knowing there were no words sufficient for the losses we'd suffered—but also the triumph we'd finally managed to achieve.

Together, we watched Inara straighten from the last injured Paladin outside, while two men hefted the woman into their arms, carrying her into the citadel, out of the rain, leaving my sister standing alone in the middle of the grounds. I stirred in Raidyn's arms, ready to go to her, when Loukas appeared, striding across the courtyard, directly toward her as though he had been watching, waiting for her to finish.

When she turned to him, the myriad of emotions rushing through her—grief and pain and weariness, yes, but others alongside those, feelings for *him*—were so strong, I couldn't ignore them, even from this distance. It was unexpected and a little alarming. With everything else that had happened, I'd almost forgotten what I'd seen when she'd let me help her heal Raidyn, the kiss she and Loukas had shared, the things she'd felt in that blinding, beautiful light.

I thought she'd been in love with Halvor. They'd certainly seemed close. But when Loukas took her into his arms, holding her in the rain, it was undeniable that what she felt for him was far stronger than anything I'd ever sensed from her toward Halvor—which was part relief and part sadness.

"Well, that's . . . unexpected," Raidyn commented.

I made a noncommittal noise, feeling a little guilty, like we were intruding on a private moment. They *were* standing in the middle of the grounds, though, in full view of anyone who happened to look, and I couldn't seem to make myself turn away.

But when Loukas took her face in his hands, his body curving toward her, and I realized he was going to kiss her again, the guilt transmuted into mortification. We definitely shouldn't stand there watching them do *that.*

Raidyn stiffened, his arms tightening so much around me, I couldn't move.

"What is he *doing*?"

I forgot Raidyn hadn't known what happened in Visimperum. I squirmed in his arms until he loosened them with a low "sorry," and turned to face him, drawing his focus to me. "There hasn't been time to tell you . . . but when we healed you, and I joined my power to hers, I saw them kissing in Visimperum."

Raidyn's mouth twisted. "He better not be taking advantage of your sister," he growled.

"I think they might be falling in love," I admitted and his eyebrows shot up.

"*Loukas?* And . . . *Inara?*"

I nodded.

"Loukas and Inara," he repeated. "My best friend and your sister."

"There are worse things that could happen."

"What about Halvor?" He glanced past me and then quickly back down at my face, the tender skin below his jaw flushing. I wasn't sure I wanted to know why. It was one thing to *know* your sister was kissing someone, but another altogether to *watch* it happen.

"I don't know. I know she cared for him . . . but I've never sensed anything from her like what she feels with Loukas."

Raidyn bent forward, until his forehead rested against mine. "I will talk to him. He's not one to kiss just anyone . . . so he must care for her. But . . . if he doesn't love her, then I will tell him to leave her alone right now, before he can hurt her more than he may already have."

Part of me bristled at the idea of him interfering—but it was *Inara* we were talking about, and if there was any chance Loukas didn't care for her as much as I suspected she was beginning to for him, well . . . "You'll have to let me know what he says."

There was a pause, when I let my eyes drift shut, our breath mingling, a sudden awareness of how close we stood, and the realization that as much as I longed to go find a secluded corner somewhere and kiss him until there was no death, no loss, no pain or exhaustion, nothing but me and him and lips and touch and fire . . . there was also no rush, because we had made it, the threat was gone, and miraculously, we had *time* for the first chance since I'd met him.

"You need to rest," Raidyn rasped, low and soft, leading me to believe rest was the last thing on his mind.

"Only if you come with me," I said, realizing an instant too late how it would sound. Raidyn drew back, eyes wide, eyebrows nearly to his hairline. My cheeks flamed with embarrassment. "Because . . . you help . . . the bad dreams . . . your stories . . ." I stammered.

"Oh, I see how it is. You only want me for my storytelling skills. And here I hoped you wanted me for *other* things." A wicked gleam lit up his beautiful eyes, sending the heat in my cheeks gliding over my entire body with a delicious shiver. A languid weakness melted through my legs at the unspoken promises in that look, in that teasing tone of voice.

"I want you for *everything*," I said, and his fingers curled into my spine, his gaze raking over me. Hunger and fire and something else . . . something even more powerful that made my heart slam against my chest. Once he'd told me he could no longer hide his feelings from me, but I'd been afraid then—afraid to believe what I felt, what I *hoped* to be true. But now, more than ever, it was so clear, there was no denying it. The emotion that filled his heart, so much that it could barely contain it, was matched only by the reflection of it in my own chest.

I loved him.

Deeply, completely. Body, heart, and soul—so fiercely, it was almost unbearable, a love so exquisite and powerful it hurt.

His eyes burned even brighter; his hands were brands through my still-damp shirt from the rain. "And I want *you*—forever, *meaula amarre*," he responded, all teasing gone, a fervency in its place that made me go very, very still.

"What does that mean?"

"The literal translation is *my soul's love*." Raidyn's gaze was unwavering. "It means you are the one my soul was meant to love, Zuhra."

I stared up at him, drinking in the beauty of his face, his eyes. "I love you too, Raidyn. So much . . . I—"

His mouth closed over mine, cutting off the need for more words. I clung to him, the heat of his touch, the fire of his kiss, and the warmth from his love far more powerful than anything else I'd ever experienced in my life. I was intoxicated by him; delirious with relief and joy and need. I stretched up on my tiptoes so I could press more fully against the sculpted planes of his body. Unbidden, an image of his charred, ruined flesh flashed through my mind, and I had to suppress a shudder, knowing how close I'd been to losing him forever.

"What is *this*?"

We broke apart and spun to face my father, but he grinned at us, one eyebrow lifted. Awareness of where we stood—only a few feet away from injured Paladin—made my cheeks grow hot yet again. And I'd been judging Inara for kissing Loukas in an empty courtyard. I would have buried my face in my hands, hiding my mortification, if Raidyn hadn't still been holding one.

"Sir, I want you to know, I have only the most honest, pure intentions with your daughter. I love her, and I fully intend to—"

"I know, Raid," my father cut into his rambling—I had never heard Raidyn speak so fast before—with a gentle smile, all teasing gone. "I know you are an honorable young man. And I can easily see how happy you make each other. The light knows we all could use some happiness right now."

He picked his way over to us, his gaze flickering past where we stood to the courtyard and back, and then he suddenly froze, his smile dropping and his eyes widening.

"What is *that*?" This time there was no teasing smile or tone, only disbelief—and maybe a touch of anger. "Is that Inara and *Loukas*?"

I winced. "Er . . . yes. But"—I pressed on when he lurched forward as though he were about to storm outside—"I'm pretty certain they're falling in love too . . . Papa," I added in hopes of softening his heart—and keeping him from rushing out there to tear them apart. If anyone deserved happiness, as he'd just said, it was Inara.

He shot me a look that was part skeptical *I know what you're trying to do* and part heart-melting *Did you just call me Papa?*

"But . . . he's so much older than her," he protested.

"She just turned sixteen. And she's always had an old soul. If they love each other, then . . ." I shrugged.

"You really think they *love* each other?" Father sounded as baffled as I was by the whole turn of events; but who were we to judge the heart? He'd fallen in love with a human girl, who'd had to leave her family for him. I'd fallen in love with a Paladin who I'd had no reason to believe I'd ever have a future with.

"If they don't yet, I really do believe they're on that path," I said.

Father exhaled, long and slow. "Well, I do have to admit, I've never seen Loukas willing to show that much . . . er . . . affection in public before. She's obviously done something to change him—and hopefully for the better. The Great God knows he deserves some joy in his life." The tenderness that filled his face was unexpected, making me remember the story Raidyn had once told me—how my father was the only one willing to take him and Loukas under his wing and let them join his battalion. How he'd been like a father to them both.

"Maybe the Great God brought them together, knowing they needed each other," I suggested. I didn't share what Inara had experienced in the light—how she'd been given the chance to truly see his heart. That was her sacred experience to share or keep to herself. But it did seem as though forces had been at work to bring them together—to give them this chance at happiness.

"Maybe," Father allowed with a shake of his head, and then his expression turned serious. "I came to tell you we're going to hold a meeting tonight, in the dining hall, after the burial, to discuss what to do now. Will you please help me spread the word to those able and willing to attend?"

"Of course."

He nodded, with one last glance out the door and another shake of his head. "Let them know too, when they're . . . finished." He jerked a thumb toward the courtyard.

I managed to summon something resembling a smile and nodded.

He walked away, and once he was out of earshot, Raidyn said, "Well, I think that went well," startling a burst of laughter out of me, making a few heads turn toward us. Guilt immediately crept in, for laughing when so many were still hurting, injured, or grieving. But then I shoved that guilt away. We were *all* hurt and grieving. And if Raidyn could get me to laugh, to snatch a moment of levity amid the heaviness of the load we all shouldered, then I had nothing to be ashamed of and everything to be grateful for.

"Come on," he said, giving my hand a squeeze. "We'd better go let them know about the meeting . . . and to warn him that I might not be the only one to corner him and interrogate him about his intentions with Inara."

I stifled another little burst of laughter, and then we hurried outside, where Loukas and Inara still embraced.

FORTY-EIGHT

INARA

The storm began to dissipate minutes after all those who were able to come out for the burial had gathered around the soberingly large pit. Glimpses of sky passed in and out of view as the clouds broke apart; rays from the setting sun painted the gray underbellies of the remaining stormclouds in shades of coral and orange, setting the heavens aflame.

Loukas stood beside me, holding my hand, scowling at anyone who dared look at us askance—even my father, who shot us more than one eyebrow-raised glance. But Mother, at his side, seemed oblivious to anything besides the body they stood closest to—the only human who had died in the battle. Our beloved Sami.

I, too, stared at her shape beneath the sheet someone had draped over her, giving her the dignity of not being on display, hiding the gruesome details of her death and allowing her to live in our memory, alive and soft and gentle, as she'd always been. I still didn't understand why she'd done it—why she'd gone to find that knife and tried to take down a madman wielding the power of at least four or five Paladin. But her sacrifice was just one of many that had ultimately enabled the rest of us to succeed in stopping Barloc and his *jaklas.* The row of bodies was devastating, and it didn't even include the gryphons who had died. They were too large to bury, and instead, would be burned by Paladin fire, the smoke carrying their souls to the Light for their eternal rest.

The burial ceremony was brief but powerful. Though the songs were in Paladin, the haunting melodies sent chills down my spine and brought tears to my eyes. When the last note ended, Loukas released my hand to step forward and help place the bodies in the pit and then cover them with dirt.

I hugged myself as I watched Sami and so many others disappear forever beneath the rich, dark soil, still heavy and damp with rain. And then an arm came around my shoulders, and I leaned into the familiar comfort of my sister's embrace.

"I can't believe she's gone," Zuhra said. "I guess part of me expected her to always be there for us."

"Me too," I said, soft and choked.

We fell silent, tears slipping silently down my cheeks.

When it was finally finished, we crossed over to the other side of the grounds, where all the gryphons who still lived—including Sukhi—sat at attention, guarding the bodies of their brothers and sisters that had fallen, including the gryphons of the Paladin who had come through the gateway with my father and Loukas and the others . . . Sachiel's and those who had remained behind—who Barloc and his *jaklas* had slaughtered. The other general stood near the gryphons' bodies, her arms wrapped around her own waist. Dried blood still streaked the sides of her shaved head. It had taken two healers working on her together to heal the majority of Sachiel's wounds, but without a gryphon, she'd been unable to join the fight. Though her wounds were gone, I knew deep scars remained—some visible and others unseen.

So many of us had lost far too much, all because of one man.

When we all had gathered with our gryphons, Sukhi bent her head to bump her beak gently into my shoulder. And then the Paladin sang another mournful song, punctuated by cries from the gryphons who had survived. When it, too, had ended, a handful of Paladin stretched their hands out and set the noble beasts' bodies aflame. Within minutes, they were consumed, turned to ash. The living gryphons stepped forward and, lifting their wings, flapped them in unison so the ashes rose up off the ground and were carried away on the wind.

This time when an arm came round my shoulders, I recognized

the height and feel of Louk's body and leaned into his embrace. He stroked one hand over my snarled hair. Someday, maybe, there would be a bath and clean clothes and not being coated in grime, sweat, and worse. But first, there was the meeting Raidyn and Zuhra had told us about—that terribly embarrassing moment when my older sister's voice intruded on a kiss that I'd partially hoped might never end.

In Louk's arms, the real world—with all of its pain and loss and exhaustion—faded away. But kissing him forever wasn't a very realistic coping mechanism, tempting as it was, and so we'd broken apart. Now his arm was around me once more, but there was a meeting to endure and whatever came after that. Which, I had to admit, part of me was afraid of facing.

The gryphons had to stay back, some huddling together on the ground outside the stable, some braving the interior with its lingering scent of death. I watched as Maddok and Sukhi lay down side by side, nuzzling their beaks together. My eyes widened, but when I glanced up to see if Louk had noticed, his gaze was trained intently on me, his eyes sharp and seeking.

Before he could speak, Sharmaine came up beside us and said, "Did you hear the rumor that they intend to destroy the gateway for good, to keep anything like this from happening again?"

"*What?* No . . . I hadn't heard that." They wanted to *destroy* it? To close off any way of traveling between our two worlds? My nameless fear grew teeth and sank them into my heart.

What did that mean for me and my family? I was Paladin again, it was true, but I'd been raised here and my mother was human. Would they expect us to stay behind?

The thought was anathema, impossible to even entertain, because that would mean never seeing Louk again. And what about Sukhi?

Possible scenarios, each more terrible than the last, swirled through my mind, until by the time we reached the dining hall, my hairline was damp with sweat and my palms were clammy and cold. I was grateful Louk's arm remained around my shoulder, holding me tight against his side, rather than taking my hand in his.

Even with the casualties and the more gravely injured Paladin not in attendance, those who came for the meeting nearly filled the once-cavernous room. Raidyn and Zuhra stood near us, but my parents took a spot at the head of the table beside Grandmother, who managed to somehow still look regal and composed, even with her hair half falling out and her face streaked with dirt.

Her gaze traveled over all those assembled, her expression grave and jaw tight. "Thank you," was all she said, voice choked, and then she bowed her head.

Silence, thick and full of sorrow, added weight to the air, pressing in on the survivors.

After several moments had passed, Father reached out and took his mother's hand in his. She breathed in deeply, her chest filling with life-sustaining air, and then she squared her shoulders and looked around the room once more.

"For the sake of my son's family, we will conduct this meeting in their language." A few heads turned toward us, but most kept their gaze on her. "I know today has already been trying, but we have more decisions ahead of us before we can return home and rest."

Father's eyes flickered to where Zuhra and I stood with Raidyn, Louk, and Sharmaine at the use of that one word: *home*. What was home to him? What was it to any of us? I looked to my sister, standing at my side but leaning into Raidyn, their fingers tightly woven together between their bodies.

Zuhra was my home. And my mother . . . even my father, now. I couldn't imagine my parents staying behind, or Zuhra letting Raidyn go through that gateway never to return to her life. And if they left . . . then this citadel would never be home to me again. Surely, they would let us come with them . . . wouldn't they?

A tiny spark of hope flickered to life in my chest.

"It has been proposed that the gateway be destroyed—completely," Grandmother continued. Murmurs rose but she lifted a hand, silencing them. "Our ancestors believed it was important to keep a way to travel between our worlds, but it has only proven to bring pain and grief to both Vamala and Visimperum. The humans don't need us—or want us. And by leaving the gateway intact, even dormant, it is inviting more Paladin like Barloc and the Five Banished to try to open it, to wreak more devastation on the humans, or drag more of us into battles we shouldn't have to fight and losses we shouldn't have to bear."

Heads began to nod, and even I could agree that though my heart balked at the idea of the gateway being gone—*forever*—it was probably for the best.

"I know the entire council isn't here to vote on this matter, but all of you have earned the right to help me make this decision by the valor you've shown here, in Vamala, and to honor those we lost, who came here knowing the risk they were taking." Grandmother's voice was unsteady, hoarse with barely suppressed emotion, but she pushed on. "And so I am asking you to vote—and I will remind you that, according to our laws, voting on an issue of this magnitude must be unanimous to pass. So unless we are all in agreement, the gateway will remain as it is. We will open it long enough for all those who wish to return to Visimperum to come through and then we will close it and continue keeping watch over it as best as we can with our battalions."

She paused, letting her words—and the options before us—sink in.

I hesitantly lifted my hand.

"Did you have a question?" She looked to me, her face impassive and gaze sharp. In that moment, I knew she was Ederra, leader of the High Council, not Grandmother, and I almost lost my nerve. Especially when most of those gathered turned to stare at me as well.

But Louk squeezed my shoulders encouragingly and I nodded.

"Yes . . . I, ah, I was wondering . . . can *anyone* who wishes to live in Visimperum come with you?"

There was a softening at the corner of her eyes, so subtle I almost missed it, more an absence of tightness that I hadn't realized was there until it left. But her voice was much more gentle when she said, "Yes. Anyone who wishes to."

I nodded again, my cheeks hot, grateful when the Paladin turned back to her.

"Then, if there are no more questions, we will put it to a vote. All those in favor of destroying the gateway?"

A resounding chorus of "ayes" filled the room, raising bumps over my skin.

"Are there any opposed?"

The silence again held weight, but this time, it was the gravity of the decision being made—the finality of it. There was no reason for any of us to stay in Vamala . . . but to have the option to return taken away was more painful than I'd expected.

Grandmother waited and waited, making sure no one was thinking it over and struggling to oppose the majority. But when no one spoke up, she nodded. "It's decided, then. We will destroy the gateway once we pass through it. But this brings up new questions. There's the matter of the books and treasures here in the citadel. Do we leave them, to possibly be found and looted, should the *custovitan* hedge ever fail? Or do we try to bring as much as we can through to Visimperum?"

As the details of what to bring back and how to do that were bandied back and forth, Loukas leaned down and whispered, "I don't think they need us for this part. Do you want to go?"

I nodded, and he slipped his arm off my shoulder, taking my hand in his and guiding me toward the door.

Once we were alone in the quiet, cool hallway, the door shut behind us, Louk turned to me. "I thought you might want to go check on Sukhi. Or rest. Or eat. You haven't had anything since before we left Soluselis."

I marveled at the reality that this beautiful, haunted boy was by my side, holding my hand, watching so closely he knew how long it had been since I'd eaten. "Thank you," I said, though I wanted to say so much more.

Instead of moving, though, his hand tightened on mine, and his eyes glistened as he stared down at me, the green-fire that I'd come to adore flaring bright and clear in the shadowed hallway. "I don't deserve you," he said at last, hoarse and heartbreakingly quiet.

"How can you say that?" I stepped even closer to him, so the heat of his body filled the small space between us. "I'm grateful I was given the gift of truly seeing you when you took me to the *luxem magnam*. I wish you could see yourself the way I do."

Louk brushed my cheek with the back of his knuckles, running his thumb across my bottom lip, instantly silencing me. "You asked me once if I wished I weren't different, and I thought maybe I did. But if being different—if all the loneliness and pain—made it so we could have *this,* then I'm beginning to think it might have been worth it." He bent down and brushed a soft, sweet kiss over my mouth. "I don't know what the future holds . . . I only know that I've never felt this way with anyone before in my life."

His words still filled me with warmth, with *hope.* He kissed me again, but it was all too brief, leaving heat racing over my skin and my heart thudding. I lifted my chin, wanting more, but instead, his mouth quirked up into a smile, a full, genuine smile that crinkled the corners of his eyes.

He had always been so beautiful, he almost didn't seem real, but in a tragic hero, stoic and full of buried pain kind of way, like some of the stories Zuhra had read to me. We'd laughed and called them ridiculous because we hadn't believed we'd ever have a chance at love—tragic or not. But *this* smile, the mischievous light in his eyes, transformed him from achingly beautiful to *breathtaking*; he wore happiness very well.

"And now that you're coming back with me, we will have a lifetime to figure it out—together."

Lifetime and *together*—two words that on their own didn't mean nearly as much, but when Louk said them, about *us* . . . My heart swelled in my chest, until I felt like I might burst from the thought of spending a lifetime with him.

"But for now, you still didn't answer my question. Sukhi, rest, or food? Or all three? I'm not going to force you to choose only one."

I grinned up at him, matching his happiness with my own. "I don't care what we do, as long as it's together."

FORTY-NINE

ZUHRA

The cliff face was as close as I remembered when Naiki soared through it, Raidyn's body pressed against mine, holding us both against her neck. This time, I had no trouble keeping my eyes open, not wanting to miss that first breathtaking view of Soluselis—a view I'd believed I would never see again.

The wind was cold and strong, but the tears in my eyes had nothing to do with it as Naiki straightened and the city became visible in the valley below us, glimmering in the distance. As we sat back up and Naiki stretched her wings to soar back home—*home,* here with the Paladin, with my entire family, with *Raidyn*—he slid his arm around my waist, drawing me back against his warm, solid body. He pressed a kiss to my temple; I tilted my face toward him, so his lips could leave a heated trail down my chilled skin, skimming my cheekbone, landing on the corner of my mouth.

"I'm afraid I'm going to wake up any minute and find out none of this is real," Raidyn murmured.

"Luckily, if you're having trouble staying awake, my sister has been giving me lessons on riding a gryphon. I think I could get us to the castle safely."

Raidyn made a noise that was half laugh, half growl, and sat back, but paused to press another kiss to the groove between my jaw and neck, his teeth grazing the tendon. I moaned, a jolt of need rippling through me.

"That's not playing fair," I complained.

He laughed fully this time, his fingers stroking my hip, just as he had on our second ride together. But this time, I had no qualms about twisting around, ready to give him a taste of his own temptations—

Then caught sight of my sister on Sukhi, just off to our left side, her blue-fire eyes wide, staring at Soluselis.

"What—is something wrong?" Raidyn caught the change in my focus and followed my gaze to Inara.

"It's like she's never seen it before." Which wasn't true; not only had she been here before, the *luxem magnam* had saved her life.

Maddok's wings beat next to Sukhi, and Inara turned toward him, responding to something Loukas said that neither of us could hear.

"Honestly, it doesn't matter how many times I leave and come back, it always takes my breath away every time," Raidyn admitted. "Maybe that's all it was."

"Maybe," I agreed, but part of me still wondered. I knew my sister, and I was certain there was more to the look I'd seen on her face.

A glance over my shoulder revealed the rest of our company, including my grandmother and my parents. My mother stared at the Paladin capital with her jaw agape, eyes wide. My father was trying and failing to hide a grin as his wife finally got to see his home, at long last.

It had taken days for the Paladin to go through the belongings and books left in the citadel, choosing only the most vital items to bring back. There had been meetings between the Paladin and the army that showed up outside the hedge, drawn by the rumors of a battle at the citadel, the events of that terrible afternoon overheard by the townspeople of Gateskeep. Ederra had promised them the gateway would be destroyed, that their people would never again be forced to deal with Paladin or rakasa, and they had eventually left us in peace. It also allowed the Paladin gathered enough time to recover the power necessary to open the gateway and deal with the potential rakasa that might try to get through.

But there had been none. Instead, we found three more

battalions waiting for our return, brought there by the rest of the council, who had come to the castle only to find Ederra and half their Riders gone. They'd come as quickly as they could without leaving the city completely defenseless, and had only arrived an hour before we all came through.

Now the entire group, a sea of Paladin and gryphons filling the sky like a storm made of blue-fire and wings, soared across the valley toward the castle that glowed like a beacon.

A beacon of peace and rest and hope.

"She'll be happy here," I said at last. "We all will."

"I hope so. Because I'm not planning on letting you leave ever again. Unless I'm with you, of course."

I smiled and wrapped my arm over his, snuggling back into his chest. "I wouldn't mind seeing more of Visimperum sometime. I've spent a lot of years behind a wall, you know."

His immediate regret was palpable. "You're right, I'm sorry. I never meant to imply that I would trap—"

"Raid," I cut in with a laugh, "I'm only teasing."

"Oh . . . are you certain? Because I truly didn't mean—"

"Truly," I insisted, running my nails over the veins in his hand, up his wrist, and on to his forearm, where I could feel the goose bumps rising on his skin from my touch. His breath quickened. "I really do want to explore the city and the rest of Visimperum with you, and if I ever feel like I need a break, we can take Naiki out for a flight. But I love the castle. And I'm actually excited to start training with you again. I think I may have discovered a weak spot or two I fully intend to capitalize on the next time we spar."

He shivered when I dragged my nails back down his arm and laced my fingers through his. "Now who isn't playing fair?" His voice was low and husky.

My laugh was carried back to him by the wind.

I loved it. I loved *him*.

And I loved that as we soared above the city's rooftops, painted golden by the setting sun, over the hedge and into the field to land, the castle rising above us, it truly felt *right*.

It felt like coming home.

At last.

* * *

The first few hours after our arrival were chaotic and wonderful and exhausting. Explanations were given, tears were shed, food was served, rooms assigned, baths drawn and savored, new clothes slipped over skin that was finally clean . . . and suddenly, there was silence and solitude. Raidyn had kissed me good night and left me to my bath and pajamas and down-filled pillows with the promise—and knowledge—that I would see him first thing in the morning when we met in the ring to spar, fulfilling my pledge to exploit the weaknesses I thought I'd discovered. Something he claimed he couldn't wait to experience.

I ran my hands over the silken material of the nightgown I wore. The weariness in my body delved far past mind and muscle, to heart, bone, *soul*—so deeply imbedded, I wondered if I would ever *not* be tired again. But though the bed in my room was large and clean and inviting, the sheets so white, they rivaled the milky moonlight streaming through my window, and a fire burned cheerfully behind the grate, making my room warm and cozy and my eyelids heavy—I knew I couldn't go to bed. Not quite yet.

I located a robe in the bureau and after pulling it on, slipped out into the quiet hallway, softly shutting the door behind me. Inara's room was next to mine, but when I tapped gently on her door, there was no answer.

"Inara?" I called out barely above a whisper, not wanting to disrupt anyone trying to sleep nearby.

When no answer came, I tried the handle. It turned easily, the door swung open, but the room was empty.

I knew there was a chance she might have gone off to find Loukas, but I had a suspicion that I might find her elsewhere.

Following that instinct, and hoping I still knew my sister as well as I once had, I moved silently through the slumbering castle. Though it had been a while, I was still able to find my way to the center of the castle, following the pull that was stronger than ever and my own memory of the way to reach my destination—the *luxem magnam*.

I turned the corner to that last hallway, the undulating light that never dimmed up ahead, and saw an outline of someone standing at the diamond banister, her arms folded as if in prayer.

Inara.

I moved forward slowly, giving her plenty of time to hear or sense my approach. I was only a few feet away when she glanced over her shoulder at me and smiled, the light of the *luxem magnam* illuminating her, wrapping around her—almost as if it *held* her, somehow. As if after healing her and giving Inara her power back, she was still connected to it in some way.

"I thought I might find you here," I said softly. "But I hope I'm not interrupting."

"Of course not," she responded immediately. "You could never be an interruption."

I stepped up beside her, staring down at the undulating light below us. It didn't look solid enough to support a body, but it *had* somehow from what Loukas had described to me when I'd asked him for more details—the light had held and healed her.

"The first time I saw the *luxem magnam,* all I could think was how much you would have loved it—and how badly I wished I could bring you to see it. I thought it was an impossible wish." I paused as warmth melted into my body, a little bit of the exhaustion releasing its hold on me, like a sigh. "And now look at us—here, at the *luxem magnam,* together."

"I still can't believe it." When Inara spoke, her voice was hushed.

There were so many things she could have been referring to, I just waited.

Her eyes glistened, the blue-fire almost as bright as it had been during the battle. "I keep thinking that it'll come back—that the cost for all of this is that one morning the roar will return, erasing everything else. But every day I wake up and I can talk to you whenever I wish. I can't believe I am truly healed. That we're *here*—with our parents. That *Louk* . . ." She trailed off with a shake of her head and turned away from the *luxem magnam* to face me fully. "I'm *so* happy . . . but I keep feeling like I *shouldn't* be. That it isn't fair, not when my happiness exists because of so much sorrow and loss."

My heart lurched for her, because I knew all too well what she was feeling. It was something Raidyn and I had talked about the night before we left Vamala forever.

I wrapped my arms around my sister, pulling her into a hug. "We'll always miss Sami. And Halvor too. And all the others. It isn't fair; you're right," I agreed, and she stiffened in my arms. "It isn't fair that when you were born, you brought so much power into the world that Papa got pulled through the gateway, leaving us trapped there with a mother who didn't know how to find happiness without him. It isn't fair that you were imprisoned in the roar for fifteen years. So much of life isn't fair." I drew back, just enough to look into her eyes, for her not only to *feel* the truth of what I wanted to tell her, but to *see* it in my face. "You told me yourself, those who lost their lives have been welcomed home to the Light. They have found true peace and endless happiness with their loved ones who went before them. So if you have managed to find even a *tiny* piece of that happiness here, the only reason to feel guilty about it would be if you rejected the chance to experience true joy, choosing to remain miserable because you're worried about them."

Inara's eyes still glittered, but the desperate beat of guilt in her heart gave way to the first bloom of hope; I could feel it unfurling in her, tender and beautiful.

"If anyone deserves to be deliriously happy, it's you, Nara. All I have ever wanted was for you to be free—and happy."

"And thanks to you, now I am," she said, pulling me back into a tight hug. "I love you, Zuzu," she murmured into my hair.

"I love you too." I squeezed her tight.

After a few moments, I pulled away and turned to face the *luxem magnam* once more, running my hands over the diamond balustrade. "It's honestly too bad the gateway was destroyed. Think of the fortune we could have made if we'd been able to smuggle even one beam from this thing back to Vamala."

"Zuhra!" Inara's scandalized outcry was followed by a burst of laughter that echoed up to the glass ceiling far overhead, where the moonlight broke into soft beams of white, caught up in a dance with the shards of dazzling light of the *luxem magnam,* refracted and multiplied by the diamonds we leaned on. The sound of that laughter was one of the most beautiful things I'd ever heard.

"You know I'm not serious. I'm nowhere near strong enough to break off an entire beam. Maybe just a chunk from the top."

Inara laughed again, and this time I joined her. We laughed and laughed, until our stomachs hurt.

"Come on, we should get to bed," I finally said. "I don't know if you remember what the beds are like here, but if my memory is right, I'm pretty sure it's like sleeping on a cloud."

"Having now flown *through* clouds, I'm not sure I'd want to try to sleep on one. I think we'd just fall through."

Our giggles followed us as we wandered through the castle, trying to remember the way to our rooms. I wondered if this was what it would have been like to grow up like normal sisters, without a roar or a hedge or a hidden gateway . . . but ultimately it didn't matter. I couldn't change the past. I could only be thankful for the fact that we were together in that hallway, that we could wander through a castle in Soluselis, giggling and lost, and not caring because it was our home now. Because our parents were there, somewhere, and our grandmother, too. Because Raidyn and Loukas would be there in the morning when we woke—or to find us if we were still lost.

But above all else, despite whatever else the future held, we had each other.

Now—and forever.

ACKNOWLEDGMENTS

As I sit and try to compose my thoughts to write the acknowledgments for my seventh (!!) published book, I'm feeling overwhelmed with gratitude. It is a very strange and difficult time right now—in the midst of a worldwide pandemic that has devastating consequences for so many in various ways. Having life change so drastically so quickly has forced many of us to step back and think about what is truly important in our lives. For me, that is God, my family, my health, nature, and story—for the beauty and magic that is the gift of escaping into the pages of a book and finding pieces of ourselves or ways to make sense of our world through the lens of another's eyes. Now, more than ever, I am deeply indebted to all those who have enabled me to continue to tell my stories—especially this one about the bond between sisters, something so dear to my heart.

I will never be able to express in words my gratitude to Melissa Frain for loving my sisters and these books as much as I do, and for giving me the chance to bring them to life. Mel, I am so grateful for you—it was my honor to work with you on this series. Thank you to the entire team at Tor Teen for your amazing work on this series! Special thanks to Susan Chang for stepping in and being so understanding, Lauren Levite and Anneliese Merz for all of your support and work on these books, Saraciea Fennell for your excitement and support, Jim Tierney for another incredibly gorgeous cover, Christa Désir for not getting mad about my inability to use farther/further correctly and for such an incredibly kind comment that it made me cry (in a good way), and Melanie Sanders, Jim Kapp, Heather Saunders, Peter Lutjen, Lesley Worrell, Devi Pillai, Lucille Rettino, Eileen Lawrence, Anthony Parisi, and Isa Caban, who work so hard to get these books on shelves and into the hands of readers, especially right now during such a hard time.

Thank you, as always, to the inimitable Josh Adams, my agent extraordinaire, and the entire team at Adams Literary for continuing to make my dreams come true and always having my back!

Kathryn Purdie—no acknowledgments page would be complete without you, just as I would never survive this journey without you. Thank you for everything, especially all the karaoke.

As always, I am so grateful for my family and their unflagging support. My incredible parents and of course my sisters—whom I love so deeply, that love inspired this entire series. And thank you to my in-laws also. I'm so lucky to have such amazing cheerleaders in my corner!

To all of my author friends who have supported me on this journey—whether it's cheering for one another or commiserating together—this career would be a hundred times harder without all of you. During the creation of this book, special thanks must go out to Danielle Jensen, Becky Wallace, Kate Watson, Demetra Brodsky, Emily King, Caitlin Sangster, Tricia Levenseller, Julie Olsen, Charlie Holmberg, Kerry Kletter, C. J. Redwine, Sarah Goodman, Nadine Brandes, Samantha Hastings, and so many more. I am blessed with amazing friends and support in my life.

Thank you to the incredible book bloggers, readers, librarians, and booksellers who have been such a huge support throughout the years—I can never thank you enough for all you do! Special thanks to Bridget and Kristen from Storygram Tours; Krysti and Sarah from the YA and Wine book club; Jenn Kelly, teacher extraordinaire; the entire staff at King's English Bookshop; and so many others for your continued and unwavering support of my career!

So much gratitude to my dear friends and sisters of my heart—Sarah Cox, Marie Rappleye, Jessica Knab, Janessa Taylor, Abby Degraff, and Emelie Lasson—for keeping me sane and always being there for me in this crazy thing called life. Thank you to Cathy Blake for your kindness, love, example, and support.

To my incredible readers who have either stuck with me this long or are just finding me with these books, a simple thank-you will never be adequate for taking the chance on picking up one of my books and allowing me the honor of sharing my stories with you. Your messages and posts about how much you love my characters and the worlds and words I create mean more than you can ever know.

I always save the most important ones for last. Travis, my best friend and soulmate. I believe in the ability to fall in love in a matter of weeks because I knew I was in love with you on our first date. Thank you for loving me as much as you do, and for making our life together so amazing. I adore you. To my four incredible children—I love you so much, I'm not sure you will understand until you are parents yourselves. Thank you for giving me the gift of being your mommy.

And finally, my eternal gratitude to my Heavenly Father. Thank You for giving me the gift of story and every other good thing in my life.